INTERSECTING ETERNITY

INTERSECTING ETERNITY

AN EDEN.2 SEQUEL

Margaret A. Babcock

QUEER SPACE

New Orleans & New York

Published in the United States of America by
Queer Space
A Rebel Satori Imprint
www.rebelsatoripress.com

This is a work of fiction. Names, characters, places, and incidents are the product of the author's imagination and are used fictitiously and any resemblance to actual persons, living or dead, business establishments, events, or locales is entirely coincidental. The publisher does not have any control over and does not assume any responsibility for author or third-party websites or their content.

Library of Congress Control Number:

For Neil and Eugene:
Loved now and through eternity

"The present moment is the intersection of eternity with time, and when our consciousness is stayed on this, it rests and finds peace, because it is released from the fantasies of the ego and is in touch with reality."
—Beatrice Bruteau, *Radical Optimism*

PROLOGUE

The tiny bulb blinked on, flashing green in the dim light of the communications room. Mistral smiled as he toggled the switch to receive the message. "Planet KOI-3284, this is Earth Station One. Acknowledge your launch date is a go. Will send next transmission directly to Glenn 2. Looking forward to welcoming you home. Over."

As he reached for the typing pad to respond, he heard footsteps in the hall behind him. He swung around, expecting Kama, who would care for this facility after he left, but the face appearing at the door was even more familiar and loved than hers.

He sang, "Jerry-O, Granddad dear, delight to see you here. Is all well with Daddy-O and all who dwell in town?"

The old man hummed notes of greeting but limped to a stool and sat before venturing a reply. Mistral noted that his breath came short and his hand shook a bit as he leaned his walking stick against the console.

"Could we speak today, dear? I have no energy for singing, and my head works better when I talk."

"Of course, of course, we can speak, not sing. Just to be together—that's the cherished thing.... Oh, sorry, it's hard to switch. But yes, let's just use words. I need the practice before I get to the silent planet."

Jerry sighed, his faded blue eyes taking in the blinking light and pad in his grandson's hands. "Practice referring to it as Earth, too. For all we know, the planet isn't silent. It may not communicate in

1

the same way Goldie does." He smiled and pointed his chin at the keyboard. "Finish what you were doing. I can wait."

Mistral nodded and typed in his response, which would arrive several months from now, when he and the mission crew were already on their way. Then he directed his attention to his grandfather, tilting his head as he took in the sunken cheeks and lines etched deep from nostrils to mouth. The gray fog, which had settled around Jerry in the days after both his partners, Rob and Lily, had passed, had never quite dissipated. But today, two revs after their deaths, it was back in force.

"You are sad and distraught. Are you mourning me before I'm even gone? You know I'll keep in touch with you. Kama and Goldie will see to that."

The wry smile returned but did nothing to dispel the emotional gloom. "I will miss you, Mistral, more than you realize. But I don't expect I'll have to bear it too long. I wanted to talk to you about something else before you leave, though. May I address you as Mission Commander today, instead of grandson?"

"Of course. You have a concern about the launch?"

"I worry about who is on the crew—specifically, Goldilocks."

"Goldie? She's been part of this mission from the beginning, but I would hardly call her a crew member. I think of her as the heart of our endeavor."

Jerry nodded. "Yes, from the time Grandpa Rob heard Earth people trying to communicate with us, Goldie wished to contact another living planet. I think it's more than just a desire. It's a biological drive to connect with a similar entity—someone closer to her nature than we can ever be. And her willingness to assist in the effort to send a spaceship back to our original home makes this mission possible. We never could have located the metals and materials for fuel and repairs without her guidance and cooperation."

"So?" Mistral felt his eyes widen.

"For the last few months, I've experienced Goldie growing

more distant. Your father has noticed it too. We understand that her attention is more and more focused on this journey, but did you know that out in Far Meadow, where they're just beginning to set up a farming village, a windstorm flattened several fields of barley grass?"

Mistral straightened his spine and narrowed his eyes. "We've had problems with wind before. It's hard for Goldie to keep in touch with every aspect of herself at once."

"Exactly. And it may be harder for her the farther her consciousness gets from this world. Grandpa Rob had a theory about how Goldie actually travelled around."

An image surfaced in Mistral's mind, bringing with it both the warmth of love and the pain of loss: a kind, round face under a shiny bald pate, laughing as the boy he had been struggled to get a yo-yo to climb back up its string. "He called it the Yo-Yo Effect, didn't he?"

"Yes. He speculated that Goldie's ability to connect with anyone is similar to human dreaming. When you dream, your consciousness drops out of time and space to wander around through memories, hopes, and fears, and then, on waking, snaps back automatically to your body's reality, like a yo-yo following its string back home to the hand. Goldie's consciousness appears to be able to travel anywhere, to anyone, but it too stays connected to her body—this planet. The big difference is that she seems to be in control of the string, sending her consciousness wherever she wants and bringing it home at will."

"Right, I remember him explaining this to me. He thought her ability had something to do with existing concurrently within the present moment and outside of it."

"Yes, he said to imagine her string being tied firmly to time and space here in this world, but she is free to fling herself through eternity to other points of space and time. Of course, it's easier for her if we meet her in our dreams, when we are off the timeline too. But through the years, she's learned to connect with us even when we're awake."

Mistral frowned. He sensed the presence of the planet listening to the conversation through him. Glancing at his grandfather, he saw in the sad, wise eyes that he recognized she was there too. This was now a three-way meeting.

"She feels sure that all will be well. There may be challenges which arise here, but nothing that she and you all won't be able to address."

The old man bowed his head and shut his eyes, concentrating. The connection always came harder for him. "I witness her confidence too."

"So, you are comforted?" Mistral asked, although both he and Goldie still felt his anxiety.

Instead of answering, Jerry leveraged himself up, reached for his staff, and hobbled toward the door. He put his hand on the wall to connect more closely with Goldilocks. Closing his eyes, he spoke into the space between the three of them.

"Do you remember, Mistral, when you were in your third rev, your folks and Grandpa Rob and I took you to Seaside? You loved to swim. One day, you decided you could make it from the beach to Sandpoint Island, about two miles out in the bay."

Mistral closed his eyes too, and suddenly, there they were, watching the scene unfold through Goldie's memory. His youthful body, lean and tan, running carefree on the sand, headed for the open water while his mother admonished him not to be foolish. He had been so certain he could swim that distance, so dismissive of her concern. As he waded in to prove his ability, she ceased trying to win his agreement and instead ran to a nearby fisherman and borrowed a rowboat.

Two-thirds of the way to the island, his spindly arms and legs had become so heavy he couldn't lift them. He felt waves close over his head and had the sense to roll over and float until she reached him. As she pulled him on board and rowed him back to shore, she never said a word. But Goldie's song had followed them, confused and anxious. Even now, the remembrance held the tinge of her bewilderment.

Jerry's rough voice broke the spell. "Humans learn their limitations when they are young. If we're lucky, people who love us provide a safety net while we test the boundaries of our strength and mortality. Goldie has never tested the limits of her being."

"So, you're worried about what will happen to her if her consciousness goes with us to Earth?"

"Yes. I also wonder what will happen to those left behind."

"But Grandpa Jerry, she contacted you while you were still on the silent planet. We're sure she can stretch that far. Our scientists have all of Grandpa Rob's papers and notes. They agree with his theories. Their best guess is that space and time don't limit her as they do humans."

"I appreciate that, and I'm not trying to dissuade Goldie from going. My heart is relieved that she'll be with you on this journey. But guesses are not certainties. As far as we know, Goldie has never dropped into multiple timelines at once, and as you travel through space, your time will be different than ours on the planet. You will also be asking her to communicate with you in a more focused way than we did when we first encountered her in our dreams. It may not be a problem, but I want you both to pay attention to the connection between Goldie's conscious being and this world. If distance does make a difference, if she isn't strong enough to go all the way, turn back to us—or, at the very least, don't be away too long."

His eyes opened, seeking his grandson. "Remember, Mistral, she doesn't experience time like we do. The twenty to thirty years you plan to be gone is just a blink of an eye to her, but her absence will affect every person here. If contact ceases completely, if the string snaps, this planet and everything belonging to it, including Goldie, might die."

A wave of concern surrounded them, and emotion erupted out

of Mistral as his words and Goldie's music: "Jerry-O, Grand-dad dear, know we love you so. While we move among the stars, we'll watch for you below. Never think we do not care. Never fear, we will be near."

A soft smile spread across the old man's face as he patted the wall. "That's all I ask, dear hearts. We won't forget you either. Go with God, both of you, and come back soon and safe."

He opened the door and waved. "See you tomorrow at the launch."

Mistral rotated his stool to face the console, the last sweet tinges of emotion wafting away as Goldie elected to accompany Jerry out, still sending a tune of concern and care. He had been waiting and working for this mission since he was in his third rev. His mind calculated, practicing the switch to Earth time: They had kept their native twelve months, but on Goldilocks, one revolution around the sun took three cycles of those months with an extra one to round it out. So, he had been eight years old when people on the home planet got themselves organized to imagine how some of the settlers might return. Goldie, however, had been with him long before that. All his life, the song of Goldie had intertwined with his breath. He never experienced a moment without her presence. All children born to this world had a similar connection. Well, almost all. There were the religious zealots who refused to merge with the larger community and hid away deep in the forest, preserving their bloodlines and traditions. The last Mistral heard, there was one struggling Christian group and another Muslim settlement left. Inbred and rigid, neither had grown beyond a few households.

There were also those few voices which protested when Goldie insisted they close the mines after finishing repairs to the spaceship. That, and her injunction against fishing in certain rich areas of the sea, had annoyed those who valued human progress and ease above the health of the whole. Yet altogether, he figured, only five to ten percent of the population wasn't in sync with the entity which nurtured them and was their home. That amount of dissent posed no threat. It just kept the rest honest about their choice to acknowledge their interdependence.

Mistral turned to the communications panel and read again the message from Earth. Now he was thirty-five years old, in their reckoning. During the last twenty-six years, they had reconstructed the science of the original space dwellers and rebuilt the abandoned communications equipment, the shuttles, and then later the still-orbiting Glenn. For twenty-six years, they worked with the Earth scientists, gathering all they understood about interstellar travel into the mission plan which would take them home. For twenty-six years, Goldie and the best minds and hearts in the universe had prepared for this moment. That was almost nine revs of calculating and exploring everything imaginable which could go wrong. They investigated every mistake the two ships which had brought the colonists to this planet had made, anticipating how to deal with catastrophes. None of those scenarios included a problem with Goldilocks.

The Mission Commander swiveled his chair toward the door, the vision of the old man limping away vivid in his mind. He cherished Grandpa Jerry and respected him as one of the few remaining first settlers, but he felt certainty rising in his heart. He knew Goldie better, deeper, than his grandfather ever could. She was the one thing they all could count on without fail. With her on their side, what could possibly go wrong?

CHAPTER ONE

DATE: REV 43.2/2204 CE

Alice kneeled on the rough kitchen rug, cleaning her little brother's skinned knee with barely contained haste. The shadows thrown by the table already reached the wall in front of her. She didn't want to be late taking Nainai her dinner, today of all days. Why couldn't Ma or Nettie take care of this child for once? Jaren's grateful hug smeared tears and snot on her worn tunic. Dropping a swift kiss onto his rumpled red curls, a shorter version of her own hair, she ladled him a small bowl of the evening's stew. Then she filled a larger one for her elderly aunt and herself, wrapping it in a clean towel, before hurrying out toward the dusty footpath leading to the village center.

Almost tripping over her own feet, she ran down the steps into the old woman's courtyard. She slowed a bit to push the door open with her elbow, the dish scalding her hands even through the cloth. Alice wanted time to talk tonight, to get her request out, so Nainai couldn't refuse to help her. She still didn't know quite how to ask, though. *Breathe*, she told herself. *With Nainai, slow and deliberate works best.*

Her great-great aunt had her back toward the entrance, but Alice caught the stealthy movement of her hands hiding a com-pad underneath the throw on her lap.

"It's only me," she called, kicking the door closed with her foot. "What have you been writing?"

"I've just finished a story." Nainai's smile set wrinkles in motion, like ripples made by wind on high grass, spreading to the boundaries of her face. "I'm hungry now. Why don't you read while we have dinner?"

Alice divided the stew into smaller bowls and put water in the boiler for tea as the older woman shuffled to the table. She was relieved her elderly aunt's appetite had returned. Alice worried she would forget to eat if no one came to check on her and sighed as she remembered what she needed to talk to her about today.

Then she propped the com-pad against the saltshaker and began reading as she shoveled in warm mouthfuls of beans and barley with a few greens mixed in. Across from her, Elena, whom everyone in their little village called Nainai, watched, smiling as she savored her meal. A few minutes later, Alice glanced up to give the old woman a bemused look. Her mouth too full to say anything, she shrugged and dived back into the story.

Bridge to Before

(This occurred in the first third of Goldie's twelfth revolution around the sun. I was not yet four revs old or just eleven years in the old Earth counting.)

We entered the house where Old Ma had died, solemnly, quietly, respecting the dignity of the dead. Even before crossing the threshold, I smelled old smoke, damp and heavy. No fire had burned on the hearth for a day and a night. None would crackle again, warm and welcoming, until they completed the funeral and the house found new inhabitants.

Old Ma's daughters (Pop's elderly aunts) had performed the family rites, washing and arranging the corpse. It lay on the sleeping platform, wrapped in dark blue cloth like a cocooned bilbug waiting to sprout wings. Pausing in the doorway, I eyed it warily, unnerved by its absolute stillness. I told myself, "It's only great-grandma's body, worn out and ready to return to dirt." I had seen death before.

Emptiness claimed the dwelling. A sad tension hung in the air. Still, it was a dwelling like all the rest in the village: One large, round room in a sunken courtyard with an arching roof and smooth, bowed-out walls. More shelves had been dug into the rear wall than usual, but the heavy door and narrow windows set high to catch the sunlight could have been in my house. I patted the great timber of the door frame as I passed through. The rough wood felt sturdy. "It's not fearsome," I told myself, breathing in and out. "It's just hollow." I studied the shadowed interior.

Pops and Da intended to pack up all Old Ma's belongings. Later, they would spread them on the grass by the side of the hole embracing her body. Everyone in the village would choose a remembrance or necessity. Like a birthday party in reverse, the dead gave all they had to the living. It is right: a holy ceremony of distribution, carefully done, slowly, with everything seen, touched, and honored.

All her closest kin—Pops, her grandson, with his heart-bond, Da, along with her two daughters, a nephew, and my two cousins—crowded into the room around me. The emptiness lurked, impatient for the rituals to be completed. We silently spread a large sheet of woven grass on the floor and collected items out of corners and off shelves to put onto it. My littlest cousin, Jenn, took the broom hidden behind the door with both hands, hauling it over to the mat. An auntie helped her set it down gently.

Dylan, my cousin older by one rev, rushed to the worktable, taking up a knife. From the way he caressed it, weighing its heft, eying its thin, dangerous blade, I knew he planned to claim it. You weren't supposed to covet the dead's possessions. I turned away, embarrassed for him.

Da moved to a chest and lifted out clothes and blankets.

I stood for a moment, watching him. Then I closed my eyes, listening for something to call me. There it was: a dark nook by the head of the bed, whispering to me.

I knew what was there, desiring it as Dylan had the knife. I wanted to go, but Old Ma's body rested right beneath it. Steeling myself, I took a deep breath. Then I tiptoed over, keeping my sight fixed on the long hole high in the wall. As I got closer, I spotted the figure of a small animal carved in light, foreign wood. Old Ma often let me hold it on my palm while she told stories of animals who populated the home world, flying in the air, hiding in the ground, and swimming like people in the waters.

As my hand closed around the tiny statue, this being's name drifted up from memory: otter. It ran on land and fished in rivers. Old Ma had seen him, loved him. This was a remembrance from Before. Old Ma, the last of the travelers, had bridged us back to that long-ago place and time. But now the stories followed her into the void.

Behind the otter, another shape loomed—something I didn't recognize. With my free hand, I reached into the nook and pulled out a bundle of rough cloth, deep blue like the shroud. Retreating a few feet from the bed, I squatted down. I set the figurine aside and unfolded the wad. I encountered two long rows of small metal teeth. This came from Before as well. It was a bag, a carryall. I tried to see it clearly in the dim light. I felt around inside and touched its slick black interior.

Time stopped.

Darkness ran up my arm and wrapped around my body, sealing me off from the familiar house, my family, even my own senses. A solid shadow crowded me up and away. It seemed I teetered on the edge of a high balcony, looking down at the bag from twice my height. Hands placed things into the carryall, brightly patterned cloth items. I sensed the movement of those muscles and the softness of material against fingers, but it was wrong, all wrong, somehow.

With a wrench of terror and vertigo, I realized that my hands, the short digits and chewed fingernails of a girl, had transformed into smooth, tapered adult fingers. Thoughts that were not my thoughts filled my mind. Foreign emotions rose like waves, threatening to swamp me. I tried to lift my arms to fend off the onslaught, but I couldn't connect, couldn't move my limbs. I shrank back, struggling to hold onto consciousness, to make sense of this overwhelming otherness thrust upon me.

Like binoculars coming into focus, color and forms, sounds and thoughts settled into patterns. The boundary between me and my strange host solidified. Curiosity bested terror, and I opened myself to the sensory input streaming by.

The beautiful long hands were still folding and packing.

"These won't last forever, but for a few years, we can sleep comfortably." The thought rose, shadowed by a wry chuckle. "I guess pajamas aren't a necessity. In fact, almost nothing we own is...."

A woman, I guessed. But where was she? I detected no smoke, new or old, yet clearly this was a house. The air tasted sterile, dry and thin. No sound of other people intruded, no children playing or adults working. *Maybe she's a hermit*, I thought.

The strange person moved a few feet, entering a smaller room, brightly lit. As her eyes panned over a narrow table with a set-in bowl, I noticed a scattering of combs and brushes, small tubes and jars and other foreign objects.

"Sherry's taking all her makeup and that infernal straightening iron she swears by," the thoughts came, tinged now with impatience. "Why bother? They'll only run out, break down. Might as well embrace the natural look." An elegant hand swept all the items, except for a small brush, into a wastebasket.

Her eyes looked up, and I caught a glimpse in the mirror of a young woman: round face, long chestnut hair pulled back into a ponytail, serious hazel eyes, and firmness around full lips, promising decisiveness. The reflection held no interest for my host. She sighed and yanked out a drawer, rummaging among its contents. "I'd better take all the bands I can to keep my hair out of my face." She filled a small metal box with a rainbow of circles.

She turned, walking back into the first room, and put the tin and brush into the carryall. As she leaned forward, something alive—dark, sleek, and alien—poked out of the bag.

I gasped, retreating to my corner until the vision fell into place. *It's an animal,* I realized, fascination taking over. *So different from the pictures.*

The woman laughed, but then wept as she lifted a long, lithe cat, cradling it in her arms, smoothing the silken fur over and over. Undeterred by her distress, it rumbled against her chest. My host bent her head and exhaled onto the creature's neck, receiving her breath back warm and dusty with a scent as familiar as her own.

"Pip, how can I leave you?" She whispered, "Why are you the only one it's breaking my heart to give up?"

Her words, spoken aloud, reverberated in my hidden space like a prayer. The intensity of her sadness bewildered me.

The woman sat on the edge of her bed and released the animal to the ground. She stared straight ahead at a picture on the wall, intricate and colorful. Her eyes lost focus, the energy of her soul consumed with reflection.

I tried to concentrate on the thoughts and feelings rising now, nonstop.

"It's true," my host contemplated, radiating guilt, "I can give up my folks and friends with astounding calmness. As long as I have Peter, I have enough love to survive. We can make a family to replace the one I'm leaving. I guess I'm just not that tied to anyone else. But the animals...." Her eyes sought and concentrated on Pip, stretched out in a patch of sunlight angling across the carpet. "How can I lose the animals of Earth and stay human?"

Sadness flowed from her again, but now I realized dread made up a significant part of that wave. The contagion of the woman's fear lapped at me, so I focused on the strange animal, the cat, to preserve stability. Light glinted off its dark fur like the sun on a deep, still pond. Its four legs spread out to one side with the tail pointing straight behind. It tilted back its triangular head to watch the woman, yellow eyes half-closed.

She stood and, stepping over the cat, moved toward a break in the wall through which she gazed at an expanse of sky and grass. No breath of fresh air penetrated the gap, though I could see through it. It took me a moment to comprehend—a vast stretch of glass sealed the opening. I had never seen such an extravagant sheet of that precious material. My attention bounced between the strangeness of looking through it and my host's churning feelings.

"I will remember," the woman thought, clenching her teeth, balling her fists. "Forget the prayer book.... This will be my evening meditation. Three is a holy number. I'll pick three. Every night I'll remind myself how they are a part of me. I won't fail. Every night. Which three shall they be?"

I perceived her gathering up pictures, some from long ago, some closer to the surface, shifting and sorting as she chose her memories:

On a mountain trail in a dry pine forest, spicy with the afternoon heat, she came upon fresh spoor. A group of people crowded around to examine it, whispering a word: "Bear." She looked down, then up the path. There it was: a huge, humped presence blocking their way. "Get down," she hissed. "Stay still."

They crouched, watching as the pointed snout swung back and forth. It saw her. For many heartbeats, bear and woman weighed together the pros and cons of confrontation. Someone whispered, "What shall we do?"

"Wait, wait," she breathed.

I shrank into the darkness, appalled at the woman's competing terror and attraction for the beast. *How can it be so big?* I wondered, overwhelmed by its wildness.

Then the memory faded and, both relieved and bereft, I allowed my attention to turn with my host's.

"Otters...." She visited them first in an enclosure, fascinated by their coasting between the elements of earth and water. Then, in a canoe on a broad river, gliding serenely, looking languidly at the bank, she noticed a slick black branch as long as her arm curving up from the ground—but it wasn't a stick. An otter paused there, watching her with bright jet eyes as she watched it, astounded as she that they met in freedom.

Time suspended. Beast and human hearts beat in unison. The expanse of water between them dwindled to nothing. High in the sky, a bird cried. The otter slid, long and heavy, into the river. Its face, bristly whiskers dripping, surfaced on the other side of her boat, checking whether she was still there and seemed trustworthy. Then he was gone. She kept her eyes on the ripples, longing to connect with him again, yearning as for a lost child.

I recognized the otter. The stiff little statue was both true and false as well. The creature incarnated so much more in its streamlined body. I ached with my host to touch such careless grace.

"Now, closer to home," thought the woman. "Cats—my dear Pip." I observed through her eyes the black fur speckled with caramel, the long, thin tail straight up in the air, the small, angular face topped by stiff, pointed ears. Memory faded as Pip, present and attentive, wove her smooth body around the woman's calves, in and out, a pattern familiar and teasing. As my host gazed down, the cat paused and looked up, round eyes with curious vertical slits meeting hers in recognition.

They belong to each other, I realized. *It's her cousin, like my little Jen. How strange to have kin so different from you.*

"Bear, otter, and cat. I'll get totems of each and hold them close. Even if I never see them again, I'll carry them with me in my soul." The woman said it out loud. She stooped, picked up Pip, and turned to walk back to the bag.

As she crossed the room, a voice rang out. She pivoted to look through a doorway leading into other rooms. "Ann! Annie, are you ready to go? We have the briefing in thirty minutes."

The masculine tone, round with well-being and eagerness, triggered the desire to…comply? Nurture? Ah—to protect.

A face appeared in the door frame, blue eyes smiling under unruly brown hair. I knew those eyes. They were the same shape and same color as Pop's—so rare, so beautiful. Then the man's smile faded. Her host noticed his gaze fix on her arms, holding the cat. She looked away from his face.

"Oh, Annie, Pip will be fine. It'll be OK, you'll see. C'mon, you have all day tomorrow to pack."

The woman crouched, setting the cat down, running

her hand along its back. I felt the throat we shared tighten, fighting for control. Still bent, she said, with feigned lightness, "Yup, you go start the truck. I'll just be a second."

I understood she didn't want him to detect her pain. She was hiding this part of her soul, as I sometimes hid my own. The guilt of withholding the center of her being warred inside her with the need to shelter his joy. A tear escaped, landing on Pip's dark coat like a tiny star in the deep night sky. The man didn't see it. He had already turned and gone.

As she stood, the woman's gaze encountered a shelf on the opposite wall. There was the otter carving, catching her attention, validating her purpose. She reached out and took it in her hand. On my hidden balcony, I noticed pressure on my own palm.

With a violent spasm, my eyes flew open and found the ceiling of Old Ma's house above me. The smallness of my body shocked me. I lifted my hand, which did indeed hold the otter figure, but my fingers looked warped, short and stubby. Where had she gone, the woman with the cat? Where were Pip and the other animals, her relatives so strange and wonderful?

I sat up, tears coursing down my cheeks. Someone squatted directly in front of me, face to face, startling me. I gasped in panic before I recognized Da's bushy beard, with Pops beside him. They stared at me, but didn't reach out, didn't comfort me. I looked right, then left, and saw my uncle and Old Ma's daughters sitting, ranged in a circle around me.

"Da!" I cried, holding out my hands but not daring to move.

"Hush," Da said. "Be still and breathe."

"We can't touch you until you tell us." Pops' voice trembled. "You've had a vision, darling girl. You must share it. Be brave now and speak."

"There was a woman with a cat...." I gasped.

"No," One of Old Ma's daughters broke in. "Start at the beginning. Tell us everything, both what you saw and what the woman thought and felt. Take us there with you. Sit a moment, then try again."

I closed my eyes, and the loneliness enveloped me. My shoulders shook as sobs pounded at my clenched teeth, trying to break loose into howls. When the tears wound down, the emptiness waiting in Old Ma's house made a home in my soul. I felt desolate and calm, swept clean.

I wiped my nose on my sleeve and began. "The otter called and when I took it, I found the carryall. Darkness in the bag swallowed me. I became a woman in a different place. Before—I think it was Before."

Shadows crept up the wall of Old Ma's house as I stumbled through my telling. The eyes of those watching grew sad and moist. An auntie rocked back and forth as though she stifled the keening of sorrow.

Da said, "Thank you, child. You rest now and eat."

"We will remember with you," said one of Old Ma's daughters.

"We will remember," each person around me echoed.

"Come, my daughter," said Pops. "You are not alone."

But I knew no comfort for the desolation of leaving the animals, which I now shared with the Before woman. I stood on shaky legs and moved to place the otter figure on the mat with Old Ma's things.

Both of Old Ma's daughters spoke at once.

"You must keep the otter," said one.

"This is yours now," said the second.

I looked up into their wrinkled faces and intent eyes.

"Where are the others?" I asked.

The old women glanced at each other. They reached to

leather cords around their necks, pulling pouches made of woven bark from under their shirts. One took out a figure, humped and black, carved from wood like the otter: small eyes; soft, rounded ears; long snout—the bear. The other opened her hand to show a tiny pottery figurine, white with painted yellow eyes and black whiskers, a long tail curved about its toes.

"Pip was black and gold," I told her.

"Yes," the old woman replied in a whisper. "This was the closest Ma could find. She didn't have much time to gather them up, you see."

I looked up into her face, beginning to understand: Death was not to be feared. The enemy that killed was forgetting who you were part of. This family I didn't know I had, who no longer shared my time and space, still belonged to me. I must always remember.

CHAPTER TWO

Alice came to the end of the story and noticed she hadn't finished more than half her stew, now cold and congealing in its bowl. This tale differed from the children's stories and folktales her aunt had told her before. It rang true. Nainai had had two fathers, Pops and Da. Was she old enough to have known a first colonist? She considered the elderly woman across the table.

"Nainai, is this an actual memory?"

Nainai paused her eating. She unfolded her old limbs, pushing up from her chair, and shuffled around to the wall lined with built-in shelves behind Alice. Reaching for something in the shadows, she set a hand on the girl's shoulder, then bent to place before her—the otter. Alice had seen nothing like it before. She took it in her hands and ran her fingers over the light wood, smooth as Jaren's young cheek. "It's beautiful," she said, "but I don't understand. How can this be real?"

She didn't want to question this person whom she loved more than her parents, but she remembered Pa's criticism of her. He vetoed Alice's request to have Nainai teach history in the village school. "That woman would have us all believe in fairy tales," he'd said, scowling at her. "I hope you don't swallow whole anything she tells you." His harsh words troubled her then. Her own doubt shocked her now.

As she sat down again, Nainai said, "I was born the year that the settlers launched the spaceship back to Earth. My fathers told me that before the Glenn 2 left, mystics on our planet had visions—

sometimes of Goldilocks, sometimes of Earth. But in the four revs since my birth, few visionaries remained. Children no longer sang before they spoke. Many concluded that people shouldn't listen to the old tales. I don't know why this vision visited me. I only know that I remember it as clearly as you barging through my door half an hour ago."

"You said nothing about this before. Why did you write it now?"

Elena turned her head and stared into the interior of her dark hut. She sighed and then faced Alice again, a sad smile deepening her wrinkles. "When I was young—your age—I believed everything would work out alright. I had faith that both God and Goldie existed. I bonded with a man whose essential goodness carried us through many difficulties—the bad times of crop failures, plagues. We always had to be discreet, but somehow, even when my little Mary died, we held onto faith and trusted in a divine pattern.

"Then Jay died. My courage failed. As worry about survival grew, I just carried on. I didn't challenge the bitterness and anger growing in this village. I lost my confidence in grace. People didn't want to hear about what mattered to their neighbors, in case they disagreed. I couldn't leave, but to stay I had to change—keep my head down and my tongue quiet." Her dark eyes searched Alice's face for understanding.

"And now?" Alice asked. "Do you still have faith?"

Nainai nodded. "That's the question, isn't it?" She sighed.

"The faith I have now differs from when I was young. Somehow, I used to think other people made things right—that our society couldn't let us down. I know better now. I wish I had done more, been braver, spoken up for the values of patience and community and the importance of everyone." She reached out to touch the otter in front of Alice.

"You belong to the present, dear girl; I'm halfway to eternity. Soon, I'll leave this time altogether. I don't know if my story can right what's wrong with us, but it's all I have to offer. I feel this truth needs to be remembered, even after I die."

"Who do you want to remember it?" Alice asked, knowing the answer. The responsibility weighed on her shoulders already. She gazed at the old woman's hands resting on the table, brown skin loose, ridged with veins and gnarled knuckles. They still had strength in them but mapped a lifetime of work and struggle. She looked up to see the dark, gold-flecked eyes focused on her.

"Not just this story. There are others I need to tell. History always interested you—not only the settlers, but back to our origins on Earth. I'd like to give you all my memories. I'm not sure what you should do with them, though. Perhaps someone at the Academy can help you make sense of them."

The Academy...Alice's heart jumped at the words. Nainai wanted her to enter the Academy. This made her request easier, even though she didn't want to be a historian. She yearned to study nature: not just plants and insects, but daks as well. Although her folks could see nothing good about the winged reptiles which often threatened their crops, they fascinated her. Still, she'd agree to anything if only, somehow, they gave her permission to go. And preserving the stories might make leaving more bearable. It would be like taking a bit of Nainai's soul with her.

Alice reached over and placed her hand on top of the old woman's fingers, her lighter skin shining on the darker base. "I will take your stories, Nainai. I'll keep them safe. We'll figure out together what to do with them. But I need to tell you something before you give them to me."

Again, gold glinted in dark brown eyes as Nainai read her face. "Something you need from me?"

Alice laughed. "Am I so transparent?" She put her hand back in her lap and took a deep breath, reminding herself to go slow and explain her dilemma.

"You like Dinah, don't you, Nainai?"

"The scientist from Seaside who studied bilbugs and taught here last rev? She seemed quite competent. I know you learned a lot from her. I thought she returned home."

"She did." Alice looked toward the door and sighed. "This is the thing.... Dinah and I...well, we're in love. We want to heart-bond, Nainai. I always planned to attend the Academy. Now, knowing Dinah, I want to go even more. And Ma and Pa don't mind us being together, but they keep talking about me making a first-bond and having a baby soon."

Alice's eyes darted back to the older woman's face, rewarded by her quiet attention. Taking courage, she went on.

"I need to get Pa's permission to leave after this crop comes in. Dinah teaches at the Academy. She'll recommend me for admission and then find me a first-bond in Seaside. I could start my studies now and live with her. She'll take care of me."

Alice paused again. She saw no signs of distress on Nainai's face to cause caution. The older woman nodded, showing that she should continue, but somehow, Alice couldn't raise any more words. Nainai eventually broke the silence.

"You're of age. It's your choice. Our society expects you to have a baby soon, but it's your decision where to go, who will father the child, and what to do with the rest of your life. If you're asking me how I feel about this, well.... My emotions are mixed. I'll miss you terribly. I knew the day would come when you would leave, though. You must act now, in the present. This is your time. I'm happy and proud that you will study at the Academy. You'll succeed in any field of study you choose."

Alice scanned her elderly aunt's face, noting the soft gaze and slight smile playing there. Yes, she thought, I can trust Nainai with anything. She nodded, showing she still listened, and the old woman continued.

"As for your relationship with Dinah: She is much older than you, but the heart knows no age, does it? You're too young to bond permanently. Have a child or two. Then, if your love for Dinah weathers well and matures, make the arrangement permanent. You'll know when the right time comes."

The words fell like a blessing on Alice. She ducked her head to hide how deeply the old woman's acceptance touched her. "Thank you," she whispered. She gathered her courage again and continued.

"This is my problem, though. I want to do what you have said, but Pa claims he's become a Glad—you know, joined the Gladiator movement. We've been arguing a lot about whether anyone should leave Far Meadow. He got mad at Liam's family last third for letting him go to Seaside because he maintains a boy's duty is here, with his household and village. I'm afraid that when I tell Pa that I want to go, he'll forbid it."

Nainai frowned and took a deep breath. "A Gladiator, huh? I heard the speech that started that movement a long time ago. Have you learned about the first gladiators?"

Alice shook her head, and the old woman sat up straighter in her chair, squaring her shoulders to the task of teaching.

"In our ancient Earth past, a people called Romans enslaved others and made them fight each other in an enclosed space, an arena, while they watched, betting on who would live and who would die. When George Seaside preached his vision of how humans must conquer any world they inhabit, his followers took the name 'gladiator' because he said the planet pits us against her elements like those slaves. That was back in—oh let me see—rev twenty-five. George was a fool. I'm sorry to hear Humphrey is giving in to that simplistic way of viewing the world."

Alice chewed her lip. "Glads don't want kids to go away to school anymore, even if they promise they'll return. Pa voted against starting our village classes back up two revs ago, after the plague. He said we should apprentice kids to farmers or blacksmiths or something practical. That's why I'm worried. My folks like Dinah, though. She really helped with the bilbug infestation. I'm interested in natural sciences, but I want to study daks, not bugs. Pa doesn't see any value in daks. He says they're about as useful as fairy dragons. But Nainai, I'll major in bugs if that's what gets me to Seaside. I could learn about daks and Earth animals—as a hobby. I can do history too."

Alice heard her voice pitch higher, taking on a wheedling tone as she rambled through arguments which had been running through her head all week. *This is exactly how I don't wish to sound*, she fumed. She hoped the old woman didn't notice the blush on her face.

Nainai sighed again and nodded. "Let's think this through, Alice. The Academy is the first hurdle. We need your folks, and the mayor too, to understand how valuable you'll be if you get an education which can help us solve farmers' problems. If we emphasize usefulness rather than your native curiosity about creation, we might have a chance of convincing them to make this investment.

"However, birthing your first-bond child at Seaside will be harder for all the elders here to swallow. We just didn't have enough children survive the last two revs to replace our older population. Perhaps that's our bargaining chip, though. Would you agree to bring the baby back for Janelle and Humphrey to raise?"

Alice looked down at the table. She dreaded this part of the conversation. She also resented having to disclose her private conversations with her lover. They fantasized a lot during the time Dinah spent in Far Meadow about finding Alice a first-bond mate in Seaside among the Academy professors. All the settlements craved children. The last two revs had devastated the entire planet. A liaison producing a healthy baby for a professor's household would be extremely valuable. The teacher who facilitated such a partnership... well, Dinah said it would allow her to achieve her much-deserved tenure.

"It would be OK with me," Alice admitted, not meeting Elena's eyes. "But Dinah thinks the first child should stay in Seaside. I would bring the second one to Far Meadow, though."

The old woman simply sat, nodding for her to continue. *It's not fair to make me have to decide between my lover and my family*, Alice fumed silently. She felt the familiar heat of anger flood into her blood.

"It's not like I haven't given five revs of my life to my household and this village. I was in the fields with Pa and Ma at one rev old. But Dinah wants to advance at college too. She's earned that. She just could use a little help. If my first child goes to an Academy family, it might be the boost she needs to get ahead." She glared at Nainai, who continued to sit quietly, raising her white eyebrows in question.

"Look, I'd promise to bring my second, even a third, baby back here. That should make them happy, don't you think?" Her desperation echoed loudly in the small room, but Alice kept her eyes focused on Nainai. To her surprise, the elderly woman nodded and lowered her gaze to the table.

"I think I see where this went wrong," she said. "It's my fault. I suggested using a child as a bargaining chip. Now you're considering the lives of two or three babies as the payment for your freedom. This never would have happened in the old days."

Alice eyed her warily. "What do you mean?"

"Children aren't objects to be used to suit our needs, even when those needs are desperate." The ancient voice strengthened, finding its footing with these words. "The settlers promised each child would be equally valuable, and the entire colony would put their best interests first. We always allowed the mother to choose the father and household for her children, trusting that a mother considers her baby's welfare first and then the good of all humanity. But we're losing that perspective. Now, we consider the interest of our individual villages primary. That is the Gladiator's viewpoint. It leads to death, Alice—death for us all."

Nainai's words shocked Alice to her core. Was she being selfish? Often, elders told her she was, but this implicated the complete village. The critique included Dinah too, and Alice realized that a niggling worry somewhere deep inside her resonated with that judgment. She shook her head, opting for cleansing anger instead of doubt.

"Well, I don't know what you want me to do about it, Nainai." Her conflicting emotions bled into her voice. "If I stay here, my parents and village get a child. If I go to Seaside, that community gets it. I don't have much say in it at all."

"No, it's difficult for you to discern the complete picture right now. That is clear." Elena spoke deliberately, watching Alice, who continued to stare defiantly. "You're in a tight turnaround spot, my dear, and don't have the tools for this task. I wonder how we can carve out time and space for you to experience more of life. Let's see if we can get permission for you to enter the Academy and wait a few thirds before your first-bond. You are still very young. I'd like you to enjoy your love affair with Dinah before taking on too many responsibilities."

"Then you'll help me convince them to let me go?" Hope blossomed up, pushing anger aside.

"I'll speak to the mayor and your parents with you tomorrow after lunch. We'll have to catch Humphrey before he gets back into the fields. Will that do, dear?"

"Oh, yes, Nainai. Thank you. They'll listen to you." In her excitement, Alice jumped up, and the otter clattered to the floor. She stooped to pick it up and, cradling it in her palm, held it out to the old woman. "I will keep your stories, Nainai. I'll have a com-pad too, at the academy. You can send me any new ones you write, and I'll read them, I swear."

Elena reached out, closing the young fingers around the little figure. "I'll hold you to that promise, dear. The otter is yours now as a pledge between us."

Alice moved around the table and bent to kiss Nainai's age-softened cheek before gathering up her household's bowl and leaving. She straightened and turned, seeing the door had swung open. Someone stood on the other side: Nettie, come to fetch her. How much had she heard?

Alice charged through Nainai's door without acknowledging the girl and headed across the sunken courtyard. If Nettie told her folks what Alice was up to, she'd lose the advantage of surprise. They might think up excuses to make her stay home before the old woman convinced them otherwise. Her Pa rarely changed his mind once it was made up, and Ma never crossed him.

"Can I see the otter?" Her younger sister's voice halted her before she mounted the stairs to ground level and the howling wind.

"OK, but you have to keep it a secret, Nettles. Do you understand? You can't tell Ma or Pa about anything you heard here today."

"How come? Did you do something bad?"

Her sister was a rev and a third younger, her face still full and round, with a sprinkling of freckles across her sunburned nose. They had been inseparable until Dinah came and Alice stepped into an adult love affair.

Alice sighed. "No, silly. I did nothing wrong, but you know how Pa is. If he thinks I'm spending too much time talking to Nainai, he won't let me come over anymore." She placed the little figurine in her sister's hands.

"I could bring Nainai's supper sometimes." The younger girl stroked the statue. "She might give me something too."

"You know what, Nettie? That's a good idea. After harvest, you could start. But the best thing about coming here isn't getting stuff. The very best thing is hearing Nainai's stories. So, let's not tell the folks about this, OK? In fact, you can come tomorrow, if Ma doesn't need you, and help me here."

The trick to controlling Nettie, Alice knew, was to convince her she was on your team. It only worked until someone else offered her allegiance. She would say yes to anyone who needed her. But it might be enough to keep her silent until tomorrow noon. Luckily, this close to the harvest, the elders' attention was on weather and calculating how many hands they needed to bring in the grain. It was a good bet no one would notice Nettie had a secret for a few days. She reclaimed the otter and tucked it into her tunic pocket.

As the two girls climbed out of Nainai's sunken courtyard, the full strength of the wind hit them hard. They pulled on their goggles, linked arms, and bowed into the rising gale. Such weather would delay the harvest, but even that didn't discourage Alice now. Maybe, just maybe, she thought, I'm on my way.

CHAPTER THREE

By morning, the planet seemed to have spent her ire. As Alice got up, the stillness of the air startled her. Calm weather was cause for rejoicing, but it made most people nervous. They had so little of it. At breakfast, Humphrey laid out tasks for the day. He charged Alice with rounding up extra hands for the harvest he expected to be ready soon.

"You go over to Micah's, daughter. Tell him that if he and his household can help us for a few days next week, we'll join his crew the week after. His barley runs behind ours, so that should work out."

Alice knew her father favored Micah. They often helped each other, but Pa usually arranged this himself. She realized, as she stepped out into the still air and honeyed sunlight, that he wanted to throw her together with his friend. She sighed. If Pa set his heart on her bonding with Micah, that would be another hurdle to overcome.

Far Meadow village, like the other four farming settlements on Goldilocks, comprised a public round of lawn about half an acre in circumference, ringed by concentric circles of dwellings in narrow, sunken courtyards. Alice's household lived in one of the bigger, outer-ring houses on the northern side. She headed into the hamlet, passing the inner circle of older huts, to cross the commons and reach Micah's. As she approached the village center, Alice noticed all twelve of the community children playing outside. Their own Jaren, just one and two-thirds revs old, practiced somersaults on the yellow grass. A few kids kicked a ball around, cheerfully yelling.

Her sister Nettie and another girl her age swung a rope for Liam's younger brother, who jumped it to a rhyme so familiar she didn't even have to hear the words to find the chant in her head.

"Five full harvests in one rev,

Then comes Bleak and you're dead.

If plagues don't kill you, hunger will.

How many baskets can you fill?"

She came close enough to catch the girls chanting the number of jumps young Pauly managed.

"One. Two. Three...."

Not long ago, a windless day like this would have found her playing without a care too, the words of the rhyme just a meaningless beat to follow. When had she grown into the realization that this poem held the truth of their lives on Goldilocks? For as many revs as anyone but Nainai could remember, the pressure to produce sufficient food in the thirty months before Goldie began the farthest curve in her loop around the sun dictated their every decision, every action—especially in the farming villages. Once the second half of the final third of the rev hit, nothing would grow in the fields. The month of Bleak, that odd thirty days which followed third December, marked the epitome of darkness and cold. Despair nipped at everyone's heels then, even when the days started to lengthen and brighten, for it would be three more months before the ground warmed enough to plant again.

"Ten. Eleven. Twelve...."

Only three more harvests in this cycle. And the dark months brought the most sickness too, mowing down a population worn out by hunger and cold. It hadn't always been this way. The first colonists consistently had an abundance to carry them through. But for three generations....

"Eighteen. Nineteen. Twenty...oh no! You're out, Pauly."

The boy had stumbled and fallen, but Alice watched him laugh and get up, moving to take his turn at swinging the rope. *Twenty baskets of food will never see us through,* she mused, hoping the game didn't predict disaster.

Occupied with these thoughts as she walked around the lawn, she nearly missed hearing a familiar voice calling to her. Her elderly aunt waved, standing on the stairs to her sunken courtyard, her head just clearing ground level.

"Nainai, you're up early."

"Do you have a minute, dear? It occurred to me after you left that I have a story which might clarify the choices before you."

"Sure. I have a message for Micah, but I'll walk back this way."

"Come now, Alice. I saw Micah go to his daughter's a few minutes ago. It will be awhile before he gets home."

As Alice stepped down the stairs to join her on a narrow bench by the hut's front door, Nainai handed her the com-pad.

"I've been thinking of my entrance into the Academy," the old woman said. "I was about a rev younger than you when I started. The school may have changed since I studied there, but the experience of leaving home and having to fit into a new community—that will be similar, I'm afraid. I wanted you to read this before we talk to your folks today."

"Do you want me to change my mind about going?" Alice frowned as she took the com-pad in her hands.

"No, dear, not at all." Nainai's voice lowered, caressing the worry out of her. "I hope you'll understand what you are committing to, and also what you are asking of your family."

At Alice's sharp, sidewise glance, Nainai tilted her head. "Remember that Elders, especially your parents, have complicated emotions tied up in you, Alice. While Humphrey and Janelle seem to use you, beneath that need to control is love. It will come out eventually. When you see it, accept it as the gift it is."

The younger woman pursed her lips, then gave a quick nod and bent to her reading.

A School Girl's Tale

(This occurred in the second third of Goldie's fourteenth revolution around the sun. I was over five revs old, or sixteen years in the old Earth counting.)

I look upon myself—a girl, almost a woman—from a great distance, as if gazing from a moon above. There I am—Elena Forest Edge, a little tall for my five revs, brown skinned and with wild curly black hair corralled into a broad braid on my neck. I'm skinny to the brink of emaciation, stalking up to the portal of the Academy complex, which will be my home.

Da follows me, a protective shadow hovering. I've always been his favorite. We share inquisitive minds but also the need for acceptance, the warm embrace of kindred spirits. His is the hand I most often reach for. Mine is the company he finds comfort in. I wonder how we'll survive without each other.

We hurry through the short hall connecting the portal to the main room and step into an enclosed space larger than any I have seen before. Foreign impressions flood my senses. The still air smells of coffee and stale sweat. The light, diffuse from the transparent wall, softens the squares of doors and desks scattered around the room. I struggle to make out the pattern and purpose of the area in front of me.

A person with shockingly short hair stands up from behind a desk to greet us. The pale, smooth face appears to belong to a very tall boy or an ill woman, but the voice sounds like Pops—a solid tenor. I know I'm staring, but I can't seem to stop.

Da steps forward, covering my confusion. "I am Armel Forest Edge. I bring our daughter Elena Forest Edge to be enrolled in the college."

"Ah, yes." The man consults a square of plastic he holds in his hands—a com-pad. The rest of the conversation fades for me. I covet this gift given to every Academy student: a real computer with the memory of all humankind locked within. I spent most of the last rev trying to get my aunt Rena to lend hers to me, but this one possession nobody is required to share. My breath quickens.

"Elena?" Da's voice intrudes. "Answer the question."

"I'm sorry. I wasn't paying attention." Looking down at the smooth floor, my face flames with shame. Coveting and not attending. Maybe they won't accept me.

But the man laughs. "Don't worry, youngster. It's a bit overwhelming at first. Just tell me your genealogy so I can make sure our records are correct, and then we'll get you settled."

I breathe deeply, then dare to peer into the strange face. His gray eyes, unlined with age or wind, attend. I recite: "I am Elena Forest Edge out of Kama Seaside and Stefan Forest Edge. I am of the household of Stefan and Armel Forest Edge."

"OK, then. That checks out. Bring your carryall, and we'll get you settled with the other beginners. Say goodbye to your father."

The moment I dread. "Can't he come with me?" my voice squeaks. I hope my brown skin camouflages my blush.

"Oh, no, sorry. We allow no men except staff in the girls' dormitory." He looks at our sorrowful faces and relents. "Step into the waiting area to say your goodbyes. Find me when you're ready to go." His waving hand shows a door to the left, and we gratefully comply.

I see us in that little room now, from the distance of all those revs.

Ignoring the pristine white chairs and sofa, we stand

sheltered, arms encircling each other, my head on his broad chest, rubbing against the stiff bristle of his beard. I smell the fields and sunlight and wind on his sweater. I hear his heart thumping. His rough hands smooth back my unruly hair, and he presses a kiss to my forehead. Neither of us knows that this will be our last embrace. I will lie awake many nights in the long, dark months ahead, savoring that hug, recalling every detail, every word.

"Remember always, you are loved," he murmurs and then lifts my chin to gaze into my eyes. He winks. "I'll come for you at harvest. You don't get to be lazy just because you're a scholar now."

And I let him go, foolishly fearing more for myself than for him.

I return to the entrance hall, allowing the man with the strange face and hair to lead me back through the warren of corridors joining Quonset huts and domes. These buildings all sit on top of the earth, connected, so a person never has to leave the shelter of their walls. In the dormitory, one of my older village cousins appears and shows me to my niche. The narrow bed, the box at the foot to hold my belongings, and a little fold-down desk and chair will be my own for two whole revs. It seems stark compared to the room I had to myself in the sunken house at Forest Edge, but the overflowing plenty of knowledge balances out this poverty of space and possessions—and even the lack of close family and friends.

I know, with the first class, grasping my com-pad as the teacher brings up a holograph of Earth, our parent planet: I belong here. The faltering and sporadic lessons of my youth prepared me for this by teaching me hunger. Here, people will explain everything I wonder about. Here, they study the world we came from, which races around its sun three times as fast as Goldilocks circumvents hers. There are pictures and descriptions of Earth animals I recognize from my vision and others as well. There are heavenly maps, naming not only the stars I can see, but also those burning in galaxies I didn't realize existed. Our settlers' history, which once seemed so vague and unimportant, takes on a shape and weight and reality which alters me. Even the math I despise becomes a language to unlock the secrets our mysterious ancestors left for us.

And the people.... The experience of being surrounded by strangers when, all my life, I've known every neighbor, shocks me more than anything else. At an early communal dinner served in the cavernous cafeteria, my cousin leaves to sit with her friends, telling me to find my own age group. I accept a tray and then perch by a girl about my height, offering to give her some of my bread.

"You don't have to share your food here," she says. "Look, I have my dinner. There's plenty to go around."

"Excuse me, but in my village, even if you have a meal in front of you, we offer some of ours. It's just something polite to say."

"Well, that's stupid, if there's enough for everyone." She sounds so definite, but softens when she sees my distress. "We have plenty of dumb traditions in my home too. When I came here, I thought every girl with a braid like yours was partnered. Braids mean bonded in my town."

I reach behind to touch my thick rope of hair. "I'm too young for even a first-bond." Fumbling with the cord that holds it in place, I feel like a hick. I wish I had a beautiful straight mane falling down my back like this girl.

"No, no," she laughs. "Don't change it for me. People here wear their hair any way they want. See that boy over there?" She points with abandon at a youth with a shaved skull. "He comes from my village. Yesterday, he had a ponytail down to his shoulders. He's going to catch it when he goes home." She sticks out her tongue at him as he catches the gist of her comment and shakes his head at her.

She giggles. "You're new, aren't you? What's your name?"

The boldness of the request startles me. Nobody but elders ever ask direct questions in my home. I decide I like this strange girl very much. "I'm Elena Forest Edge. May I ask you your name too?"

My bench mate nods. "Oh, from way outback. That explains a lot. I'm Susanne Touch Down, but everyone calls me Suz."

See them there, two fledgling girls, one with a fat black braid and the other with straight ebony hair spread over her narrow shoulders, bending their heads over bowls of lentil stew and soy bread. In another instant, they'll laugh at a young man who winks at them. They'll sit together in classes the next day and become the best of friends. The irrepressible good nature of Suz buoys me up. It reveals the wonders of friendship between those who are different—for no one can be more opposite to the shy, awkward youngster I am than the exuberant Suz.

During that whole third of rev fourteen, the universe discloses new vistas to me every day. The air at the Academy vibrates with energy, making my heart beat faster. Even news that the pox returned, coming when it did, just before the harvest, couldn't frighten me. No one at school falls ill. My mind, feasting on the banquet of learning, shies from the fact that people out back are getting sick. I set that information aside, saying, "It's too bad, but what can I do about it?"

I feel just a pinch of guilty relief when Da sends word that it's too dangerous to come home and help with the farm. The End of Third holiday means backbreaking labor in the outback, in windy fields, cutting down and stacking stalks of grain, digging potatoes and carrots, picking rows of peas and beans. Safe in Seaside, though, I sit down to a family feast at my biology teacher's house, which I don't even have to cook. It's a luxury of exotic foods and the joy of being included in an inner circle of this foreign life.

How innocent that happiness was. Only a week later, when I return to the rhythm of my studies, getting ready for exams, word comes that the youngest of my household, a baby girl born just after I left, died of the plague. Pops pens the letter himself, noting Da is too busy with work to write. I search his words for evidence of tragic feelings but find only plain information: The child had been alive and now is dead. They are sad, but life goes on. They are taking good care not to fall ill themselves. I wasn't to worry but was charged with studying hard and making them proud.

The note gives me permission to do what I want to do anyway, so I embrace it without question. My test scores on this third are among the highest in my class, and I float on a cloud of confidence. I wish to spend my whole life here. I'll become anything—doctor, teacher, scientist—to stay in this wide world.

Heading into second supper the day after they announced the grades, the man who greeted me when I first arrived with Da, whom I now know is dean of students, calls my name and hurries toward me. His urgency frightens me. Did I do something wrong? Is he coming today to kick me out?

And indeed, his words do exactly that: All my family is dead. They burn my village to the ground to stop the spread of disease.

I stayed at the college for the rest of that rev and two more. I pledged my first-bond and bore two children, while still a student, then taught, and finally left its halls with regret. Never again would I experience the innocent wonder

and excitement of that first third. I look back now, knowing
I could not have saved them—not Pops or Da, not Davy or
the babe. But I never knew if they died frightened, in pain,
and alone, while I luxuriated in my magic bubble, watching
the heavens of other worlds and paying no attention to the
needs of my family. The cost—to lose those loved ones of my
early life without even saying goodbye: That price was high.

A cloud drifted over the sun as Alice finished reading Nainai's
story. In the shadow, she looked up to see her elderly relative more
clearly than in the sunlight. The old woman's hands rested in her
lap. She stared at the wall in front of them, seeing something beyond
the bricks.

"Oh, Nainai, I didn't know.... I'm so sorry you lost your family."

The gold-brown eyes focused on her and a smile bloomed among
the wrinkles.

"Thank you, Alice. I'm not looking for sympathy, though. I give
you this tale because I want you to understand both the wonder and
the wound of the Academy. Be aware there's a cost to the journey you
embark on. It may not be the same price I paid, but you can't come
back home unchanged from this experience. I pray our village won't
meet with disaster while you're gone, but it will never be the same
for you. Life in the present always changes. It's good and exciting,
even when painful. May you be blessed as I was with friends to pull
you through the gaps. May you be such a friend to others."

Alice reached out and took Nainai's thin hand in her own. "You'll
always be here, Nainai. I'll always come home to you."

As if she didn't hear her, the older woman said, "What you do
in the present impacts eternity, Alice. You usually can't know how. I
hope love does not leave when the pattern of our existence changes,
though." Then she sat up straight, pointing with her chin to the path
above. "Go on. I saw Micah cross the commons. He'll be waiting for
you at his hut."

Reluctantly, Alice stood and bent to kiss the white head before climbing the stairs to continue her task.

CHAPTER FOUR

Coming down the steps into the sunken courtyard at Micah's, Alice noticed the door propped wide, spilling sunlight into the dark interior. Few windows graced the walls of this old inside-ring dwelling, built by the first settlers of Far Meadow. The kitchen and family room were one, like Nainai's. Micah, a big, muscled man with thinning black hair tied back from a generous round face, seemed to Alice to resemble his house. He felt familiar: grounded, limited, but always there, welcoming neighbors. *No wonder he's Pa's best friend,* Alice thought to herself, frowning. *He's the only one who puts up with Pa in his nasty mood.* She amended her critique—*just like my moods*—then adjusted her mouth into a smile as her eyes, getting used to the shadows, saw Micah sitting at the old, square table.

"Alice, have you come for a visit this fine morning?"

"Pa sent me to ask if you can help with the yellow grass harvest next week. We need someone to reap and two or three to bind. With more people, we could finish in a few days. Then he'll pledge our household to work with you."

"Sit down, girl. Here, I'll pour you a cup of coffee. My Jenny baked this morning. Have a bun."

Alice perched on the bench across from him, looking around. Micah had three adult children—Jenny and her two brothers. She knew they no longer lived with their father, but she had never been to his house when one of them wasn't present.

"Where are your children today?"

"Oh, busy with this and that." The huge hand delicately placed a bun on a small plate and set it in front of her. "I visited Jenny this morning. She's a wonderful daughter, but she has a family of her own. I need to stay out of her way."

He looked down at her, his smile sad with the shadow she expected. Micah's heart-bond, Mimi, succumbed to the last sickness, a rev ago now. And before Mimi died, they endured the loss of two children in their household, including Jackie, a special friend of Alice's, just a third younger than she. After leaving the big house to his grown sons, Micah moved into this small hut.

Alice ducked her head, looking at the perfect breakfast bun. "Thank you," she said, taking a bite. It was impolite to refuse food and anyway, who would turn down one of Jenny's creations? She sighed. "This tastes wonderful." She tried to put more enthusiasm into her voice than she usually bestowed on pastry, hoping to cheer him.

Micah settled back in his chair to watch her eat and sipped at his own coffee. "Do you consider me elderly, Alice? You're just six revs, and I'm approaching fourteen."

Startled, Alice glanced up at him. What was she supposed to say? She covered her confusion by taking another bite and shrugging.

Unfortunately, Micah knew how to wait. He wasn't going to let her duck out of this conversation. She swallowed. "I guess you're as old as Pa? Maybe older, because Jennie and your boys are all grown."

Micah nodded and frowned as he sipped his coffee. "I'm more than a rev younger than your father. Mimi was older than me. Her first partner died, and she brought their three teenagers into our household. Jackie and little Ned—they were our blood children." He paused, looking into the bottom of his mug. "Of course, they're gone now."

"I'm sorry. I miss Jackie too." Alice bit her lower lip, glancing at his face, rough and weather-beaten. His eyes caught and held hers.

"Yes, it's been hard these last few revs," Micah said. Then he sat straighter, putting down his cup. "You know, I wouldn't bring this up without your folks' permission, Alice, but I talked to your Pa yesterday, and he gave me encouragement. You're coming of age to have a first-bond. I'm young enough to father a child and lonely enough to want one more try at parenting. I wonder if you might consider me a potential partner?"

There it is, thought Alice, *the trap to keep me here*. She turned her face from him and stared at the thick wall of the hut, anger flushing her cheeks. Neither Pa nor Ma had warned her. How could they ambush her like that? What could she say to him?

She knew that getting up and walking out wouldn't solve anything. Finally, in the silence that Micah let gather, she spoke, still facing away. "No disrespect to you, Micah, but my parents haven't included me in this discussion. I'm not ready to make this decision yet. I wish you hadn't brought it up."

"Ah." The soft sigh escaped from the big man across the table. "Then pretend those words weren't said."

He took a breath, and Alice thought with relief that now she could escape. Instead, as she turned her face toward him, he leaned in, demanding her attention. "But Alice, when you are ready, I'll move us into one of the bigger houses, give you all the comforts of life, even—"

She stood abruptly, cutting him off. "I am not ready. Don't think you can buy me. Shall I tell my father you'll help him with the harvest, or was that part of your deal with him too—that you will only work if I agree to bond with you?"

The shocked look on Micah's face shamed her. She stomped toward the door to get some space between them, but then stopped to wait for his answer, struggling to hold onto her fury so the fear and embarrassment of the moment wouldn't overtake her.

The older man stood, his bulk taking up most of the small kitchen. Alice raised her face defiantly, but instead of meeting answering anger, she saw only concern.

"You may tell your Pa that I and my sons will come to his harvest. Jenny will help too if she can. No one is selling or buying you, Alice. I'm sorry I took you by surprise. I hope you can forgive me."

She turned on her heel and left without saying another word. What was there to say? She bounded up the stairs and let instinct guide her away. Tears welled behind her eyes, and she wanted to be angry, just angry.

It's all Pa's fault, she convinced herself. *Now I've hurt Micah, my friend's father and an honorable man. If they didn't force me into a corner, I wouldn't be so rude.* Her remorse at hurting someone who was already wounded threatened to steal away her righteous fury. She knew she had to get control over herself before she got home.

She found herself at the stairway leading down to the town's community center, a lodge near the commons which served as school and gathering place for the village. With the children gone, one of the small rooms was likely free. She'd regroup there and pretend this whole thing hadn't happened.

The front door was open when she reached the bottom of the steps. At the end of the large meeting area, she spotted the mayor ushering a stranger into the middle conference room. They were deep in conversation and didn't notice her as they closed the door behind them. The glimpse she got of the outsider intrigued her. This was someone from the Academy. Like Dinah, the man wore his hair cropped and carried a small case which she knew contained a com-pad. Very few people out back had computers which worked and, if they did, kept them home, protected from elements and accidents. Alice hesitated for a moment, not wanting to be discovered but still desiring solitude. Surely, she thought, I can get into one of the other rooms without being noticed.

She entered the right-hand room on silent feet, easing the door shut. As she sat at a little desk lit by a small clerestory window, she realized curiosity about the Academy visitor had already edged out the anger and confusion of the morning's adventure. *He may be recruiting scholars*, Alice mused. *I have to get my name in front of him before I lose my chance. Perhaps good fortune drove me here today.*

She rose and wandered toward the wall between her and the middle room, but the earthwork on the buildings was sturdy and thick. She couldn't hear a word. Could she just drop in on them and confess her heart's desire? Dinah might have already mentioned her to him, and he had come to interview her. Pressure built in her chest. If only she could get accepted before her parents forbade it. Surely, they would be too proud to refuse this honor.

Alice tried to weigh her options. She seldom met, much less spoke to, people outside the village. How could she impress this man? She gathered courage, telling herself that she would not let this opportunity slide. *I'll hang around until they exit that room*, she decided. The mayor will have to feed him lunch, and if I'm here when they leave, she'll have to introduce me.

The middle room's door was shut when she moved into the assembly area. *Alright, they're still in there*, she realized. *What should I say when they come out?*

Sunlight poured in through the courtyard entrance. Alice saw by its slanting rays that mealtime was fast approaching. Nainai had promised to speak to her folks. *I should go get her soon*, she fretted. Her discomfort escalated, and her mind, pulled in two different directions, refused to concentrate on producing a plan. Just when she decided to fetch Nainai, deserting the pipe dream of talking to the Academy representative, the door to the middle room opened.

Alice froze in the courtyard entrance, staring over her shoulder. The mayor, leading her guest out, saw her. "Why, Alice, what are you doing here this morning? The children are playing in the commons today."

"Oh yes, I've seen them," Alice stammered. *I need to say something else*, she realized. *Anything else....* "Um, I just was getting a little quiet time."

The woman looked at her closely. Barbara Far Meadow was a

popular leader. She had held the top position in this village for four revs, ever since Nainai had retired from it. She'd guided the hamlet through good times and bad, relishing the responsibility. Her salt-and-pepper hair, tied back in a tight braid, emphasized her no-nonsense approach to life. For the mayor, unambiguous answers, even if difficult, were necessary. Once she decided on what was in the best interest of the community, she made sure the council members backed her.

Now she nodded and turned to her companion. "Arthur Seaside, I'd like you to meet Alice Far Meadow. She's a student we spoke of this morning."

The young man stepped up beside the mayor and raised his hand in the greeting required during the plagues. Alice looked up into his face, noticing the smooth skin of one who lived indoors most revs. She raised her palm in response and said, "Oh, have you come to recruit students for the Academy? I would so love to go. I'm sure my household and village will support me. Isn't that right, Barbara?"

She immediately regretted her enthusiastic speech as the man frowned and looked down at the floor. The mayor spoke up. "I mentioned you as a possibility, Alice, but I'm afraid that Arthur came to tell us the Academy is not interested in outback students this rev."

"What?" Alice's voice squeaked.

"Yes." The stranger nodded. "I'm sorry to be the bearer of bad news, but unless the villages can send more provisions, we'll have to cut our services to the outlying areas."

Alice noticed the man's narrowed eyes and scowl, and decided he sounded peeved. Had there been failed negotiations? Her chest tightened with fear. "But my pa says we should have a good harvest this third. I'm sure we'll have some to share."

Barbara said, "There are only three more harvests before Bleak. Our own stockpiles need replenishing. The village can't bridge the gulf between what we can spare and what they demand." The mayor directed the bite of her words toward the uncomfortable man at her side. "They even want to send Liam home if we don't increase our gifts to them."

"Well, as I said, Liam is an excellent student. He'll be a valuable asset to you once his education is complete." Neither of them looked at Alice now, as they rehashed the argument just finished.

"He'll be an asset only if he comes back here. Our educated offspring don't return or stay only for a season. As I told you, when you count up the resources we lose and the children who desert us, we are better off keeping our young people home. Take Alice here: Even if you accepted her, she's at the height of her strength and productivity. If we let her go to Seaside, she'll bond with someone there. We'll never see her again and have none of her offspring in our community."

"Oh, but I would bring a child here." Alice looked wildly back and forth between the angry pair in front of her. "I must attend college, Mayor. There's stuff there I can't learn in Far Meadow, but I promise I'll come home."

"Alice, what you need to live a good life and help your village lies right here under your nose." The mayor scowled at her and sniffed. "Higher education gives you a lot of facts and figures but has little to do with keeping us alive and getting in the next harvest. Your family will bring you more joy than you'll ever achieve from studying far away." She directed a disdainful glance at the Academy rep and then ushered him out the door, brushing Alice aside.

Could this day get any worse? Alice recalled that Nainai always said windless days caused her nightmares. Well, here was a waking nightmare: pressure to bond with a man old enough to be her father and to relinquish her dream of a meaningful future. What was she going to do?

Nainai waited for her. She would help her.

She stumbled up the stairs of the meeting room's moat, hurrying to her great-great aunt's house.

***

The elderly woman was exiting the courtyard door of her little inner-ring hut. Her left hand grasped a walking stick, which her creaky hips made necessary these days. Alice's appearance over the edge of the wall halted her slow progress.

"Oh, Nainai," Alice began as she climbed down the steep stairs toward her. But instead of pouring out her story of woe, she was surprised by hot tears springing out of her eyes and tracking down her cheeks.

"Ah. I'm guessing we're having lunch here today," Nainai remarked, turning around and setting her stick against the wall. She directed the girl back inside to a seat at the little kitchen table and set the tea water on to boil, reaching for the soy bread and nut butter with the ease of long practice. Then she made herself comfortable on the chair across from her weeping niece and began making sandwiches.

Alice gulped her feelings down as well as she could. "It's just that I'm so furious, Nainai. I can't keep it in."

"There's no need to here. Take your time. Reach over and hand me the bumble berry jam, would you? This nut butter is too dry by itself."

Alice turned and fumbled for the jar. Her breathing steadied as she pivoted back. She wiped her eyes with her sleeve.

"Bite, chew, and swallow," Elena instructed, shoving a sandwich in her direction. "I'll get the tea." She grabbed the ancient teapot and sprinkled in a generous amount of mint. The fresh smell filled the small room as the boiling water activated the leaves. Then she retrieved two chunky pottery cups, made by Alice and Nettie a rev ago, and set them next to the pot. "Let's give this a couple of minutes to steep, shall we?"

"Yes, Nainai." Alice fought with herself, biting her tongue to stifle the wail which rose in her throat. She clung to the old woman's calm.

Elena settled herself again and raised her eyes to Alice's flushed and still-damp face. "Now, dear, tell me step by step what happened today."

Drawing an unsteady breath, Alice began. "Pa sent me to ask Micah if he would help with the harvest next week. He promised Micah I would make my first-bond with him. He didn't even talk to me about it. I tried not to be rude, but Nainai, he's Jackie's father." Alice heard the panic rising in her voice and stopped to take in air and calm herself.

Elena nodded, tapping her forefinger on her upper lip. As Alice paused, she said, "I'm astounded Micah would broach this subject with Humphrey before speaking to Janelle or even me. I wonder why he's broken with tradition. I'm not surprised he's offered you a first-bond, though. Unless he goes to another village, there are no other available women. And if he wants to keep the offspring of the union, you would be his best bet."

"Why can't a heart-bonded woman here have his child?" Alice asked. "Liam's mom isn't too old, or even Janelle."

Elena picked up her sandwich. Before she took a bite, she said, "Because if all three people are in close proximity, it causes jealousy. It's easier if your forever partner goes away for a third or two, returning home with a child to rejoice in. You should know that already, Alice. You've heard these discussions."

As Alice began to argue, a knock startled them both. Nainai twisted her head around, her mouth full of bread, to see a young man standing in her doorway. Alice jumped to her feet and went to meet him.

"Nainai, this is Arthur Seaside. I meant to tell you—he visited the mayor today. She says no one from Far Meadow will study at the Academy this year because they are asking for more provisions." As she shared this second blow to her day, tears welled again in her eyes. She turned to hide them, retreating to her seat.

"Elena Far Meadow?" The stranger gave her time to swallow

before expecting her to reply. As she rose to greet him, he stepped over the threshold. "Please, don't get up. I'm sorry to intrude, but I wanted to speak to Alice before I left. The teacher on the commons guessed she'd be here."

"Welcome to my home, Arthur Seaside," Elena managed, stifling a cough over crumbs that had gone down the wrong way as she collapsed back into her seat. "Do come in. I think this tea is done. If you don't mind, Alice, pull up the extra chair and grab another mug. We may have much to talk about."

As the three of them settled again, Elena poured, and Arthur sipped his drink before stating his business. On either side of him, the two women waited—one more patiently than the other. As he put his cup down on the table, Alice noticed his long, smooth fingers. *He doesn't have to do much labor*, she reflected, imagining those digits tapping out code on a com-pad.

Finally, he was ready and addressed his host. "I came to tell your young relative there's another way to enter the Academy, which your mayor failed to mention today. I hesitated to bring it up in her presence because she seemed so set against it, but Dinah insisted she would want to know."

"Dinah? She spoke up for me?" Alice grasped at the hope he extended.

"Yes, she considers you the best candidate in the whole outback this year, but we knew our requirements might be out of your village's reach." He smiled at Alice's brightening eyes. "It's clear our biology professor wants you to come."

"What is this other path to acceptance?" Nainai's voice sounded pointed and clipped.

Arthur considered the old woman. With a nod, he acknowledged her concern. "We rarely suggest this, it's true. But times in Seaside are difficult. When the pox hit the coastal communities, many people died. Your mayor judges us as unfair to ask for so much food, but we lost several farms closer to home. If we are to keep the Academy open at all, we need to either shrink our student population or get more resources from the outlying villages."

"I'm not questioning your motives, Arthur. I'm asking what you are suggesting." Nainai sat still. Across from her, Alice frowned with concern. Why was she annoyed?

"Yes, well...." The young man glanced between the two women. "Dinah assumed Alice could live with her and have her first-bond in Seaside. That way, she'd qualify as a resident and the college would be open to her."

Alice beamed at him. "What did I tell you, Nainai? Dinah will take care of me. I'll have my first child there, and then I'll bring my second one back to Far Meadow."

Nainai didn't move a muscle. Her eyes stayed on the Academy rep as she said, "I suspect Arthur has more to say, Alice."

The young man sipped his tea. "You should know that once you start your classes, the rules don't allow home visits until you're through with your studies—two or three revs at least. We can't have students bouncing in and out of their courses. It disrupts the rest of the student body."

Alice stared at him while Elena dropped her gaze and deliberately raised her tea mug to her lips.

"Three revs!" The younger woman gasped. "But I'll be nine revs old by then. Here, women have at least three children by then."

"They know that." Nainai's voice sounded calm, but Alice could hear the anger in it. "They're counting on you staying the rest of your life at Seaside."

Arthur looked into his tea mug. "We lost a third of our population in the last few revs. You're right, Elena Far Meadow. We need more people, especially young women. But consider this: How many doctors serve the outback? What education is available? What choice do women have among eligible men here?

"If Alice comes to Seaside, she'll have many potential mates. Her children will be healthy, and their DNA will contribute to the diversity of our humanity. She'll receive the best care available on the planet. She might even learn enough to become a contributor to our future—discovering cures or more productive species of plants. Don't allow her to bury her mind and prospects out here. Let her come and join in the struggle to build our society."

"Our society?" The old woman raised a white eyebrow, highlighted on her brown face. "Are farmers no longer considered part of human culture?"

Arthur scowled at her. "You're not a fool, Elena Far Meadow. I've looked up your history. Your contributions at the Academy were stellar. It may have been noble of you to come to the outback with your heart-bond when they called for a medical team, but you're too bright not to see what's happening. When Dinah first came here two revs ago, she reported a thriving community with thirty or forty children. I counted a bare dozen on the commons today. And how many adults remain? Maybe fifty, most elderly? The mayor claims the coming harvest can barely feed everyone in this failing village, and the dark months are coming. Far Meadow can't sustain much loss. In another rev, villagers will have to move to the larger towns."

"My question is, will the old places, Seaside and Touch Down, accept the farmers?" Elena's gold-flecked eyes flashed at him. "It sounds to me as if someone has decided we're expendable."

Arthur's voice mirrored her anger. "Survival is the issue for you and for us."

"There used to not be a 'you and us,' young man. Goldilocks once meant everyone together—live or die."

"Well, times change." He set his mug on the table and turned to Alice, whose face had paled during the exchange.

"Alice, would you like me to wait until you make your decision? I'll be happy to escort you to Dinah and see you enrolled in the Academy."

Alice's gaze flashed between him and her great aunt, her throat constricting so breath could hardly pass. "Nainai, I don't know...."

And then anger rose in her chest, forcing out the fear. She stood up and backed away from the table. "How can you ask me to choose? Either I give up my dream of being educated or I desert my family, my home, and everyone I've ever loved, forever?"

Nainai held up her hand, forestalling a response from Arthur. "She's right. You set before her a wrenching decision. She needs time to consider all aspects of her choice. We thank you for being so honest about the stakes."

"I can't wait long for her to decide." The young man directed his bluntness to Nainai, ignoring Alice's outburst. "Your mayor made it clear I wasn't welcome here."

"I can see why." She sighed. "Where do you go from here? Back to Seaside?"

"No, I'm going to one more village, Mountain View."

"Then you'll return this way in a day or two. Let her have that time to decide."

"All right, but Alice...." He stood and faced her across the table. "Dinah won't return here. If you want to be with her, you must come to the Academy."

He moved toward the door, nodding to Nainai as he left, but before he could cross the threshold, she spoke again. "Arthur, does Barbara know where you go next?"

"No, I don't believe I mentioned it. She surely didn't ask. Why?"

"We won't tell anyone where you're headed." She nodded at Alice to make sure she understood the promise included her. "The villagers won't take it well when they figure out what the Academy is doing. You may face a beating or worse, if they find you're moving to steal young women from the outback."

Arthur's brow creased as he took in her meaning. He chewed his lip. "How can I know if Alice wants to return with me?"

Elena shook her head. "I don't think it's safe for you to escort her. Even if she leaves with you voluntarily, it will look like coercion. Go back home after you visit Mountain View. Either Alice will find her way herself or she'll stay here."

"Fine. The next semester starts in three months. If you come, be on time." With a last nod, Arthur crossed the threshold. The women watched as he ran up the stairs and disappeared down the path.

Alice sank into her chair, and elbows on the table, and put her head in her hands. "Oh Nainai, what should I do?"

"Have some more tea, child. Let's figure this out." As she sipped the fragrant brew, Nainai's eyes focused on a point beyond the walls of the hut.

Alice, watching her, wondered what she was seeing, but didn't dare interrupt her train of thought. She weighed the different choices herself: If she consulted only her own wishes, she would have gone with Arthur then and there. But Alice, growing up on the farm, knew what one less person meant to the already-scarce team they had for harvesting. She understood her place, her importance in her family and what complete desertion would mean to them: hardship, maybe even more starvation and death.

It had never been her plan to leave them completely. She always intended to come home and help with the hard labor. *Caught*, she concluded. *I'm stuck in a trap as sure as any bilbug that's fallen in the vinegar bottles they set to protect the fruit trees. And it will kill me, slowly and surely, just as the bilbugs drown. Either choice makes me the villain of my own story.*

Her feet could no longer stay still. She rose and paced the floor, ten strides to the far wall, pivot, then ten strides back. On her third trip, Nainai looked up and laughed.

"You're not going anywhere like that, are you, dear?" she asked.

"I'm not going anywhere, no matter what I do," Alice snapped. "Nothing I choose will be right."

The old woman sighed. "Yes. Life is often that way. Whatever we do has both negative and positive consequences. Still, more options may surface than Arthur Seaside offered."

"What other options?" Alice stood, staring down at Elena. "Both

Far Meadow and the Academy want to use me and spit me out. I'm going to hurt myself and others no matter what I do. Show me this other way, Nainai, because I see none. "

"Alright, sit down, and let me tell you what I'm thinking." While the young woman sank into her chair, Nainai rose to shut the door, which Arthur had left open. She returned to her seat and looked straight into Alice's eyes. "If Barbara rejected the Academy's request for more food out of hand, she overstepped her bounds. That's a decision the entire village council should consider. I doubt they will disagree with her, but the question must be raised and her authority properly limited. I'll challenge her on this. We need to know exactly what the college requires so we can gauge how serious this threat is."

"That doesn't sound very hopeful." Alice's mouth turned down in a pout. "If the council votes to let students go, I'll still have to get my folks to agree. It won't solve the problem with Micah."

"One step at a time, dear. Despair cuts off all avenues to action, so guard against that in your soul." Elena threw off the advice casually, her fingers tapping out a rhythm on the table, her eyes unfocused.

She looked up from her meditation and sighed. "Alice, there may be a different path open to you as well, but it's dark and dangerous. I'm afraid it could separate you from both our village and the Academy. If it comes down to the choice laid before you, we can explore this third way. For now, I'll talk to the mayor and then your parents. Hopefully, the situation is not as dire as Arthur Seaside expressed."

CHAPTER FIVE

Later that night, in the glow of the Rose Moon after first supper, Alice sat on the assembly building's courtyard wall, waiting for the council to finish its meeting. Nainai's age and standing as former mayor provided some clout, and Barbara had reluctantly agreed to consult the village council. The ten members, including both Nainai and her Pa, had been discussing the situation for over an hour. Alice kicked against the stones with her heels, attempting to hurry them on to the right decision.

Finally, the door to the sunken patio opened, spilling warm light out into the shadows, and the Elders emerged by ones and twos, climbing up the stairs and heading to their homes. She strained but failed to read her fate in the set of their shoulders or the indistinct murmurs of their goodbyes. Finally, she saw her father turning to give a hand to Nainai with the mayor behind them. Barbara shut the door as Pa helped his elderly relative up the steps and then spoke to them before they could disappear.

"Elena, I hope this decision satisfies you. You see, it's not only me who knows our village must pull back from the old alliances."

The old woman paused at the top of the stairs, waiting with Pa for the mayor to join them. Alice stepped out of the shadows as she responded. "My desire, Barbara, is to be one people on Goldilocks, sharing all she's given us, so everyone thrives. I never condoned Seaside's stance any more than I do yours. I hope both communities' fortunes improve so that we can be generous once again."

"Well, we'll see what happens with Liam. If he returns to us with the skills of a doctor, the council may be inclined to invest other children's futures with the Academy."

Humphrey looked at his daughter standing just outside their little circle. "Yes, if Liam comes home, that will help. But Alice's chance has gone, I'm afraid. You must make the best you can of your life here with us, my dear."

Alice's breath caught in her throat as she took in the confirmation of Nainai's failure to sway the council. But before she could react, Nainai put out her hand and patted her arm. "There may yet be time, Nephew. Alice is still young. If she has her first-bond child here, wouldn't you support her in following her dreams to higher education?"

Humphrey glanced at Alice and the two women across from him. "We'll see. I wish times were better. I wanted to attend college myself." He looked again at his daughter, staring up at him, eyes liquid in the moonlight. "I know you have the brains to do well at the Academy, Alice. You're a sharper student than Liam ever was. Give the village a baby, help us the next few seasons, and then we'll try to scrape together whatever the Academy requires." He set his face toward home, and Alice took Nainai's arm.

"I'll settle Nainai and then come home, Pa."

"That's a good girl. Goodnight, Elena." As he headed toward the outer ring of huts, Barbara fell in beside him, and Alice turned to lead her aunt across the commons to her hut.

When they got there, Alice started second supper. She put the soup on the stove to heat and stirred up the embers on the hearth. Then she set the table, glancing often at Nainai's face, waiting to hear the details of the council's discussion. But when the old woman sat silent, staring into the fire, she couldn't contain her need to know. "So, no one wanted to give the Academy what they were asking?"

Nainai startled, then shook her head. "What? Oh, no—actually, it was close. It lost by only two votes, which is pretty rare. Barbara's used to unanimous agreement with her decisions."

"I bet Pa voted not to pay." Alice gave the soup a vicious stir.

"Well, yes, but don't be too hard on him, dear. Our problems in this village are greater than I realized. Your father and the four other farmers on the council, including Liam's mother, say the crops they put in this year will barely yield enough to feed us and provide seed for next season. We'll be very lucky if we have any left to begin our stockpile for Bleak. There is a razor-thin margin for error when it comes to the weather. One unexpected gale during harvest, and that leeway is gone. Arthur Seaside was right about us hanging on the edge of failure."

Alice felt a dark despair settle on her shoulders. "I guess I'm selfish to want to leave," she said.

"No, dear—you're young, and your time is now. It's not selfishness, it's nature. If you don't strike out to fulfill your dreams soon, they'll fade. But I wonder: Could you give your father's plan a try? It surprised me to hear Humphrey agree he would be open to supporting you at the Academy if you have a baby here first. You could stipulate the relationship with Micah will only last a third. After twelve months, you'd either be free to make another decision or be pregnant. At the most, you'd lose twenty-four months before the child is ready to live with its sire."

"Two-thirds of a rev," Alice sighed. "I guess that's better than deserting everyone here. Do you think Pa will let me leave?"

"I haven't known my great-nephew to break his word, but ultimately, you know, it's not up to him. The woman in a bond sets the terms. The man you partner with either agrees or finds someone else. And once you cross the threshold into bonding contracts, none of your parents, blood or household, have legal rights to make you do anything. You become an Elder then, responsible for your own choices. Humphrey could withhold payment to the college, but he can't keep you here."

By the stove, Alice gave one last stir to the soup, ladled it into bowls, and brought them over to the worn table, setting them on the cloth. "Nainai, do you think Micah is a good match? Don't you imagine he might be too old to father kids?"

Elena smiled, her eyes soft in the firelight. "He had two children with Mimi. And he's a gentle, moral man. Here again, Arthur Seaside spoke the truth—there's not much choice in this village. You could ask for Billy. He's closer to your age and not yet heart-bonded, but if I remember right, he's your first cousin. That's genetically dangerous, and the council might not allow it."

"Ew—I don't even like to spend time with Billy at family gatherings. All he talks about is how much stronger he is than anyone else. He's pretty self-centered, Nainai."

The older woman laughed. "Yes, it's often best when you're young to have temporary bonds with older men you respect. Do you feel you could care for Micah?"

"For a third I could do it. It's not that I dislike him, Nainai. It's just, I don't know.... We don't have much in common other than Jackie, and that's weird now." Alice picked up a piece of bread and tore it into bits, floating them in her soup.

Elena considered her with a tilt of her head. "Has Janelle explained first-bonds to you, dear? Has she told you of her own?"

"No, she's too busy. And I spent most of my breaks with Dinah when she was here. I guess I've been thinking of bonding with her more than having children."

"Life's been disrupted in the last few revs," Elena said, frowning. "I'm afraid we haven't prepared you for this responsibility very well. A household or blood mother should discuss this with you, but since we're together here...I've written about my first-bond. Would you like to read it?"

Alice nodded, and the old woman levered herself up out of her chair, moving to retrieve the com-pad hidden in the quilt at the end of her bed. When she returned to the table, she opened it and handed it over.

My First-Bond

(This occurred in the last third of Rev Fifteen, just as I turned six, or eighteen in the old reckoning.)

After the plague destroyed my village and family, the child I was chose to survive. The only way I knew how to endure was to turn my back on pain and work. Good choice, little girl! I won honors every third. The professors at first gave me extra attention due to the tragedy and then continued because I showed such promise. But my victories brought with them no pride or smugness. I realized even then that I excelled only because studying hard helped me stay ahead of the grief.

But the crossroad of turning six revs took me by surprise. I had neither blood mother nor household parent to prepare me. My cousin, who long ago guided me to a cot in the dormitories, told me I must now share my bed and get a child.

Why did it come as a shock? Suzy and Luna had been giggling about choosing partners for months, their mothers and aunts flooding their letters with suggestions of suitable mates. Maybe I hadn't noticed because I spent more and more time with Jay. Boys his age could bond, but they didn't talk about it as much. Instead, Jay and I talked about science, speculating about new theories for curing the sicknesses, which never seemed to end.

I can't recall now why it never occurred to that budding woman that she would need to choose as well. It came as a jolt when my cousin Angel read a letter from our nearest surviving relative, an aunt who lived in Touch Down, saying she would soon arrive to consult with the record keepers and professors. I was living so much in the present, avoiding the painful past, I forgot the future also had to be faced.

Tanta Marnie arrived and went to work. In a week, she had a list of names: eligible men, all of them. The only conditions I insisted on were that this partner live in Seaside, so I could continue my studies, and that he would raise the baby in his household. Lying in bed at night, I told myself, *this makes no difference. I'll go sleep somewhere else for a third, but still study. I'll bear a baby, but nothing will change. It's just a civic duty, like picking up trash on the commons or weeding the college garden.*

I pored over the list my aunt gave me, studying the attributes of the five men selected as suitable. They were all older, but that didn't matter. One was a successful fisherman whom I had never seen. The other four worked for the Academy. Tanta Marnie impressed on me that the teachers and professors held my academic success in high value. The suitors were eager to have me bear a child who would come home to them.

I remember now that little frisson of pleasure young Elena felt at having the power to choose. Seaside found me acceptable, desirable. I had stepped over the threshold from being an outback hick to an insider. Although Angel tried to convince me to accept the fisherman, a man I'd never have to see again, I knew I'd pick an academic. This was my place. My child, even if I gave it up, would have the advantages I valued most. Already, I was thinking like a mother.

I chose a calculus professor. Math came hard to me, and this man's kindness in tutoring me made him stand out. I also learned he had a heart-bond partner and three children at home. If our union proved fruitful, the baby would pass to experienced parents and the company of siblings.

Traditionally, a girl met the family of her first-bond before spelling out the details of a contract. Women, then as now, hold all rights in this relationship—justified because they stand to lose the most. So, I went with Tanta Marnie to spend an afternoon with Paulo Seaside's household.

I see myself again from the vantage of all these revs, looking at the small room which would be mine from after the baby is born until it weans. Paulo's partner, Nessa, appears calm and serious, explaining how they want one more child. They have two boys of their own bond and a girl, twenty months old, sired by another man. They respect the need to have genetic diversity. I moved through this all as if in a dream. I was thinking of a paper which needed revision before submission. Even today, I remember that.

Only a month later, during the golden days' break, we celebrated the ceremony for first-bonds at the Harvest Festival. I stood on a raised dais with couples which included Suzy and Luna. Beside me, the math professor, tall and solid, shifted to glance over his shoulder at his heart-bond partner. I reminded myself, *that's who he bonded with for life* and searched his face for remorse. He must have felt the gaze, for he refocused on me, giving me a warm, reassuring smile.

The record keeper began reciting our heritages, the list of dams and sires which assured the community our unions would be healthy. We'd already gone over this, of course, so it captured none of my attention. Instead, I looked out into the crowd. My aunt stood on the perimeter, straight and serious, with Angel grinning at her side. She'd tell the extended family, those who survived in more fortunate villages, about this ceremony, including how I comported myself. I tried to look happy. The effort must have wobbled a bit, because I noticed Tanta Marnie frown.

Someone behind my aunt caught my attention. Jay stood there. My smile steadied and became real, my heart warmed. My friend came to witness this first-bond. In my mind, the gap between us closed, and I saw him as he had been the day before: the freckles on his nose barely visible against his caramel skin, green eyes angled up and sparkling with amusement at my awkwardness. He had wished me well then, with no undercurrent of envy. He wanted me to be happy in this initial experience of sex and childbearing.

Why didn't he ask for me himself? The question popped into my head, annoying me. I hadn't wondered this before, but as the keeper droned on, I considered it. He was old enough to request a first-bond with me. Perhaps he did, but Tanta Marnie didn't consider him worthy of even cursory consideration. Since he was still in school himself, the baby would have gone to his hometown of Far Meadow, deep in the outback. He wasn't handsome like Suzy's mate or a gifted fisherman like Luna's. No, he was as nondescript as me. But it pleased me he had come, his grin reassuring across the courtyard.

The record keeper finished the last recitation for our first-bond group, just five couples this season. In the corner of my mind, always tuned to patterns, I noted the recorder had indicated Suzy's partner was also her second cousin. That was close. They were lucky to be allowed this union. I glanced at my friend and saw how genuinely excited and happy she looked. Hers was a love match. Jenner begged her to choose him months ago. Their baby would go to Touch Down to be raised by her mother.

The minister read the contracts and signed them. It was all for show. These papers had been reviewed and approved already. I smelled the savory bean stew prepared for the feast and heard the crowd's impatient rustling as the long ceremony wound down.

The record keeper beckoned all five couples forward and wrapped the red ribbon for a twelve-month bond around each pair of joined right hands. The minister, a gray-haired matronly woman who had done this a million times, cleared her throat to address us. Ignoring both wind and restless crowd, she acted as if nothing else in the world mattered but this one moment, these pairings.

She spoke about love: "Love comes in many forms, and you will experience them all in life. Know that this temporary bond can give you much joy—but hold it lightly. It's not the main course, but an appetizer for the feast of mature and lasting relationships. Don't mistake it for what it is not."

Had she focused on Paulo and me more than the others? Our partnership was the most disparate in terms of age. Was there a warning in that blessing? Before I could figure it out, the usual words about duty and bearing healthy progeny rained down. I searched the crowd. Jay had disappeared.

The minister lifted her head, speaking so the whole gathering heard: "Go forth, be fruitful and multiply."

The people replied as one, a wave breaking over the newly bonded: "The children you bear belong to all, daughters and sons of our future."

My hand in Paulo's felt small, the red ribbon gashing across it.

My cousin warned me of the danger of falling in love with a first-bond partner. I confess, young Elena slid into that temptation right away. Perhaps the early and abrupt demise of my household parents left me yearning for the attentions of an older man, someone to guide and adore me. I wonder why only Angel saw this coming.

Paulo followed the rules meticulously. He set us up in a small hut close to the Academy and said goodbye to his family. They knew they might not see him for twelve months. While we both kept up our responsibilities at college—he teaching and me studying—in the evening, we'd come together in the softening light of first supper. The space between then and last meal we spent tying up loose ends from the day and then reading or playing card games. He often would help me with difficult homework or listen while I read out a paper I needed to edit. He asked me about my life. I did not ask him personal questions. When it came time to slide into bed, his loving was slow and gentle. I realized how deeply I craved intimacy—to be known not only in body but in soul. I began to reveal more of who I was becoming with him. After the first few times, we sought our bed earlier and earlier, both eager to enjoy the other.

It's normal for new partners to retreat from friendships for a while. I had little time for lunch with girlfriends or long conversations with Jay. It only took a few weeks for Paulo to become all I thought about. I began looking for him in the hallways to exchange a secret smile. I found excuses to drop by his lecture room to give him small presents or ask what he wanted for dinner. Others smiled indulgently, but those who knew me best worried. My heart would not disengage with ease.

Luckily, I conceived quickly. Only two months into the bond, my period didn't come. I refused to believe it at first, going back to my calendar every day for a month to convince myself I was wrong. When I couldn't put it off any longer, I went to the health center and took the test.

That evening at last meal, I told him. Paulo, uncharacteristically obtuse, missed the tears in my eyes and grinned from ear to ear. *He's happy,* I realized. *He doesn't want me. He never wanted me.* I got up and fumbled to cut the bread, hiding my despair. We shared one more night together, but I felt no ecstasy, no closure. Only bleakness stretched out before me.

The next day, I stayed home from school, trying to find

some ground under my feet. I told Paulo it was morning sickness and spent an hour in the toilet while he got ready for work. When the hut was quiet, I ventured out, touching his chair at the table, the coat he had left hanging, smelling his pillow. The stillness of the rooms spoke to me of what was to come.

By noon, I had settled enough that I started reading one of my textbooks, trying to find my way back to my former self. A gentle knock sounded on the door, and Paulo's partner stepped through.

"Come in, please. I'll make tea." I stumbled over the courtesy and busied myself with preparing the drink. He's told her already, I realized.

Nessa, a tall woman, whom I noticed now was quite striking, with her dark hair just revealing gray at the temples and solemn, long-lashed eyes, smiled down at me. "That's alright, dear. I wanted to see how you're doing. I brought some broth and crackers. These saved my life during my first few months."

Color rose to my cheeks as I realized my fib had produced this generosity. "Thanks." I continued to arrange the teacups, not knowing what else to do.

Nessa put her offering on the table and sat, signaling me to sit as well.

"We have the room prepared for you at the house, Elena. Whenever you're ready to move, we'll settle you there."

"At the house?"

"Yes, remember? I showed it to you when you came to visit. You can live with us until you wean the baby."

"I think I'd rather stay here if you don't mind." Panic began rising in my throat. I didn't want to face his real family—not yet.

As if she understood, Nessa nodded and said, "Whenever

you're ready, dear. But remember—you'll be on your own now. Paulo won't come here anymore."

The words, gently spoken, were firm and unequivocal. She claimed her right to get her heart-bond back. I bowed my head, finding no other response.

In my eighth month of pregnancy, I joined them when I dreamed of bursting open with no one there to hold me together. Paulo rarely spoke to me. When the contractions came, Nessa rushed me to the clinic.

Another danger for a first-bond woman, emphasized to me by Tanta Marnie, is that she won't want to give up her child. We all go through this struggle. I was no different, for the baby was a perfect miracle and wonder.

I tried not to love him too much but found it impossible. I considered claiming my right to raise him myself, a right all women have. The temptation chewed at my heart every time he latched onto my nipple, every time I woke in the night to smell his warm breath and sweet hair. I pretended, during the long hours of recovery, that the sun-filled room belonged to me and the infant and we could continue there forever. I ignored Nessa's presence as much as possible when she held him, distracting and comforting him while I ate. Listening to the older woman's advice on how often to change his diaper or burp him, I barely heard the words over the cacophony of denial in my soul.

Paulo's visits were even worse. Hate rose in my gorge now, stronger than the love I thought I bore him, as he feasted his eyes on this son which would be his and not mine. It was only when the other household children came in to play with the baby, tickling him and cooing over his smiles, telling him about all the toys and games they would share, that my selfishness disgusted me.

On naming day, I stood alone with the minister while

Nessa, Paulo, and the older kids hung together. Then I returned to the dormitory and eased back into my studies at the Academy, expressing my milk and packing the bottles on ice to give to Nessa for another three months. They promised I could see the baby whenever I wanted, inviting me for dinners and play dates, but I declined. I found I couldn't talk to other girls about my experience. I avoided conversation about it, even with Suzy. Only to Jay, a neutral observer, did I confess how close I came to committing the ultimate social sin. Only Jay held me while I cried for all the loss, all the sacrifice, which society claims so casually from young women.

By the end of the rev, it all seemed like a fever dream that had never happened, except when Paulo's face surfaced in the halls and the eyes of my child looked out at me. I understood at last why my blood mother never visited me.

Alice put down the com-pad, raising her head to view her great-great aunt, whose head drooped on her bosom. The fire filled the room with warmth and shadows. Quietly, she got up and knelt beside her, reaching out to touch her hand lightly. "Nainai," she breathed.

Her great-great aunt opened her eyes and smiled at her. "I must have dozed off. Did you like the story?"

"You're my hero," Alice said. "If you could bond with a man you knew so little about, I can stand to partner with Micah for a while. At least I know what I'm getting into with him. I don't think having romantic feelings for him is going to be a problem."

"That is one advantage of the match." Nainai chuckled, her gray head bent close to Alice. "Tell your ma in the morning, dear. I'll help with the contract if you like. I admit, I'll love having you around a little longer."

CHAPTER SIX

In the morning, Alice rose, feeling a sad calmness. She met her mother in the kitchen, falling into her role as helper by starting porridge while Janelle cut bread and shooed Jaren back to his room to get on his school clothes. Alice spoke when he had disappeared.

"Ma, I know Pa wants me to bond with Micah, and I'm willing to do that if I can go to the Academy after I have a child. Is that what you want me to do?"

The middle-aged woman turned to face her daughter. "Micah? I hadn't heard that's who he meant. I thought it would be someone closer to your age."

"Nainai says it's easier to make a first-bond with a more mature man. Who was your first partner?"

"Oh, no one you know, but yes—he was two revs older. His name was Brent. He had a forever mate in Mountain View. That's where they raised the child."

"You think an older man is better too?"

"Yes, for a temporary partner when a girl is young. But I wouldn't have wanted to stay with Brent until he died."

Alice considered her household mother. Janelle sometimes wandered in her thoughts when she was multitasking, but this segue made no sense.

"What do you mean, Ma? I'd only sign a contract for twelve months with Micah, like most first-bonds. He's not sick or anything. I saw him yesterday, and he seemed fine."

Instead of answering her, Janelle turned away, busying herself by getting out plates and spoons.

Anxiety churned in Alice's stomach. "Ma, what are you not telling me?" She put her hand on her household mother's arm, forcing her to stop.

Janelle frowned, looking at the restraining fingers. "You should talk to your father and Barbara about this. They came in before you last night and spent about an hour drinking wine, discussing the council meeting."

"I know they decided not to pay what the Academy wants. But Pa said if I have a child for Far Meadow, I can go next rev."

Janelle sighed and turned to face her daughter. "They weren't planning that last night. Look—I don't want you to leave the village. I have more to do here than I can handle and so does your Pa. We need you here. But it's not right to make you heart-bond with someone at your age." She shook her head. "It's not right. I tried to tell them, but they don't listen."

"What do you mean, 'heart-bond'?" Unease morphed into full-fledged fear, clawing up into Alice's throat. Her voice squeaked. "I said I would do a first-bond with Micah, not a permanent partnership."

"Well, Barbara wants all young adults to stay here now. She says the life of our village depends on it, because Seaside and Touch Down withdrew their support and service. The only way they could think of to keep you all here is to bring back the marriages they had on Earth."

"But...but that's crazy. What about mixing up the DNA? How can we make sure children are healthy? And anyway, they can't force anyone to partner. That's always been a free choice."

"They have a point, Alice. No one will be healthy or free if we starve."

"That's right." Humphrey appeared in the kitchen doorway, and both women jumped at the sound of his voice. "Put our community above your selfish desires, daughter. We fed, clothed, and housed you your whole life. Now it's time for you to give back."

"Pa, I want to help. I was telling Ma that I'll agree to a first-bond with Micah. You told me if I did, you would let me go to the Academy next rev. Don't you remember?"

"I said 'maybe.' That was before Barbara came up with her plan." Humphrey glared at his partner and scowled. "It's an excellent strategy, Janelle. It will give us stability here that we've never had."

She looked at the floor, then picked up the plates and stepped away into the dining area.

Alice reclaimed his attention. "What's the plan, Pa? To make me heart-bond with a person I don't love?"

"Micah is a good man." Humphrey hurled the words at her like stones. "And it's not just you, Alice. You'll be first because you're the oldest. You're my blood daughter and need to set an example for the rest. We're cutting out the system of different bonds. You'll marry just as the women of Earth did and bring children into this world with one partner. Your offspring will stay with us and enrich our village—*ours*, not some other town far away."

Alice leaned into her father's anger with a passion of her own. "You can't change the rules just because you don't like them anymore. I'm almost an Elder. I get to choose. And I do not choose this."

She spun around to leave, but Humphrey grabbed her upper arm, shoving his face close to hers. "You owe me," he hissed. "You owe this village. Daughter, you'll do as the mayor says or I'll throw you out on your ear."

"You're hurting me!" Alice cried, more startled by his action than scared. He had never been so unreasonable before.

He let go abruptly, and Alice stalked through the outside door, slamming it shut behind her.

There was only one place to retreat to. She ran across the common to Nainai's house. Would she be awake? She jumped down the stairs to the tiny courtyard and tapped on the door. As it swung open, she felt her knees shaking.

"Child, what's the matter? You're ashen. Is someone ill?" Elena put out her hand to steady Alice and guide her into the hut. As the younger woman collapsed onto a chair, she continued to keep her fingers on her arm, bending to scan her face. "What happened?"

"The mayor and Pa—they're planning to change the rules about bonding. Nainai, they want me to marry Micah—like the old days on Earth. They're going to make all young people have one partner and stay here forever."

It was Nainai's turn to sink into a chair. "Why? Whatever do they think they'll gain from that strategy?"

"Stability is what Pa said."

"Stability," the old woman snorted. "What they'll get is stagnation. This is no solution to our problems."

"I can't do it, Nainai."

"No, of course you can't. I wonder if Micah knows what they're planning. This never came up at the council."

"But what am I going to do?"

Elena looked her niece in the eyes. "You're not in this alone, Alice. I'll go see Barbara right now." She went to grab her cape and then paused. Alice watched as she hung the wrap up and took her seat again.

"Perhaps that's not the best idea," she said. "If Barbara and Humphrey are planning things behind the council's back, they could shut me up or deny what you've discovered. We need to be smart about our next move, Alice."

"They can't force me to marry, can they? When the minister comes up from Near Meadow for the ceremony on the next golden days, they won't be able to change the contract promises, will they?"

Elena shrugged. "Perhaps they're breaking with customs as well as traditional values. Mayors are allowed to perform the ceremonies if the minister isn't available."

Alice felt fear clawing at her throat again and reached for

righteous indignation to suppress it. "I'll go to Seaside and never return."

Nainai nodded. "It could come to that. But what happens to Nettie then, or Billy, or any of the other children who will soon be adults? No, we can't allow them to take away your rights, but it may require further sacrifice on both our parts to ensure they fetter no one else's freedom, either. Neither Barbara nor Humphrey are stupid. Why do they think this can work? I wonder...." She sank into herself as she focused on the problem in her mind.

Alice stood, looking for an outlet for her anxiety. She noticed Nainai had been fixing breakfast, so she put on the kettle for tea and cut bread for toast. As Nainai remained lost in her own thoughts, she set the table and soon had a meager meal before them both.

Nainai looked up and smiled. "Thanks, dear. You're right to get food ready. You and I are going to need energy to figure this out." She twisted around and began to spread her bread with the nut butter. "I suspect Barbara has been talking to the other small villages, like Mountain View and Near Meadow, maybe even Last Stop. If they're frustrated with the larger towns too, she may gather allies. That would make sense. In fact, I wonder if they mean to have you marry Micah at all. They might look for a match in another village and leverage their plan by bargaining you off."

"Pa still wants me to be with Micah. He said he was a good man."

"Yes," Nainai nodded and put down the bread she was about to bite, "and since he's already talked to him about bonding with you, he can't honorably begin negotiating some other partnership unless you refuse him. I wonder if he's pushing you into rejecting Micah, only to trap you into marriage with someone else."

"Micah may turn down a permanent bond with me too. I could see him doing that," Alice offered.

The two women sat in silence for a few minutes, both chewing their food meditatively.

"Alice," Elena broke their reverie, "do you remember I told you there might be a third way for you to deal with your dilemma—different from either staying here and bonding or going to the Academy with Dinah?"

"Yeah, I do." The young woman put down her bread and sat up straight. "What did you mean, Nainai?"

"The Singers.... It may be time to rouse the Singers and see if they can help us."

"Singers?" Alice frowned. "I thought they died out long ago. Weren't they the ones who believed the planet talked to them?"

"They are mystics who have a special understanding of our world and, at least in the early days, communicated with her. I have two questions now. First: How many of them remain? And second: Can they revive that relationship with Goldilocks?"

Nainai's eyes wandered to the clerestory window as she spoke. Alice, watching her, felt a shiver of something—fear or awe—go up her spine. "But they haven't spoken to the planet since you were a little girl, right? How could they benefit us now?"

"I had a dream last night, Alice. It's a dream I've never had before, but my husband told me about it. I'm missing Jay and so it could have come from him. But somehow, I don't think so. Goldie might be speaking again."

Alice shook her head. "Still, how does that help? Did the dream tell you something?"

Elena looked at her niece and smiled. "Not really. When I first mentioned this third way, I was thinking of sending you to spend some time with the Singers, learning about the woods and the daks from them instead of attending the Academy right away. You could disappear into the forest. They'd never find you there. The Singers are a strange bunch but tuned into natural life on Goldilocks. They're also very self-sufficient and could teach you to live off the land. We're losing so much of that wisdom. It might be a wonderful adventure for you."

"I thought thieves and murderers were the only ones who lived in woods," Alice said, wondering if Nainai was tracking alright. "Ma says it's dangerous even to travel to Seaside because the road lies so close to the forest."

Elena nodded. "Yes, people are terrified of it now. And they may be right that some inhabitants are unsavory, but that fear also provides cover for others who live there, not only the Singers but the throwback groups—you know, Jewish, Muslim, and Christian families who refused to join interreligious community."

"Those still exist?" Alice had never considered this.

"Before Jay died, we visited the forest pretty often. I'm not sure how many have survived, but they were a hardy lot."

Alice looked at her plate, thinking about this new information. "I don't know, Nainai. Even if I can find the Singers, how would that help Nettie and the other youngsters. Why would they care what happens to us?"

"That's a fair question." Nainai's smile seemed sad to Alice, lost in the wrinkles on her face. "Some of them are anarchists, waiting for most humanity to destroy themselves so their kind can reassert dominance. But Jay never thought like that. He believed the fate of all people intersected with the planet. He wanted everyone to work together. And if they are able to reach Goldie, we may find some answers to our environmental problems, at least."

Alice looked at the old woman wide-eyed. "Are you saying great-Uncle was a Singer?"

"Yes, dear. He dreamed Goldilocks and went back to the woods to sing. But he married me, who never sang, and dedicated himself to being a doctor for all humanity."

Alice digested this revelation while her aunt lost herself in memories. Then Nainai shook off the past. "Jay believed the planet would reestablish contact some day and help us learn to live with her." She stood up stiffly and reached for her com-pad, hidden under a blanket on her rocking chair. "Alice, I want you to read a story about the Singers, so you'll know at least a bit about them."

She pulled up the file and handed the tablet to her young niece. "I'm going to talk to Micah and see what he knows of the mayor's plans. I feel in my bones that this is more dangerous than any plague we have faced."

Alice set the com-pad on the table and rose to help her up the courtyard steps. Then she returned, poured herself another cup of tea, and settled in to read.

Meeting the Mystics

(This happened in the last third of Goldilocks' twenty-first revolution. I was almost eight revs, or twenty-four in the old reckoning.)

I write this memory now, long after my Jay has gone, missing the gift of his presence more than words can convey. I loved him rather recklessly when I was little more than a schoolgirl. This experience first gave me a glimpse of how deep his soul proved to be.

See me then: I have borne and let go of two children already. My hips are rounded and my breasts heavier, but my hair is still a wild, curly black mess that I fight back daily into a braid, and my eyes, though sadder, continue to know wonder. I am going to Far Meadow with my lover, Jay. We haven't heart-bonded, but we soon will, and then I'll bear my third baby and not part with her until she grows up. But not yet.... That child is only a dream, not even conceived. Tonight, something else is born.

We left Seaside early in the morning, traveling with Jay's best friend Pete in the hummie he borrowed from the Academy. The little open-air electric vehicle bounced up the rutted road all day. By the time we reached the wayfarer's hut, we three gladly climbed out to rest. I recognized this place. My vanished village sat just a half mile up the track.

The forest, with its distinctive spicy smell, loomed only yards away. I turned my eyes from the men to hide my tears.

We plugged the car into the solar array on the side of the cabin, rejoicing that nobody else had arrived to disturb our solitude. After a simple last meal of steamed veg and tofu cooked over the little one-burner stove, Jay and I chose a bedroom and Pete retired to the other. It was just after Rose Moon set, the light of Second Moon casting a pale-yellow glow, which Jay shut out by pulling the shade. I slept hard, falling far from the reality of the world.

How long was I out? It seemed only minutes when an unfamiliar rustle and scrape awakened me. Confused at first, I scanned my surroundings and saw through the window opening, now free of its curtain, a dark sky studded with brilliant stars. It had to be after Second Moon set. Where was Jay? I sat up and spotted him in the shadows, struggling into his pants.

"What is it?" I whispered, mindful of Pete in the adjoining room. "Are you ill?"

Jay came over and perched on the bed, folding me into his long arms, keeping me from the nighttime chill. "Sweet love, I have to go somewhere tonight. I thought I could sneak out and let you sleep."

"What are you talking about? We're in the middle of nowhere and it's nighttime. Did you have a nightmare?" When Jay didn't answer, I tried reasoning. "Honey, no one starts a journey when it's dark out."

"We do if we're called."

He said this so gravely, his bass voice reverberating in his chest against my cheek. I shivered with a sudden fear that he was being lured away from me. "Well," I replied, mustering resolve, "if you go, I'll go too."

He sat tall, holding me at arm's length so he could see my

face in the starlight. "Did you have the dream too?"

"What dream?"

Jay sighed, cuddling me close again. "I don't think you should join me if you didn't have the dream."

"Oh, really?" I pushed back from him, alarms clamoring now. Why should a nightmare determine my actions? Was this some kind of test? If it was, I would not fail it.

"You woke me up so suddenly, I might have been dreaming and just forgot it. Anyway, why should that matter? I thought we were a couple. I thought you wanted me with you."

"Laney, I want you with me. But I'm not the only one this involves."

I could tell I had hit a soft spot. His voice held a note of pleading and, even though shadows hid his face, I knew he was frowning.

Thrusting home the guilt, I said, "You would choose someone else to travel with tonight?"

A tentative knock at the door interrupted his exasperated intake of breath. Pete's head poked into the room. Jay snapped, "Give me a minute here."

I slipped out of his arms and began throwing on my clothes as he rose and went into the common area. Buttoning up my shirt, I heard them whispering together with great urgency. Were they arguing? Pete and Jay never fought.

As I joined them in the bigger room, still fragrant with our late meal, both men ceased talking and stared at me. Finally, Pete spoke up. "Look, Elena, we'll be back before morning. Don't worry about this."

Jay stopped him with a hand on his arm. "But she does need to worry about it, if she partners with me. She should know what she's getting into." His face stern, he looked me in the eye. "Will you promise to keep this a secret, Laney?

Whether or not you decide to go, whether or not you bond with me, can you swear not to betray us?"

It seemed the planet under our feet stopped spinning. The lantern, ready on the table, softened the outline of the men in front of me, throwing shadows on the wall twice their size. I nodded, then reached out to take my beloved's hand.

"I swear to you I will guard your secrets with my life. Only don't shut me out, Jay. Let me into your world."

"Pete too," he insisted, grasping me like a drowning man being pulled from the sea.

This was no lover's game, but an event of utmost seriousness. I turned my gaze to his friend, who shifted from foot to foot. Stepping closer, I reached out my disengaged fingers to Pete, who accepted them. "I promise I will tell no one this secret of yours. Please believe me. I am committed to Jay, even though we haven't had the bonding ceremony yet."

Pete nodded, shot a glance at his companion, and shrugged. "We've got to go now if we're doing this."

"Right. Laney, we're going into the forest. You don't have to come. I'll still love you if you choose not to. But if you join us, understand the danger. Some crazies live there, as well as our friends. And, if the professors at the Academy find out who we associate with, they'll ruin our reputations. I may never get a job as a doctor, and Pete could lose his position at the college. If you collaborate with us, you take a similar risk."

As he delivered this mini-lecture, my mind stuck on the first sentence: "We're going into the forest." No one entered the woods at night, not even back when I was a child. Murderers and rapists got banned to that desolate place. Deranged people hanging onto useless religions buried themselves there, waiting to die. Even in daylight, we approached the trees with care. And now Jay was daring me to go with him under the dark branches. My heart felt as cold as my feet on the flagstones.

"I'm coming with you. Let me get my things." The rash commitment necessitated instant follow-up. I put on my boots and grabbed my coat. We followed the weak, bobbing light of Pete's lantern into the frosty night.

Walking abreast over the stubble of grass, we quickly reached the forest's canopy. Then the men searched for a trail, a faint track through the undergrowth. Clearly, they had been there before. I never would have recognized it as a path. Before they stepped onto it and into the deeper darkness, Pete checked his wristband.

"We've got about ten hours before we need to be back, if we're going to keep to our scheduled arrival in Far Meadow."

Jay nodded. "That should give us plenty of time. We might even catch some more sleep before we leave." He pulled my hand, guiding me into position behind Pete. "I'll bring up the rear. Laney, stay close to Pete. We'll go single file from here."

I said nothing, swallowing my fear, catching a quick glance at the shivering stars overhead before plunging into the shadows.

Pete strode down the faint path, the electric lantern raised before him, throwing his shadow back over my smaller figure as I hurried and stumbled, trying to keep up. The trees blocked the middling wind, which had ruffled our hair and chilled our skin as we walked across the meadow, and the chilly night muted the spice of the woods. The sounds were crisper, though, carried farther by the cool air. Jay put out his fingers, steadying me when I jumped at the sound of a branch cracking. I glanced behind and saw light glint off a thin blade he held ready in his other hand. I hadn't even known he owned a knife.

We walked for about an hour in silence. Eventually, I peered ahead to see the glow of the lantern diffuse into the space around Pete. The woods here widened into a small clearing. Looking past him, I spotted the round roof of a traditional hut sprouting like a gigantic mushroom from the opposite side of the meadow. Set in the ground, it looked like the older huts of my village—one or two rooms at the most—nestled in its protective courtyard. A warm, buttered gleam shone from a narrow window. The sunken door opened, and more light spilled out onto the descending steps. Pete quickened his pace, but I held back until Jay stepped up beside me, draped his arm across my shoulders, and swept me forward.

A thin, stooped figure waited at the entrance. I followed Pete down the steep, leaf-strewn stairs and registered a man, bowed and gnarled with age, waving us inside. Beyond him was a warm and cozy great room, with fire burning on an old-fashioned hearth, kettle steaming, and some kind of stew bubbling in a pot on the stove. A table set for four stood in the center. He expected the men, but why put out four plates? He couldn't have known I was coming with them.

The old man hugged Pete and reached out to pull Jay into the embrace too. Still holding them, he crooned a sweet tune. My friends hummed the music back to him, then stepped away, grinning. Jay took my hand, and I realized he was going to present me. Instead of speaking, though, he sang in his rich deep voice,

"Yieyie man, teacher san, hear these words of mine: This is my beloved, come to see you too. Elena, heart's love, born in Forest Edge, braved the forest dark this night, to walk with us to you."

Our host, I now saw, was not just old but ancient. He took my icy hand in a warm grip, strong for such knotty fingers.

"We will not sing when a speaker is present, eh, Jay? I receive your beloved gladly, and I sense she has other gifts besides singing. Be welcome, Elena Forest Edge. I knew your fathers, Stefan and Armel, and still feel the emptiness of their passing from this world."

"You knew my parents?" I whispered the question, stunned. It had been so long since anyone had acknowledged their existence.

"Oh, yes." His back curved, so he stood hunched, just shorter than me. He twisted his neck so his bright eyes found mine. "I probably met you, too, when you were only a baby. You must miss your family. Shall we tell their tales tonight? Is that why you braved the forest?"

"I would love to hear any stories you have about them. I mourn them every day." Swallowing hard, I blinked back tears. "But no, that's not why I came. I didn't even know where we were going."

"Then why did you risk the journey?"

I hesitated a moment, looking at his face, so open to anything I would share. "I want the truth."

It sounded like a dare. My words surprised me. I was supposed to say something about love and following my man, wasn't I? My brow wrinkled in a frown, but my host nodded, reaching out to take my hand again.

"Ah, don't we all, dear, don't we all? Come, have dinner. We'll try to find the truth together."

I allowed him to lead me to the plain square table and sat with Pete and Jay flanked on either side. The old man ladled stew and poured tea before settling across from me. As he sat, I gathered my courage.

"You haven't told me your name, sir. Is it a secret? Would you tell me how you came to live in the forest?" Jay's hand found my thigh under the table, but I couldn't say if he wanted to warn me or offer comfort. I ignored him.

"My name is secret," the old man said, unruffled. "I will not share it tonight, but you may call me Yieyie, as these two, and most others, do. As to how I came to dwell here, don't worry. Society didn't force me out. I grew bored with its banality. Here, I can think and pray freely, without offending my neighbors."

No rancor tinged his voice, only a gentle amusement. I cocked my head and asked, "But isn't it dangerous, especially at your age?"

"Child, why would anybody harm me?" The gnome grinned. "I'm too old to be a threat. There are no valuable possessions in this hut. Anyone who comes to me in need, I help. I assure you, it's safer for me here than in any of the villages or towns. There, people fear my ideas and seek to change me. In the forest, I'm a hero to the broken and desperate." His eyes, full of light, sparkled with amusement.

"So, you're a hero now, are you, Yieyie?" Pete teased.

"Ah yes, so the brigands tell me. The family of Christians down by the river have named me a saint. I'm collecting titles and honors galore."

Jay joined the banter, and, for a while, the three men traded stories about acquaintances, both in the forest and from the Academy. I let the words run over me as I sipped my tea and looked over the one-room cabin. Someone had organized the spare space into separate areas for sleeping, study, cooking, and eating. I recognized the style of fold-down desk from my student days. The shelves made from pockets inset in the half-submerged walls reminded me of Old Ma's hut in my home village.

As I gazed over my host's head, looking at such a shelf, my eyes caught sight of a small statue surrounded by leaves and flowers.

"Oh...!" I gasped, jumping to my feet, startling the men into silence. Ignoring them, I crossed the room to stand in front of the shrine. My hands stretched out to touch the little bear, carved from foreign black wood, humped back rising over four paws planted square, with the small, rounded ears above the tiny eyes, the blunt snout.

"It's the bear. Old Ma's daughter had one like this."

"What's a bear?" asked Pete.

"Honey?"

I felt Jay hover just behind me, almost smelling his concern. But Yieyie spoke up. "It's alright. Pick him up, dear. Bring him over here. You're right. It's Old Ma's bear."

"How did you get it? I assumed it burned up with everything else in Forest Edge."

"It came to me through Janet, her daughter. She brought it and the cat to the forest when the pox hit the village."

"The cat?" I looked around, searching the other shelves.

Yieyie reached under his shirt and pulled out a pouch, just like the one they had given me so many revs ago. He loosened the strings. "Here she is." He lifted out the tiny clay statue and put it on the table next to the bear.

Tears sprang to my eyes seeing these splinters of a past broken and thought lost. I fumbled for the cord around my neck and freed the otter from its little bag. I set it, creamy wood gleaming, alongside the dark bear and delicate white cat. "But the real Pip had black fur," I whispered. "Black with golden patches and an orange star between her ears."

"You're the Bridge," Yieyie said, stroking my otter with a crooked finger. "The Bridge to Before. Janet told me one existed, but she never came back. I never spoke to her or anyone from Forest Edge again."

Behind me, Jay reached out and touched my shoulder. "What's a Bridge to Before?"

The old man answered for me. "A Bridge is someone who has visions of our history. They experience what others learn about only on their com-pads. It's a gift, like seeing through a window which opens onto a particular time and space to connect with something we need to remember. Does that sound right, Elena? I expect it was a rather frightening encounter."

"It was scary, but wonderful too." I couldn't take my eyes off the statues. "No one else knows. All my family is gone, and I didn't tell anyone in Seaside."

"You didn't tell me either."

Jay's tone, taut with annoyance, reminded me of where we were. I turned to face him.

"And what are you not telling me, Jay? You're not here tonight just to gossip with an old friend. What's your connection with the forest? Why did you and Pete come here?"

"Let's sit down and have some more tea." Yieyie's voice cracked as he leaned over, arranging the three figurines on the table. "All will be revealed. A Bridge is a splendid gift, indeed. We Singers welcome you."

"Singers? A group of Singers came to Forest Edge when I was a child, but they never returned. I thought they didn't exist anymore."

"And yet, here we are." The old man spread his hands to indicate her fiancé and friend, as well as himself.

She shivered, feeling unsteady in this new reality, but found no words to reply.

As they settled down into their seats, Pete glanced at his wristband. "Yieyie, we have an hour before we should head back. We have to talk about the dream."

"Ah yes, the dream. You see, my dear," the old man looked at me, smiling under his sagging eyes, "we have visions too.

They come to us in dreams—shared, similar dreams—which, unlike the clarity of your vision, have to be deciphered."

"You mean you all dream the same thing?" I remembered Jay had asked if I had dreamed that night.

"Pretty much. It comes filtered through our own personalities or through our individual fears and wishes. That's why we try to get together as soon as possible after one visits us. We winnow through each version to see if we can discern commonalities. We hope to find an essential message."

"Message? So, it shows you something new? Is it like the woman from Before who loved animals?"

The three men all sat still. I couldn't tell if the insight into my vision shocked them, or they just didn't want to explain their own. I scanned their faces, settling my gaze on Jay, who took my hand in his.

"Dear heart, I don't know your woman from Before, but I hope you'll tell us more about her. In our case, we believe the dream comes from Goldilocks, our world. There is historical evidence, quite clear in the journals of Jerry, but also referenced by Xander and others of the original settlers, that the planet spoke to them through emotions. They first realized this in a shared dream, while they were in outer space."

Pete interrupted, "Don't forget Jerry had the vision even before they left Earth."

"Yes, that's right." Jay nodded. "Which tells us she can project across great distances, although more people received the dream as they came closer to this planet. Children born on the ship and during the early years of the settlement connected with Goldilocks even while waking. They sang to her because music carries feelings better than words. In the first seventeen revs of our history, more colonists communicated by singing than speaking."

"So, you talk to the planet?" I surprised myself with my willingness to consider this phenomenon.

"No, dear," Yieyie picked up the explanation. "We've lost the ability to initiate contact with her. At this point, we just receive. It's like we pick up random radio signals she's sending out. We hope to re-establish a relationship with her, but so far we've had little luck."

"We know some of the old songs the settlers used to celebrate her, though." Jay nodded toward her with a mischievous smile. "Remember, you caught me practicing one when we were first at college together?"

I bowed my head, overwhelmed by all the fresh revelations. "Yes, you told me it was your family's tradition to preserve the songs, but you had to keep it hidden because the Academy objected to traditional spirituality. They claim it muddles students' focus on their studies."

"And you kept my secret." The wattage of his smile increased.

I laughed. "Well, I kind of forgot about it," I admitted. "Do you know why the planet stopped talking to us?"

Pete snorted. "That's the question. In the old records, it's mentioned that Goldie went back to Earth with the failed mission in rev 16. They don't say how that happened. It could be that she died with those voyagers. But if she did, why do we still receive dreams from her? Singers like Yieyie have spent their whole lives trying to figure out what's wrong."

"It's not just a problem for us people," the elderly man said, leaning forward into the conversation. "Fairy dragons are much harder to find these days. The settlers' journals show they used to be quite interested in humans. And the winds seem more intractable and unpredictable, according to records kept since the landing. But I don't think Goldilocks is gone completely. It's more like she has shut down or drifted away."

Pete tapped his wrist com. "Well, my friends, if we don't start talking about the dream pretty soon, we'll miss the opportunity to get a fresh critique of it to add to your studies."

"Alright." I lifted my hands in surrender. "I'll quit asking questions. Jay can fill me in later."

The old Singer sat back in his chair with a sigh. "I hope you'll come again, though, and share your vision with us. But Pete is right. We should look at our dream while it's fresh in our minds. Who will go first?"

I sipped at my cooling tea, listening with suspended judgment as the three men took turns telling their version of the vision which had visited them that evening. The basic outline was simple: Each had found himself standing in a mist, unable to see anything around him. The fog clung and obscured their vision, even though they could hear a howling wind blowing. Someone out of sight was singing a sad and lonely song. Here, the dreamers differed a bit: Jay was sure the singer was a child. Pete thought it could be a woman. Yieyie detected several voices in the music. They all tried to move toward the singer. Jay swore he lifted one foot and took a step in its direction, which excited the other two men, who hadn't moved at all. Jay also sensed being called personally, which neither Pete nor Yieyie could confirm.

Our host had gotten out an ancient com-pad, taking notes throughout the conversation. As their talk wound down, he said, "Well, boys, did we learn anything new?"

Pete frowned at the spoon he had just used to stir honey into his tea. "Nothing significant. I still felt like a blind observer."

"Don't you think the singing is a little louder?" Jay leaned his elbows on the table and set his chin on his balled fists. "I recognized more urgency in the song. And I moved. That's a first, right?"

"Yes, definitely, for our generation of Singers," agreed Yieyie. "And remember—the last dream was just two months ago. We've gone years without hearing from Goldilocks before."

Pete tapped his spoon on the table. "If she is increasing her efforts to reach us, we should match that effort. Could we have a choir on the next golden days? Maybe boost our singing to four times a rev?"

The old Singer nodded his ancient head, which kept moving even when it was clear he had told it to stop. "Good idea, if we can convince our people to gather. It's getting harder, you realize." He looked up. "Were you the only ones who had the dream tonight?"

"We don't know." Jay sat up straighter. "It is strange. Of course, we were close by at the wayfarer's hut. Perhaps the others couldn't get away."

"I somehow didn't expect anyone else, even though there are Singers in Far Meadow and Mountain Top who could have arrived by now."

"What does it mean?" Pete asked. "Do you think Goldie targeted us to receive it?"

"Or it's because of Elena," Yieyie said.

"I didn't dream tonight." My color rose as they all looked at me. "How many of you are there, anyway? I thought this died out years ago." Even I realized I was deflecting the conversation.

I felt they might ignore my redirection, but, after a pause, Jay said, "Sometimes we have thirty gather. Lately, it's been more like fifteen or twenty when we rehearse. We haven't disappeared yet, but we're not getting any stronger. All

Singers dream Goldie at least once, though."

"So, sharing the dream makes you a Singer?"

"Not for you, dear." Yieyie didn't hesitate to respond. "You're part of our family now, through the bond you have with Jay and also through your gift of vision to Before." He reached across the table to place his weathered hand over my smooth fingers. "Promise me you'll come back and see me soon. And I promise you that when you do, we'll share stories of your fathers and Forest Edge."

Again, the pricking of tears in my eyes surprised me. I nodded, afraid I would break down if I opened my mouth. It had been so long since I felt like I belonged. Jay's love sustained me, but this was a true family.

"OK, folks," Pete said, rising from his seat. "We better go. I need some sleep before I get in that damn hummie again."

Watch them with me in my memory now, as they leave the old man and his little hut, tearing themselves away from the warmth of his hospitality, following the bobbing yellow gleam of the lantern bouncing off the path with the shadowed trees crowding in. I traveled there as an orphan, only to find my beloved had a family beyond my wildest dreams, ready to fold me in—a family which not only accepted me, but helped me discover who I am. I never forgot that night. It changed the course of my life.

Alice finished reading and put Elena's com-pad down. Leaning back, she reached for her tea, now stone cold. Everyone knew about Singers, but she never thought of them as real. She remembered joshing Nettie about them, telling her they were like Santa Claus. Could Nainai's heart-bond really have been one? And did this validate the story of her great aunt's vision? Well, why should any of this matter today, anyway?

CHAPTER SEVEN

Impatient with her thoughts, Alice stood to clear the table, then looked up as she heard quick footsteps on the courtyard stairs. She considered hiding, but, looking around, realized there wasn't much chance of concealing herself. Instead, she went to the door and opened it to see Nettie raising her fist to knock.

"Oh, Alice, there you are. Pa told me to go find you. You're supposed to come home right away."

"Why? What does he want?"

"I don't know. Is Nainai here? Did she give you another present?"

The girl's innocent eagerness brought an involuntary smile to Alice's face. "No, Nettles. Just a story today." Her heart ached with the responsibility she now had to protect her sister's future. If the Singers could help...

"Come in while I clean up and then we'll go home together, OK?"

"Alright. Can I have some bread? Where's Nainai?" Her younger sister bounced over the threshold, gravitating to the table and jam jar.

As Alice washed up the few dishes and Nettie ate her snack, they heard the slow, careful footfalls of Nainai navigating the courtyard steps. "You finish your snack here, Nettie," Alice said, wiping her hands and pushing the door open.

The wind skimmed over the dry moat, leaving the well around the hut comfortable. She met the old woman and handed her down the last steps, where Nainai caught her breath before saying, "I talked to Micah. It's like we thought—he knew nothing of a permanent bond."

"Nettie's inside. Pa wants me home."

Nainai nodded. "Yes, he'll want to keep an eye on you."

"What can I do? If I find the Singers, how will they help us?" She whispered, knowing she couldn't trust her sister with a secret.

"I told Micah to go along with your father's plan for now. I suggest you do the same."

"But Nainai...."

She held up a hand, forestalling her protest.

"We're just buying time before you can get out. If you lull your pa into thinking you're compliant, he may drop his guard. We need you to leave to convince the rest of the council of how serious this is."

The door to the hut cracked open, and Nettie leaned out. "Hi, Nainai. Alice is supposed to go home now."

"Yes, dear, I know. Let me finish giving her some instructions and then she can come with you."

The girl joined them, licking the jam off her fingers, eyes wide and attentive. Nainai looked at her and sighed. Then she turned to Alice again.

"Micah's family has two of the newer huts in the outer circle. I told him I expected him to give you the biggest of these, even if his son has to move out. It took a little convincing, but he has agreed." She regarded Alice and then glanced at her younger sister before continuing. "It will take a while to sort out, but it's time well spent, if you can be content with the best home in town. Your father values things like fine houses, so I think he'll understand that this is an acceptable compromise for you."

Alice frowned and then nodded. "Come on, Nettie. Let's go. I'll be back to bring you first supper, Nainai."

"Good," the old woman said. "We have much to talk about before your bonding. You've never set up a household before and, as your oldest female relative, it's my place to instruct you." Turning to Nettie, she smiled. "I'm sure your sister will fill in on any chores that you can't attend to in this time of preparation, won't you, Nettie?"

"Yes, Nainai." The younger girl beamed. "And when Alice can't come anymore, I'll bring your dinner."

"Thank you, dear. I'd like that." And she shooed both girls up the stairs, watching their progress over the lawn before turning and entering her hut.

Later that evening, Nainai got right to the point, not even waiting until her grandniece settled down to eat. "Did you convince Humphrey that you would go along with his wishes?"

"Yes, I think so," Alice replied, putting tofu cutlets and carrots on the table for the two of them. "Micah was already with him when I came home, telling him about your visit and how you made him promise the big house. Nettie confirmed it. You were right, Pa did seem pleased. Neither Micah nor I did a great job of appearing thrilled, but we were polite to each other. He looked a little embarrassed, really."

"Well, that's sounds normal. If either of you had been enthusiastic, your pa would have become suspicious."

"I don't understand, Nainai. What's the plan? Why is Micah helping? Does he expect me to do a first-bond with him still?"

The old woman smiled sadly. "Micah is a decent man. It appalled him that your father and the mayor tried to maneuver you into a permanent commitment. He resisted even seeming to condone it, but I convinced him I need time to figure out how to extinguish this movement."

"Movement?" Alice blanched at the word. It seemed so big.

"I know. It took me by surprise too. Barbara and Humphrey are not the only ones trying to return to Earth traditions. I talked to several members of the council. Two had heard that Near Meadow was considering a similar move. They're afraid if our community doesn't match them, we won't be viable for long."

"Well, only a couple." Alice perked up. "That means four members with my pa and the mayor. The others might follow your lead and vote it down."

"Yes, that's what I tried to find out today." The old woman nodded slowly. "The other five are ambivalent, though. They don't see how dangerous a move like this would be. Even Liam's mother sounded as if she wanted to have her children stay in our village forever. I don't think we could win a vote if it comes to one right now."

Alice looked down at her plate and shook her head. "I'll have to leave then, won't I?"

"I'm afraid so. My ruse with the house might buy us time, but I'm concerned that will only let the mayor bring her plan into the open and Micah's seeming compliance may mislead others. The quicker you disappear, the faster we'll confront the implications for individuals, as well as the community. The question is—where should you go, and how can we get you there safely?"

Elena studied her niece, who stared at her untouched meal. "You don't have to run, Alice. We could try to fight this with you here, but I'm afraid Humphrey will end up throwing you out of his house. I'd love to have you here with me, but it's not much of a future."

"No." The young woman sat up straight and met her great aunt's gaze. "Actually, this makes the break easier. I'm not just doing it for myself, but for Nettie and the other children. I don't know where to go, though. If I set out for Seaside, Pa may catch up with me before I can get there. I'd hate to fight with him on the open road, and if he's really determined—well, he's a lot stronger than I am."

"I've thought about that too. If we didn't have several months until college begins, it might be worth the risk. I doubt the Academy would let him jerk you out once you've started your studies. But you won't begin your courses for twelve weeks yet, and you'd be vulnerable all that time."

"I could stay with Dinah."

"How will she protect you if your father wants you back? She has no legal hold."

"Maybe I should go to Mountain View and live with my blood mother for a while." Alice tilted her head as she said this, making it a question.

"When did you last see Marna?"

"I think I was three revs old. Pa took me along to deliver soybeans to the village, and she came over to say hi. She didn't talk to me at all." Alice shrugged. "She's never actually wanted to connect."

"She'd take you in for a while, but it might be uncomfortable for both of you. Also, it's the second place Humphrey would look, and Marna won't cross him."

"That leaves the Singers."

"Yes, the Singers."

Alice and Elena sat in silence for a while.

"I read your story about meeting Yieyie with Jay and Pete. He sounded ancient. He must be dead by now."

"Yes, but Pete left Seaside soon after that adventure. He and his heart-bond Lyssa still live in Yieyie's hut. At least, I have not heard that they died."

"Do you believe they would let me stay with them until school starts?"

"I think that's your best bet, Alice." Nainai sighed, and her frowning face collapsed even further into wrinkles. "If you find them, I'm sure they will help you. You'll learn things that no one at the Academy can teach you if you spend time there. I wish I were younger, so I could guide you myself."

Alice stood. "I'll go to the forest. Pa and I stayed at the wayfarer's hut when we took produce down to Seaside once. I'll walk there tonight and find the path when the sun comes up."

After the rest of her household had gone to bed, Alice waited until she heard Humphrey snoring in the big bedroom and then slipped into traveling clothes and boots, stuffed a pack with an extra shirt and underwear she had tucked under her pillow, and snuck out the kitchen door. Rose Moon and Second Moon vied for dominance in the night sky, and her shadow crossed itself in front of her as she slid through the waving grass to Nainai's hut. Descending the stairs into the deep shelter of the courtyard, she felt safe. She eased the door open and stepped in.

Nainai sat at the kitchen table, tying up a bundle in the dim light of one lantern. Alice noticed the dark shadows under her eyes, the thin knobby fingers, and thought, *she is so old and trying so hard to help me. I may never see her again.* For a moment, regret swelled like a threatening illness, but she pushed it down.

"I can't stay long, Nainai. I should get going while the moons are still up."

"Yes, dear, I won't keep you. I've got some bread and dried fruit for you to stick in your bag. Do you have water?"

"Oh, no," Alice stammered. "I should have thought of that. I don't know where Ma keeps the canteens." How could she have forgotten this elemental necessity?

"I have one here for you. Don't stress." The old woman shuffled as she moved to the sink and filled a large, round canteen nestled in a cloth sling. "Fill it up from the cistern in the hut before you go into the forest."

"OK." She put the food in her pack, slipped her arms through the loops, and slung the water on her hip.

"Just a moment," Nainai said. "You have the otter?"

Alice fumbled at her neck and eased the little bag out of her shirt to show her.

"Good. I have two other gifts for you tonight." She reached into her pocket and brought out a small blue rectangle about the length of her thumb. On one end, it had a transparent case, and Alice could see metal through it. "This is called a jump drive, dear. I loaded all my stories on it. When you get a com-pad, insert this into a hole in the side, and you'll be able to read them. Keep it safe with the otter until you have use for it."

"Oh Nainai, thank you. I'll have you near me always with this." Alice beamed as she put the tiny storage device into the pouch and hid it back under her shirt.

"Just one more thing." Elena reached into her pocket and brought out a bright red oval about five inches long with shiny silver sides. Someone had embossed a cross on the top of the object, and when Nainai set it in her hand, it weighed more than she expected. It felt ancient, precious—an Earth relic.

Alice traced its smooth exterior with a tentative finger. "It's beautiful, Nainai, but I'm not sure what it is."

"Let me show you how it works." She took the strange item into her gnarled fingers, searching for a dent incised in a layered side surface, and pried a slice of the silver from the oval. She held it up and said, "They called these Swiss Army knives. I don't know why. This is the biggest blade. There is another small one, tiny scissors, and a blunt tool to dig or poke with. It also has this curly-cue thing, but I never knew what it was for. My Pops told me an ivory toothpick used to go in this slot, but he lost it long ago."

Alice's eyes had grown wide throughout this demonstration. "Oh, Nainai, it's wonderful. It's like magic. But why give it to me?"

"Because it's an explorer's device, a scientist's tool." Her eyes gleamed in the lantern light. "An excellent implement when you don't know what the next day or even the next hour will bring." She held it up so Alice could see it. "Look, fold the blade back in this way. Keep your fingers clear. And don't run with it open. It might collapse and cut you."

"Right." The young woman accepted the knife gingerly and tried to unfold it.

"It's stiff. I haven't used it much since my arthritis got bad. You may have trouble, but if you keep it clean, I think it will get easier the more you use it."

Alice had already flipped out both blades and discovered the scissors. She folded everything in and weighed the bright oval in her hand before slipping it into her pocket.

"You've given me the best gifts I've ever had." Her face clouded over. "I wish you would come with me." The last came out as a whisper.

Nainai stepped close and wrapped her in a hug. "I wish I could too, dear girl. I love you." She leaned back, taking a breath. "Look for the path south of the wayfarer's hut. Remember—it's an hour's walk to Pete's place. And if it's empty, Alice, it might be a good idea to stay there a week and then take the road to Seaside."

"Yes, I'd thought of that too."

"Be careful, darling girl."

"I will. I love you, Nainai." Alice dropped one more kiss on her soft, wrinkled cheek and opened the door to the night.

She had about six hours of walking ahead of her, but Alice knew the way well. The main thing she feared was being detected, but few people traveled after last supper, so she set off confidently. In her pocket, nestled next to the wondrous knife, was a small flashlight she borrowed from the solar charging station on her mother's kitchen windowsill. She would return it someday, she told herself. But she wouldn't turn it on until it got so dark she couldn't see the track. A wave of gratitude for the two moons washed over her. They'd give enough light to walk by for at least half the night if no clouds appeared.

As she hurried through the outer ring of the village, she registered sounds of human talk and laughter carried on the wind behind her, as if in a lingering farewell. Some neighbors were still up, but she saw no one else outside. She looked once over her shoulder as she reached the dirt lane nestled in the hip-high grass that surrounded the town. The warm yellow light from clerestory windows peeking above sunken courtyards illuminated the ground in pools around a few houses. She impressed the scene on her mind. *This isn't my place anymore,* she told herself. And yet, turning and setting her foot on the road, she knew she took part of Far Meadow with her. She confronted her path, following the dark gash through the waving stalks. Soon, the breeze sang only its own song, with no other voices riding on it.

Alice was used to hard labor, being a child of the farms. She had been on her feet all day, yet setting her body into the rhythm of a steady trek felt peaceful, almost restful. When the Rose Moon set, her eyes had become so accustomed to the dimness that she hardly noticed. As the yellow Second Moon followed suit and true darkness descended, she came out of a trance to take stock of her position. The night grew chilly, and she shivered when she stopped, wrapping her arms around herself, scant protection from the wind which pushed against her back.

A brief rest revived her, chewing a portion of the bread Elena provided, as well as a long drink from the canteen slung across her chest. She shook it to determine how much remained. About half, she guessed. She wasn't sure how far she'd come. The old woman claimed the hut had water, but what if she was wrong? Dehydration always threatened travelers on Goldilocks. The wind sucked moisture out of anybody who spent time outdoors. *If Nainai hadn't looked out for me, I would have already failed,* she thought, grimacing. *I guess I'll have to trust she knows what she's talking about.*

Alice drained her canteen an hour before she stumbled onto the wide lawn surrounding the wayfarers' hut, a few miles past the ruins of Forest Edge. The darkness had become an old friend by that time, and Alice, seeing the dawn breaking before she reached her sanctuary, felt exposed by the light. She checked her first impulse to take cover in the sunken cabin when she saw a hummie parked by the courtyard steps. *Damn,* she swore to herself. *I didn't expect other people to be here.* She cast about for a hiding place, crouching in the high grass that surrounded the yard, where she could watch the single entrance into the dwelling. Someone had piled dry fish into the bed of the vehicle, and she guessed it was on its way outback to trade them for produce.

Settling in the meadow, the sun warming her back and protected from the teasing breeze, sleep snuck up on Alice. When the hut's door banged shut, she startled, almost jumping up before she remembered she was hiding. She parted her lips to quiet her frightened breathing, peering through the long blades to see two travelers preparing to take off. An older woman packed carryalls into the hummie while a youth checked the cargo. The murmur of their conversation reached her, but she couldn't make out the words. The track from the road to the hut went right by her haven, and Alice knew, if they looked in her direction, they'd discover her. Her tongue stuck to the roof of her mouth, and her head throbbed. She needed water and rest. *Please,* she thought at them, *please leave now.*

As if moved by her plea, the hummie started up and carried the two occupants past her. Intent on quarreling, they didn't discover her. As soon as they were out of sight, Alice stumbled forward toward the sunken hut. She paused above the well-worn steps, listening for any movement. The windmill rising above the roof whirred reassuringly, but no other sound disturbed the solitude.

Inside, her eyes adjusting to the dim light, she surveyed the small kitchen area with its little table, an electric burner, and sink. Yes, there it was—a familiar pottery cistern with spigot. *Be full,* she prayed, as it occurred to her that the former occupants might have already depleted the precious liquid. As she turned the handle, water poured into her cupped hands. She drank and filled her canteen.

Her first need met, she looked around and saw the two doors she remembered from her childhood trip with her father. She chose the one farthest from the front entrance. Slinging her pack onto a bed, she noted the clerestory window opened with enough room to escape if someone came by. She felt pretty safe, though. It wasn't likely anyone else would stop before evening. That gave her about six hours to sleep, and then she'd use the remaining daylight to find the path and begin her trek into the forest. She turned the sign outside the bedroom door to "occupied" and collapsed on the thin mattress.

When she woke, twilight shadowed the walls. Alice guessed she had overslept and tensed with fear as she listened for any hint of movement in the great room. The wind, grown into a tempest, obstructed all other sounds. She risked a peek out to the hall and was met with complete solitude. With a sigh of relief, she sat back on the bed.

Well, I can't stay here long, she reasoned. *The couple in the hummie probably assured Pa that I wasn't here, but he'll have found out by now I'm not in Mountain View either. Likely, he'll borrow the village vehicle and head this way shortly. I need to get moving as soon as possible.* Her stomach reminded her she hadn't eaten in hours, but she decided she would take shelter under the trees before she sat down to make a meal. Hoisting her pack and grabbing another swig of water, she was just about to leave when she remembered—the cistern was full this morning. *If Pa finds it half empty, he'll know I stopped here.*

She found a pump between the hut and the forest. Dogged by anxiety, she filled the pail which hung at its side, replenished the crock, and finally was ready to look for the trail.

"South of the cabin," she recalled Elena saying. The shadows laying long on the grass reminded her she had little daylight left. Indentations of dirt dotted the border between lawn and woods. Which led to an actual path? The trees loomed up, throwing a deeper shade of their own, as if to protect their secrets.

She had traveled a quarter mile down the forest edge and thought about retracing her steps when the wind carried the sound of a hummie to her. Without thinking, she ducked under the canopy, crouching behind the phalanx of trunks to peer out at the yard surrounding the wayfarer's hut. Bumping down the track was the electric car so valued in her village, with Pa and Micah in the front seat. Alice retreated further into the trees. They didn't see her, but how would she find the trail now?

Desperate, she scanned the forest floor, moving farther in as she searched. A ray of sun, penetrating between the dark branches, glinted off something to her left, and she peered ahead: a dak's feather, bright copper in the light. Despite her fear, Alice felt a thrill of pleasure, turning to see it more clearly. There, as if the pinion feather pointed it out, a narrow, dusty trail emerged.

She stood looking at the faint path for a moment, recognizing this as the turning point from which she could not return. If she chose, she might reverse and go back to the hut, picking up familiar conflict with her father, trusting her body to steady Micah, and returning to a life where a circle of friends and family knew and accepted her. Or she could set her feet on this slender line that led into an unknown world of strangers and become someone strange herself. What should she do?

Her house mother had taught Alice to pray nightly, a listing of concerns and thanksgivings thrown up for a generalized deity to catch as he or she would. The entire clan always attended monthly gatherings on the golden days, which gave a nod to all three religions—Jewish, Christian, and Muslim—which the settlers brought with them from Earth. Those were the time for bondings, namings, and funerals. But other than blessings over planted fields and curses when gales or drought ruined the crops, Alice's family never felt a need to converse with God.

Now, though, the immensity of the choice before her quickened her heartbeat, and she cast around for some sign, some help in making this ultimate decision. The wind, stilled by the trees, found its way between the branches, ruffling her hair, dancing among the stiff needles. She turned her face into it, eyes closed, comforted by the sense of life beyond her small self. She breathed a plea into the roiling air: *What should I do?* When she opened her eyes, she saw the feather stuttering down the path into the woods. She hurried to pick it up, stuck it in a buttonhole, and continued forward toward the unknown. No shelter existed for her outside the forest now.

CHAPTER EIGHT

The trees Alice now walked among were familiar to her. They called them christmas trees, after a kind on Earth the settlers had loved. Slender, rough trunks held up branches with small, teal, needle-like leaves. In one version, the bottom-most limbs grew long enough to arch out and sweep the ground, creating little mini-huts in which children played. Most of the trees surrounding this path, though, were of the shorter-branched variety, their branches sticking out straight, beginning about six feet off the ground. Where saplings sprouted, she had to step over or push her way through the boughs, but the trail remained clear, even in the waning light. She sniffed the air, appreciating both the stillness and the musty, earthy scent.

She thought about the tales of madmen and murderers exiled to the forest. Most of them, she comforted herself, must be closer to the big towns in the broccoli-tree forests of Touch Down. Her hand wrapped around the little knife in her pocket, though, just in case.

Noticing how dim the light was growing, with the woods getting denser and the sun going down, she wondered whether she would reach her destination by nightfall. Then, she looked up to see the path brightening. Slowing, she inched forward, noting the christmas trees giving way to a new species, with squat, smooth trunks and broad, dark red leaves. She realized these must be the bilbos she had heard about, but never seen. The familiar timber stopped before the line of these other trees, as if they knew their territory had ended here. Standing in their last row, she noticed the bilbos stood only two or three deep before a meadow took over the landscape. As she ventured into the clearing, she saw the crimson forest formed a perfect circle, about the size of a soybean field, within which short grasses and flowers flourished. Across the glade, she made out the windmill and roof of a house sunk low in the ground. The trail led directly to it.

Now, she had to decide: Should she knock at the hut, trusting this was the correct cabin and that Nainai's friend would welcome her? Or should she wait until she could tell who was in there? If this wasn't the right place, where would she go from here? Maybe it was empty, and she could find shelter without the complication of strangers.

Unable to sort out the best action, she took the safest course. *It's at least an hour before full sunset*, she reckoned. She stepped aside and found a spot protected by a bush. She eased off her canteen and pack, making a seat for herself among the brittle old leaves of the bilbos.

Within minutes of settling, the door of the hut opened, dashing her hope that the place was deserted. She saw immediately that this wasn't the old fellow Nainai had led her to expect. Instead, the person bouncing up the courtyard steps and walking the track toward her was a young man about her age. Alice assessed her position. She was off the path, but was she hidden enough to elude his sight? As quietly as she could, she eased around to the far side of the wide bilbo trunk and squatted, breathing through her open mouth.

The youth stepped off the trail as soon as it met the forest and headed in her direction. Just as she thought, *He knows I'm here*, he veered to the left and strode toward the line of christmas trees. She shifted her position and spotted him about twenty feet from her hiding place, staring up at an especially grand christmas tree, the kind with drooping boughs. With a triumphant laugh, he ducked under the branches, only to appear a moment later, climbing up the trunk.

Alice watched, her mouth agape, as he climbed at least fifteen feet off the ground. She held her breath as he eased onto skinnier and skinnier limbs, which creaked under his weight. Then she identified his goal: a mess of moss and twigs, resembling a basket made by a blind person. The young man stretched out a long arm and pulled something from the tangle, stashing it in his shirt. He reached again, and then a third time, as a loud squawking call broke through the quiet woods. Beating wings collided with needles as a furious dak descended on him. Not giving way, the youth grabbed at whatever he sought. Alice saw an ivory orb, the size of a man's fist, slip into his tunic. Then he clambered down the trunk as fast as he could, with the beautiful copper vengeance calling him out, clinging to the branch her home was on, reaching out her snake-like neck to threaten him with a beak filled with tiny teeth.

As the young man emerged from underneath the tree, Alice realized she had risen to watch. She crouched low again. She didn't think he noticed her, but as he walked past her, clutching the eggs in his shirt, he said over his shoulder, "These will make an omelet for three people. You're welcome to join us, if you're hungry. We don't bite."

Surprised, her first reaction was to stay put. She wanted to go look at the dak. She'd never been this close to a nest before. And, as she thought about it, annoyance sparked at the man's causal acceptance of her presence. How did he know she wasn't dangerous?

She looked around and observed that darkness had descended further in the woods. Soon, she wouldn't be able to see the nest or even the path. Common sense kicked in, telling her that there was no purpose in hiding from someone who already saw she was there.

Trying not to look like a scolded child, Alice shouldered her pack and canteen and followed the stranger. *He could teach me more about the daks*, she encouraged herself. Too quickly, she stood looking down at the hut's entrance, into which the young man had disappeared.

"Come on in," a deep, hoarse voice called from the sunken interior. "Shut the door before the wind takes up residence." It didn't sound like a youth, but something about the rebuke, which all parents in Far Meadow used to chastise their offspring, reassured Alice. Her feet tripped down the steps and through the doorway, and she swung the door closed behind her.

The yellow light inside, provided by an electric lantern in the middle of a table, shed shadows around a great room, which included kitchen, dining, and living areas. She suspected the curtain spanning the length of the wall at the back concealed sleeping cots.

The young man stood at a counter between an old stove and sink, scanning her while mixing something in a pottery bowl. He appeared taller than he had outside—Alice guessed about the same height as her Pa. His dark eyes, wide for his narrow face, returned to his task. His long hands, brown against the cream-colored dish, whisked a yellow liquid. Beside the basin, she recognized the pale shells of the eggs he had filched. She walked over and touched them, wondering at the leathery quality of the dry outsides and the slimy, emptied interiors. A blaze of anger shot through her, and she turned to confront him.

"How could you kill these baby daks?" she demanded, without thinking. As soon as the words escaped her mouth, she clamped her lips together hard. This was not the way to start a relationship that she hoped would help her.

The youth looked at her with amusement. "What?" he asked. "You mean these eggs? Don't worry. I left the old girl three to hatch. Six is more than she can care for, anyway."

"She'll not complain once she's sampled your omelet, Sami."

Alice spun around, recognizing this voice as the one which invited her in. The corner of the room contained an old-fashioned rocker and an electric radiator, as well as a stone hearth. The man sitting there was old, as old as Nainai, his faced etched with deep wrinkles and his shoulders hunched. In his hand, he held a whittling knife, and she noted a small pile of shavings at his feet.

"Welcome to our home, girl." His blue eyes twinkled from

beneath unruly gray eyebrows. "I'm Pete. The cook there is Sami. We're not too dangerous, at least if you're not looking to steal anything or kill us yourself."

"Me?" she stuttered, thrown off base by this vision of herself as a threat. "No. I mean, I'm just Alice. I wouldn't hurt you."

"Well then, just Alice, now that we've established that we're all peace-loving, harmless creatures in this cabin, why don't you relieve yourself of your burden and sit down here by the heater?" The gnome-like creature had no sting. He appeared to laugh at himself as much as her.

Sami, moving to chop vegetables, snorted and said, "Don't mind Pete. He missed his nap waiting for you and is cranky now."

"Waiting for me?" Alice slipped off her canteen and pack and laid both next to the door. She addressed the Elder. "How did you know I was coming? I didn't tell anyone but Nainai, and she's in Far Meadow."

"Didn't you?" The gnarled fingers resumed their work on a piece of christmas tree wood, and the scent of pitch was sharp in the close room. "Anyway, you're late. I thought you'd be here hours ago."

Alice felt her jaw drop open in astonishment and shut it with a snap. What was going on here? She slipped her hand into her pocket and touched the reassuring oval of her knife.

"Give her a break, for goodness' sake." The younger man pulled out a chair at the table and nodded to it. "Come and sit down, Alice. Pete thought Goldie meant you'd arrive here before noon, but it must have been exhausting walking from Far Meadow yesterday. No wonder you didn't get going earlier."

She stepped forward and sat on the edge of the seat, her hand grasping the knife in her pocket.

Sami smiled at her. "Are you cold? I can build a fire in the fireplace if you like. We have plenty of electricity for the heater, but sometimes a wood blaze is nice too."

"No, no, I'm fine. Just confused. You seem to recognize me, but

I don't know you at all."

"Don't you?" The raspy voice taunted her. "Didn't you come to meet the Singers?"

"Yes, that's right. And you must be Nainai's friend, Pete. Nainai is Elena Far Meadow."

"Now you're tracking." The old man cackled with delight.

"But how could she tell you I was coming? I just left last night. And I wasn't sure I'd find the path. I almost didn't." Alice couldn't seem to keep her balance in this conversation, and it didn't help that whatever concoction Sami had gone back to stir on the stove smelled heavenly. Her stomach growled, and she felt her face heat, but neither of them seemed to notice.

Neither man answered, and the room settled into quiet. The young man concentrated on his cooking, and Pete was content to watch. Alice looked around again, feeling at home in the little cabin despite the strange conversation. Next to the kitchen area, she noticed a pile of dirt and a wheelbarrow and realized that the hut was being worked on.

"Are you building on a new room?" she asked, grateful to find a safe subject.

The old man considered the earth works. "Yes, we didn't want to mash you in here with us. Some neighbors will be over soon, and it shouldn't take long to finish with their help."

Reality shifted under Alice's feet again. "What?" she exclaimed, trying to catch her breath.

Sami intervened. "Pete, come and do something useful. These eggs are ready. Get the plates down, would you?"

The Elder pressed himself up out of the chair and shuffled across the room in a manner of walking that Alice recognized from observing Nainai. In the kitchen, he reached up to take plates, one at a time, from a stack of homemade ceramics on the shelf built into the wall closest to the table. The dishes were thick, but almost perfectly round and smooth, glazed in a beautiful cerulean blue, decorated with doodles of bright green. Alice viewed them with a critical eye. She made pottery, too, and loved the hours she had spent creating sets for her family and friends. She understood the difficulty of getting plates to turn out flawless and uniform, matching each other as these did.

Pete noted her attention. As he began handing them to the youth, one by one, to be filled with a fragrant yellow heap peppered through with bits of red and green, he said, "Sami's mom made all our pottery. She had a genuine gift for it, bless her heart."

Sami supplied the essential information as he settled across from Alice at the table. "May she rest in peace."

"May God and Goldie ease your loss." She voiced the polite words, but with such emotion that both men looked at her.

The young man nodded, tracing the rim of his plate. "Thanks. We miss her."

Neither of her hosts picked up the chopsticks lying beside their plates, so Alice let hers lie still too, although her mouth salivated in response to the delicious aroma rising from the yellow mound. As she tried to anticipate what they expected next, Pete tapped three times on the tabletop, and then he and Sami sang.

The tune wove around in their two voices, a deep, faltering bass and a light, clear tenor. Startled, Alice caught a few words but missed their meaning. In a minute, the impromptu concert ceased, and her hosts picked up their chopsticks and dove into their food.

"Oh, that was lovely," she stammered. "Thank you."

Pete snorted. "It wasn't for you, sweetie."

"We do it every meal," Sami explained with a half-smile. "It's a traditional Singer grace. You know, a prayer of thanksgiving."

Alice felt her face grow warm again. How could she keep making silly mistakes like this? She picked up her chopsticks to hide her confusion and tried the eggs. They tasted as delicious as Pete had said they would. She forgot her embarrassment and even her squeamishness at eating young daks as she filled her grateful belly with the best meal she'd gotten in ages.

They ate the rest of the food in silence, Alice not daring to ask more questions and the men comfortable in their companionable quiet. After clearing the plates, Sami set the kettle on the stove, then got out two long sticks, both split at one end.

"Would you help me make some toast? Pete's hands shake and the bread burns more often than not."

She accepted a stick and watched as he cut three thick slices, then put one across the forked end. Following his example, she held it over a burner, letting him flip it over for her when he judged it done. He did one more and then, slathering on jam Pete conjured up from somewhere, they all sat down to a second course.

By this time, the clerestory windows had gone dark. Full of good food and feeling drowsy in the warm, cozy hut, Alice let herself believe she might be safe. The old man took his tea and retreated to the rocker, where he drifted off into a post-dinner nap. Her focus strayed to the wall with a chalk outline and dirt beside it, and she frowned, reminded of the unsolved mystery.

As if reading her mind, Sami murmured, "The room won't be ready for several days, maybe a week. You can use the bed behind the curtain while Pete and I sleep out here. Will that be OK?"

"It's certainly generous of you." Alice matched his subdued tone, not wanting to disturb the old fellow. "But I don't understand how you knew I was coming."

"Pete dreamed it." The young man sounded matter-of-fact.

Alice shook her head. "I still don't get it. Can Singers see the future?"

"No, but when Goldilocks pays attention, she knows what's going on. And Pete is the best at hearing her."

"The planet?"

"Yes, didn't your great aunt tell you about the dreams?"

"She wrote a story about when she first met Singers. I read it last night. I only know you all exist and have a connection with our world. That part really baffled me." Alice examined the cup she held in her lap. "Nainai figured I could hide here until it's time to register for the Academy."

Sami's eyes opened wide. "The Academy? Pete said nothing about that. I thought you came to live with us—you know, like a member of our family."

"I don't need another family." Alice's words came out sharper than she intended. She took breath before going on. "Look, I'm so grateful for the dinner and the hospitality you've already shown me. But college starts in three months, and if I can get there, they'll take me."

Pete's hoarse voice sounded across the room. "Why did Elena send you to us if not to stay here?"

Alice turned to address him. "Nainai told me there's lots you might teach me about the forest and daks that no one at the school knows. I'd like to learn from you. But I had to come now because my father and the mayor of Far Meadow are changing the rules about partnering. They want me to bond permanently with an older man in the village. I think Nainai wants the Singers to help change their minds, but I don't understand how you can do that." She glanced at Sami, biting her lip. "I'm sorry. It all happened so fast. I had to escape before we had a good plan in place."

"I see," he said with a frown. Alice thought he looked more sad than angry. He focused on Pete. "Well, at least we'll have a new room and a guest to occupy it for a while."

Their disappointment weighed down the air. *They expected something else*, she realized. *Do they want me to keep house for them? Cook and clean and take care of them?* Pride sparked and a flush rose to her face. "Look, if you need some help, I'm glad to work for my bed and board until I leave. But I won't stay here forever. I have plans for my life."

"Oh, we all have plans," Pete sighed. "The question is, how do our plans fit with the pattern Goldie offers us?"

"What is that supposed to mean?"

Sami interceded again, shaking his head and releasing some tight black curls from their tie-back. "He's just disappointed, Alice. We got a little ahead of ourselves in thinking we understood what you wanted. There are so few Singers now. When we heard you were coming, we thought you might be the first of a wave of young people returning to the tradition, the Singer ways. I guess we expected help from you, in the same way that Elena hoped we could assist your village."

Alice scrutinized him, taking her time before answering. She felt a reserve, as if he held a shield in front of something he wanted hid. It stunk somehow, like when Pa sent her to ask Micah for help with the harvest. Finally, she said, "I don't have much to offer you all. I work hard, though. Could you use a hand getting your garden harvested and replanted in the three months I'm here? Cooking and cleaning don't scare me either. If that's not enough, well...I hope you'll let me at least stay the night. I can leave when the sun is up."

The men locked eyes over her head. Alice, examining Sami's face, saw a warning flash to the older man and then his features smoothed over to neutral. She turned to look at Pete, finding it harder to read his wrinkled visage.

He smiled at her then, becoming the lovable old gnome he had at first appeared to be. "Don't mind me, dear. I miss my women— my heart-bond and my daughter. I think having a lovely girl at the table made me nostalgic. You're welcome to stay whatever amount of time seems right to you."

"And the truth is, we could use some help with the garden," Sami said, matching Pete's smile. "Twelve weeks of someone who knows her way around vegetables might get our production up. In our last crop, the potatoes got a blight, and we haven't had a good mash for two-thirds rev."

"OK." Alice's voice came across as tentative, and Sami, as if eager to please, continued.

"I could show you a few more daks' nests tomorrow. I spotted at least three bordering the clearing. We might find some more."

She nodded as she searched his dark eyes for a truth that would reassure her.

Pete stood up from his rocking chair and stretched. "Well, if you're getting up early in the morning, we should turn in now. Sami, come help me shift our stuff out here so Alice can have the bedroom. And young woman, you might want a shower before you sleep. The water heater is full, and the wind blew all day, so it should be nice and hot."

As they moved to rearrange the furniture, Alice grabbed her knapsack and ducked into the simple bathroom. Still worried by the men's attitude, she considered escaping out the high window, which provided ventilation, but the temptation to get clean overwhelmed her. Anyway, the portal was tiny, and the night was very black. Where would be safer than here?

On reflection, she didn't think either man would hurt her. Some unspoken need lay between them; that seemed clear. Until they asked, though, she couldn't judge how they'd react if she denied compliance. *One evening shouldn't be too dangerous*, she consoled herself. *If necessary, I can escape them the same way I did Pa. I'll take another look at where the path begins tomorrow, so I'm able to find it in the dark.*

She ran the shower as hot as she could stand it, stopping the stream after getting wet to soap up and then rinsing efficiently. They considered warm water a luxury at home, and here it would be no different with three people sharing. As she dried off, she noticed the sound of the men speaking and leaned her head toward the door. The hushed tones sounded intense, if not angry. Pete's bass rumbled something she couldn't make out. Sami's clear voice, easier to hear, said, "Don't push me, man. Let's just see how things unfold. She'll be here awhile if you don't scare her off." And then, as if they realized the shower no longer drowned out their conversation, the voices ceased.

A fragrant cloud of steam followed Alice into the common room. She saw the men had arranged a narrow cot and pallet across from the curtained-off area. Sami stepped to the partition, holding it back so she could see a little nook containing a bed with a wooden box at the end. Shelves of various sizes and depths were dug into the far wall and, although they cleared several of the lowest for her things, the rest held assorted goods and knick-knacks. She noted a few of Pete's carvings, a dak and a bilbo tree, and then her gaze met a computer.

"Oh, you have a com-pad," she said. "Does it work?"

"Sure it does. I use it when I'm at the Academy." Sami dropped this information as casually as he had made the omelet.

She stared at the young man, wide eyed. "What? You go to college?"

Pete laughed in the background. "I wondered when he would tell you that."

"Yeah, I started last rev. I took this third off, though, after Mom died. I needed some time to recoup and help get Pete set up." He looked at Alice, his deep eyes shadowed. "If you still want to travel to Seaside in three months, I'll take you. I know a back way your pa won't find you on."

"Oh, thank you, Sami." Relief flooded through her. This might work out after all.

Then a sudden revelation hit. This was the expectation that she couldn't fulfill: They hoped she would stay to care for Pete. Immediately, she felt the pull of unwanted responsibility. She looked at the old man settling himself in his rocker and thought of Nainai all alone in Far Meadow. At least Nainai had Nettie to bring her food and help.

"Pete, do you have to remain in the forest? You could go live with Nainai. I'm sure she'd be happy to have you."

"Yeah, and I'd be glad to see her. But you and I know, Alice, another mouth to feed won't be welcome in your village, especially when I don't have the strength to work on the farm." He assessed her crestfallen face and smiled. "Don't worry about me. I like it out here. You and Sami can visit me during vacations. Go on and rest up now."

"Yes, get some sleep, Alice. And if you want me to show you the com-pad in the morning, I'll be glad to start it up for you. Of course, once you enter the Academy, they'll give you one of your own."

"I know. That's one reason I have to go." Alice sighed. "Well, good night, then. Thanks so much for everything."

Behind the drape, light filtered in, dim and red. She kicked off her shoes, then shrugged off her outer clothes, folding them beside her pack on the chest. Her mind tugged at the problem of the old man living alone in the forest, but she had come so far in such a short amount of time. The mattress, covered in smooth cloth, was so soft, and the blankets warmed with her body heat. Before she even said her evening prayer, consciousness fled. The quiet voices on the other side of the curtain, thick with worry, barely clouded her dreams.

CHAPTER NINE

A delicious smell found its way into Alice's nose before she woke the next morning and, drowsing, she dreamed she was home, her Ma fixing pancakes for a holiday breakfast. As her stomach demanded sustenance, she woke in a short state of confusion before remembering where she was. The scent of baked goods got stronger, and she stretched, noting the sunlight pouring through the clerestory window above the shelves, then pulled on her outer clothes to investigate.

"Here she is." Pete grinned as she emerged around the curtain. He set a teapot on the table, which already had three plates on it. "Just in time for breakfast, dear. Sami has outdone himself in your honor."

"It smells wonderful, whatever it is." Alice watched the youth lean over to pull something from the stove. "May I help?"

"Could you grab the soy milk out of the cooler? And that bowl of berries? We're almost ready here. I've got some hot cereal and these muffins my mom used to make." Sami's brown face, flushed with the heat of the oven, beamed at her.

As they sat, the men paused to sing their thanksgiving before diving into breakfast. Alice again felt the music's power, but this time, a sense of being home swept over her. She bent over her food to hide her confusion at the depth of joy it brought her.

Pete broke the silence of the enthusiastic diners first. "We have people coming in this afternoon to help build the new room. I'd like you to give them a hand, Sami. You too, Alice, if you don't mind meeting the neighbors."

"I'd love to meet them. Are they Singers, as well?"

"Yes, there aren't many left, but we stick together."

Sami said, "They're older folk. They'll need us both to do any heavy lifting."

The old man snorted. "I'm not sure Jamie and Manuel would agree with your assessment of them."

"Are they coming? This will be a breeze, then."

Pete grinned at his enthusiasm. "You two should do your dak watching this morning before they show up."

"Is that OK with you, Alice? Would you like to use the com-pad first?"

The young woman paused, her spoon suspended mid-air. She thought of the small drive in the pouch around her neck. She wanted to read Nainai's stories privately. "Oh, it's probably best to see the daks this morning. You can show me the com-pad tonight, if you don't mind."

"Sounds like a plan." Sami finished up his last bites and got up to wash the dishes.

They didn't get to the computer until several days later. When the two young people returned from a hike around the clearing, neighbors had already assembled. They found Pete inside with a couple of other men a generation younger, shifting furniture from one side of the room to the other. Sami stepped in to help, and Alice made for the kitchen to begin lunch.

The rest of the crew filtered in soon after, helping themselves to sandwiches, fruit, and tea. Altogether, there were eight neighbors, ranging in age from the brothers, Manuel and Jamie, who were a rev older than Sami, to the gentlemen who had arrived first. Only two women were with them, Alice noted, both more elderly than her house mother but still hearty and full of energy and laughter.

Pete divided them into teams and assigned the labor: He and his older friends would cut through the existing wall. The three young men and one of the older women he selected to raise frames and stack bales of straw to create the walls, extending to the courtyard boundary. The others, Alice and a couple named Sarai and Michel, would make and apply adobe mud to seal the sides, inside and out. Straw-bale houses preserved a comfortable temperature and, as grass was a limitless commodity on Goldilocks, this was a preferred building method. Sami had shown Alice the blocks of dried grass that stood ready for this project, stacked behind the garden. How they came to be there was a mystery he didn't reveal.

Except for receiving concise instruction from her workmates, Alice found little time or energy for conversation. All three of them dug dirt from the outer bank of the courtyard, helping to extend its boundaries past the bulge which the room would create in its circle. Then she and Micah dumped water and soil into a makeshift mixer as Sarai pedaled the old bicycle modified to run it. They hauled the mud to a rising wall and plastered until their buckets ran out. She lost count of the number of times they repeated this procedure. *Obviously*, she concluded, *these people have worked together on similar projects.*

They had almost finished the small room when Pete stuck his head through the new doorway to call a break. His trio had completed their task early and used the rest of the afternoon to fix a feast worthy of the work party.

Before serving even a spoonful, though, everyone walked to the meadow above the courtyard. Alice followed them, halting by the moat's steps as they arranged themselves into a pattern: the women standing together, facing the forest, with Sami and three other men lined behind them, then Pete, Manuel, and Michel a step to the rear in the gaps of the second row. Sarai lifted her hand and let it fall. Alice heard them take a collective breath and then....

Sami and Pete's thanksgiving song had been beautiful. This music shook her to her core, transporting her out of herself with a purity and richness of complex sound, both ethereal and grounded in the very bones of the planet. It lasted less than five minutes, the air reverberating in the silence after the last notes. She realized her face was wet with tears and looked away as the Singers descended into the hut.

Sami paused and touched her hand as he passed by. "You OK?"

"Yeah, I think so. I never heard anything that powerful before." She swiped at her eyes with shaking fingers.

"C'mon. You're starving. You worked hard today." He took her elbow and guided her down the steps.

They crowded into the kitchen, where the smells of vegetable stew and savory biscuits mingled with the sweet aroma of two berry pies. Pete loaded plates and bowls, and everyone found a place to settle. Alice made herself useful by filling mugs with tea and delivering them before finding a corner to hunker down in. The other guests seemed to sense her reticence and, after a few comments on how glad they were for her help, directed their attention elsewhere.

She ate with gusto, for Sami was right about her being starved, but she also attended to the conversation swirling around her—the young men talking about the Academy, the older folks discussing weather and illnesses. These people loved and respected each other, just like her Far Meadow family and friends. She felt a stab of homesickness.

After eating, Sami and Alice cleaned up while Pete and his cronies settled on blankets for a siesta. The younger men said they would take their rest beneath the trees in the forest, and Sami joined them there. The two women shared the bed behind the curtain, inviting Alice to join them. She felt stifled in the small space after the day outside, though, and told them she would find a napping place in the courtyard. Young adults often skipped the traditional after-first-supper nap, but today even she needed a break before returning to the challenging work of finishing the walls and roof of the bedroom before last meal.

She stepped around already prone and snoring bodies and let herself out into the narrow channel of the courtyard within which the hut sheltered. In some of these classic dry moats, people set up patios with furniture and lounges to enjoy the sun while escaping the endless wind of the planet. Pete's small yard, however, held only pots of herbs and vegetables.

On the side farthest from the door, she found a patch of sunlight beside an enormous pot of rosemary and sank down to rest her back against the outer wall while stretching out her legs. She was just drifting off when the crunch of dirt under shoes warned her that someone was approaching.

She looked up to see Sami, who stopped in his tracks on seeing her.

"Oh, I didn't know this spot was taken. You found my favorite hideout."

She squinted up at him. "There's room for two."

"Thanks. I love Manuel and Jamie, but I needed a break." The young man sank down on the other side of the herb pot and leaned against the wall.

She could smell the tang of his dried sweat mixing with the pungent fragrance of rosemary but didn't bother to shift so she could view him. "Do they go to the Academy too?"

"Yeah. They started a rev ahead of me. They're twins, you know—fraternal."

"I didn't, but now that you say it, I can see it. Are they on a break from their studies?"

"Not like me. They took the weekend off and thumbed a ride with a hummie. They'll hitch back tomorrow and finish out the semester before taking an actual vacation."

"They came all this way to build the room?" Alice moved slightly, peeking around the plant to catch Sami's face. "How did they hear you needed help?"

He shrugged, frowning. "Sometimes Singers just realize they're wanted. It surprised me too, that the twins got the message." He chuckled. "Usually, they're focused on other subjects, and if they're required, someone has to go get them."

"What other subjects?"

"You know—women. They're old enough to bond, but they don't have much to offer. Few mates want to send a child to the outback."

"Oh." Alice hadn't thought about bonding all day. She realized it was a relief. But she also hadn't remembered Dinah and felt a twinge of guilt. "So, what do they study when they aren't chasing women?"

"They're both interested in technology—computers and windmill generators and stuff like that. They're quite good. We'll be lucky if they come back to the forest with their skills."

"And you're studying medicine, right?"

"Yup."

Alice paused, angling her face away to catch the sun, looking toward the opposite wall. "Have you met a science teacher at the Academy named Dinah Seaside? She's not a full professor yet, but she teaches some of the basic courses."

"Yeah, we've all had her intro to biology class. She also does one on botany, but I think her actual area of expertise is bugs, isn't it? How do you know her?" It was Sami's turn now to crane his neck so he could read her face.

Alice kept her gaze fixed away from him. "She came to Far Meadow to research bilbugs, and a few of us older kids studied with her."

"So, you'll be ahead of the other freshmen—at least in biology."

His voice held a smile but, even so, she didn't look at him. "What is she like? When she's at the Academy, I mean."

"I don't know.... Pretty much the same as the rest of the teachers, I guess. She gives a hard test. Some students complained, but I had no trouble with her."

"She has to be rigorous." Alice turned to him, her green eyes intense. "Science requires exact observations, and if you don't learn that early, you become sloppy."

Sami tilted his head and nodded. "Yeah, that sounds like her. She must have impressed you."

She almost confessed then. The words "I love her" sat on the tip of her tongue. But before she could speak, two pairs of legs swung over the courtyard wall and the twins jumped down to join them.

"Have your lazy butts had enough of a siesta?" Manuel grabbed Sami by the wrists and pulled him to his feet. "We've got to raise that roof so we can get back to school tomorrow."

Jamie put out his hand to assist Alice more gently. She said, "I don't think anyone in the hut is up yet."

"If you're not sleepy, would you mind helping? We can get most of the supports up ourselves, with four of us working."

She realized she was beginning to tell them apart. Even though he was taller and broader than his brother, Jamie seemed the calmer soul. And after what Sami had told her about them, she also suspected he was trying to impress her. With a wry smile and a glance at her host, she said, "I'm ready to go."

The remainder of the afternoon sped by. They got half the roof supports up before the rest of the crew appeared and Alice went back to applying adobe on the walls. The older men were expert roofers, and they had a rounded top in place by sunset. The plaster had to dry before being whitewashed, and the floor needed to be packed down, but the bedroom was essentially done.

As they cleaned up, putting away tools and washing mud off the mixer, Pete brought out leftovers for everyone. The wind came up as the sun went down, so the Singers offered thanks gathered around the table. Then the twins stuffed sandwiches into knapsacks and headed out to hike to the wayside cabin, to catch a ride back to Seaside. The other men bedded down on comforters for the night, while Alice joined the older women behind the curtain. She opted to lie on the floor beside the bed while they shared the mattress. She heard them murmuring, sharing gossip about family and friends for a few minutes before sleep took her.

In the morning, Alice awoke to find her companions already out of her nook. She stretched, feeling muscles sore from the unaccustomed work and the hard floor. Conversation and movement in the outer area told her breakfast was underway, but she dressed slowly, folding up her blankets and making the rumpled bed, before joining the crowded great room.

It wasn't as cramped as she expected. Sarai and Michel had already departed. The others were taking their leave and wished Alice goodbye, hoping she would enjoy the new bedroom. She added her thanks to Pete's before settling at the table with a muffin and mug of tea.

Her elderly host cleared dishes, preparing to wash up.

"I'll get that when I finish eating," Alice said. "You've already done enough work today and I'm the last one awake. In my household, the latest to breakfast always cleans up."

Pete nodded, sitting down with his own cup. "That's the rule we live by too. I'm glad you're making yourself at home and not acting like a guest."

"Where is Sami this morning?"

The old man shrugged, frowning. "He left last night to check in with his dad. He'll be back before first supper."

Alice peered over her mug. "What village does his father live in?"

"Wood Lawn." Pete shot her a sharp glance. "They established Wood Lawn after they burned down Forest Edge, when Elena and I were in school. It's the closest settlement to the forest now. Sarai and Michel and many of my friends have houses there, as well as here among the trees."

"I heard about Wood Lawn, but I haven't been there. Pa traded with Near Meadow and once or twice with Seaside. Those and Mountainside are the only villages I've visited."

"Well, you'll have time to travel. There's a lot of Goldilocks no one has ever seen. An entire continent that people haven't yet set foot on lies across the sea, even though we've been here over forty-three revs."

Alice grinned. "Sounds as if you wish you were an explorer."

He nodded his balding head. "Yeah, that was my dream. It kinda got waylaid when the plagues struck."

"Did your family die in Forest Edge like Nainai's?"

"My folks settled Last Stop, so I grew up on the edges of the geography we recognize. That's when people welcomed Singers everywhere. When I was three revs old, they moved down to Near Meadow, where my blood mother had a home. The epidemic hit there too, but not as bad as Forest Edge. I was at the Academy, so I wasn't around when they began to blame the Singers for their troubles."

Alice leaned forward. "What happened to them?"

"My family? They were pretty lucky. My grandfather—Yieyie, we called him—already lived in the forest, in this house, in fact. My parents stayed with him until they built a hut of their own a few miles from here in another clearing."

"Oh, I read Nainai's story of meeting Yieyie for the first time with Jay and you."

"She wrote it down?" Pete's crinkled face lit with pleasure. "She always was the cleverest of us."

"Nainai's written a lot of her memories down," Alice said. "She hasn't shared them much, though." Pausing, she remembered Elena's last words to her. "She'd like other people to pay attention to how things were back then. I have some of her stories with me."

"Hmmm." The old eyes looked away. "I wonder if anyone would be interested. Or, perhaps the question is, how to get them interested?" He considered her for a moment. "I believe Goldilocks may be ready to speak to us again."

"How do you know?" Alice asked.

"Well, that's the problem. I'm not sure. There have been periods when people dream of her more, but then contact drops off. I've been aware of her more often and more vividly than before, though. In fact, I wonder...." He broke off his stream of thought to examine her again.

"Wonder what?" she prompted, knitting her brows.

"Do you dream her, Alice?" The old man's white eyebrows lifted.

"Dream of Goldilocks?" She shook her head. "No, I'm not a mystic. I only heard about you guys recently."

"You realize that Elena—well, she's not a Singer, but she is a Bridge."

"Yes, I read that story. It was wonderful, but I didn't think it was true at first. I thought she made it up."

"Nope, she's the real deal. And we haven't had another Bridge since her." Pete sighed. "These gifts often get passed down through generations. You may have the potential to be a Singer or a Bridge yourself, being blood related to Elena."

"I'm sorry, Pete." She looked into her mug. "I don't seem to have any special powers. I'm just a farmer's child who wants to become a scientist."

"Hey," the old man reached out to lift her chin, "being smart enough to get into the Academy is a wonderful ability. As for the others, don't worry about it. Sometimes dreaming comes later in life, but one thing I've learned—and Elena taught this to me: Everyone has just the right gift to give."

He drained his cup and stood up from the table. "We simply need to find the best time and way to offer what's special about us."

"Yeah, well, I'm a great dish washer," Alice said, rising. "I'll give that gift right now."

Later that day, when Pete had gone out into the garden, Alice lifted the com-pad down from the shelf. Sami hadn't had time to show it to her yet, and she told herself she should wait until he got home, but the conversation with Pete gnawed at her. Why did people blame the plagues on Singers? Why were they shunned and not even talked about anymore? It made little sense. They appeared kind and dear to her, a family she would be proud of.

So, though she realized she stepped over a personal boundary, when she held the com-pad in her hands, she also knew she would try to get it to reveal Nainai's stories. She looked it over, running her fingers around the edges. Sure enough, a little port nestled in the side, protected by a rubber cover she pried off. She took the drive from the pouch around her neck and pushed the bright metal end in. It fit—but nothing happened. The screen didn't come on, nor did anything else indicate it worked.

Alice sighed, taking the stick out to examine. It seemed unharmed. She set it aside and addressed the com-pad again. She had used the computer in Far Meadow's common hut, of course. Every school child learned to read and type on the slates which synced with the village's network. But they were cut off from the primary processing system in Touch Down and had been since before she was born. Com-pads connected with all the knowledge of humanity—everything the settlers brought from Earth and what they had discovered since then. Just holding one awed her.

She found and pushed a button on top of the rectangle. Bing... the screen lit up, and a slight whirring emanated from the pad. *Well, that's something,* she thought. Clearly, she needed to write in the blank space outlined there. She touched the shadowed oval, and three lines of letters sprang up—a typing board. What did it want?

"You have to put a password in."

Alice almost dropped the com-pad and, blushing, turned her head to see Sami standing at the curtained entrance, which she had not pulled closed.

"Oh, I'm so sorry. I didn't think you'd be home until later. My curiosity got the better of me." She rose from her seat on the bed, stretching out her hands to give the precious machine back to him.

The young man brushed her apology aside, coming further into the nook and sitting down beside her. "Look, when you get one of these, you choose a password and use it to log in. Don't pick something easy that anyone can guess. You'll want to keep things on this that are secret."

"Like what?"

"Oh, love letters, signed confessions, deep, dark journals—stuff like that. Actually, I have nothing that interesting on mine, so I don't care if you know my password. It's 'forestson'—all one word."

Alice watched as he hit the virtual keys. "Why did you choose that?"

"It's my identity—at least that's how I think about myself. Now, what did you want to do?" He reached out and picked up the drive she had left lying on the blanket. "Is there something on here you need to access?"

She felt uneasy about revealing the gift, but he had been so kind.... "It's from Nainai," she stammered. "She said she would put her stories on it for me."

Sami studied her. "Are they private? Do you want to look at them alone?"

She considered his willingness to leave but realized that, in her gut, she trusted him. Even if he found Elena's writing fantastical, he wouldn't make fun of her. "No, that's alright. In fact, I'd like you to read them and tell me what you think. For a while, I suspected Nainai made stories up, though she called them memories. Now, I realize the things she wrote about this house and Pete turned out to be true."

"Kind of flipped your world upside down, huh? Well, let's see what we've got." Sami slid the jump drive into the side slot. A long list appeared on the glowing screen. Sami said, "Wow, she's written a lot. What do you want to start with?"

Again, Alice considered, watching the dark eyes flitting down the list. Maybe he would help her understand. He could be her ally. "Pete told me this morning that people blamed the Singers for the plagues, and they had to hide out in the forest. I wondered if Nainai knew about that. She might have a story about why it happened or how it started."

Sami nodded. "Yeah, I'd like to learn her take on that too. Let's see what we have here." They sat in silence for a while as he moved his fingers over the screen. Alice watched, noting how he manipulated it. He settled on one file and read aloud, "Meeting the Mystics."

"No, you can read that later. That's how she first met Pete's grandfather. It's a good tale, but I've already seen it."

"OK. How about this: The Singers' Last Visit."

"Yeah, that might do it. How do you get the story?"

He tapped the title. It darkened, and then the whole screen bloomed into light and words.

"See, nothing to it." He handed her the com-pad and leaned back, half reclining on the bed. "Shall I look over your shoulder?"

Again, she felt a shiver of discomfort, thinking of Pete just outside the curtain. "Why don't we move to the courtyard, and I'll read it to you there. We could sit by the rosemary pot."

"Sure." The young man sat upright and hopped off the bed. "Let's go."

CHAPTER TEN

They relaxed as they had the day before, one on each side of the potted plant, their backs against the sun-warmed outer wall. Alice held the com-pad, sheltered by her shadow looming over it, and read. In a moment, the story enveloped her, and she forgot Sami even existed.

The Singers' Last Visit

(This occurred in the final third of our eighteenth revolution around the sun. I was in my third rev, about eight years old in the old Earth reckoning.)

It was the month of Bleak, the coldest, darkest season on Goldilocks. The initial two-thirds of the rev yielded disappointing crops, barely replacing the stores used in the last winter. Then, for the first time since the settlers landed, bilbugs infested the yellow grass harvest, and the soybeans failed. Even fishermen seemed doomed to poor catches.

Hunger stalked our village, and people calculated how much they could eat and still survive until spring. I remember Pops hunched over the kitchen table while Da cooked up a few withered carrots with a stunted squash, trying to figure out how to make the flour hold out until June, the earliest we could hope for more wheat or soybeans.

See that skinny child now, haloed in wild curls, thin ankles and wrists exposed to the wind: young Elena, escaping the gloom in the house to climb a christmas tree some settler had planted near the turnoff from the main road to our little village. The forest loomed dark behind the huts as I climbed up through the dense branches of that lonely tree standing sentinel on the plain. I felt weightless and free. I peeked through the sheltering needles to spy a group of six people I didn't recognize coming down the track. They were not villagers or the regular traders. Should I slide down and go alert the Elders?

Just as I concluded this was my responsibility, an Elder out on some chore spotted the travelers approaching as well. This man scurried back into town, so I stayed in my place. Soon, ten of my neighbors ambled out to the boundary of our acreage.

Strangers and villagers converged under my perch, and I thought about slipping down the trunk to join my clan. But I could see much better there, high above everyone's heads. The wind whistled, but I held tight, peering down at the action.

Two women and four men were traveling. They carried packs on their backs and had staffs in their hands to help them walk. All had their hair pulled back into tails, which the breeze blew about. I wondered why they didn't plait it like we did, pushing at my own curls, which refused to be corralled even in a braid. The hairstyle and walking sticks were the only differences I could see from my community's clothing and basic looks. But they had to be outsiders, or someone would have called their names, claiming them.

Peering down directly over the meeting, I noticed one other detail. The staffs the strangers carried were intricately carved. A woman's stick showed a face peeping out of swirls of water. The other staves looked plainer, just whirls and decorations. I hung almost upside down to get a better look at the patterns. The travelers stood still, waiting for the villagers to speak first.

Old Ma, our eldest resident, moved through the small crowd, ending up at the front of the pack.

"Welcome, People of Goldilocks, kin of our kin. Be at peace in this place."

The woman with the beautiful staff stepped forward and opened her mouth, but instead of the reply I expected, a rich melody wove around her words and carried them dancing into the wind. "We come as family with peace in our hearts. Thank you, thank you for your welcome."

A murmur coursed through my neighbors. No Singers had visited in more than a rev. I could recall the last song fest only vaguely. I remembered there was eating and laughter along with the music, though. Da had held me close and told me not to forget, but I had been so young. As I listened to the crowd below me now, I thought I caught troubled grumblings.

Then Old Ma began to hum. Her daughters caught the tune, and then all the adults joined in the buzzing as the few children with them giggled. The woman with the staff laughed too. The strangers picked up the music, humming and singing, until even the wind danced with merriment. Old Ma reached out her hand to the lead Singer, who took it and tucked it into the crook of her arm. Together, they led everyone into the village.

I slipped down the christmas-tree trunk and popped through its foliage, which swept like a skirt to the ground, breaking into a run even before I shook the last branches from my shoulders. Instead of following the crowd, I headed around the outer edge of town to my house, closest to the forest on the second ring. Neither of my fathers had been among the neighbors who welcomed the travelers. They would want to know.

I spotted Pops before I reached our home, coming from the communal greenhouse. His back slumped, and I saw he carried only a bunch of carrots in his right hand, his other stuck deep in his pocket against the cold.

"Singers have come," I called to him. "Old Ma met them and is taking them into town."

He straightened when he heard me, turning to meet me with a grimace. "Singers? How many?"

"Six. They have walking sticks with pictures on them, Pops."

"Do they, dear?" His frown faded, and he attempted a grin. "They have appetites too, I'll bet. Here, Laney, take these carrots into the house and tell Da your news. I'll go to the town hall to see what's happening. Ask Da to meet me there, OK?"

He took the shortcut into the middle of the village after thrusting the withered vegetables into my hands. I considered ignoring his directions and following him, but then sighed and trotted on to our house. I found Da with Davy, my little brother, in the kitchen, putting beans on to soak, and I told him the news.

"Hmmm," the big man hummed in his beard. "Do you remember the last song fest, Laney? You must have been Davy's age."

"I was almost two revs old," I protested. "Davy just turned a rev."

"Well, well. You're probably right," Da laughed. "Still, it was a long time ago."

"Pa says the Singers will be hungry. He wants you to meet him at the town hall." Da moved a lot slower than fiery Pops. I didn't want to miss all the action. I danced my impatience as he wrapped the wiggling toddler in a warm quilt and pulled on his own coat, but finally we too started toward the community hut.

As we came near, I noticed many of our neighbors headed that way too. We streamed together down the courtyard steps and into the crowded common room. At the big table in the front, used for council meetings and potlucks, Old Ma and the mayor, a man named Denys, sat with the guests. Other people milled around, listening in on the conversation, making whispered comments on the strangers' appearance, and trading stories about festivals in the past. Not everyone looked pleased.

Da, taller than most other men, spotted Pops and made his way to him, hoisting Davy high to keep him out of the fray. Just as they reached him, the mayor stood up and called the villagers to order.

"People of Forest Edge: Singers have come to share the stories of Goldilocks with us."

"What do they want in return?" The question shot from the back of the crowd. Sharon, her anger sharp as her cheekbones, had five children in her household, and her partner had never returned from a trip to Seaside last Winter Festival. An uneasy murmur rippled through the group.

The woman with the beautiful staff, the leader of the Singers, rose and sang, "No fear, no fear. If you have nothing to share, you still can hear. We will give our songs freely and leave."

More shifting and murmurs. Even in poverty, the villagers weren't comfortable holding back hospitality.

Old Ma stood, leaning on her chair, and the hall fell silent to listen. "Let's go home and find one thing—a carrot, a handful of beans, a spoonful of tea—or, if you are not willing to share food, maybe a cup or plate you can spare. We will put our gifts on this table in an hour. If you have nothing, that's alright too, as the Singer promised. But let's gather to hearken to the songs and remember who we are tonight. God has sent this gift. Let us not refuse it."

I saw relief on people's faces. Yes, every household could find one small thing. The grand feast would not happen, but it had been a long, relentless rev. To have an evening's entertainment? The excitement had permission to spread.

As the room emptied, I saw Pops approach and speak with Denys. Always tense, he angled toward the harried mayor, signaling a warning. Da had followed with Davy still in his massive arms, adding his deeper voice to the conversation. I tried to overhear, but by the time I fought through the exiting crowd, my fathers turned to leave. Together, our little family made its way home.

"What will we give, Pops?" I asked.

"Oh, I'm not sure. What do you think we can spare, Armel?"

"Hmmm, if they spend the night, we'll serve them porridge for breakfast. But I feel we should also put something on the table. What about a small jar of jam?"

Not the jam, I thought, but resisted confessing my selfishness. On further reflection, I decided that if the Singers stayed with our family, it would be worth not having a sweetener for our bread. The excitement of exotic strangers in my house intoxicated me. What could I learn from them?

"Pops," I asked, trotting to keep up with the adults, "where will they sleep? They can have my room."

But Pops didn't answer. His head bent forward, and his shoulders slumped again. He seemed preoccupied with something ahead.

Da said, "That's generous of you, Laney. We may need your bed." His attention was focused more on his husband than me, but Da always heard me, even when he was busy with other things.

I felt small and powerless. I slipped my hand into the crook of Da's elbow and huddled close for the rest of the short walk home.

When we returned to the common hall, we noticed Sharon and another couple stomping in the cold on either side of the door, haranguing villagers as they entered. I caught her words as we approached the entrance.

"God is already angry enough. Don't stir up His wrath by listening to heathen songs. We should hold prayer vigils, not indulge in this spiritualism."

Most people slipped by without acknowledging her protests, and Pops glared as he helped Davy down the steps and across the threshold. Da, following him, slowed and murmured to the three angry adults as if they were children. "Now, now, all will be well here. Singers tell good stories and love God too."

The man in the trio shot back, "It's fine for you, Armel. You only have two kids. But what if Sharon's right, and we are being judged for our infidelity? I have four to feed, and she has five."

Da reached out and patted the frightened father on the arm, like he comforted me sometimes, saying, "God loves you, Harold. You needn't worry about judgment. Come and listen to the songs. Remember that warmth and fellowship are important." Without waiting for a response, he took my hand and continued through the door.

The Singers had piled their backpacks and walking sticks near the entrance and stood facing each other in a corner. The mayor and Old Ma oversaw the gifts, nodding approval as each family brought forth their offerings and then settled in for the concert. Soon, the hall filled up with neighbors sitting on the floor, waiting with anticipation while the children milled around and played.

My household claimed a spot close to the table where the Singers would stand to perform, but as the six strangers broke their circle and moved to rearrange themselves in the front, Pops stooped to whisper something to Da and left us. Craning my neck, I noted he stationed himself by their belongings. Again, I felt a wave of confusion and smallness wash over me and leaned against Da for comfort.

With the night lights on, I saw the strangers in sharper relief, details of their faces and clothes highlighted by the artificial glare. Their tunics and pants appeared patched in many places, some more skillfully than others. With sunken eyes and cheeks, they looked as hungry as I felt, my tummy cramping to remind me I hadn't eaten since lunch. There had been no time for first supper, which we often skipped now, anyway. *Will we have enough to feed them last meal?* I wondered. But their presence, when they stood up shoulder to shoulder in front of the seated crowd, bore a peacefulness rich with confidence and joy. A deep calmness settled over me.

And then they sang.

The first piece the villagers hummed along to, filling the crowded room with an intimate, stimulating vibration. *This is my family*, I thought, feeling the rumble deep in my throat too, so that I tried a tiny hum of my own. Da looked down and smiled at me. When that song ended, a woman in the back asked for a favorite, which the Singers offered. Then came another request and another. I saw smiles and tears as I glanced around. Da was right, I realized. They have brought us warmth and love.

The leader stepped forward to announce the last piece. "My friends," she said in her clear voice, "we have enjoyed remembering the old songs with you. Before we go, though, we must sing a new song, which may be hard for you to bear." With that, she fell back into line. The Singers inhaled and started again.

Now, so many revs later, I still remember it—beautiful and terrible at the same time. I couldn't catch all the words, but the music accused us. It promised death and destruction. And then it repented and gave grief and sadness that eclipsed anything I had ever known. When they finished, there was stunned silence.

The mayor, pale and trembling, stood up and confronted them. "Why have you sung such a thing to those who welcomed you?" His voice shook, agitation moving his fingers as well.

The leader faced him, her profile now to the rest of the room, showing her beaked nose and gaunt neck. "Be at peace. It is a hard song, but Goldilocks gave it to all people, just as she did the others. We share it with you now because discovering its meaning is as much your task as ours."

"How should we know what it means?" someone in the crowd cried. "If the planet doesn't speak to you, why should you expect it to speak to us?"

"She used to connect with everyone." The Singer's voice remained calm and sure. "She still communicates, although far fewer listen for her. Take this last message, bitter though it is, and think on it. If Goldie whispers to any of you, come and tell us of your dream, your insight. Maybe together we can mend our friendship with her."

The crowd grew restless, mumbling and gathering up their belongings, all the light and happiness gone. The mayor called for one last song to soothe the hurt. Our guests obliged with a gentle lullaby...but even as the music poured forth, some villagers headed out, grumbling.

By the door, Pops guarded the Singers' possessions as our friends trickled out. When the song ended and all the neighbors were gone, Da and he joined the performers, the mayor, and Old Ma, leaving me to care for Davy while they talked. Even at a distance, distracting my brother with the wooden puzzle Da had brought to amuse him, I could see the mayor's beet-red face and clenched fists. Old Ma and my parents appeared as serene as the Singers, though, who finally gathered their packs and staves, ready to go.

On the walk to our home, the travelers remained silent, and I felt too shy to ask them questions. The Rose Moon had already set. It was late for last supper, but Da put water on for tea, and the guests spread out their gifts on the table, urging him to use whatever they had to create a meal. Da chose some vegetables and a block of tofu. He started cooking while our guests went into my room to rest. I could hear their low voices humming and singing about the villagers' reactions to the new song. Pops put Davy down in the main bedroom, which didn't take long, as the boy had already fallen asleep. Then, he listened with me at my room's entrance. He sighed, then slipped in and shut the door.

There was little talk at the table when Da served the meal. Even though the Singers' stomachs lay flat as ours, they paused before sitting down to sing a short grace of thanksgiving, which I noticed included both God and Goldilocks. One man considered me with a kind smile. "You're getting so big. Last time I was here, you could barely reach the table, even kneeling on your chair."

"You know me?" I asked, eyes wide.

"We all know you," the leader said. "Your fathers have been our friends for many years."

I checked the faces around the table, but no memory of them surfaced. Da looked at her, smiling, but Pops ignored the conversation, having gone to some other place in his active brain.

I dared to speak. "Sharon says you don't like God, only Goldilocks, but you thanked God for this food."

There was a pause, and then the man who first spoke to me nodded. "You wonder if your neighbor speaks the truth. You try to decide if we are good people or bad, wise or foolish. Sometimes it's hard to tell. Let me ask you, do you love your brother or your fathers?"

"I love all of them." Even to myself, I sounded shocked.

"Really? You know how to love and help your fathers— so capable, big and strong—and, at the same time, you love and help your little brother, who can't yet cook or plow or sweep the floor."

"Yes." I looked at Da for encouragement. "But helping Davy usually means taking care of him for Pops and Da."

"I think that makes you both good and wise," said the Singer. "We're like that too. We love our parent God, striving to walk in God's ways. But we love our sister Goldilocks and try to help her as well. Helping both is often about caring for our sisters and brothers."

The leader smiled and added, "But remember, Gabe, we are the little siblings to our older sister Goldilocks. She helps us much more than we do her."

At that point, another Singer entered the conversation, and it became too complex for me to follow. Soon, the meager supper was over, and everyone retired.

Later, in a deep sleep, I didn't hear people stirring and would never have wakened if someone hadn't stumbled over me where I lay on cushions in the common room. I cried out in alarm, and Pops was there, shushing me. "Be quiet, dear heart. Our guests are just leaving. All will be well."

I scooted out of the way so I wouldn't get stepped on again. The Singers were all around the table, shrugging into their coats and shouldering their packs. Pops went over to

Da, who was filling their canteens with water. They disagreed about something, and Pops looked over at me. His brows knit. Da appeared to win the argument because he grinned and came over to hug me.

"I'm going to get our guests started on their journey, and then I'll come right home. You go to sleep. I should be back before breakfast."

"Don't they know their way?" I whispered.

"They are taking a new path tonight. Don't give Pops a hard time, huh?"

The door opened, the moonless sky sparkling with bright stars, when the leader hesitated and turned back into the room. She approached me and bent to kiss my forehead. "Blessings on you, my child. May you grow to always see what is true."

And then they were gone.

Dawn had broken, and I had already started cooking the breakfast porridge when Da returned and sat down at the table with Pops. A few minutes later, a crowd of villagers stomped down our courtyard stairs, demanding the Singers. Sharon led them, but the mayor hovered in the back. Pops informed them our guests had traveled on and, after several snooped around inside to witness their absence, they left.

There was never another song fest in Forest Edge. We were lucky because even after the Singers no longer came to us, sometimes my fathers and other villagers sought them out for counsel, comfort, and stories of the past. We didn't lose them as completely as the bigger towns and the farther-flung villages. Still, when I entered the Academy, I never thought of them. I assumed, with a young girl's arrogance, that being out of my sight, their worries ceased to exist. This memory, though, remains vivid in my mind's eye.

Alice paused after the last words of the story, coming back to the present, sensing again the warm berm she leaned against and smelling the rosemary in the fading heat. When Sami offered no comment, she peeked around the herb pot to see him staring into the cloud-flecked sky.

"Well, what do you think?" she asked.

"I wonder...." The young man shifted a bit and turned his head to meet her eyes. "People think speaking with the planet is like an outdated religion, something throwbacks try to resurrect from our past. But that wasn't true about the Singers in Nainai's story, and it's not the truth now. We always sing of finding God with Goldilocks. The tradition shows that she is as committed to her relationship with God as we are and that when we communicated, the contact with her expanded our faith. We hoped it helped her connection with the divine too."

"The misunderstanding goes back a long way." Alice wrinkled her brow and concentrated on the math. "Nainai was three revs old when this happened. She's twenty-three now, so the seeds of this conflict took root over twenty revs ago."

"Yeah. What I wonder is why the Singers never corrected the impression. Why didn't they show everyone that they were wrong?"

Alice scooted forward on the gravel and sat cross-legged, facing Sami. "When my father became a Glad, saying that he wanted to go back to old Earth ways, Nainai told me about George Seaside, the guy that started the Gladiator movement. This was when the plagues ran rampant, and everyone worried about extinction. So, he framed his entire theory on how to live here as a fight against Goldilocks. I suppose people like Sharon bought into that idea then, just as they do now."

"Yeah," Sami sighed. "When you feel threatened, you look for someone outside yourself to accuse. There's nothing too logical about it."

"Perhaps we should ask a different question then: Why didn't the Singers blame Goldilocks? Why did they think the blights and sickness took over?"

The young man looked down at his hands resting between his knees. "Not all Singers followed a rational path either, I'm afraid. Some insisted that we isolate from the world in the forest. That faction believed the disconnect with the planet created the atmosphere for our disasters. They thought it happened because most people no longer sang Goldie's songs. They didn't want anyone to go to the Academy or bond outside our community anymore. There was a big fight before I was born. I guess some Singers still think that way."

"Wow." Alice frowned, then looked closely at Sami. "Is that why Pete wants me to stay here? Does he believe people who don't sing cause the problems?"

He shrugged, not meeting her eyes.

Alice shook her head. "That doesn't make sense, though. If he thought that, he never would have welcomed me into his home. And he lets you go to the Academy and even sounds proud of you."

Silence settled over the two for a moment, as Alice tried to figure out how Pete and Sami had accepted her, given the rift between Singers and non-Singers. A sadness welled up in her, as if a welcoming family had just showed her the door. Before grief turned into anger, Sami reached over and touched her gently on the arm.

"Look, Alice, maybe I shouldn't tell you, but I think you have a right to know. Pete used to believe that everything wrong with this world was the fault of the human-centrics—the non-Singers. That's why I never met him when I was little. My mom was his granddaughter, but she lived in Wood Lawn with her mother all her life because Gran partnered with a non-Singer. Pete wouldn't talk to them. Not until my grandmother passed. Not until my mom needed his help and claimed the relationship. My great-grandmother had died earlier, which left him awfully lonely, so it wasn't hard for Ma to connect with him. We came to live with him when I was five revs old."

"So that's why you call him Pete instead of Yieyie?"

"Yeah. We started more formal and just continued."

"I wondered. But that doesn't explain why he wants me to stay, does it?"

"Yes, and no. The isolationists insisted on not bonding with non-Singers. They shunned young adults who found partners, especially heart-bonds, elsewhere. Your Nainai and Pete's best friend, Jay, opted to leave, although Pete always thought they could have stayed because she's a Bridge. I gather he felt deserted by them."

"Oh...."

"Yeah, but that's not the issue now. The Singer community is too small. We barely birth enough healthy babies to take the place of Singers who die. For some reason, we have more boys than girls too, making it hard for men to find even temporary mates. So now, the Elders promote outside bonds, but encourage selecting partners who have Singer blood in them. They hope to raise more children who will communicate with Goldie."

"So, it's an inherited trait?"

"No one really knows. History says that in the beginning, everyone born on Goldilocks could connect with her. I guess it's only a theory that babies bred from parents related to Singers might dream and sing like us."

A realization hit her hard, and she drew away from Sami. "That's why you want me to stay." She fairly spit the words at him. "You and Pete expect me to produce a child who can sing. Even though I don't dream, you think because I'm part of Nainai and Jay's family, I'm a prime candidate."

"Alice, I—"

She jumped to her feet, glowering at the young man, who also scrambled up. Her anger rooted her in place, trembling, until he faced her. "I'll leave tomorrow, as soon as it's light."

As she spun on her heel, he reached out and caught her arm. "I told Pete this was a terrible plan. I told him I would have nothing to do with it. That's why I went home to see my father. Pete needed to cool down."

She looked over her shoulder. "How can I stay here now?"

Sami took a deep breath. "You can stay because Pete agreed I'm right. Do you know how often I win an argument with him? This might be a first."

"What do you mean?"

"When I came back today, I met him in the garden. He admitted that Goldie never guaranteed you would stick around, but that she only wanted us to shelter you. He apologized for scheming and said he realizes how selfish that was—like with my grandmother. Pete's not a bad guy. He's just worried about the future. He promised you can live here on whatever terms you want."

"Really?" She scanned Sami's face, trying to read the truth, and saw nothing but sadness.

He nodded. "I know you love someone else, Alice. My father sells produce to the Academy and hears all the gossip. There was a big upset the day before yesterday when your Pa arrived and demanded to interview the biology professor—Dinah Seaside. Evidently, she offered to bond with you so you could stay in Seaside, and he found out. I figured that's why you asked about her. You two want to be together."

The blazing fury sank away so suddenly it left her weak. "Yes. I tried to tell you when the twins dropped in on us."

"Poor Jamie. He hoped you liked him." Sami's voice teased, but she sensed it took an effort. He lifted his hand off her arm and put it on his chest. "I promise, Alice: no more plots involving your future, here or anywhere else. Pete promised too. I'll take you to Seaside myself in September and make sure you find Dinah."

Alice met his eyes and saw only sincerity. Her heart still beat hard, but softened as she considered his assurance. Taking a deep breath, she found she believed him. He would not betray her but be a loyal friend. "OK then," she said. "OK."

CHAPTER ELEVEN

Three months after Alice arrived in the forest, she began consolidating her belongings on one side of the small guest room the Singers had constructed for her. Sami brought in a used produce box, now lined with an old, soft towel.

"I think you could store your egg collection in this," he offered. "If we're careful, we can get the dak skeleton in too, and put the feathers you've collected on top."

"It's perfect. Thanks." She removed her treasures, gathered during many forest walks, from the niches in the wall. The young man squatted, helping her nestle them into the container, then tucked the towel around them before settling the lid and straightening up.

"No one else has a collection like this in Seaside," Sami said, grinning. "You'll impress Dinah for sure."

She looked up into his warm brown eyes with a responding smile. "I just hope she's glad to see me. She must wonder what happened to me after all these months."

"Don't stress, Alice. Dinah's smart. She'll have figured out that you've gone underground until school starts and your father can't prevent your bonding. She probably expects you any day."

The young woman nodded and looked away. While she had initially dreaded this enforced hideout, she now felt how much she would miss this little household. The time had flown by with harvesting and then expanding the garden so Pete would have enough food to get through the coming dark months, learning how to use the com-pad, and exploring the forest. Nainai had been right.

She had learned more about Goldilocks' plants and insects here than she had in all the years she spent in Far Meadow. And the daks—she had kept a journal of observations on each sighting and every feather, egg, and bone she found. They proved as wonderful and mysterious as she imagined. *After I graduate,* she thought, *I'll come back and discover even more about them.*

She would miss Pete too, she realized. Before she explored that approaching emptiness, she directed her attention to the now-bare wall.

"How many shelves can we fit in here?"

"Maybe eight? We should go all the way up to the ceiling." Sami eyed the area. "I guess we'd better anchor them well, though. I don't want Pete pulling something over on himself."

"Right. I'm glad we have enough food to warrant more storage space, but I worry about him being alone here." Alice frowned.

"Hey, Sarai and Michel will check in on him, and I'll come home for the next harvest and planting. He'll be OK." Sami turned to her, registering the depth of her concern. "His chance of survival has doubled with all the help you've given us in the garden. The yield is better than we ever hoped for, and, with luck, we'll have two more bumper crops. We'll fill this room with food before the dark months. It's a good thing we built it."

"Yeah, well, I wish there was a bio-dome he could use too. We might bring him fresh fish from Seaside sometimes."

"We?" Sami grinned at her. "I like the sound of that. Pete will be happy that you want to visit again."

She punched him in the arm. "Of course, I'll come back. You guys need all the help you can get." She turned, intent on fetching the shelving, but the young man put his hand on her shoulder.

"Alice, we should talk before we leave for Seaside."

His eyes mirrored the solemnity of his voice, and she nodded. "What is it?"

They heard a shout in the kitchen.

"Hey, I could use a hand here. Are you going to make the old guy do the heavy lifting?"

"Oh, for crying out loud, Pete," Sami called back, hurrying out of the room. "You're supposed to be peeling tomatoes for canning. Leave the boards for me."

After first supper, the two young people finally had time to talk in private. They finished the dishes and, as the ancient resident of the hut dozed in his rocking chair, they ventured out into the meadow. Sometimes the daks would alight in the dusk, snapping up the little bugs hovering over the grass stalks. Once, Alice got close enough to see one of the winged lizards bobbing its long, thin neck and pointed nose toward another dak, who seemed oblivious. She watched until the disinterested party spun around and chased the bobber. Then they both took off on their coppery wings and disappeared into the woods. She had never seen adult daks interact before, and, sharing it with Sami, they decided it must be some kind of mating ritual.

Now, as they sat together on a boulder nestled under the bilbo trees, she resolved, *I'll come back and study them. Even if no one else is interested, I'll discover their secrets.*

Sami broke into her train of thought. "That thing we need to talk about…can I share now?"

"Oh, sure," she said, not taking her eyes off the meadow. "We got sidetracked, didn't we? What's up?"

"When you go to the Academy, please don't tell anyone where you've been for these three months. It'd be dangerous for Pete if certain people knew he was out here, and your reputation will take a hit if professors know you associate with us."

She swung her head around to consider him, noting his tense shoulders and the crease between his dark brows. "Someone is still threatening Singers?"

"Yeah. It's dicey for Manuel, Jamie, and me as well. If it becomes known that we identify as Singers, they'd probably kick us out of the Academy. Just hanging out in the forest makes you suspect. That's why Sarai and Michel live in Wood Lawn. The twins come from their household, and my blood father lives there, so I claim his family. Do you think you can keep quiet about it?"

"Of course, but what do I say to Dinah?"

Sami sighed and looked away. "I knew you'd want to tell her."

She scowled. "It's important to be honest with… Well, you know--with a lover. Would you lie to someone you wanted to bond with?"

"There's a difference between lying and keeping a confidence," he shot back. "Couldn't you just ask her to trust you?"

"Like you told me this morning, Dinah is smart. Don't you expect she'll figure out what the secret is about?" Alice wrapped her arms tight around her middle, containing the uneasiness rising in her. She already fretted that her lover had moved on, and now she had to reenter the relationship with the burden of deception?

"I do think she might suspect." Sami's voice sounded gentler, and she noticed him lean forward and hug his knee as he spoke. "Maybe you could view this as protecting her. Even if she guesses you've been with us, as long as she doesn't know for sure, she won't have to tell the authorities. You save her from having to decide to turn you in or not."

Alice's mouth fell open in surprise, and she took in a sharp gasp. "Being with Singers is a crime? Sami, you never told me that before. What have I done?"

"No, no, don't get upset." He put a hand on her arm to reassure her. "It's not technically a violation of law; just a terrible social misstep."

He looked down now and his brown skin flushed. She could see it even in the dimming light.

"We should have told you—yes, Dinah's job would be in jeopardy if she bonds with a Singer. But remember, you didn't tell us about your relationship with her at first and then, well…you'd already been here awhile, and you don't sing or dream of Goldilocks, so there didn't seem any point in worrying you."

"Thanks for deciding how to run my life," she spat back at him.

She heard him take in a deep breath and let it out slowly, but she refused to look at him. *God, he's annoying*, she thought. *He's trying to be so grown-up. It just makes me madder.* She considered jumping off the rock and huffing away, but Sami's restraint, as much as she wanted to deny it, affected her. She ground her teeth and stayed put.

"You must feel betrayed and undermined again," he murmured.

"Wouldn't you?" Alice felt tears pricking under her eyelids. Damn it—she'd rather have him arrogant than understanding. She wrapped her arms tighter around herself.

"Yeah, I think I would. I just hope you realize I didn't intend to hurt you."

"Well, what was your intention, then?" She spat the words out from between her teeth and angled further away from him.

Again, she sensed the deep breath and slow consideration in the man beside her. "I read Elena's story about going to the Academy for the first time. I know you have too. The best friend she made, the knowledge freely shared, and the sheer number of new things enthralled her. I felt that too. But the college has changed since your Nainai went there, Alice."

He paused. Alice still faced away, but she nodded to show she was listening.

"Elena's story doesn't tell you about the power struggle brewing there today. It doesn't let you in on how deeply divided our culture has become in the school and the towns. Even those who don't call themselves Gladiators think they have to beat the planet into submission, and that means suppressing any person who wants to befriend Goldilocks. And right now, most professors and students hold that attitude."

"Look, Sami, I don't want to get embroiled in a cause. I just want to study and be with someone I love. Is that too much to ask?" She looked over her shoulder to assess the impact of this declaration. He wasn't looking at her, but at the meadow.

He sighed. "Now that you've been in the forest, that may be difficult. You can try to stay above the fray, and I don't know for sure where Dinah stands. All I'm asking is that you not betray Pete and me and the twins. And I want you to walk into the Academy with your eyes open."

His face settled into stillness as the dusk descended on them. Alice had never seen him so sad, and her anger trickled off, leaving only concern for her friend. She scooted around to face him and reached out to touch his arm.

"Hey, you know I'd never do anything to hurt you and Pete. If you need me to keep this secret, I will. Dinah will just have to understand." She sighed. "I'm sure she has parts of her life that she doesn't want to share with me."

Sami turned toward her, but a sudden swoosh and a hoarse caw announced a dak descending. Both young people watched as it stumbled to a landing and started snapping at bugs.

Sami stifled a laugh. "For beings so graceful in the air, they sure are klutzy on the ground."

"Ah, that's what makes them so interesting, though," Alice responded. "Creatures of contradiction."

"As are we all," he whispered.

They left for Seaside three days later. Pete filled their backpacks with sandwiches and hardtack for the trek, which would follow the back paths through the woods. As he handed his great-grandson a canteen, he said in a low voice, "Remember, Sami, steer clear of the settlement down by the river when you cross over into the broccoli-tree forest. I've heard that they are getting more contentious. You'd be alright, but I don't want them to abduct Alice."

"Right. I'll go around to the north and hit the main track. Don't worry. I'll keep her safe."

Alice stepped from behind the curtain serving as the guest-room door. "Like I need protection. Who kept this idiot from bleeding to death last month when he fell out of a tree and sliced his arm on the rake he left below?" She came up to the table and began stuffing her coat into the top of an already-fattened pack.

Pete laughed but continued to caution. "Well, don't get cocky. We're not the only ones who use this path through the woods. Deeper in, there are some strange characters—mostly harmless. You two watch out for each other."

"Don't fret, old man." Sami reached out to embrace him. "I'll be back for the next harvest."

"I'll come too, if I can." Alice opened her arms for a hug as well. Before releasing him, she said, "I've left my box of daks' eggs and bones under the bed. It was too big to pack. I'll have to return for that." She kissed him on a leathery cheek. "Thanks for letting me stay with you, Pete—and for letting me go."

The old man nodded, turning away, but not before she noticed his eyes mist over. He hobbled to the sink and said, "Get going now before you waste any more daylight hours. I've got to put these carrots up. The curse of a good harvest is having to can all this stuff."

The young people glanced at each other, then ambushed him with another quick hug before hoisting packs onto their backs, slinging canteens across their shoulders, and heading out the door. When they looked back from the edge of the bilbo trees, they saw Pete had climbed the courtyard stairs to watch them leave. They waved and then plunged into the cool shadow of the forest.

It wasn't the same path that she had come in on twelve weeks ago. Barely visible under the scattered red leaves mixed with pine needles, it departed from the meadow on the west end. Alice had already trodden its first few winding miles on trips with Sami to find daks' nests and berries, but, in an hour, they were beyond the terrain she knew. Back at the hut, the men had shown her a crude map tracing this circuitous route to Seaside. It doubled the journey time, but she'd be safe from detection by Humphrey or anyone who might report to him.

I'll have to write Nainai as soon as I get to Dinah's house, Alice thought. *She'll want to know everything that's happened to me so far. I'll have to write it like a story, disguising the characters a bit, so other people will think it's just made up.* The idea tickled her, and she began to compose the narrative in her head as they paced the track.

Sami, busy with his own thoughts, walked in front of her. They could hear the wind blowing high in the treetops, but here, surrounded by christmas trees, the forest was still. When the young man stopped without warning, Alice ran into him.

"What's up?" she whispered, unwilling to disturb the quiet of the woods.

"Time for lunch. See that outcropping of rock up ahead?"

"Yeah, now I do."

"When I was here before, there was a stream. I'm trying to remember how we got to it. We should refill our canteens after we eat."

"Sounds good to me," Alice said, waking to the realization that she did indeed feel hungry.

They stepped off the trail, picking a path through the sparse undergrowth toward the stony cliffside. Before they reached it, the christmas trees gave ground to bilbos, and they saw a meadow before them and heard running water. Stepping out into the short grass and sunshine revealed a rambling silver creek wending its way through the middle of the clearing. Alice would have run to the brook, but Sami's hand landed on her arm.

"Wait," he whispered, scanning the area. "Other people use this place too."

"Like who?" Her brow creased with worry, but she couldn't see anyone else in the open space before her.

"Like whoever made that fire ring." Sami nodded downstream, and Alice realized that beside the brook, someone had indeed placed a circle of stones which contained the blackened remains of a log.

"Do you think they're still around?" She noticed her whisper quivered.

"Stay here. I'll go see whether the ashes are cold. Whoever was here may be long gone."

She wasn't crazy about being separated, even by the few yards to the creek, but bit her tongue to keep from admitting her nervousness. Sami slid his pack and canteen off and then cautiously crossed the meadow. She watched him crouch down beside the deserted cinders, then look back at her with a smile and wave.

Just as Alice gave a sigh of relief, something heavy settled on her shoulder. She jumped, spun around, and found herself face to face with a man at least a foot taller and many pounds heavier than she was. Her first thought—Run!—canceled itself as she realized she had no idea where to go. She couldn't lead him to Sami, and she'd lost the direction back to their path. So, she dug in her heels and glared at him, hoping to appear fierce.

"Hey," the giant grunted. "God's peace. You want to fish?"

"Fish?" She noticed now, balanced on the broad shoulder, a ridiculously long, thin stick with a line of string attached. The man nodded a massive head, topped with graying curls like a cap. His eyes, shining electric blue out of his dark brown skin, skimmed over her.

"You can use my pole if you forgot yours."

"Uh, thanks."

"Hey, Corey." Sami came up so quietly behind her that Alice jumped again. He spoke in a calm voice to the man in front of her. "I'm Sami, remember? Pete's great-grandson. I met you at Pete's house a long time ago when I was a kid."

Corey held up his left hand in the greeting gesture. Alice noted calluses and scars on the huge paw. The pinkie finger bent at an awkward angle, as if broken and not set right. Then she studied his face, noticing a shy smile exposing a gap in his teeth. *Obviously,* she realized, *this guy lives outside of society, and it's been hard on him.*

She shifted her gaze to her friend, who returned the salute, but still looked wary.

Sami continued. "We're just passing through. We thought we might sit by the creek and have lunch. Would you like a sandwich?"

The man put down his hand and let silence settle between them. Then he nodded, saying, "I'll fish. If I catch one, you can take it for your dinner."

"Fair enough." Sami picked up his pack and canteen. "Where's your favorite fishing spot?"

As Corey led them into the meadow, Alice stepped up beside Sami and whispered, "Is he safe?"

Her friend shrugged. "Kind of. No quick moves or loud noises, though. I'll tell you more later."

When they reached the firepit, the giant indicated they should sit, while he continued another three yards to where an eddy in the creek had hollowed out a kind of pool. There, he cast his line into the water and reeled it in, over and over. Alice watched him, wondering how such a big man managed such delicate movements. As she and Sami spread out their coats for a makeshift table, she asked, "So, what's his story?"

"I only know a bit. I met him when my mother and I first moved in with Pete. He traded some with other people in the forest. Pete said he made the best fishing lures and poles he'd ever seen. Mom knew him from her time in Wood Lawn and warned me to be hushed and slow around him."

"Why?"

"His childhood household lived in Forest Edge, and he lost them all in the plague. He was visiting relatives in another village. He eventually moved to Wood Lawn. I think he helped establish it, and they considered him a leader. He may even have been mayor at one point. But then, his partner and all his kids died in some accident or illness—I can't remember what—and he went crazy. Mom said the neighbors tried to be understanding, but he showed up to meetings bleeding from cuts on his arm, picked fights with both men and women, and flew into rages at the drop of a hat. The last straw came when he mistook a little girl for his dead daughter and insisted she come home with him. The villagers banned him to the woods. Mom thought he would commit suicide, but somehow he's survived all this time."

Sami paused and pointed his chin to signal Alice should look toward the creek. Corey was pulling out a fish as long as his forearm, silver flashing in the sunlight.

"Wow, he really is a good fisherman."

"I guess he's had to be."

"How many revs has he been out here?" Alice whispered as Corey approached.

"Three at least."

The big man nodded as he came up, continuing past them to the forest's edge. There he squatted, and the young people watched him gut his catch and bury the offal. Then he picked up a handful of red leaves and strode back to the creek side, nodding at them silently again. He rinsed the fish, then rolled it in the leaves, tying it with string he retrieved from a pouch on his hip, before returning to them.

"Here," he said, holding out the packet to Sami. "This will keep until your dinner tonight."

"Thanks, Corey. Are you ready to eat?" He held up a thick nut-butter and jam sandwich.

"Yeah. I haven't eaten bread for a while." The big man made himself comfortable on a flat rock and took a bite. "Good," he mumbled around the mouthful.

He looked so like Jaren, eyelids half closed in delight and crumbs on his lips, that Alice almost told him not to talk with his mouth full. Instead, she stifled a laugh. The shocking blue eyes opened wide and stared at her as he swallowed.

"Sorry. My manners aren't what they used to be."

"No, pardon me," she said. "It's just that you reminded me of my little brother and how much he likes nut-butter sandwiches. I guess I'm missing him."

He nodded his head, taking another bite while the travelers joined him. After a few minutes of eating in silence, Corey spoke in his deep, soft voice. "I know what it's like to miss someone."

Alice hesitated. *What's the right response to that?* She wondered, glancing at Sami, who paused as well. She swallowed, drew a breath, and said, "My brother lives in Far Meadow. I haven't seen him for three months, but I hope to visit him after a semester at the Academy."

"Ah, you're going to Seaside." He didn't look at the travelers but took another bite before continuing. "There are shorter ways to get there."

"There are," Sami admitted. "We're trying not to be noticed."

Again, a long, reflective silence with chewing. "Not many come this way. I will not tell."

"Thanks."

Alice frowned, wondering what might be safe to say. Her gaze settled on his feet, tethered in makeshift sandals. How would he manage when the dark months came?

"Corey, how do you live out here when it gets cold? Do the fish still bite?"

He looked up from the disappearing sandwich, eyes calm and round. Instead of answering right away, he swallowed the last morsel and licked the jam off his thick fingers. "The fish bite, but not as well. There isn't much left after the last berries. I will be hungry."

Sami frowned, glancing at Alice, before he said, "We had a bumper crop this harvest. There should be enough to share in the dark times. If you visit Pete, he'll help you."

Corey nodded. "Pete is a good man."

"Well, I guess we better go. We have a long way to walk." The younger man got to his feet, grabbing their two canteens. "I'll get these filled if you want to pack up, Alice."

"No problem." She brushed off her hands, but before she could rise, Corey put a hand on her knee. Startled, she saw Sami already walking away and felt a moment's panic.

"I have a picture of my daughter. She died just before she turned six revs." The big man stared into her eyes.

Alice swallowed and said, "I'm six revs old."

"I thought so."

"May I see your picture?" She caught Sami watching them from a few feet off.

"Yes." Corey sat back and reached into his pouch, bringing out a small square of plastic and metal. He faced toward Sami. "You can look too. I only turn it on for a few seconds, though, because it's very old. It might not last much longer."

The young man returned and kneeled beside the others. Corey placed the device on his left palm and deftly found a hidden button. A six-inch 3-D image leapt up from the platform: a young woman with Corey's blue eyes; thick, curly, black hair; and a shy smile balanced there in his hand. Alice glanced from the picture to the giant, who gazed at it without expression before he shut it down with a flick of his finger.

"She was beautiful, Corey." Alice breathed.

Corey studied the photo square. "They all were beautiful," he said. He replaced the device in his pouch. He looked at her with desolate eyes. "I only have this one left."

"I'm so sorry."

Corey turned from Alice and focused on Sami, who still kneeled beside him. "Pete is a Singer. Are you a Singer too?"

Alice saw her friend hesitate, a worry line creasing his brow. But then he nodded.

"Yes, but I'm not as accomplished as Pete or the other Elders."

Corey frowned. "I was angry at Goldilocks for a long time. She should have been with us, like in the old days. She could have saved my family."

The friends glanced at each other. They were on either side of the big man, separated by his bulk. Alice put out her hand and grasped a pack. If he attacked them, she had a vague thought of hitting him with it. Sami stayed still.

Corey shifted a bit and sighed. "I had a dream last night from Goldie. You should tell the Singers."

"What was it?" the younger man asked.

"She is sorry. She didn't know. She grieves." Corey bowed his head. Tears dripped from his eyes, splotching his faded tan shirt. He slowly rose to his feet and looked down at Sami and Alice. "Tell them."

Before they could react, he grabbed his fishing pole and strode off toward the woods.

The travelers packed up and got on the trail. As they headed down the path, Alice asked, "What did he mean—Goldie grieves?"

"I wonder too," said Sami. "I wish Pete was here to ask. I never heard that Corey joined the Singers, but the planet used to speak to everyone."

Alice paused, bringing them both to a halt. "Maybe we should go tell Pete. Corey wanted the Singers to know. It could be urgent."

Her friend narrowed his eyes in thought, then shook his head. "No, I can contact Singers that live in Seaside when we get there. We'd lose at least a day and a half, probably two, if we go back now. I have to connect with the twins." He shrugged his pack into a more comfortable position and walked again. Alice followed, mulling over her first encounter with a real fugitive.

They reached Seaside without further incident. Their route had taken them deep into the broccoli-tree woods, which delighted Alice, who had never experienced it before. On the morning of the fourth day, when Sami said they would be in town before Second Moon set, she wished they could spend more time there. If anyone had asked her why, she would have spoken of the beauty of the trees: the way their trunks rose like gray pillars to the blueish-green buds and leaves of their crowns, leaving an open forest floor dappled with shadows and sunlight among low bushes and flowers smelling of spice. In her heart, though, she felt how anxiety about her reunion with Dinah grew the nearer they got to their destination, dragging at her footsteps. The tension between remembering that initial passion they shared in Far Meadow and the insecurity of not communicating with her lover for three months roiled her stomach.

Soon after first supper, they broke through the last line of trees and stood on the verge of the plain which flanked the sea, a faint track showing them the way through hip-high yellow grass. They couldn't see the ocean, but when Sami mentioned he could smell salt water, Alice found she too could detect the tang in the wind.

They hiked on, mostly silent for the last hours of their trek. As they neared Seaside, their path took them around several small compounds of sunken huts. Alice noted they were all deserted. Stopping for a break, she asked her companion, "Why are these houses out here?"

"Families used to live out this far before the population shrank. People stay pretty close to the city center now."

"Are we almost there?"

"Yep. Just over that little rise, we should be able to see it." Sami pointed with his chin to the swell in the grass field before them, which blocked some of the wind.

Alice faced toward town. "Should we go to Dinah's tonight?"

"Sure," Sami said. "Her place is on this side of the city. No one will notice us."

"What if she isn't home, Sami?" This sudden thought brought her head around to face her friend. "What if she has someone else with her?"

"Hey, it's OK. I have some friends you can stay with if Dinah's busy." He smiled to reassure her, but she looked away. They planned to separate when they got to town—Alice to her lover's house and Sami to the main road where he would hook up with the twins and be seen arriving with them. The deception was necessary to protect him, but Alice already missed the security of his friendship. However, there was nothing else to do but shoulder their packs and go on.

The memory of going to Seaside with her father rose in her as they walked. The city had seemed enormous to the little outback girl, but her recollections were of sailboats, fish, and a bustling market. In the dim light of descending night, they now approached the crest of the plain, looking down on gathered huts and buildings close to the edge of the sea. She identified the docks with their bobbing fishing boats, extending out into the white-capped water. Closer to their vantage point and on higher ground, she saw the depressions of courtyards far bigger than any in her village. Between the harbor and the residences was the Academy complex, domes and lodges sitting high on at least ten acres of land.

Sami pointed out a bright line snaking in from the left on level terrain which ended at the water's edge. "There's the main road. We're almost exactly across from it. Hardly anyone comes into Seaside from the neighborhood approach."

She nodded. "So, where do we go now?"

"Manuel told me Dinah lives in a house two clusters down to the north. Look for a blue door. The number sixteen should be painted on it."

So, that's how they keep track of their houses, Alice thought. In Far Meadow, people just knew where everyone lived, but here.... As they approached the courtyards, she looked to her left and right, not seeing an end to the sunken circles. Sami seemed sure of his way, though. There was no one about, which was not surprising as Second Moon had almost set. It was time to eat last supper and get into bed. Did she hear the murmur of voices?

Sami touched her arm and guided her toward a depression. As

they approached, she realized that instead of individual courtyards, six to ten small huts shared a communal moat with a common space in the center of the ring. They paused at the stairs leading into this area and, peering down through the growing gloom, found the door with sixteen painted on it.

Sami put his mouth close to her ear and whispered, "I'll wait here until you're in. If she's not home, come back to me."

Alice nodded. "Thanks. I'll see you at the Academy, won't I?"

"Yep. I'll introduce myself as if we're just meeting. Don't worry, Alice. I'll keep an eye on you."

"OK. Be careful. I'll miss you, friend." She gave him an awkward hug, their backpacks thumping together. His dark curls had escaped the tie-back and blew around his face, so she couldn't see his expression. Then he was gone, melting into the shadows, and she stood alone at the top of the steps.

CHAPTER TWELVE

Alice descended the steps and crossed the courtyard to the door, which held her future. In her village, she would have called out from the top of the stairs to announce her presence, but Sami had schooled her in the art of knocking, so she rapped the wood with her knuckles, holding her breath. Someone was home. Light shone out of a curtained window which faced her. She heard footsteps and then the door swung open, spilling brightness all around her.

As her sight adjusted, she saw her lover and mentor standing there with a small pottery cup in one hand, her wiry body wrapped in a robe and a slight frown on her lips. As she registered who stood before her, the frown flipped to a wide smile and her sharp green eyes brightened.

"My God, is that you, Alice? Where the hell have you been? Come in, come in! I've been so worried about you." She reached out her free hand and pulled the young woman across the threshold into a half embrace.

Alice, burying her face into the fold of Dinah's neck, began to shake. "Oh Dinah, I'm so glad you're here."

"Wait, wait. Let's get that pack off you. Is anyone with you?" She peered out the door before kicking it shut. Taking Alice by the arm, she drew her farther into the house and directed her to a chair at the kitchen table. "Sweet girl, you must be exhausted and famished. I had supper, but I'll see what I can do for you."

"It's OK. I'm just so glad to see you, Dinah." She searched the face of her lover, noting the freshly cut salt-and-pepper hair and her fading tan.

The emerald eyes crinkled in response as she plunked down bread on the table. "I'm delighted you're here too dear. Your father showed up looking for you yesterday, but when I told him I hadn't seen you, he assumed you must be dead."

"Pa came here?"

"Yes, three times. The first visit, he accused me of harboring a minor, because you hadn't turned six revs yet. This time, I insisted I'd call the community guards if he didn't leave me alone." Dinah sawed at the loaf and set a generous slice before Alice, along with a knife and jam. "Do you want tea, dear? Or something a little stronger? I'm having wine myself."

"Oh, um, OK. I'll take some too." Alice could count on one hand the number of times she had tasted alcohol. It was a rare luxury in Far Meadow, and she had never seen it at Pete's. She didn't want to seem uncouth, though.

The drink went down smooth and sweet, warming her immediately. She set the cup down and said, "How was he?"

"Your Pa?" Dinah sat down beside her, having filled her cup again. "Well, he swore at me and blamed me for making you run away, but he looked like he'd weathered the last harvest alright. Before he got mad, he thanked me once more for stopping the bilbug infestation."

The wicked little grin in which Alice delighted lit her countenance, and the weary traveler smiled in return. "Poor Pa. I'll let him know I'm here after I've started school."

Dinah's face clouded over. "I'm not sure that's smart. Look," she leaned her elbows on the table, closing the gap between them, "I spent a long time figuring out what we could do if you showed up. We need to register you under a different name so that no one can challenge your status here. The deans continue to refuse entry to anyone from the outback not bringing in enough food, and if your father finds out you're here and makes trouble, they could very well kick you out."

Alice took a sip from her glass before responding. "Won't they find out, anyway?"

"No, I'll take care of you. I've got some strings I can pull, favors I'll call in, to get you set up. Once we have you partnered to a professor, you'll be untouchable." The older woman patted Alice's hand and downed her wine. She stood to retrieve the bottle she had left on the counter, filling her cup, missing the frown on her young lover's face.

Alice stared into the dark red liquid in her own glass. "I assumed if we bonded, even with a one- or two-year commitment, I would satisfy the residency requirement."

"Nope, not anymore." The older woman tightened her robe's belt and sat down. "But you need a female relative to get you your first-bond, so I'll pose as your auntie. Do you like the name Allie? I thought we could call you Allie Touch Down and say you're a niece from my brother's bloodline."

"Won't they guess who I really am? Allie isn't too different from Alice, and if my pa's been around asking for me...."

Dinah rolled her eyes. "Anyone who's paying attention should get it. But there are no students left from Far Meadow now that Liam's gone home, and the officials will leave us alone when they realize you're going to produce a child for Seaside. They'll claim they didn't know who you are. It's called 'plausible deniability.' Of course, you'll live in the dorms until your first-bond. People expect that of a niece."

Alice's eyes narrowed as she looked into Dinah's smiling face. "I thought you wanted to commit to me. If everyone believes we're related, the registrar won't allow us to partner."

Her lover snorted. "When two women pair, nobody cares. And even if someone objects that it's not traditional, by the time we're ready, they'll have forgotten we said we're aunt and niece." She reached over for Alice's hand again. "Don't worry, little one. I've got this figured out. We have to play the game for a while, but it will work out the way we dreamed in the end. I promise."

After studying her beloved's face for a second, Alice let go of her tension. Squeezing the firm fingers which held hers, she nodded, exhaustion blunting her emotions. She understood so little about the rules and labyrinthine customs of the larger settlements, but Dinah still loved her, still wanted her. *Trust that love*, she told herself.

Later that night, after a hot shower and the physical reassurance of shared passion, she lay staring into the dark while her partner snored gently beside her. *It will be OK*, she hoped. *If we can't notify Pa and Ma, perhaps Sami can smuggle a letter to Nainai. It's not fair to leave her thinking she sent me to my death.* But even as she planned this, she knew she would not tell Dinah.

Sami didn't connect with her for over two weeks. *He probably can't get near me*, Alice reflected. The first-year girls moved in a pack, like a swarm of gnats in the forest meadow. It wasn't that she disliked her fellow students. She just missed time alone to think. Even her nook in the dormitory offered a meager respite from the continual chatter, except for the enforced study hours. She found Dinah had been wise to choose Touch Down as her supposed home: It was large enough that she could tell the locals she lived on the opposite end of the city and often visited her birth mother at Mountain Side. The kind Touch Down pupils, though, considered it important to help their less-cultured sister fit in and never neglected a chance to pull her along with the group.

Manuel and Jamie finally created the opportunity for them to meet "naturally." The twins swooped in behind the freshman women as they got in line for first supper at the cafeteria. Flirting with the prettiest, Shanna and Dion, they pulled in Sami and introduced him as well. The three older students invited the whole group to a play being given in the auditorium after the meal that evening. Soon, Alice found herself seated next to her dear friend in a darkened room watching a farcical comedy. Fortunately, hers was an aisle seat, so when he bent over and, under cover of a burst of laughter, whispered, "Let's go outside for a minute," she eased herself out of her chair.

In the deserted hallway, Sami led her to a door she had not yet been through. It belonged to a greenhouse, and they wound their way through raised beds of plant experiments until they were hidden from the view of anyone entering.

"We can't be gone long. How you're doing? What's with the alias?"

Her friend kept his voice low and his eyes on the entrance.

"Dinah thinks the deans might still kick me out if Pa comes looking for me." Alice sighed. "She's posing as my aunt, so we don't even live together yet."

"Are you OK with that?"

"Yeah, I guess." She sighed again. "It's like I'm living Nainai's early life. I'm stuck in the dormitory with all these friendly girls, and I love the classes. I'm so happy to have a com-pad. It's just that I'm not myself." She searched his face for understanding. "I didn't realize this would be the price I'd need to pay."

"Oh, Alice...." He frowned, his dark eyes clouded. "Do you want out?"

She gave a sharp laugh. "Out to what? I can't go back to Far Meadow."

"I could get you to Pete."

"What future would I have there?" She regretted the irritation in her voice. This wasn't Sami's fault. "No, I'll make the best of it. Dinah says once I have a child, we can drop the pretense. It's not so bad. I am glad to see you, though."

Her friend's smile warmed her. "I'm happy you're here, Alice. Oh, I'll be careful to call you Allie."

They both were silent for a second.

"I guess we better get you back before you're missed." Sami said.

At the greenhouse door, he instructed her, "Say you went to the bathroom, if anyone asks. I won't go in again, but I'll check on you later. It will be easy with the twins pursuing your friends."

She saw Dinah every day. Indeed, she had her as an instructor in beginning biology. Because of their supposed aunt-niece relationship, no one thought it odd that they snatched a few minutes of time between classes to talk. But Alice wondered if her lover liked the distance that pretense put between them. The professor showed no anxiety about the situation, joking that it helped her grade Alice more fairly. If she hadn't been so intrigued by her studies, she might have questioned what she was doing there. As it was, those questions didn't surface until after the first quarter.

She made the dean's list, reveling in her good grades and ability to focus. Dinah seemed proud of her efforts, and they planned to celebrate during a three-day weekend holiday before the second term started. Alice turned down invitations from her Touch Down friends to travel home with them, claiming commitments to her 'aunt.' She rejoiced that soon she and her lover would be alone for the first time since she appeared on Dinah's doorstep.

The initial night of vacation, wine on the table and laughing at the foibles of other freshmen, Alice felt like she stepped into the identity she longed for. *An adult life at last,* she thought to herself, flushed with the praise of her older mentor. Dinah had even splurged on a bigger bed, squeezed into the small bedroom and supplied with cheerful pillows and quilts. The two women showered together and then took their time exploring the advantages of the expanded space.

As they lay in each other's arms, drifting off to sleep, Dinah whispered into Alice's hair, "You're the best thing that ever happened to me, little one."

The affirmation created a pool of warmth at the center of Alice's soul. She breathed into the curve of her dear one's neck, "I love you too. I wish we could be together like this forever."

"Soon, darling. We have to be patient—but soon."

Alice felt a gentle kiss on the crown of her head. Then the older woman rolled away, pulling the covers around her shoulders. With that assurance, she too drifted off into contented sleep.

The next day, the women returned to the almost-deserted Academy. Dinah's experiment on grass-whirler beetles needed tending, and Alice offered her help. She had often taken the role of data recorder, even helping with observations, when still in Far Meadow. They entered the empty laboratory and settled down to work, dropping into their old rhythm of the professor calling out the number of bug eggs in different environments and her protégé making notes. They both started when a deep voice broke their concentration. "Well, Dinah, it looks like you've got a helper today."

Alice looked up at a smiling, middle-aged man, thin and taller than her father. She took in the prominent forehead, made even more distinctive by a receding hairline. Indeed, with the close haircut, he appeared almost bald. She recalled seeing him somewhere around the school but couldn't pin down where.

Dinah, straightening up from her counting, seemed unsurprised to see him. "Ah Darryl, there you are. How are your fish doing today?"

That's who it is, Alice realized—the head of the biology department, who specializes in aquatics.

"This is my niece, Allie Touch Down." The older woman jiggled Alice's elbow, reminding her to raise her hand in greeting. "She just joined us last semester."

Dean Darryl returned the gesture, his broad fingers lingering in the air a second longer than Alice's. "I've heard good things about you, Allie. You already impressed the dean of freshman students."

"Thank you, sir." Alice blushed, not from the compliment, but from the suspicion that he perceived she wasn't who she said she was. Or was it from the quick flip she made from partner and lover to niece and student? She looked at his gray eyes, twinkling with amusement as he observed her, then stared at the floor.

He turned his attention back to Dinah. "Could you spare a moment to look over lab assignments with me? I need to get them to administration for approval before Monday."

"Sure." The older woman was grinning too, Alice noticed. "Um, Allie, could you stay here and keep counting these eggs? I shouldn't be too long."

"OK." She turned to the trays of bugs. As the professors moved away, she glanced over her shoulder to see the man studying her, even as he held the door open for his colleague. Then they were gone.

Dinah returned in less than fifteen minutes, getting back to work without a word about the dean. Alice forgot about the whole incident until breakfast the next day.

She emerged that morning from the shower, luxuriating again in the wonder of waking next to the person she loved and reflecting on how special Dinah made her feel when she cooked for her. Whistling, she got into her clothes and then sat down to a meal of toast, nut butter, and tea. She smiled at her lover across the table.

"So, more egg counting today?" she asked as she picked up her mug and took a sip.

"Yep, we'll spend the morning at the labs and then come home for lunch. I'm afraid we'll have to share our space with company at first supper tonight, though."

"What?" Alice set her drink down. "I thought we had the whole vacation to ourselves."

Dinah's mouth quirked into a wry smile. "Vacations are for students. If you haven't noticed, I still have responsibilities."

"I don't mind the work. I just don't enjoy sharing you with anyone." Alice sighed. "So, who's coming over?"

"Darryl and his heart-bond, Jocelyn. They've been together, I'd say, three revs now."

"So, is this a school meeting? I should find somewhere else to be. I wouldn't want to blow our cover."

Dinah, holding her mug of tea in both hands, leaned back in her chair, considering her lover. "No, you need to be here, dear. They're coming to get to know you."

"Me? Why would they be interested in me?" Alice sensed a chill of suspicion trickle through the warm security of the morning. Her eyes narrowed, taking in the self-satisfied grin on Dinah's lips.

"Why do you think, little one? You awed them with your obvious intelligence in those semester grades. Darryl got a good look at you yesterday and found you satisfactory in every other way too. If his partner agrees, he'll ask for a first-bond with you."

"So soon? Why didn't you say something?"

Dinah frowned and sat up straight, setting her mug on the table. "Because I didn't want to upset you. I planned a nice evening together, and that's what we had. I was trying to do you a favor. If you think about this for half a second, you'll see what a brilliant match this is. Darryl is head of the biology department, for God's sake. How could I get any better pairing for us?"

"But I've only been here one semester. Aren't there supposed to be men for me to choose from? Did you speak to anyone else?" The chill became full-blown panic, squeezing Alice's throat, so the words sounded shrill.

"Look, I see you hanging around with those boys from Wood Lawn. There's no future in them, girl. First-bonds should be with mature men who have influence. Darryl is the cream of the crop. Trust me, Allie...."

"My name is Alice." She sprang up, the chair crashing to the floor. Inside, ice morphed into boiling rage.

Dinah stood too, reaching out for her. "Don't be a baby. If you make this match and produce a child, we're that much closer to bonding ourselves."

But Alice had reached the front door and slammed it behind her.

There was no Nainai's hut to run to here. Sami, Manuel, and Jamie had all gone home to help with the berry picking. Alice's steps slowed as soon as she left her lover's compound. The wind, fierce and cold, battered against her, whipping frustrated tears out of her eyes and cooling her anger. Of their own accord, her feet headed back to the dorm, her tiny slice of private space.

Fortunately, she kept her com-pad locked in the trunk at the end of her bed. She retrieved it and let her hands caress the smooth metal before she turned it on. *This is my purpose*, she reflected: *to learn, to grow, to be with Dinah. Why am I so angry? I am six revs old. This is expected of me.*

Missing her confidant with all her heart, she reached into the little bag she still wore around her neck and took out the jump drive Nainai had given her. She hadn't looked at the stories all semester. *Something on this might help*, she thought. *At least, I'll hear her voice when I read these.*

She called up the list of her great-grand aunt's entries. *I haven't seen that one yet*, she realized, and clicked on the title: "Of Girls and Dragons".

Of Girls and Dragons

(This happened so long ago—near the end of Rev 18. It's one of my earliest memories. I still think of it, mulling over the story and the men who cared for me, teaching me by example and stories and always by love.)

I remember the giggle my little brother gave. He had just begun to toddle around and somehow grabbed my special doll, the one Da made for me, which I'd laid by the side of the field as I helped with the weeding. Even before I raised my head, I knew he had stolen her away, getting grubby hands all over her. Fury surged in me as I straightened up, blowing me across the rows of carrot tops onto the path, depositing me before him. As I screamed in anger, he fell backward into the dirt, the toy tumbling out of his chubby fingers. I didn't touch him, but the wail he sent up brought Pops running.

"Dammit, Elena. You're over two revs old now. You know better than that."

"But he took Betsy."

"I don't care. You need to...."

My fury blew his words away. I scooped up the doll and ran. *Pops didn't care. He never cared.* The anger of injustice fueled my feet as I left both father and brother in the dust. *Da would care.*

I found him in the workshop, banging on some broken tool brought in by a neighbor. He turned as I pounded into his space, setting aside everything else to wrap his massive arms around me. I cried, sobbing out the unfairness of the world. Then Da settled on the bench by the door, pulling me into his lap. I leaned my head against his broad chest and wriggled up under his wide beard. This was my fort, where I was protected from all attacks, all woes.

"Hmmm...." Da hummed as I told him of Davy's stealing and Pop's meanness. The rumble came from deep inside of him and made the stiff hairs on his chin vibrate. "Hmmm.... Makes me remember an old story I heard from my mom."

"A story?" My tears ceased. Da knew the best tales. Usually, he would only share them at bedtime.

"It's called 'The Dragon in the Girl.' Shall I tell it to you tonight?"

"Oh, now. Tell me right now, Da."

He gave a low chuckle, followed by a resettling of limbs and lap. I stayed tucked up under his beard, head pressed against his heart. "Well, OK. I need a break anyway."

This is the story he told me:

Once upon a time, fruit was ripe for picking on a faraway planet called Earth. Wonderful apples grew on trees deep in the woods, where a well-trodden path wound, shadowed and cool in the scorching summer sun, smelling both rich with life and dusty. On that trail, a girl trotted along with her younger brother, empty bags in hand, searching for the makings of an apple pie promised by their mother.

Soon, the boy spotted a tree with bright red fruit ready to eat. In his excitement, he grabbed his sister's sack to pull her off the track toward the prize. The bag tore in half, and the girl, furious, screamed, "What are you doing, you idiot? You've ruined my sack," and hit the child hard on his arm. Her brother wailed.

The sister, ashamed of what she had done and confused by the anger coursing through her, threw down the torn bag and ran farther into the forest.

Now, although they hadn't seen her, an old wise woman stood hidden, well off the path in a tangle of brambles. When the children quarreled, she examined them. And when the girl dashed off into the trees, she followed her. You know you aren't supposed to talk to strangers, but this child was so angry she forgot. She stopped to catch her breath and, seeing the Elder, she spoke right up.

"Who are you? What are you staring at?"

"You hit your little brother."

"It was his fault," the girl said. "He tore my bag. Now I can't bring home any apples."

"Yes, I saw what happened." The wise woman had a low, gentle voice. "Did that make you angry?"

"Of course, that's why I got mad. He's always wrecking my stuff."

"Oh," said the woman. "I thought it might be your dragon."

"My dragon? What dragon?"

"Why, the one wrapped around your heart. Didn't you

know it was there? Your brother stepped on its big toe."

(At this point, I shifted under Da's beard, whispering, "Was it a fairy dragon, like the settlers saw?"

"No," said Da. "Remember, these children were on Earth. I think Earth's dragons are fiercer, and they breathe fire. Be still and listen.")

"A dragon inside me?" the girl asked, forgetting her anger. "How do you know?"

"Well, I have special eyes, but you can use these glasses to see it." And from somewhere in her long, twirly skirt, she retrieved a pair of old spectacles, the kind with dark lenses and a thick square frame.

When the girl slipped them on her face, everything in the woods disappeared. Then she peered down at her own chest and, sure enough, she could see, standing in front of her thumping heart, a tiny, shiny red dragon. It had black ridges above its flashing yellow eyes and a sawtooth of ebony points down its back. As she watched in fascination, it lowered its head and stretched out so it lay curled around her heart, settling in for a nap.

"That dragon made me hit my brother," the girl murmured, relieved by this revelation. "If I get rid of it, I'll never become mad again."

"Well," the old woman said, her eyes twinkling, "how do you propose to kick the dragon out? You already know you can't run away from it. Everywhere you go, it will be with you."

"I could trick it by offering something to eat, so it would come out."

"That might work...but since it feeds on your feelings, it's very full. You have a lot of emotions—not only angry, but sad and happy and confused and scared. You're stuffing that dragon pretty well."

The girl panicked. When she looked through the glasses into her chest once more, she saw the beast getting restless, beginning to stir and lifting its head. "Oh, no. It's waking up again," she said. "I know—I just won't feel anything. That will starve it out." And she tried very hard not to be scared. But it's difficult pretending not to feel anything when you really do. Her fear still fed her dragon while she feigned being brave. She thought she could even see it growing bigger.

"Please, take this thing out of me." She begged the old woman. "I'll do anything to get rid of it."

"Yes." The mysterious woman nodded. "If you don't do something, it will soon grow big enough to eat your heart, and then you will become the dragon."

"Oh no, tell me what to do. Quick!"

"I don't know how to make it leave, dear. But I'll share a secret with you: That dragon belongs to you and, if you want to, you can tame it."

"Tame it?" The girl was skeptical. She had never tamed anything before. "How do I do that?"

"Well, first, make friends with it. Convince it that you're glad it's your dragon."

"But I'm not glad," wailed the girl. "It's going to eat me, and I'm scared!"

"I promise I'll stay with you," the wise woman said, settling down on the grass. "I'll wait as long as it takes for you to find your bravery. Come sit beside me and look for it."

It took some time, but the girl found her courage and addressed the dragon.

"Hi, dragon," she said. "I didn't realize you were there, but now that I see you, well...I think you're very pretty."

Her dragon perked up and, to the girl's amazement, spoke back. "Why thank you. I am astoundingly beautiful, aren't I?" ("You should know dragons are very vain," Da said in an aside to me.)

"I wonder," the child ventured, "could you not make me angry from now on?"

"Oh no," the dragon answered. "When someone does or says something mean, it's like they stepped on my toe and that hurts terribly, so you get mad." Here the beast lifted its front forepaw, and the girl could see that indeed, its big scaly toe looked swollen and sore. "It's very painful, but then you feel angry, and anger is one of my favorite dishes. So spicy!"

"But when you hurt, I do dumb things, like hitting my brother," the girl said.

"Well, I don't make you hit," said the dragon. "I just stand up and roar so you know you're mad. Can't you decide to do something different with the feeling?"

"If the roar wasn't so loud, I might think of other things to do. Could you be quieter?"

The dragon frowned. "No, it really hurts. And anyway, I like how I sound. It's part of me and you. I wouldn't be as beautiful if I couldn't roar."

"Oh, what shall I do then?" cried the girl.

"What if you kept your mouth shut, so the feeling doesn't get out?" said the dragon.

"I'm afraid I'll burst," said the girl. "That's what getting angry is like: so much feeling I might explode."

"Could you make me a sturdy house? When I need to roar really loud, I'll go in there and let it rip, but you won't have to be so full of it. The shelter will keep in the mad, so you can just use a little of it, if you want to."

"What a good idea," said the old woman, who was listening to their conversation. "I'll help you build a hut around your heart so you feel everything but can decide with your dragon how much to let out."

And that's what the girl did, with the wise woman's

assistance. But first she went back to see her brother. He had already picked a big bag of beautiful red apples and was ready to go home.

"I'm sorry I hit you," his sister said, "but I found out that I have a dragon wrapped around my heart. Now that I know how to work with it, I hope I won't lose my temper with you again."

"A dragon!" The boy's eyes got big. "I bet it's just like mine. Maybe they can be friends."

"How did she build the heart house?" I asked Da through the cloud of his beard.

"Hmmm...." he hummed. "Let me think. My mom told me they built it from love and friendship, but it took them a long time."

"Did she have blue eyes?"

"Who? The old woman?"

"No." I snorted with disgust. "The girl."

"I think she had dark eyes with gold flecks, just like yours. And I'm sure she had curly black hair."

"And brown skin?"

"Beautiful brown skin, the color of my bilbo tree planks."

"Do you suspect there's a dragon around my heart, Da?"

"I'm sure there is, but I don't have the old woman's glasses, so I can't show it to you. I bet it's the same kind Pops has though—beautiful, red, and fierce as they come."

"Like Pops?" I came out of my hiding place, looking Da in the face. "I want one like yours. What is yours like?"

Da smiled and said, "Mine is lazy and fat. I don't think it has much fire in it at all."

"Don't you believe him, Laney." Pops must have snuck in during the story. He stood now facing Da and put his hand on my head. "Da's dragon is silver and gold, full of the best feelings in the world. Maybe someday our dragons will learn to be more like his."

Alice sat cross-legged on her bed, com-pad resting on both knees. *I didn't know Nainai ever got furious,* she reflected. *That two-rev-old girl could be me.* The realization made her smile, even as she wiped her eyes. I need to control my dragon if I want to grow up wise as Nainai.

She sighed again as she set the computer aside and lay back on the narrow bed, seeking counsel from the ceiling. Had she done irreparable damage to her relationship with her lover by stomping out like she had? They never fought in Far Meadow. But, she realized, she never questioned Dinah's guidance before. Was she right to challenge her now?

One part of her mind said, *If we're partners, Dinah must include me in decisions which affect me.* The other side of her argued, *I didn't give her a chance to explain how she concluded Darryl was the perfect first-bond for me. I never let her know I wanted choices in the matter. In fact, I avoided thinking about it all semester, even though my roommates all talk about their upcoming pairings. This fight is as much my fault as hers.*

In Far Meadow, when she got angry and stomped out of her parents' house, they left her alone to deal with her fury. Ma often warned her that her temper hurt her more than anyone else. Pa's decisions always stood, and the rest of them had to just conform, at least until Alice ran away. But neither conformity nor separation was what she wanted with her lover.

So, channel Nainai, Alice told herself. *Go back and listen. Then dig up what I'm feeling and get Dinah to understand. Maybe we can find a way forward that makes us both happy.*

She sat up, swinging her legs over the edge of the bed, and retrieved the jump drive from the com-pad. If she was going to try this, she needed to do it before she lost her nerve.

CHAPTER THIRTEEN

Dinah had come down to the Academy to continue her work. When Alice stepped through the lab's door, she looked up and then returned to recording her data.

"Could you use some help?" Alice asked, navigating the room crowded with tables and wire bug boxes.

The older woman fixed her with a steely eye. "Yeah, if you're done pouting."

Ouch. Dinah's no Nainai or Da, Alice thought, struggling to hold back a defensive reply. She took a breath and managed, "I guess I am for today. How about I record while you count?"

The two women worked for a while with only numbers flowing between them. Finishing a row of insect cages, Dinah said, "Do you want to eat lunch in the dining hall? I hear they're putting out sandwiches for those of us who are working through the holiday."

"I'm OK with eating here, but I'd like a chance to talk with you about this morning."

The scientist frowned but nodded. "We should go home then. It will be more private."

They crossed the field and walked up the hill to Dinah's house in complete silence, Alice growing more uncomfortable. She took the lead in making sandwiches and tea, aware that her lover avoided even looking at her. She breathed deeply as they sat down together. "So, I just want you to know I'm sorry I got angry and huffed out of here this morning. You put a lot of thought into who I should bond with, and I'm sure Darryl is a good match."

"Damn right." Dinah took a savage bite out of her sandwich and chewed without looking up.

"You must feel as if I don't appreciate you."

The older woman looked at her for the first time since arriving. "Exactly. You're acting like a little kid, Alice. You don't understand how critical your first-bond is. When I think of those Wood Lawn boys wanting to get in your pants and ruin our plans for the future, it makes me want to scream."

"Wood Lawn boys?" *What do they have to do with this?* Alice asked herself. *Did she find out I spent the summer in the forest?*

"Don't play innocent with me, kiddo. I know you've been meeting that Sami in the greenhouse. And one of those twins asked to partner with Dion already. Her household mother complained to the head dean, furious. The baby would go to that godforsaken village. What a tragic waste."

Alice let the comment about her friend slide as she tried to fathom what fantasy Dinah had concocted. "You think I want a first-bond with Sami?"

"Isn't that why you're balking at Darryl? An older man isn't exciting, but I thought you were into women, anyway. Why are you hoping for a young stud?"

"No, no, no—you've got it all wrong." Her copper hair swished with the vehemence of her denial. "I don't want to partner with Sami. We're just friends."

Her lover sat back, crossed her arms, and studied her for a moment. "Then why fuss about partnering with the dean?"

Alice glimpsed something more than annoyance in the green eyes. Was it jealousy? Was Dinah worried she would leave her for a young man? The idea softened her heart.

"Dearest, the problem is, I don't want anyone but you." She breathed into her belly, trying to connect with the truth of her emotions. "When I was waiting to come here, and throughout this semester, I thought only about sharing my life with you. I understand it's my duty to produce a child, but I avoided thinking about it altogether because it meant more time away from us." She snuck a look at the older woman across from her, whose expression had softened. "You surprised me this morning, and it felt like you stepped on my heart-dragon's toe."

Dinah actually smiled. "I know that old tale. My ma used to tell it to me."

"So, are we good?"

"You're willing to meet Darryl and his heart-bond tonight?"

"Sure."

They still had hours before they needed to make first supper. Their afternoon nap turned into a lovers' reconciliation, and Alice received confirmation of Dinah's desire for her. As they snuggled in the afterglow, her head resting underneath her darling's chin, she heard Dinah murmur, "So, if you don't want to screw Sami, what do you find so fascinating about him?"

She's not letting this go, Alice realized. She sighed, trying to gather a truthful but harmless answer. "Well, he tells me things about the forest I didn't know. You've seen how obsessed I am with daks. They nest in the woods."

Dinah stroked the sleek head on her breast. "You need to be careful. You might not be interested in those boys, but they have designs on you."

"Don't worry. I can take care of myself."

"It's not just what they want from you that concerns me, little one. I heard rumors they may be kicked out of the Academy altogether before long."

Alice raised herself on an elbow to look her lover in the face. She tried to keep distress out of her eyes as she asked, "But why? I thought all three got good grades."

"Well, asking for Dion is a strike against them. And some profs suspect they're promoting the ancient religion—you know, that old shtick about the planet being sentient. I don't want you to get mixed up with that, Alice." She reached up and brushed a stray lock of hair aside to look into her eyes. "It might be better if you didn't spend time with them anymore."

Alice felt the sharp heat of anger rise in her again. She bit her tongue to keep from retorting and sat up in the rumpled sheets, circling her arms around her bent knees. "Dinah, I left home because my father wanted to tell me who to love and who not to love. I think I've had enough of that in my life."

The older woman considered her companion and then turned her back, swinging her legs off the bed. "I'm just trying to give you a friendly warning, dear." She began putting on her clothes. As she went out the door, she muttered, "You won't have time for anyone else once you bond, anyway."

Dinah proved right on several counts. When Alice returned to school for the next semester, neither Manuel nor Sami showed up. She watched for a chance to speak with Jamie, but he avoided all the freshman students. Finally, she caught him between classes in a crowded hall and whispered, "I'll break into your dorm if you don't talk to me soon. I need to understand what's happened."

"Fine. Tomorrow at lunch, be late. I'll be sitting in the far north corner." He hissed the words through clenched teeth.

He was almost done with his meal when she sat down the next day. "I can't speak to you after this," he prefaced his remarks, "unless it's an emergency. I'm on probation myself."

"Oh, Jamie, what happened?" Alice kept her voice low, but it shook as she considered the implications of what he was saying. "Is it my fault?"

"No, nothing to do with you. Well, except my brother wouldn't have met Dion and made a fool of himself over her if we hadn't been helping Sami connect with you." The young man sighed. "But it's not your responsibility. He knew better than to call attention to himself."

"How can they kick him out? And why Sami too?"

"Dion's household had someone shadow Manuel, trying to find something to scare Dion off. They caught him and Sami at a meeting of Singers. Luckily, I had a study group that evening." The young man pondered the scraps on his plate. "The dean gave them a choice: promise never to attend a gathering again or leave school. So, technically, no one dismissed them. They chose to quit. They might let them back in next semester, which means after Dion bonds with somebody else."

Alice's face flushed, and her breathing grew shallow. "That's so unfair. They can't dictate who people are friends with."

"Open your eyes, girl." Jamie looked up and frowned at her. "The school holds all the cards. As long as they don't want anyone to remember our link with Goldie, they'll repress every connection to her. And that's why I can't talk to you anymore. It's not to protect me. It's to keep you safe and in classes." He rose and grabbed his tray.

"Wait." She reached up and seized his sleeve. "How do I find the other Singers here in town?"

Jamie sat down on the edge of the seat. "Haven't you been listening? It's too dangerous. Sami would kill me if I got you into trouble."

"I need to know where he is. What's he going to do now?"

"He'll be OK."

The young man tried leaving again, but Alice gripped his arm harder. "Pete and he are like family. I have to stay in contact with them."

Jamie scowled, then sighed. "Sami's still in town. I'll tell him you're concerned. That's all I can do, Alice."

Nodding reluctantly, she released him. She fought to keep tears at bay, staring at her own plate of uneaten soy cutlets and summer squash.

"Do you mind if I join you?"

Dion materialized, standing where Jamie had vanished. A wrinkled forehead marred her smooth oval face, her mouth trembling a bit.

"Oh, of course," Alice brushed her eyes dry. "I was, ah, just talking to Jamie."

"Yes, I saw." The tall young woman flowed into his vacated seat. "Did he say anything about Manuel?" She shrugged an apology. "I don't want to pry, but he won't talk to me at all."

"Yeah, I know what you mean. It took a threat to get him to meet with me." Alice studied her beautiful classmate, noting puffiness around the wide hazel eyes. They hadn't been all that close last semester, but then Alice had been intent on solidifying her cover as a Touch Down girl, and Dion was Seaside born and bred. That's one reason her relatives opposed a match with Manuel, she realized. The bigger towns felt superior to the villages, even though they depended on them for food.

"So, did he say anything about what happened to Manuel?" Dion picked up her chopsticks and stirred her lunch, keeping her voice low.

"Not much. I guess he and Sami got caught at a Singers' gathering. They either had to promise not to go back or leave school."

"He chose to quit?"

The pain-laden words lanced Alice's heart. "It wasn't much of an option. Jamie hopes they might let him return next semester."

Dion leaned in, her eyes glistening. "But why did he have to go? Was it my fault? I told them I'd do the first-bond with someone else. Manuel was OK with that. He said he would wait until we could partner forever."

Alice bit her lip, wondering how much of the truth she should tell this suffering woman. *This is what Pa tried to do to me*, she thought. "Dion, have you lined up a first-bond mate yet?"

"Well, my household ma has a list of three possibilities, all from here. I guess it's just a matter of me making a choice." She leaned back, frowning.

"Maybe after you give a baby to Seaside, you can settle down with Manuel. But I don't think they'll let you alone until you fulfill that responsibility. Your family seems pretty influential here. They won't let him return until that happens."

"Responsibility." The young woman spat the word at Alice. "That's all I get from my ma and pa and aunties. But there's supposed to be freedom within that obligation. Have you read the old journals? Women had complete choice over who fathered their babies."

"I know we can refuse anyone, but how will we keep the gene pool healthy if we don't agree to multiple partners? Back in my village, the Gladiators are talking about only allowing permanent bonds, and my Nainai says that will be a disaster."

"If the first-bonds existed just for the health of children and the community, that would be one thing. But don't you wonder about how much control people have over us, Alice? You're promised to the biology dean, but how did that come about? Were you consulted on the bloodlines of his family? Did anyone ask you if you are ready to bear a child? Or does your aunt benefit more than anybody else from bringing a baby into the dean's household? The bottom line is that being a young, fertile woman means you're a pawn in everyone else's power games, and I'm sick of it." Dion's dark skin glowed with anger, and her eyes flashed.

"I have thought of that," Alice admitted. She sat back in her chair, intimidated by this view of the world. "It's what we've always done, right? We do it for the community once or twice, and then we're free to heart-bond with whomever we want, and the children we bear can stay with us."

The woman across from her scowled. "In the old days, no one forced women. They choose how, when, and with whom they would mate. Lots of them heart-bonded first. Then, later, because of the community's need, they had babies with other partners. They took responsibility because they had freedom. They weren't required to earn that freedom."

That's what I've been missing, Alice realized. *Nainai tried to tell me. People are using our offspring as bargaining chips instead of putting mothers and children first.* She leaned in and whispered, "How do I learn about this history? Where did you find the journals, Dion?"

"Manuel's not the only one who goes to the Singer gatherings."

From this time on, the second semester of her schooling unfolded in two different directions. One way, hidden even from Dinah, connected her with the Singers. The night after meeting with her in the cafeteria, Dion touched Alice's shoulder after lights out. They snuck through the dark streets of Seaside and climbed the outer sand dunes, finding themselves at the door of a deserted hut on the outskirts of town.

Inside, a handful of disparate people gathered. A fire burned in the old-fashioned hearth, lending warmth to the cool evening. A woman, bent and wrinkled with age, greeted Dion. When she introduced Alice as her classmate Allie, the grandma frowned and, taking Alice's hand in hers, said, "We know who you are, dear. Sami told us about you and asked us to get word to him if we heard you needed him. He left a few days ago to help Pete. We hope he'll be back soon. The Academy offered him a job guiding students doing fieldwork in the broccoli-tree forest."

"Is Pete alright?" Alice asked, fear rising in her throat.

"Well, we don't know. News is scarce from that portion of the woods. Sami said he'd return in a few weeks if everything checked out."

Before she could ask more questions, a middle-aged man came up and claimed the grandma's attention.

Dion grabbed Alice's elbow and pulled her aside, whispering, "Did you know Sami and his family before you got to the Academy?"

"Oh, Dion..." Alice realized she needed to give her new friend some version of her history, but how much? "The truth is that I stayed with Sami and his great-grandfather, Pete, all last summer, hiding from my father, who didn't want me to go away to school. I even had to change my name so Pa wouldn't know I had enrolled."

"Wow, you have more secrets than Manuel and his brother."

"Will you help me keep them?"

"Of course. You're lucky to have your Aunt Dinah helping you out, too."

Alice bit her lip, wanting to reveal the whole truth but thinking, *Dion doesn't need the burden of knowing everything about me.* "Yes, I am fortunate. My aunt knows how unreasonable Pa can be."

Just then, the man who had interrupted them earlier stepped closer, facing Alice. "Why are you here? You're not a Singer."

"Neither am I, but you let me in." Dion stepped up beside her friend.

Alice, grateful but determined to stand on her own two feet, said, "I was hoping to see Sami or Manuel. They left so abruptly. But I'm also interested in the journals Dion told me about. I want to study the first settlers."

As she spoke, three other Singers walked across the room to join them. A middle-aged woman, tall and thin, exuding a quiet confidence, addressed her. "You are welcome, Allie, but your presence puts us all at risk. If school officials discover you here, or you reveal any of our identities, the consequences might be more severe than Sami or Manuel experienced. You are, after all, bonding with a dean."

With a jolt, Alice recognized the woman. She was Dean Agatha, who headed the English department. A senior professor who was a Singer....

"I understand. I promise I won't tell."

"Yes, but I must also ask you not to return until you complete your contract with Darryl. And Dion, I'm afraid the same goes for you, if you bond this semester." Her voice, compassionate and clear, became even warmer when she turned to the beautiful young woman.

Dion hung her head. "If that's how you want it. I guess it's just one more thing that they're taking away from me."

"You know we count you as family, dear. This is a temporary setback. Hopefully, Manuel will be back at the Academy next semester, and you'll be free to partner in the new rev." Agatha studied the student, reaching out to touch her shoulder.

"Time to sing." A younger woman, dressed in coveralls which marked her as a sailor and fisher, urged the group. "I have to get some sleep tonight." Alice noted the bright red knit cap atop her glistening black curls and thought, *she must be about my age.*

"Right, Edie." Agatha agreed. "Let's go over by the fire. Girls, if you want to stay and listen, we're practicing some of the old songs this evening."

The two friends sat on the ground as the group of Singers formed an arc around the hearth. Because they were outside the circle, Alice couldn't see their faces, and yet it seemed the fire's glow intensified with the sound of their music, as if they flung energy into the flames. Some tunes were familiar from her summer with Pete, but most were new to Alice. When they stopped after an hour, she sighed, replete with beauty and peace.

The young fisherwoman exited with a wave to all. Then Agatha urged Alice and Dion to make their way home. The rest would leave in a staggered exit designed not to attract attention.

Before they stepped out the door, Alice asked again about the first settlers' journals. "Could I borrow the writings some time? I'd like to go over them."

A man not much older than the young women spoke up. "We never loan those out. The Academy has a copy, but it's not in the library. You need special permission."

"Which I don't recommend you requesting," warned Dean Agatha. "That's asking for attention you don't want."

"How can I get hold of them, then?" Alice frowned, pushing down the temptation to snap at the professor.

"Come have tea with me someday, dear." The elderly woman who had greeted them inserted herself into the conversation. "I'll let you read them at my place. If anyone asks, you're just visiting a friend of you great-grand aunt's."

The generosity of the old soul warmed Alice's heart. "Oh, thank you, I'd love that. And perhaps you'd like to read the stories of her life my Nainai wrote. I can bring those to share with you."

Suddenly, all other conversations halted.

"Elena Far Meadow recorded her history?" Agatha's gray eyes grew wide. "How far back does it go?"

Alice, sensing the tension in the room, took a step toward her classmate. "Well, I haven't read them all, but one is from when she was two revs old."

"What about being a Bridge to Before?" In the shadows, a fifth Singer spoke up. His had been the deep baritone grounding the songs. Alice saw now that his dark skin and bald head hid his age. He might be ancient as the grandma.

"How do you know she's a Bridge?" she asked with a slight tremble in her voice.

The elderly man smiled, calming her fears. "I'm Lucio Seaside, her blood son, given to another household when she was young. But I connected with her and Jay when I was traveling. She is dear to me. I'd love to read those stories."

"We'd all like to study them," Agatha said, her brow creased. "They might hold the key to why we're not hearing Goldie speak to us. Where are you keeping them, Allie? You mustn't let them fall into the wrong hands."

"They're on a jump drive." Alice's hand moved to the bag on its string under her shirt. "Where do you think I should hide them?"

"Well, for sure not there." The younger man spoke with disdain.

"Hey, I can understand why she wants to keep them close."

Lucio smiled at her again. "I wonder if you would let me and Emily take your drive and get it copied. Then, when you come to tea, we'll give you back your original. That way, even if it gets confiscated, we'll save the stories."

The old woman, whom Alice now realized was Lucio's partner, nodded her white head. Dion shrugged her shoulders. Alice drew out the soft cloth bag and spilled the otter and jump drive out onto her palm. Again, the room grew still and tense.

"That must be ancient, from Earth," Agatha said.

"Yes, it's Nainai's otter. It came from Before."

The English dean reached out, stroking it with her long forefinger.

"There's no time now, Agatha." Emily's soft voice carried a deep sadness. "We all need to get going."

"You're right. I'd love to see this again, Allie."

"OK." The young woman replaced the little figure in her bag and gave the drive to Lucio. As it left her hand, she shivered.

"Don't worry, dear. We'll keep it safe." Emily patted Alice's arm. "You come for tea next Saturday and we'll have this copied and the journals ready for you to read."

Then Alice and Dion found themselves outside in the darkest hour of the night, stars piercing the heaven above them, cold, sharp air in their nostrils.

Heading back to the dorm, Alice felt the lightness of her pouch and wondered if she'd trusted the right people. She didn't speak her fear, though. What was done was done.

Before Alice could continue on her way with the Singers, though, her lover redirected her. She couldn't get away to visit Emily and Lucio on Saturday, as Dinah insisted on her being present at the preparations for the first-bond ceremony. She invited her young paramour to spend the weekend with her and took her to the traditional meeting with the family that would receive her child.

Although she had previously met Darryl and his partner, Alice's heart rejoiced in the three other children who gathered around her and chattered about their delight at getting a new playmate. The youngest, a curly-haired one-rev-old, pulled on her hand, insisting, "I want a sister, please. I already have two brothers."

"So I see." Alice eyed the rambunctious boys who had begun wrestling each other. She smiled at the little girl. "I'll do my best, dear."

Darryl's partner Jocelyn, gracious and calm, showed her around their spacious house and courtyard. There wasn't a room for the birth mother, as there had been in Nainai's day.

Next, Dinah and Alice toured the birthing center, built two revs ago, which housed the newborns and their mothers until the infants were weaned and ready to go home. Household parents visited daily, giving the younger women free time to work or continue their studies. Alice noted the small, spare rooms for the nursing mothers, the common study areas, and several comfortable playrooms where outside family could bond with the babies. In the bigger towns, the connection between birth parents and the child's household was less encouraged than in the older generations or in the villages.

"How long will I live here?" she asked her partner.

Dinah shrugged. "The average stay is three months—just enough to give kids the immunities which come from breast milk. You don't have to nurse if you don't want to, though. Some women can't make enough milk, and the kids do fine on bottles."

"When you had your children, how long did you stick around?"

"Well, mine were born before they built the center, so I had to live with the household parents. I found it very uncomfortable being in someone else's space. With the first kid, I made it for two months. I left within a week of the second birth. The household mom seemed fine with that. She was glad to get rid of me, I suspect." Dinah gave a snort of laughter. "I don't blame her. I wasn't the happiest of guests."

Looking at the wiry, intense woman walking beside her, Alice smiled too. She found it hard to imagine her work-obsessed lover as a mother at all, but Dinah fulfilled her obligation to society. Her genes now enriched humanity. *If she could do it, I can too,* she thought, raising her head.

The next day, Sunday, brought an unexpected development. After a lazy breakfast, Dinah said, "Well, I guess we should get you settled in your apartment. Darryl had your things moved over yesterday. I wanted you to myself for one last night."

Alice looked up from the book she was reading. "What do you mean?"

"Honey, haven't you been listening to anything your friends are talking about? Everyone in a first-bond moves into the temporary partnering huts and then, when ready to give birth, they shift over to the birthing center. Your roommates all moved yesterday. But don't worry—Darryl pulled strings to get you the best room."

Alice frowned. "I guess I haven't been paying attention. Shanna and Dion discussed getting rooms next to each other, but I thought that all got sorted out after the ceremony."

"The tradition is to go to the hut with your partner after bonding. From then on, you're at the apartment or the Academy. No more visits with anyone else." Dinah's casual voice belied the sharp glance she directed at her lover.

Alice bit down hard on rising anxiety, which threatened to spill over into outrage. She took a breath. "You mean we can't be together again until after a baby is born?"

"No, just until we know you're pregnant." Dinah moved over to sit close to her, putting an arm around her shoulder. "It's a stupid custom, isn't it? I suspect it started to ensure that the bond partner's genes were the ones that fathered the child. But I don't think we can flaunt tradition now, little one. We have to make this pay for ourselves."

"I wish you wouldn't spring things like this on me." Alice found tears in her eyes and gnawed her lip. She refused to ask for pity. She'd rather be mad.

Dinah sighed and removed her arm. "Everyone in Seaside knows this. Your ma should have prepared you."

Again, Alice bit her tongue and scowled. "She might have if I'd been there. I left suddenly, if you remember, so I could be with you."

Dinah nodded. "You're right. I should be more understanding. That's not my long suit. I don't know why you put up with me."

"No, let's not fight." Alice sighed and envisioned shutting her heart dragon up in its house and locking the door. "OK. Where are these apartments, anyway?"

"Between the Academy buildings and town. You'll meet a few women who aren't in school, but most are your roommates."

It turned out that only eight of the twenty rooms which formed a circle around the deep courtyard of the apartment complex held occupants. Six students from Alice's class congregated on the east side of the yard. The others, from fisher families, took accommodations to the west. As Dinah and Alice walked down the steps into the patio, occupied by a wooden picnic table and a few chairs, Dion appeared and waved. "Hey, over here. You've got number four."

Alice smiled. At least she would be with friends. She opened the white door with the turquoise numeral painted on it and pulled up short. Her trunk, sitting in the middle of the double bed, gaped open, the lid askew and contents strewn in disarray.

Dinah, who had followed her in, swore. "What the crap happened here?" She swung around to pin Dion with an angry stare.

"Hey, don't blame me." Alice's friend held up her hands. "Two guys from the janitor squad brought it in like that. Your com-pad's OK, though. I checked and put it on the desk." She nodded to the narrow table on the opposite wall of the dark room.

"Why did they go through my stuff?" Alice moved to the bed, reaching out to refold her clothes.

"I don't think the janitors did. It was open when they arrived. The hinges broke." Her friend regarded Alice. "Is everything there?"

"My knife...." It was the only thing of value she kept in the trunk.

She jerked up shirts and pants until the bright red oval fell out onto the bed. She grabbed it up and turned to Dinah and Dion. "It's OK. It looks like they didn't take anything important."

Dinah nodded. "Well, that's good. Maybe the workers dropped it on the way over. You'd better check your computer, dear, just to make sure it's not damaged."

Alice crossed to the desk and flipped on the com-pad, frowning. "It seems alright, but someone's been messing with it. I know I was working on my essay for English when I shut down last time. It's opening to a blank page now."

"When they dropped it, the bump might have made it close from sleep mode," Dinah said. "The school owes you a new trunk. I'll lodge a complaint and get one ordered for you tomorrow."

Alice nodded but didn't look at her lover.

"Do you want some help cleaning up here, dear?" The older woman surveyed the apartment again. Besides the bed and desk, there was an alcove with a hot plate and kettle, and a small sofa. A closed door promised a private bathroom. She reached to pull open curtains and sunlight spilled onto the floor but left most of the space in shadow. When Alice didn't reply, she said, "At least it's bigger than your spot in the dorm, Allie."

"Right." Alice turned and faced her with a stiff smile. "I'll be fine, Auntie. I'm sure Dion will help if I need anything."

Her friend, leaning against the doorpost, nodded.

"OK, I'll see you at school tomorrow. Try not to worry about your trunk, dear. I'll take care of it." Dinah patted Alice's arm in a friendly manner and then strode off across the courtyard.

As soon as she was out of earshot, Dion whispered, "So, is everything here? Did you have anything compromising on the com-pad?"

"No, I hadn't put the stories on it. It's a good thing Lucio took my jump drive, though." Alice began getting her clothes in order, shaking shirts out with a snap and folding them flat.

"Why?" Dion moved to the bed to help her. "Didn't you always have that with you in your pouch?"

Alice nodded, remembering that Dion didn't know how close she was to her "Aunt" Dinah, and tried to push her fear of betrayal away. "Yeah, you're right. But don't you think it's weird that somebody just happened to break my trunk and go through all my stuff?" Her hands shook, and she quit trying to get the clothes together. Instead, she collapsed on the bed. "I didn't even know I was supposed to arrive this weekend."

"Don't be paranoid. This is probably just a fluke." Dion sat down beside her and held her hand. "C'mon, we only have a week to enjoy this space by ourselves. Next Saturday, we'll have to deal with our partners. Let's get lunch at the cafeteria and bring it here. We'll grab the other girls and head over now."

Alice looked into her smiling face and found a small, lopsided grin to reciprocate. "OK. Maybe I can find Jamie and ask him to take a note to Lucio and Emily. It doesn't look like I'll have tea with them anytime soon."

CHAPTER FOURTEEN

Six months later, Alice left her little apartment and Seaside, stepping into the Academy's hummie, anticipating the freedom of a fieldwork expedition, as excited as a beetle escaping its cage. Dinah had congratulated her luck on conceiving after only two months of intimacy with Dean Darryl. The young woman was aware of her fortune too. Only one of her eight neighbors had also managed to get pregnant. Darryl's lovemaking was gentle, but she felt none of the ambivalence Nainai described when her period didn't come and the test returned positive. When she showed him the results, the dean went home rejoicing, and she gratefully slept alone again.

Now into the second trimester, she could navigate life once more as the nausea let up. This outing into the forest with a small group of students to catalog insects in an uncharted section of the broccoli-tree woods would help her claim her own path once more. That her lover included her, got special dispensation for her to go, filled her with warm gratitude.

Two hummies carried the biology professor and her four pupils inland to Touch Down, where they were to connect with guides hired to assist them in navigating the forest. About noon, they reached the rendezvous point—one of the wayside huts on the main thoroughfare north of the city—and got out a picnic lunch while they waited for the scouts to join them. They laid the food out on blankets on a lawn of short grass surrounding the hut, basking in the sunshine, with only a light wind rustling their hair and the branches of the trees several yards away.

Alice spotted the guides as they emerged from under the forest shadow. She stood and shaded her eyes, but there was no mistake. Both Sami and Manuel approached them, packs on their backs. She swung around to check on Dinah and found her wearing her smug grin.

"Surprise," the older woman said. "I thought you'd like to see your friends again."

Alice managed a small smile, but a tendril of doubt snaked into her stomach. Was this some kind of test? Dinah claimed she didn't want her to associate with these Wood Lawn boys. She looked around to check other reactions, but the two men and one woman, all upperclassmen, flirted a few yards away. They hadn't yet noticed anyone approaching.

The professor frowned. "What's the matter?"

"Nothing. I'm just kind of shocked that you would hire Sami and Manuel." She kept her voice to a whisper as the guides approached hearing range.

Dinah stood to meet them, exclaiming, "These are the most knowledgeable woodsmen I know. Welcome to our study group, boys."

As the older students ambled over to be introduced, both young men greeted the professor and gave Alice warm smiles.

"It's so good to see you," she said, setting aside her initial discomfort. *Don't be so paranoid*, she told herself, remembering Dion's advice. "How have you been?"

"Get them something to eat, Allie. I want to move soon. We've got quite a hike ahead of us before we can set up base camp." Dinah moved off to the hummies to organize the equipment packs, taking the older students with her.

Sami took the sandwich his friend offered and said in a low voice, "We're all fine. Pete sends his love."

Manuel, talking and eating, mumbled. "How's Dion? Does she

still remember me?"

Alice's heart fell. "Of course she does. If she had known you would be here, I'm sure she would have given me a message. She'll be devastated to know she missed her chance."

He leaned in as he picked up an apple and whispered, "If I give you a letter, can you take it to her?"

"Yes, certainly."

Over by the cars, Dinah shouted, "Allie, get the canteens filled in the hut, will you? There'll be time for gossip while we're walking."

Plenty of time...but no privacy, Alice discovered. They each had heavy packs, which included tents and rations for four days. Trudging down the path, Sami led and Manuel went last. The five scholars lined up single file between them. Somehow, she found herself maneuvered into the middle of the line after each rest break. She didn't speak to either of her friends until they arrived at their campsite just before first supper.

Her summer of hiking in the forest with Sami had prepared Alice for this kind of exercise, even though her muscles screamed that she should have kept them in shape while in school. Dinah and the other students collapsed when they emerged into the clearing, vowing to never work that hard again. Sami and Manuel laughed, not reminding them they obviously would have to hike out in just a few days. With good nature, the guides set up the tents while Alice got the fire going and started a meal.

They planned to split up into two groups, leaving early in the morning and returning to base camp each evening to share results. The male students, Eric and Mike, tasked with finding and counting a species of dragonfly-like insects, expected a long trek to a forest lake where the elusive bugs reportedly flourished. Manuel, having been to the site several times, would lead them. Sami would steer Dinah, Hannah, and Alice to more northern meadows in search of a pollen-gathering bug rumored to be similar to bees on Earth. They hoped to be the first to capture specimens. "If we discover they make honey," the professor said, "we'll all get medals."

The initial day of the expedition was trouble free. After much groaning and grousing about sore muscles, the groups got going on their respective tasks. Alice sensed Dinah watching her whenever she spoke to Sami, so she kept her interactions with him short and professional. Even that constraint couldn't dampen her spirits, though. To be in the forest, among the looming broccoli trees with their great branches swaying in the wind above and the spicy smell of the undergrowth in her nostrils...the tension of months in Seaside melted away.

Back in camp after first supper, the groups compared notes. Dinah's team didn't find any bee-like bugs but spotted a new species of the tiny sapsuckers which inhabited the grasslands. Sami promised them better luck on the next day with a meadow farther out. The lake proved a perfect site for Eric and Mike to get specimens and observe the flying insects which they came to study. They cheerfully entered observations and showed off the six-inch-long, bright blue and red needle-thin bugs perched on reeds in their cages, translucent wings quivering.

Mike said, "We should go to the other side of the lake tomorrow. Manuel says there are orange ones there. We'd like to get a broader sample, but that means we'll have to camp out overnight. It's an enormous body of water."

"You want to break down tents and haul everything out there for one night?" The professor frowned, still peering at their spectacular samples.

"Don't worry," Manuel said. "All they need to take is their sleeping bags. There's a cave we can sleep in. I'll fish while they catch bugs and give them a couple of meals from the lake."

Handing the cage to Eric, Dinah nodded. "Alright then. Hopefully, my group will have more luck tomorrow. We should get a good night's rest so we can leave early."

In the morning, after a quick breakfast, both groups started out in different directions, Manuel taking the men back east while Sami headed due north with the women into the thickest part of the woods.

Alice noticed no path here. *He must be leading by pure reckoning,* she thought. Then a crash to the rear halted her in her tracks.

Sami turned and sped past her to check on the sound. Alice joined him as he stooped over Hannah, who was lying on the ground. Dinah, bringing up the rear, came running up too. The older student, face white with pain, grabbed at her left foot.

"I fell over something. I think it's broken." Tears spilled, and she moaned, biting her lip.

"Stop it," Dinah commanded. "Before you panic, let's have a look."

Alice held the injured woman's hand while Sami and Dinah eased off her boot.

"You were pre-med, weren't you?" The professor addressed Sami. "Is it a fracture?"

Sami considered, manipulating the ankle gently. "No, just a bad sprain. We should take her back to camp and wrap it. If she rests it, she'll probably be able to limp out on Friday. I'll carry her pack with mine."

Dinah stood abruptly, hands on hips, and scowled down at them. "Shit, this means we won't find the bees. The only field trip I'm allowed for a third and now it's ruined."

"I'm so sorry, Professor," Hannah spoke through her tears, but Dinah waved her apology aside.

"I could still go hunt for insects with Sami." Alice kept her eyes on the fallen girl. "Let's get Hannah back and settled. We should have time to reach the meadow and make it back afterward."

Dinah studied her young lover. "That's a thought. Protocol says I have to stay with an injured student. But if it's just a sprain, and she's on the mend tomorrow, Sami can take me to the meadow, and you can nurse her."

Luckily, they hadn't gotten far from base camp. Alice and Sami, leaving their packs where they lay in the undergrowth, formed a seat between them with their interlaced hands and slowly carried Hannah. Soon, they had her ankle soaking in frigid stream water. Dinah shooed them away then, saying, "I know how to wrap a sprain. I'll take care of her. You two get going or you'll be late returning. Allie, don't forget what I told you about those specimen holders—you have to twist the tops on tight."

"Right." She practically danced in her enthusiasm to leave.

Sami, patting Hannah on the shoulder, said, "Remember to keep the foot elevated once you've wrapped it. There are more pain meds in the kit if you need them, Professor."

Then they were alone, on the vague trail into the forest. Alice felt freer than she had since last summer. It only took them twenty minutes to retrace their steps and hoist on their packs. Relieved of Dinah's presence, they fell naturally into the old rhythm of friendly chatter, filling each other in on what had happened in their lives after Sami left school. He told her how Cory made his way to Pete's and now occupied her old room, and he shared his relief that the Academy had hired him and Manuel to guide these expeditions. He felt it indicated a willingness to let them return to their studies soon. Alice held back, however, on her last months of bonded life. *It just doesn't seem important*, she thought. Instead, she let him know she had met Lucio and Emily and the others on her late-night escapade with Dion.

Sami laughed. "If you keep that up, you'll be kicked out too. I doubt Dinah has the clout to get you back in like Dion's family does."

"Yeah, I guess you're right. I should be more careful." Alice neglected to say anything of her own connection now with Dean Darryl.

They reached the meadow after lunch, a broad gem of bright green ringed by the dark forest, sparkling with highlights of tiny golden flowers. Just as he had promised, before she even stepped into the clearing, she witnessed the little fat bugs with impossibly fast wings darting in and out of the clusters of yellow, their mauve fuzz sticky with pollen. Laughing with delight, she got out her camera to take pictures. Then, together, they began the laborious task of catching the insects.

A few hours later, with several of the "bees" safely in small boxes, Alice sat on her heels and sighed. "We should head back with these. Dinah will be jealous we found them, but she can come tomorrow and do her own observations."

"There's another meadow near here I want to show you," Sami said. "I'm glad it's just you and me, Alice. I wouldn't take anyone else there."

"Can we get back to camp for first supper?"

"Probably. If not, we'll for sure arrive before last meal. But you have to promise, Alice—you can't tell anyone about it, not even Dinah." He fixed her with his most serious stare.

She laughed, "Always the man of mystery, huh? OK. I shouldn't, but it feels so good to be here. I don't want it to end. I'll be stuck in camp with Hannah tomorrow, so I better make the best of it while I can."

They packed the specimen boxes carefully, making sure the insects had plenty of air, and then he led her to the northern edge of the meadow. She looked once more at the magical glade before plunging into the shadows. They hiked in silence for an hour, with Sami leading the way. As she tailed him, again on no discernible trail, Alice noticed that not only were the trees becoming taller here, they grew closer together, and the light that filtered down from their heights took on a purple tint. The ground cover was scarcer, and the spicy smell she loved settled into a dustier version, almost musty. *This must be the heart of the forest,* she thought, *and these are the very oldest of broccoli trees.* She shivered.

"Sami, how many people have ever been here?" She whispered,

as if trying not to disturb the Elders.

He paused, facing her, his eyes bright in the dim light. "Only a few Singers. You sense it too, don't you? I think of this as Goldie's center, where her soul lives."

"You still believe she's alive, sentient?"

"I do." He nodded and then turned back to continue his way confidently through the woods.

"Why isn't she talking to us, then?" She asked gently, not wanting to provoke but really curious. She remembered how the Singers of Seaside seemed stressed about the question.

She could hear him sigh as he considered the issue.

"I don't know, Alice. Why hasn't anyone from Earth contacted us for over thirty revs? Is Earth a figment of our imagination too?"

"Good point. If we didn't have the settlers' journals, we might think so."

"Yet, the scientists say that the records of them speaking with Goldilocks are fantasy." He wove his way through the giant trunks without looking at her.

"Don't get mad, Sami," she said a bit breathlessly as she struggled to keep up. "I wish I could read the colonists' documents, but Dean Agatha warned it would be dangerous for me to ask for them in the library."

"I thought Lucio offered to share his copy with you." The young man let her catch her breath.

"I haven't visited him and Emily yet."

"I hope you have time to study them soon. Look, do you see the brighter light just ahead?" Her friend nodded in the direction they had been going. "We're almost there. Let's go quietly from here."

"OK," Alice whispered, trying to walk softly and close behind him. *If he wants to be stealthy, it could be daks he's wanting to show me,* she realized with increasing excitement. *Maybe a different variety lives in the deep woods.*

While the meadow in which they found the insects had been

enchanting, the scene she looked out on from the edge of woods stunned her. *God, it's like heaven*, she thought. A verdant lawn, twice as large as the one they left earlier, spread out in front of her. A dark blue pond sparkled to her right. She traced a stream which fed into it and then wandered off over a small waterfall back into the woods. And in the middle of the clearing, a ring of seven broccoli trees, the tallest she had ever seen, seemed to hold up the sky with their deep green and purple buds highlighted in the bright turquoise ether.

Sami took her hand. "It blows your mind, doesn't it?"

Feeling like a child, Alice stammered, "It's too beautiful. I don't know if I should go in."

"It's OK. It's for us too." He looked down at her and smiled. Then he gazed around the meadow and said, "What I really wanted to show you isn't here right now. Let's have first supper and see if it shows up."

He led her to the brook, close to the circle of trees. As she continued to gape, turning to take in every angle of the scene, he spread out a blanket and retrieved sandwiches and fruit from his pack. When Alice noticed what he was doing, she chuckled.

"I see you brought enough food for an extra meal. Did you arrange for Hannah to trip, so we'd have a chance to come here?"

"No," he laughed with her, "but I was hoping something might give us the opportunity. And now we're here."

She dropped down on the cloth facing the stream, and Sami sat beside her, looking into the central trees. They ate in comfortable silence, listening to the music of the water mixing with the light breeze shaking the nearby branches. Alice finished and stretched out prone on the turf, gazing into the sky.

"I wish we could stay here forever," she breathed.

Sami didn't reply. She looked over to see him studying the grass a few feet away. He whispered, "Look at this fellow, Alice. He must be twice as big as the bees we have. Do you want me to catch him for you?"

She propped herself up on an elbow. Sure enough, the fuzzy insect, a shade darker than the specimens they had, rustled in the golden flowers which studded the grass. But she shook her head.

"No, he belongs here. If we took him, Dinah would need to know where we found him. I don't want to lie to her." She looked up at Sami, who crouched beside her. "I think you're right to keep this place a secret."

Alice sighed then, conscious of her lover waiting for her at base camp and the passing of time. She opened her mouth to suggest that they start back....

A rush of air and dark shadow swept over them from the surrounding woods, headed for the inner trees. She scrambled to her knees while, beside her, Sami stood tall. Her friend stared at the lower branches of the closest tree, and she followed his gaze. *Was that a dak?* Clearly it flew, but it was twice the size of the flying lizards she had seen—at least four feet long—and somehow the wrong shape. She rose to her feet to see better and the creature, black against the bright sky, opened its wings. Alice gasped. Pinions, surely six feet across, shone with vibrant blues and reds, inky veins intersecting and patterning the colors. Now she also noticed the ebony tail which snaked out behind its body. This was no dak. She reached out and caught hold of her friend's upper arm.

"It's a fairy dragon, Sami. My God, a fairy dragon! They're real."

He placed his hand over hers. "Shhh. Stay still. It might come to us."

As he spoke, three other shapes swooped low over them, settling next to the first. Alice trembled, her whole body shaking. These weren't supposed to be possible. They told her fairy dragons didn't exist. But Sami must have known all along, she realized.

As she watched, the original one lifted a broad, rounded snout and sang a single pure note into the air. Then it launched itself off the branch, its wings unfurling, and rode the slight breeze down to the ground, landing only ten feet from where the two friends stood mesmerized. Fear fought with wonder within Alice, but Sami patted her hand, still clutched around his arm, and whispered, "Don't move. It just wants to meet you."

And indeed, this close, she could see the gold foil eyes intently staring at her. Fascinated, she let her dread of the alien go. The creature tilted its head on its sinuous neck, as if considering what she was, and flapped its great wings once, rising to hop onto her shoulder. Sami gripped her fingers hard and murmured, "It won't hurt you, I promise," as warm breath snuffled in her ear and cheek. She giggled nervously, delight and terror wrestling. The long, snaky tail looped around her collar, and she caught its scent: dry and earthy, like the forest dirt. She experienced each of six clawed feet grip her body, none of them piercing her skin but balancing the weight of the fairy dragon between them.

Carefully, she turned her face away from her friend, toward the creature, hardly daring to breathe. She detected the delicate pink of inner nostrils over a wide mouth delineated with rigid black lips. The golden eye found hers. For a moment, she linked with a Being, something beyond both her and the beast. Startled, she pulled her hand free from Sami's and placed it on her belly, sensing a pulse there which mirrored the beat of both her heart and the fairy dragon's. The creature gave a low trill. Alice trembled as a feeling of complete acceptance washed over her.

In the meadow, the wind rose, whipping around the frozen tableau of the two young humans and the fantastic beast. The fairy dragons in the trees all called out with one note and launched from their branches. The one on Alice's shoulder raised its head, bounding into the air to meet them. In wonder, the friends gazed at their beauty, the swirling colors of their vivid wings—green, blue, red, gold, purple, pink, orange—caught in the fading sunlight. Then the gust carried them west over the crowns of the trees, and they were gone.

Alice looked around. "Where's my pack? Quick, before I

forget. I have to get down their descriptions." She crouched down, scrambling to pull out her com-pad.

Her friend eased down beside her, gently taking the backpack out of her hands. "Not in your com-pad, Alice. We can't let anyone else know they're here. Not many are left. I've seen only ten. If the scientists suspect they're out here, they'll want to trap and study them."

"Right," she said, remembering that someone had already hacked into her computer. "You're right." She sat on her heels, but then pulled her pack toward her. "Where's some paper? That will be easier to hide. I have to write down what I observed, Sami. I have to remember it all." Even now, her mind was questioning: *Did she really see fairy dragons?*

"Here, use my sketchbook."

He handed her his unlined, homemade pad and, flipping it open, Alice saw he had already drawn the image of the beast, actually many images. Some he had painted, the dark black of their bodies emphasizing the vivid colors of their wings. She recognized the red and blue pattern of the creature who sat on her shoulder.

Choosing a blank page, she began writing a description as if these fantastic creatures were just some specimens like the bee:

Length: body 3–4 feet with tail increasing length another 2 feet.

Color: body, legs, and tail matte black with markings showing a scaled skin, smooth and dry to the touch.

Wings: 6-ft wingspan, appearing to be veined, thin membrane. Brilliant coloring which varies between individuals. They appear to function mostly as gliders. Back two legs swing the wings open. When not in use, they fold in, hiding the colors.

She paused, returning to the pictures he had made. Yes, there were three pairs of legs, with the hindmost fused to the wings. She looked up to see Sami watching her intently and asked, "How often have you come here?"

"I found this place a month ago. And there's another thing,

Alice...." He looked at her, a slight line wrinkling between his eyebrows.

She put down the notebook and gave him her attention. "What is it?"

"I perceive Goldilocks through them. It's more than just the fairy dragons themselves. I believe Goldie is waking up, or coming home, or something. I definitely feel a greater presence with them."

The young woman looked down at her fingers, still gripping the pencil, remembering the shimmering eye so close to her own. She nodded slowly. "I suspect you're right, Sami. But what does it mean?"

She told him about her pregnancy as they made their way back to base camp. "After the child goes to the dean's household, I'll have more freedom. I can go to Lucio and Emily's house and read the journals. I'll attend the Singer meetings too."

Sami silently continued to hike. They paused before crossing a brook, and he studied her face before saying, "Don't you think Dinah will object to your connection with the Singers? She didn't want you to have anything to do with me, and she just thinks I come from Wood Lawn. She doesn't know I'm part of their community."

Alice jumped over the thin line of water. "After this child is born, she'll cut me more slack. She's sure to make tenure this third."

"Yeah, thanks to your contribution." Sarcasm edged Sami's voice.

The young woman bit her tongue. It would look that way to him. But the truth was they loved each other, and that's what people in love do: aid and support each other. She would not regret her decision.

Sami sighed. "Sorry, I don't mean to be snarky. Anyway, if you can pull it off, it would be wonderful to have you more involved. With your background in biology, maybe you could help us figure out more about the fairy dragons." He shot her a sidelong look. "If you don't mind doing undercover work."

She beamed a smile at him. "These creatures are the most exciting thing ever. Of course I want to study them. I want to be wherever they are. This is kind of perfect, you know. I can tell people I'm studying daks, but really switch over to the dragons. Since no one else seems interested in daks, I should be able to do the research by myself."

Her friend laughed out loud. "Only you would consider this an excellent situation, Alice. I love your enthusiasm. But seriously, think about what committing to the Singers means for your life, especially for your relationship with Dinah, and if you want to continue at the Academy."

On their return to camp, Alice made sure to put distance between herself and Sami, hurrying to greet Dinah. Her lover showed her fury at their late arrival by refusing at first to acknowledge her. But when Alice set the boxes of buzzing insects in front of her, the excitement of success overrode her anger, especially when Sami assured her he could lead her to the same spot tomorrow.

The next morning, Sami declared Hannah to be out of any medical danger, so Alice stayed with her at base camp, finishing notes on both the bugs (on her com-pad) and the fairy dragons (on the notepad). She hid the papers, with one of Sami's sketches, in the bottom of her pack. On the last day, after a slow hike out, the researchers said goodbye to their guides at the rest stop. As they carefully loaded the insects they had collected, along with the still-limping Hannah, into their vehicle, Manuel slipped a note to Dion into Alice's hand. Navigating the hummie over the rough roads to Seaside and the Academy, Dinah talked excitedly about the bees and the paper she planned to publish. Alice nodded at appropriate intervals. Her preoccupied mind, though, threw back and forth the question Sami had posed. How could she have both realities she now knew existed: the love of Dinah with a career at the Academy and a passion for the planet with the miraculous fairy dragons? Goldilocks, she felt sure, would not require that she give up the first. But would her lover and the school be as generous? Was she meant to be a bridge between these two worlds?

CHAPTER FIFTEEN

Several months later, as Alice returned to her apartment after first supper at school, she noticed Dion sitting with a visitor at the worn picnic table in the middle of their sunken patio. Usually, only the men who had not yet fathered children visited the young women. When her friend saw her descending the stairs, she waved Alice over. The person with her turned around and recognition dawned: Emily, from the Seaside Singers, who had borrowed her jump drive of Nainai's writing. Eagerly, she joined them. Maybe there was news of Sami, Pete, and Manuel.

The old woman beamed as she met her. "I'm so glad to see you, dear. I felt awful taking your stories and not getting them back to you."

"Oh, it's no problem." Alice maneuvered her legs over the bench so she could sit next to her. At seven months pregnant, the growing weight in her womb threw her off balance. "It turned out I had to move in here the day after I met you, and I'm not allowed to visit anyone until the baby is born."

"Yes, it's a new restriction which I think ill-advised. Expectant mothers need the friendship and support of more than just their peers. Why, I practically lived at my aunt's house when I was pregnant with my first child." She inclined her head toward the younger women. "I loved that baby's father but didn't care for the household mother at all." She made a wry face as they giggled.

Dion said, "Emily brought me another letter from Manuel. Since I'm expecting now, he's trying to return to the Academy next semester. We'll have to be discreet, but at least I'll be able to see him."

"Oh, I hope it works out." Alice reached over to squeeze her friend's hand. Dion had been relieved when her test came back positive last week. Some in their group were still waiting. "Do we have any news about Pete and Sami?"

"That's one reason I wanted to visit." The white head bowed down, encouraging the young women to attend. "Pete is doing fine. Sami got Corey to move in with him and help with the garden and food storage."

"Oh, yes, I'd heard that," Alice broke in. "I met Corey last summer. He really needed a place to stay."

The sharp blue eyes, sunk in wrinkles, pondered her. "Do you think he's ready to live in society now?"

"Sami thought so when I talked to him last month. He guided our field trip last month and filled me in a bit on what he'd been doing. He was relieved that Pete would have someone with him during the dark months."

"Well, I'm glad Corey has your endorsement. But that's not what I need your advice on."

"My advice?" Alice didn't think of herself as an expert in anything, much less a counselor to an older adult.

Their visitor dropped her voice another notch, almost whispering now. "Sami's doing some research, but we're uncertain what it's about. He asked us to look in the old journals for details about the first revs after the Glenn 2 left. As far as we can tell, the messages slowed and then disappeared completely about two revs following the mission launch. Theories developed that the plague returned, which had disrupted life on Earth, or some other disaster occurred. No one knew for sure. People here gave up hope that anyone made it back to the home planet. Most had already ceased dreaming of Goldilocks, and many quit believing she was real at all."

"That's terrible," Dion said. "I wonder what happened."

"Well, we realized this part earlier, even though it's not included in the history you're taught nowadays. We found nothing new in our records. But Alice, your great aunt's stories told us something we hadn't learned before. If what she says is true, Earth may be just fine. The ship launched from here might have made it, although why Goldilocks stopped communicating is a mystery."

"What did she say?" Alice couldn't think of an entry that dealt with this subject, but she hadn't read them all.

"I take it you didn't get to the one titled 'The End of Hope'?" Emily said.

"No, that doesn't sound familiar."

The old woman reached into her shirt pocket and produced the jump drive. "Here, I've brought this back to you. Lucio made a copy for the Singers. I'd like you to read that story and tell me what you think."

Alice's fingers accepted the small rectangle, but she remained puzzled about the request. "What do you mean?"

Her elderly visitor sighed. "I don't know how to put this politely, dear. We wonder if we can trust your great aunt's memory and her integrity. Lucio hasn't seen her for revs, and so much rides on this. Do you think she told the truth when she wrote these stories?"

Alice felt anger stir in her heart, and she scowled. "Of course, Nainai is honest." Then she remembered her own doubts when she encountered the Bridge to Before entry. She took a deep breath, let it out, and said, "I didn't always believe her either. I first read about her connecting with the Earth woman and her animals and thought she was making up a fable. But Emily, she had the carving of the otter. You've seen it. And Pete has the cat and bear her daughter gave to him. If that tale is true, I trust anything else she tells us."

Her visitor nodded. "Still, I'd like to know what you make of this memory. Read it over, dear. I'll be back next week to visit, and we can talk about it then."

Dion pointed her chin toward the stairway leading down into

the patio. "Here come the Touch Down sisters."

"That's my signal to go, then." Emily accepted Alice's help in extricating herself from the picnic bench and stood up. "I'll see you both soon."

As the old woman left, nodding to the girls as she passed on the stairs, Dion disappeared into her apartment with her precious letter, and Alice retreated to read the story.

The End of Hope

(These events occurred in the first third of the eighteenth revolution around the sun. Rev eighteen was when the spaceship, Glenn 2, was projected to land on Earth and connect us to our original planet. As you will see, I was too young to understand, and my fathers didn't entrust me with the complete story until just before I moved away to the Academy. My limited memories, and what I was told, are here.)

Pops and Da took me to meet my birth mother when I was almost two revs old. This is the first time I remember her. We went to pick up a baby. Her heart-bond and Da had partnered briefly, and now the child, a boy, would come home to live with us and be my little brother.

The journey led us to the abandoned site of the Armstrong's community. The Armstrong was the second spaceship from Earth to land on Goldilocks. They arrived several revs after the first Glenn, and conflict arose between the two groups almost at once. After the death of the Armstrong's autocratic leader, the village built by this second wave of colonists was deserted. While no one had lived there since those settlers joined the Glenn's group at Touch Down, the communication array still worked and needed constant tending, especially because the Glenn's equipment had been damaged. My mother, Kama, an engineer and computer expert, volunteered for the task. She and her heart-bond, Shuggy, liked the solitude and quiet of the unpopulated spot. They set up a hut and garden in a nearby clearing, close enough that my mother could come every day to check the equipment. They had settled there before the Glenn 2 tried to go back to Earth, preparing to monitor messages from our home planet and the travelers in space.

I'm not sure why my fathers took me on this journey. They may have realized it would be hard for me to lose the total focus of their parental attention with the arrival of a new baby and hoped to cushion the blow by including me. It couldn't have been easy traveling with a child not yet two revs old, especially as they intended to add a baby on the return trip. Somehow, they got permission to use our village's hummie, so we drove the rough road to the ghost town. They planned to meet Kama at the communications center and then walk to her home.

Most of the journey escapes my memory. I only recall Da lifting me in his arms to climb the steps leading into the giant orb in which my mother worked. I asked Da if it was a star dropped from the sky. He laughed and said, "Yep, something like that." And then, we stepped inside, and both my fathers got very quiet. Later, I understood they saw destruction all around them. At the time, I didn't have any idea what was wrong, except that my mother wasn't there. They called her name, and it echoed through the empty space. Soon, we were out in the air again, my parents agitated and stressed. They put me in the pack on Da's back, and we set out to find the women at their homestead.

A clear path led into the woods. I got sleepy, bumping my head on Da's broad shoulders, and then we were there. That arrival was met with silence as well. We stopped at the edge of the garden, and even I could see that something terrible had happened: bean poles lay on the ground, just-ripening melons showed gashed sides and broken curves, a tomato plant with tiny green fruit exposed its roots to the air. Pops made us wait under the trees while he walked down the courtyard stairs. After a while, he called us to join him. No one was there.

I don't know how long my fathers waited. The next thing I recall is following another path leading farther into the woods. We stopped to eat near a stream after walking quite a while. I was playing in the water, floating sticks for boats, when my mother stepped out of the forest. Tall and elegant, I imagined for a moment that one of the christmas trees had come to life and was visiting us. Shuggy, a smaller woman with a heart-shaped face surrounded by sandy wisps of hair, followed her with the baby in her arms.

We never spoke of this trip in our family. When it came time to tell little Davy about his birth, my parents said only that his mother and mine were heart-bonds and dear friends of theirs. They claimed the mothers would visit someday, but they never did. I grew up suspecting they had died.

Many revs later, the day before I left for the Academy, Pops entered my room and sat on my bed. "I want to tell you something," he said, serious as only Pops could be. This is what he told me.

When my mother and her partner stepped into the glade where we ate and I played that afternoon so long ago, they risked their lives to get my brother to us. Davy's mother, still in shock, wept for most of their visit. Kama explained what happened.

She had walked to the communications center that morning, as she did every day, to check for messages from Glenn 2 or Earth. It had been over two months since they had heard from either, but that had occurred before. The scientists appreciated how difficult making connections across many galaxies could be. They had learned patience.

More upsetting was the spotty communication with Goldilocks. Evidently, she had not known that going on this voyage would strain her link with her physical world. Although sentient like humans, she had never experienced visceral boundaries. My Pops speculated that she also had no concept of temporal flow. No one fully understood why she committed to the journey or what form that took for her. The close connection between the planet and her people weakened the farther the spacecraft got from us, and over the two revs, Kama came to depend on the Armstrong's ancient and temperamental equipment more than dreams or other visitations from Goldie. While rumors flew in the settlements that the ship had lost its way or, worse, gotten to Earth only to be destroyed by trouble there, my mother trusted they would receive a message any day. She saw the growing Gladiator movement feed the pessimistic gossip, but at that point she wasn't worried about it. After all, didn't Truth always win in the end?

Sure enough, that morning the light signaling an incoming report invited her in with its blinking. She approached the panel, but, before reaching it, heard boots on the steps, people entering the orb, and then loud shouts and banging. A premonition of trouble led her to slip out of the control room and into a side hall. She peeked through a crack in the door, watching as ten men entered her workspace. They all held various tools: pry bars, wire cutters, and hammers. She recognized only one: a leader in the Gladiator movement. He called her name, but when she didn't respond, he turned to the mob and said, "She's not here. Let's get the metal and wires out of this. Then we can go take care of her and her family."

"What's this flashing light mean?" asked a younger man.

"It means we got here just in time," the leader replied. He took a sledgehammer out of the youngster's hands, swung it high, and crashed it down on the panel.

My mother ran, the sounds of destruction covering her footsteps. She returned to her house, grabbed her partner, their toddler, and the baby, and escaped into the forest.

Pops paused here, rubbing fingers through his salted red hair. His gaze at the floor seemed so sad. I hesitated to ask, but then decided I needed to know.

"Did the Gladiators find and kill them after they brought us Davy?" I whispered.

He took my hand in both of his and shook his head. "No, but they went into hiding. They lived with some other Singers deep in the forest, rarely coming out. Shuggy died just a rev later, and your mom never got over it. They had been so happy together."

"Didn't she ever want to see me again?" In my self-centered adolescence, I focused on my own needs.

"At first, it was hard for her to bear seeing you and your brother. Davy reminded her so much of Shuggy. But she came once. Do you recall when the Singers visited the village, and Da got them out safe?"

I remembered, and suddenly I understood. "She was the lead singer, wasn't she? The one who blessed me."

"Yes." Pops squeezed my fingers and smiled his saddest smile. "She loved you, you know."

A great anger filled my chest, and I took my hand out of his. "Why didn't you tell someone? Why did you and Da let them chase our mothers away like that?"

He sighed then, nodding his head as if he realized I would demand a reason. "They were so afraid, not only for themselves but for their little girl. We didn't have law officers back then. Nothing like this had ever happened. Kama thought about it a lot and convinced us we should stay quiet until the Gladiators calmed down. She figured the fear of sicknesses and famine led to the rise of this extremist faction, and things would get better. Unfortunately, they only got worse. I wanted you to know, Laney, but I think we must keep this a secret until the Singers feel safer."

I pondered for a moment, wondering at this timidity in my invincible father. "But Pops, what if Earth was trying to contact us? What if it was the ship? Did anyone get their message?"

He sighed and shook his head. "In both Touch Down and Seaside, people were getting sick again. This time, it hit the adults as hard as the children. All the scientists put their energy into figuring out how to stop the virus. When the health threat resolved, somehow it became common knowledge that the Glenn 2 had been lost, Goldie with it, and Earth no longer wished to reach us. The Gladiators made the metal and wires they had salvaged from the orb available for building the windmills and solar generators needed in the new settlements like Far Meadow. Since the mines had closed, these were valuable commodities, and no one wanted to question the wisdom of destroying the communication array."

"Didn't anyone care about my mother and Shuggy? Didn't they notice something happened to them?" My voice squeaked through my tight throat.

"We cared." Pops' firm tone reproached me. "Da and I let trusted friends know where they landed. But try to understand, Laney—Kama was sure those men meant to kill them and their child. When our society accepted the lie that the Gladiators spread, we thought the only thing that could help was to restore communication with Goldilocks somehow. We put our efforts into protecting the Singers. We put our hope in their faith that she still reached out to us and would someday speak more clearly. And we survived. That took all our energy."

I bowed my head, the weight of his words heavy on my neck. He spoke the truth. So many died because of drought, insect infestations, or illness. For him to send me to the Academy required great courage and generosity. Pops deserved better than my petty judgment. He not only survived, he kept me and my brother alive and thriving too, with Da's help. His intelligence and focus protected our entire village.

Of course, not even he withstood the plague, which struck less than one rev later, while I luxuriated in my studies at school. I fulfilled my promise not to tell, and indeed, I felt no real pull to enlighten anyone. We all still existed in survival mode. But Kama and Shuggy, along with Pops, Da, and Davy, have been gone a long while. There may be nobody else who knows this history but me, and I too will enter eternity soon. It is time to reveal the truth: Earth did not quit speaking to us. We stopped listening.

Propped up on her bed in the small, dark apartment, Alice read the last line over, and then over again: We stopped listening. Here was the answer to the conundrum of what was wrong in their world. But if Nainai was right... Well, this story concluded that humanity damned itself.

She shut off her com-pad and returned the jump drive to her pouch with trembling fingers. As if sensing her agitation, the baby in her womb shifted and kicked. Alice smoothed a hand over her taut belly, feeling a tiny arm or leg bulging at the surface. "What kind of world am I bringing you into?" She whispered.

Unlike Emily, she had no doubt that Nainai remembered accurately the last conversation she had with her Pops. The fragments of memory surfacing from Elena's two-rev-old self confirmed the story. Only one question remained for Alice: How do I live in a world where these awful lies—that Earth is dead and that the sentient Being which is our home doesn't exist—have triumphed over Truth?

As the darkness of that query descended, Emily's other words surfaced in her memory. "Sami's doing some research...."

Of course he is, Alice thought. *He's trying to find out if the dragon fairies amplify the connection with Goldie.* She hoisted her swollen body off the bed and kneeled, pushing her fingers deep under the mattress until they grasped the paper hidden there. Sitting back on her heels, she gazed once more at the fantastic creature which Sami revealed to her: the dragon fairy with wings spread to show vivid reds and blues against its dark frame. *Maybe*, she considered, *the lie has not yet won completely.*

CHAPTER SIXTEEN

Alice sat in the garden of the birthing center, bending her body over the compact form in her arms to shade it from the bright sun. She tickled her baby's face with the end of her braid draped over her shoulder, and the two-and-a-half-month-old rewarded her with a giggle and wild swings of her chubby hands. In this moment, this now, contentment reigned, and no outside force could touch her or this precious child. The circle of her embrace held the world.

Footsteps crunched on the gravel and halted in front of her: Dinah's feet, in the soft moccasins she wore on teaching days. Alice's eyes registered them and then returned to focus on her daughter.

"I stopped by the nurse's desk. They said the docs approved you to stay for another three and a half months." Her lover's voice was emotionless, controlled.

"Mm-hmm."

"I thought we agreed on the standard three months."

Alice looked up to assess the depth of her lover's irritation. The compression of the older woman's lips and the stressed line between her brows spoke volumes. Alice kept her eyes on the angry face as she shifted her grip on the baby. "You know she came early by a month. The docs figure nursing helps preemies catch up developmentally."

"But six months, Allie?"

"If I was keeping her, they would ask me to leave her on the breast for a third or more. Mother's milk is the best for these little ones. Why are you so upset? Darryl and Jocelyn agreed to it."

Dinah sighed, relaxing the tension in her mouth, and looked around to check if anyone else was within listening distance. Then, sitting on the edge of the narrow bench, as far as possible from Alice and her burden, she said, "I'm worried about you, little one. It's dangerous to get too attached. The way you look at that kid, the way you hold it...."

Alice gazed into the baby's unfocused blue eyes. Her nurses fretted about that too. Women who almost lost their babies, who had to fight to keep them alive, who prayed for them to breathe their first breaths—those women had the hardest time giving children up. And she had been such a woman. As if it had just happened, she slipped into the vivid memory:

Her contractions came on suddenly, four weeks before she expected them. Still wrestling with the implications of Nainai's story, her own little slice of reality changed forever.

She lived again the stabbing pain in her gut which woke her, wrapped in sodden sheets, in the middle of the night. Dion helped her, calling for a hummie and riding with her to the birthing center. She couldn't come in, of course. They allowed no pregnant woman to be present at a birth.

Dinah was out of town. Alice faced delivering with only strangers at her side, but her friend fetched Emily. The Elder stayed with her, coaching her breathing, holding her steady, calming her even when the tiny body lay still and did not cry. When the nurses gave up, Emily took the silent form and breathed into the minute nostrils, tickled the wrinkled soles of feet no bigger than commas until, with a hiccup, the baby sucked in and then whimpered. Blue to pink, death to life, horror to happiness, all in a breath.

Alice sighed. "I understand, Dinah. They warned me about it already. But what's done is done. I do love this child. Let me love her well before she goes to live with another family. It's all I have to give her."

"You know, if you don't hand it over...I'll also be in a lot of trouble."

Her lover shot her a glance. "What do you mean? I thought you got your full professorship. You're tenured now."

"Yeah, but I'd lose my best assistant." The older woman was smiling, teasing her. "The house is too quiet, little one. Nap time is so lonely."

She didn't experience the sympathy her companion asked for. Instead, she threw out the suggestion that she told herself she would never voice. "Well, if I brought the baby home, it wouldn't be quiet anymore." She tried to make the reflection light, a humorous touch.

She glanced up to see the reaction and bit her tongue. Dinah's fists clenched, and she leapt up.

"That wasn't our agreement, Allie. I'm too busy to be saddled with a kid. I wanted you, not a whole damn family."

"OK, I know. Just kidding." Alice backed out of her proposition as quickly as possible, but her eyes found their way back to the round face in her arms, and she bent to kiss the infant, apologizing for her cowardice.

"Look, kiddo, this is important." Dinah sat down, serious now in her earnestness, setting anger aside. "You're in a no-win situation here. I know the law says you can choose to keep the baby if it's too hard for you to relinquish it. They tell you that up front. But let me fill you in on reality.

"You assume if you don't give the kid to Darryl—if you decide to go home and play mommy all by yourself—they'll just kick you out of the Academy. You expect to end up marrying some old farmer and spending the rest of your life in Far Meadow. And that seems like a good choice right now.

"But little one, that's not the crossroads you're facing. Darryl wields power not only in the college but in this town. They will never allow you to keep this child."

Alice's face flushed, and she spat back, "And how could they stop me if I want her?"

Dinah nodded. *She saw what I was considering*, Alice realized. *Even now, she knows me well.*

The lecture continued: "Listen carefully. Last rev, a girl wanted out of her contract. The father was very influential, just like Darryl. She insisted it was her right to keep the infant, and the next day the doctors certified her mentally ill—crazy. They took the kid away from her and committed her to the psych ward in the hospital. Kept her there for two-thirds. Now she lives out at Last Stop. She's barred from ever coming in contact with the child or the household family."

Alice looked at her, wide eyed. *She's telling the truth*, she realized. "That's horrible," she gasped.

"No," said her lover, "that's life. Face it, Allie."

The words landed like a vicious slap on Alice's cheek. She hugged the baby hard, turning so Dinah wouldn't see the tears in her eyes. The infant cried, a small whine escalating in volume until Alice freed a breast and let her latch on. The act steeled her.

Without facing around, she said, "What if something is wrong with this child? What if Darryl and Jocelyn won't take her?"

"What do you mean, something is wrong with it?"

The sharp retort told her she had Dinah's full attention now.

"She hums, Dinah. She may be one of those throwback children who sings instead of talks."

"Shit." Her partner stood and walked around to face her. "When did this start? Does anyone else know?"

Alice shook her head no, looking at the baby, who gazed up at her while sucking. "That's the reason I'm going to stay six months, though. She might work through this just fine. Breast feeding could help."

Lying didn't come easily to Alice. She couldn't let her beloved perceive she hoped the humming would turn into singing, that her child would be a bridge to contacting Goldilocks again. She had to have time to figure out what she, as a mother, should do. *It's only a tiny white lie*, she told herself, and risked a quick glance to see if

Dinah was buying it.

The older woman faced away, looking at the garden gate through which she had come in. She held her left arm across her waist, the elbow of the other resting on it and her right fist bumping against her mouth. Alice recognized the signs of her working out a tough problem. After a moment, she turned and looked at the pair on the bench.

"Don't tell anybody, Allie. Whether it stops humming or gets worse, don't volunteer this information to Darryl or the doctors or anyone else. Your bonding contract says the dean must take the kid, whatever birth defects it has. And remember, he has connections, power. If it needs remediation, he'll get it help more readily and more quietly than you can. But let him discover the problem on his own."

Alice scowled. "Remediation? What the hell does that mean?"

"It means there are people who understand how to deal with this kind of defect. It's not so rare. A certain percentage of children, about 25 percent, suffer from this. Usually it dies away, but sometimes the kid needs therapy. I haven't studied it. I suppose they just forbid them to hum and make them learn to talk. But for sure, don't sing to that baby now. You don't want to encourage it."

"But Dinah...." Before she could get an objection out, the older woman interrupted her.

"I mean it though, Allie. Don't tell anyone. With any luck, Darryl will take the kid and not even notice until he has it home. Then, none of this reflects on you."

"On me?"

"Yes, on you. If the dean discovers this later, he'll keep it quiet. But if someone gossips about it now, while the child is with you, no one will bond with you again. They'll brand you as a carrier."

Alice felt the familiar rush of blood to her face. Before she opened her mouth to retort in anger, though, the heavy head in her lap shifted. The baby released its grip on her breast and gave a gentle snore. Biting her tongue, Alice lifted the limp body to her shoulder, patting the damp back until the required burp sounded in her ear. Then she lowered the child down to nestle in her arms. As she pulled down her shirt, she took a deep breath, preparing herself to speak calmly.

Dinah, however, preempted her. "Look, I've got to go, little one. Don't worry too much about the humming. I understand now why you want to extend to six months. I guess I can live with it. Just remember what I said, OK? Don't get too attached."

She dropped a kiss on Alice's bent head, turned on her heel, and hastened away without waiting for a response.

As the gate swung closed behind her, Alice whispered, "I told you, it's too late for that advice," and listened as her daughter hummed a two-toned note of contentment. In a second, she joined in, crooning along with her.

The humming didn't stop. Luckily, though, the baby only made the low two- or three-note vibrations when relaxed, after nursing, as she settled into sleep or as she cuddled beside her mother for naps. If a nurse checked on her or Jocelyn dropped by for a visit, the only sounds they heard were common infantile coos and squeaks.

Life at the birthing center cocooned Alice in a daily rhythm of focusing on the baby while juggling a few classes at the Academy. Jocelyn came to play with her future daughter for an hour each morning, but she gladly left the long nights punctuated by nursing for Alice. She had children at home and a busy schedule at her work as supervisor of a shipyard. She joked that she wished for the days when birth mothers lived with adopting households for six months or more. A household mother would use any help she could get.

Other than these regular visits and the occasional appearance of Darryl, there were few distractions. Dion, Emily, and sometimes even Sami dropped by on weekday afternoons when they were sure they would miss Dinah, who came on the weekends. Most often, the young mother sat alone with her child, trying to keep up with her studies between nursing, diaper changes, and naps. Before Alice knew it, three more months had flown by.

The day her daughter pushed up and rolled over, she realized the inevitable had arrived. Jocelyn returned with the baby to her room, jubilantly declaring that her girl had tried to sit up. The preemie had caught up with her age group and was ready to go home. When she noticed Alice's stricken look, she tamped down her enthusiasm and said, "I know it's hard, dear, but it won't get any easier. You've given this little one all you can. It's time for you to take your life back."

"Of course, Jocelyn." Alice controlled her urge to rip the baby out of this woman's arms.

"Well then, I'll make the arrangements. Next weekend should work, if we can find a minister to do the handing-over ceremony."

"You mean in three days?!" Alice couldn't help the panic in her voice.

"No dear, I meant the weekend after that. I think it's too short a notice to arrange this Saturday. I need to plan the welcoming party and get ready for the service. And we should put the baby on a bottle. I can have the doctor prescribe something to dry your milk up. That should help." The older woman paused her planning to look at the young mother with concern. "Does that give you enough time to prepare yourself, Allie? I'm afraid any longer will just make it more difficult for you."

"No, you're right. I'll get it together by the weekend after next. Thank you." Now, she reached out her arms for the child, not meeting Jocelyn's soft brown eyes.

As the infant was transferred between the women, the older one said, "So, Darryl and I figure Lucinda might be a good name for her. What do you think of that?"

Alice looked up at this unexpected request for advice. Household parents had the right to name their children. They announced it on the day of the handing-over ceremony. Until then, infants were just called "baby" or other terms of endearment.

"Lucinda—it means light, doesn't it? That's beautiful."

"Thank you, Allie." She reached over to kiss the child and patted Alice's arm before she turned to leave. "It will all turn out well. You'll see. I'll call the doctor for you first thing tomorrow."

"Yes," murmured the younger woman as she watched her go. But then she snuggled her face into the soft crook of her daughter's neck, smelling the sweet warmth of her, and whispered, "But your name is Aria, for you are a Singer."

As if in answer, her daughter hummed.

Alice grabbed a sandwich from the kitchen and took the baby out to the yard. Under an old christmas tree growing next to the seven-foot wall surrounding the area set aside for gardening and exercise, she settled against its trunk and arranged the child for nursing. She had gotten good at multitasking, and now she enjoyed her meal while her daughter gulped down hers.

The birthing center was quiet, the other, newer mothers either eating in the dining room or already taking naps. In the afternoon heat, the garden glowed. Alice noted the barest of breezes playing around the needles of the tree, too high up to bother her or the baby. As Aria finished and drifted off to sleep, Alice fashioned a nest out of her sweater to hold her, then leaned back, determined to work through her dilemma.

I've waited too long to figure this out, she chastised herself. *I only have ten days before Aria's future is out of my hands. Ten days. If I decide the best thing for her is to stay with me, how can I keep her? I know Dinah won't help.*

The image of her lover, even in this negative sense, evoked desire. *God*, thought Alice, *if only the baby were normal. If only I could go back to school and Dinah, not worrying about her. Everything was going so well, but I can't desert this child if she needs me. That's why I'm so indecisive. I wish I had Nainai to talk to.*

As always, when she wished for her elderly aunt, her hand crept up to caress the pouch lying at the base of her throat which held the otter, the jump drive, and the Swiss army knife. Longing to be closer to the source of these treasures, Alice loosened the little bag, and her fingers met the smooth side of the knife. She took it out and let the weight of it nestle in her palm. Her eyes unfocused, she stared down at it, letting the vibrant red and silver colors fill her senses....

Suddenly, all her awareness channeled into that compact blade. The tree, the ground, little Aria, the color red, all dropped away. The oval morphed into a silver disc over which her consciousness hovered like a dak ready to swoop down on a beetle. She couldn't move or speak. Far off, in some other space, she sensed the beating of her heart and a frisson of fear, but somehow separated from her, leaving her to concentrate on the strange scene beneath her.

Where was she? Silver was everywhere: shiny surfaces with knobs and levers and even a steely floor. She had seen this previously, but where? Before she could recall, a whooshing sound pulled her attention to a door sliding open. Two men stepped through. One was young, about her age, the other older. Both were dressed in identical dark blue coveralls. These she recognized. Every child on Goldilocks had studied pictures of the first colonists. The patches on their sleeves were not quite right though, Alice thought. Then she realized where she was. This was a spaceship. These people were from Earth.

The younger man spoke in English, accented but understandable, confirming her realization.

"So, Jackie told you three more jumps should get us there?"

"Yep. That means just twelve months, or less." The second guy, shorter and rounder, with gray flecks in his thick brown hair, moved to a horizontal panel. He glanced over his shoulder and then turned his attention to the buttons and knobs in front of him. "It seems strange to think that this time next year we'll be on Goldie's planet."

"Not her planet. We'll be on her, with her, more fully. I suspect it's completely different from being on Earth."

Focusing now on this younger man, Alice noted he looked a bit like Sami—smooth brown skin and tightly curled hair, although cropped too short to tie back. He bent toward a screen, and she saw him mirrored there: a thin face with a straight, long nose and deep creases down to a wide, bowed mouth.

The older man seated himself in front of the console and adjusted some knobs with delicate fingers. "Did you hear about the lottery Dan started yesterday?"

"No, what's he up to now? Taking wagers on the exact date of our arrival?"

"Nope. He's getting everyone to speculate on how many people are left on the planet. Bets so far range from zero to a population of fifty thousand."

His tone of voice sounded light and amused, but the first speaker grew somber as he listened. He straightened up and faced his companion. "How could anyone imagine that no one's alive? Goldie consistently shows us she's connecting with some people."

The other man swiveled around, and Alice saw his face: a circle with full cheeks and a small mouth. From his previous tone, she expected a smile, but he frowned, and his bright blue eyes clouded as he viewed his colleague. "You know, Esteban, not everyone hears her as well as you do. Even those who can connect don't have your understanding of what she's trying to convey."

The younger man (*Esteban*, Alice reminded herself) looked away. "What did you bet on, Alan?"

The round face crinkled into a grin. "I haven't put my money down yet. I figured I'd get inside info from you before I committed. So, what do you think? How many humans are we going to discover on Goldie?"

Esteban sighed and turned back to the task at his own console. Alice thought for a moment he would not answer, but then he said, "You know you can't get numbers out of her. There must be several settlements, though. She seems to connect with people from different parts of the planet."

"So, the fifty thousand theory is plausible?" Alan's eyes bored into the back of the younger man's head.

"No." The curly head shook, although Esteban continued to face his console. "There has to be a reason that humans there cut off communications with Goldie and Earth. If everything was going well, the population could have grown that big. But I'm sure something went wrong—very wrong. Whatever kind of society is left there isn't functioning properly."

"So, what happened? War? Plagues? Earthquakes, fire, and famine?"

"That's what we need to know, isn't it?" The dark young man swiveled to face his pale comrade, a furrow above his brows. "Dan's correct to raise the question of who we'll find there. The issue isn't how many, though. It's if they're friendly. That, and do they want Goldie back?"

Alan cocked his head to the side. "Why wouldn't they want Goldie back? She's the essence of who they are now, right? They're all part of her biosphere, aren't they? Like the seas and mountains and daks."

"What if they don't understand that, Al? They may be as clueless about the interdependency of life as we used to be on Earth?"

"The original settlers certainly understood it. You suspect the current population forgot her?"

Alice could tell Alan rarely entertained such shocking thoughts. He looked more bewildered than incensed. Esteban, however, scowled, shaking his head.

"Something must have happened. Maybe not to everyone but, since communication broke down, it's reasonable to assume that after so many years, Goldie faded into a memory that seems like a fairytale."

Alan frowned. "If they don't believe she's real, how does she communicate with some of them? What do they think she is?"

Esteban sighed, but leaned toward his friend. "When I ask her about that, I get a sense of the population being weak. Not as in completely broken physically, but as if their eyes are myopic so they can't focus or they're partially deaf. If I push Goldie for an explanation, she gets impatient and starts talking about time."

"Time?" Al's brow contracted with the same confusion that Alice felt.

"Yeah, it's like she wants to have this metaphysical conversation about time not really being linear. She said this morning the people of Goldilocks have trouble meeting her in the present. I asked her why, and she showed me they're looking far away—into the future. It's so frustrating. Her primary fallback when she's trying to get across an idea which is foreign to us is communicating in images, and I don't always understand."

"Is Judy getting this from her too?"

The young man leaned back in his seat. "She isn't speaking to me at all. You know we broke up."

Alan straightened, keeping his eyes on Esteban. "You and Judy are the best contacts we have with Goldie. It's your job to make sure we're communicating well with the entity. I'm sorry your personal relationship hasn't worked out, but you are professionals. I want you two to suck it up and talk to each other."

OK, Alice deduced, *this mild-mannered guy must be in charge, even if he hides his authority.*

Esteban seemed to think the same as he swung around to face his boss. "Right. I'll ask Judy about it at lunch today."

"Ask me about what?" From behind the bank of computers, a young woman appeared, dressed in coveralls matching the men's and sporting a shiny black ponytail.

"How long have you been there?" Esteban's voice held an accusatory ring.

Al said, "Glad you're here, Judy. Pull up a seat."

The woman ignored her estranged lover and complied with Alan's request, facing him on a stool and swinging her back toward the younger man.

"Esteban's briefing me on Goldie's complaint that the people on her planet don't connect well with her. Seems to have something to do with time. Have you had similar conversations with her?"

"Could be. Time is a cerebral concept, so it's hard to tell if Goldie has the same understanding of it as we do. I sense she tries with varied success to communicate with the population, and yes, the subject of time comes into it. It might be a temporal delay or some issue with the distance from them."

"I don't think it's like different time zones, if that's what you mean." Esteban spoke to the young woman's back. "I get this picture of people looking off into the horizon. They seem far-sighted, missing what's under their noses right now."

Judy swiveled her seat around and fixed bright black eyes on him. "Hmmm. I wonder why they look for her in the future, but not in the present."

"They're not searching for Goldie in the future. It's just that their focus is there, so they aren't able to concentrate on her reality in the present." Esteban frowned and directed his attention to the console.

"Huh." The young woman took in the statement, seeming to roll it around in her mind. "You know, yesterday I was stewing about the past, wondering about something that happened on Earth before we left. It was a silly thing: I had dropped off my cat at my sister's, assuming she was happy to take care of him. But, later on, I second-guessed myself. I wasn't confident that she really wanted the responsibility. I got a message from Belinda saying Paws died. It brought all that doubt up for me again." She hesitated and glanced at Esteban, who raised his eyes from the screens and knobs to search her face.

"I'm sorry about your cat, Jude," he murmured.

"And this has to do with Goldie, how?" Alan prompted.

"Oh, she kind of broke into my thoughts. She does that sometimes—hijacks an incident or emotion that becomes clear to her. She indicated something like this happened in her history too."

Al scowled, an incongruous look on his genial round face. "I don't get it."

Esteban did, though. He looked at Judy with his mouth gaping. "I wonder..." he began.

"Yeah, me too," she responded, even before he finished. "It fits with the time theme."

"Are you sure you guys broke up?" Alan growled. "'Cause it seems to me like the two of you are in sync now. Explain."

The young man raised his eyebrows, and the young woman nodded.

"OK, this might have happened," he said. "Goldie hooked into Judy's uncertainty about what she did in the past and her feelings about her cat who died. I'm guessing you feel a little guilty about leaving Paws with your sister, who maybe wasn't the best person to care for him, right?"

The proud face softened as Judy confirmed he had her pegged.

He continued. "So, Goldie had an experience of trusting that she did the correct thing in the past, but that choice produced consequences she didn't expect for someone else—I'm guessing the people on her planet. Now, as the present unfolds, she wonders if she made the best decision. And she could suffer guilt about repercussions happening there, because they didn't accept or understand whatever action she took."

The black eyes locked with his, welling with tears that threatened to fall. Taking a deep breath, Judy said, "And one more feeling I had upset her deeply: regret. I longed to change the past—to put Paws with my aunt or a friend. But as soon as I felt regret and wished to alter history, Goldie retracted. It was as if the emotion disgusted her, or it frightened her. In any event, that's where we quit exploring my emotions. She ghosted me for about eight hours after that. She rarely leaves me alone for so long."

Silence fell in the control room as they pondered Judy's admission. Meanwhile, up at her vantage point, Alice's disembodied breath came in gasps as she realized what had occurred. *Don't you see?* She thought hard at the three people below her. *That's exactly what happened. Goldie went away. We didn't comprehend how tough it would be when she left. Maybe she didn't realize what her absence would mean, either. And now, hardly anyone accepts she's real, because we've been without her so long and suffered so much.*

As these thoughts crowded into her head, she noticed a familiar smell: the rich, earthy scent of christmas trees and dak nests. Her heart suddenly overflowed with warmth, and she realized another presence permeated the room, someone trying very hard to comfort her, to reassure her. Below, both Esteban and Judy froze, attentive and still. Then, the light muddled, growing shadowed and jumbled. Alice noticed a swirling pull and then only the bright red and silver oval of the knife in her palm filled her sight.

"Alice, are you alright? Can you hear me? Alice...?"

It was Sami's voice. She felt his hand on her shoulder and smelled his warm skin right in front of her. She raised her gaze from the knife and focused on his face, just a few inches from hers, forehead wrinkled and brown eyes searching.

"Sami. Were you there? Did you see them too?" Her words emerged with a croak.

"Oh, thank God. I thought you were having a fit. Are you OK, girl?" The young man sat back on his heels.

"Did you see them, Sami?" Alice reached out to catch his forearm. *Was what happened just now real?*

"Who? I climbed the wall to make sure Dinah wasn't here and spotted you sitting there staring at your hand. I assumed something was wrong. Nobody else is around. Well, I looked at the baby, but she's OK."

Aria. Alice checked her little one snoozing on her back on the sweater in the speckled shade of the christmas tree. Still gripping her friend, she said, "I wasn't here, Sami. It was like Nainai's Bridge to Before, but now. Not here, but now. I'm sure of it."

"Oh." Sami eased from his squat to sit in the dirt, facing her. He reached over with his free hand to loosen her grip on his arm. "You've had a vision, Alice. Tell me as clearly as you can what happened. There should be other Singers here to help figure this out, but I'll have to do for now."

She nodded, clasping her hands together, trying to contain her agitation. "OK. There were Earth people, two men and a woman, arguing about Goldie on this spaceship...."

"No, wait." Sami held up a hand. "There's a protocol for this. Take your time. Describe every detail of the vision you can remember. And start with what you were doing when it took you." He settled, completely present to her and whatever she was going to say.

"Right." She breathed deep and began, keeping her eyes on her hands. "Jocelyn noticed the baby turn over today and decided that she wants to do the handing-over ceremony next weekend. So, I came out here to decide what to do. They don't know—I guess you don't either—that she hums. Dinah said if they find out, they'll try to stop her from singing. I'm wondering if I should keep my child, if it's important to let her learn how to sing—you know, for Goldie." She glanced up to see Sami's focus still on her, his lips narrowed and pressed together.

"I'm sorry I didn't tell you about the humming. Dinah warned me not to reveal it to anyone, and you haven't been around much, so...." Her apology petered out as Sami shook his head. "So, I guess I should just continue?" A small nod from her friend.

"After I finished nursing Aria, I was trying to decide the right thing to do and wishing for Nainai to give me advice. I got out the knife she gave me and was looking at it." She held out the red and silver oval for Sami to see, and he nodded again. "And as I looked, the red disappeared and everything became silver—everything. I realized my body was still here, but I floated somewhere up high in this shiny room that turned out to be a spaceship."

Alice continued, not looking at her friend, but telling her story to herself. She repeated the conversations the Earth people had in as much detail as she could, solidifying the experience in her mind. When she got to the end and mentioned the warm comfort she sensed, she paused.

"I wonder if Goldie was there," she said. "I've never dreamed of her, but somehow I'm certain it was her. Was she showing me this to encourage me to keep my child?" She asked of herself, but Sami volunteered an answer.

"That might be an accurate assessment, Alice. But I'm not an expert. We should tell Pete and see what he thinks. I'll help you remember what you saw until we can get him and some other Singers to weigh in on it."

The joyous buzz Alice experienced from remembering the vision evaporated. "I don't have time, Sami. I have to decide what to do with Aria now. If I keep her, we'll have to sneak away and hide somewhere. Dinah made it very clear that Dean Darryl won't let me out of my contract."

Sami frowned, his warm brown eyes searching her face. "So, what do you want to do?"

Alice leaned over and picked up the sleeping baby, hugging her to her chest. Tears dropped on the child's head, darkening the reddish blonde fluff. "I have to leave. Somehow, Aria and I have to escape and hide until it's safe for her to sing."

CHAPTER SEVENTEEN

They climbed over the wall that night. Alice ate first supper with the rest of the new mothers, acting unconcerned about the upcoming handing-over ceremony and joking about how good it would feel to get back to school full-time. Then she returned to her room to prepare. She left everything behind—all her clothes and baby paraphernalia, even her beloved com-pad—to disguise the seriousness of her absence as long as possible. *Maybe they'll think I'm just on a walk*, she reasoned. *At least it will give me an extra hour or two.*

She rumpled her bed to appear slept in and then loaded up Nainai's jump drive with every bit of information she had on the daks. As a precaution, she also wiped all traces of research and the stories off her computer, in case someone cracked her password and went snooping. Diapers would be a problem, she realized, and sneaked down to the laundry to borrow a dozen. How she would clean them on the road worried her, but she brushed it aside as an issue to deal with later.

After nursing the baby (thinking, *Thank goodness I kept her on the breast!*), Alice struggled to stay awake until the center quieted. The Rose Moon, in full splendor, lit the garden as she crept into the deserted space at close to one a.m. She didn't see Sami until he stepped from the shadow of the christmas tree and reached out his arms to hold the child. Then she scrambled to the top of the wall, straddled the rough concrete, and took back her infant while the young man hoisted himself up and over, ready to receive them on the other side. They accomplished all this in silence, the miracle being that Aria didn't stir once.

Then Alice cradled the child in her arms as Sami's hand on her shoulder guided her through a maze of neighborhood streets and housing wells. At last, half a mile from the birthing center, her friend stopped in the deep shadow of a small grove of trees in a public park. He shrugged off the backpack that Alice hadn't noticed he carried and motioned for her to lay the baby and the bundle of cloths on the ground. Whispering, he said, "I've modified this to carry Aria. There's about three days' worth of food in it and water bottles on both sides. Let's put the diapers on top of the bread and— see, there's still room for her."

As they eased the child into the pack, carefully pulling her chubby legs through the holes Sami had cut, she fussed. "She'll need to nurse in another hour," Alice said as she helped him swing it onto his shoulders.

"That's OK. You should be in the forest by then. I'll take you that far."

Alice patted her daughter's back as they walked, and the baby quieted, laying her head down on the pack's padded frame, lulled to sleep by the rocking of Sami's gait.

The path they followed on the outskirts of town was the same one they had traveled when she first entered Seaside. Alice sought the neighborhood well of Dinah's house as they passed but ordered her mind not to think about what her lover might be doing. She didn't dare consider other options now. *I've made my choice*, she told herself, *so just keep walking*. The tall grass, blowing in the night wind, brushed her legs with compassion.

Suddenly, the dark broccoli trees loomed in front of them. Sami and Alice slid into the darkness that pooled under their branches and halted. Sami swung the pack off his shoulders and helped Alice extricate the child. She kneeled on the short verge to change the diaper and then settled cross-legged to nurse. Aria forgot to fuss in wonder at the strange scenery all about her.

"I wish we could stay right here," Alice said, no longer wary of waking inquisitive neighbors. "It's so peaceful."

"I know." The young man rooted around in the backpack. "Here, eat some bread and nut butter. You're going to need to keep up your strength. Where did you set that dirty diaper? Here's a waterproof bag to carry it."

"Sami, you're amazing. Who else would bring something to put the laundry in?"

"It's nothing." He stashed the sack with its malodorous contents in an outside pocket and settled beside her. "You've got the hard road ahead of you. Do you still want to do this, Alice? Are you sure you can find the route alone?"

She looked away from him, across the plain of grass lit by the moon. "No, and no. If I could think of another way to let Aria grow into the person I'm certain she's supposed to be and also have a life with Dinah and the Academy, I'd do it."

Her voice sounded bitter in her own ears, and she sighed. *No fair taking it out on Sami*, she thought. She softened her tone. "But I can't figure out any other strategy. I don't know if I'm the most stupid, selfish mother on Goldilocks or if I'm doing the best thing for my child at the expense of everything I ever wanted." She closed her lips hard, setting teeth against the sobs that rose in her throat.

Next to her, Sami sat silent and still. Aria let go of her breast, and Alice shifted her up to her shoulder for the required burp. Content but curious about her surroundings, the baby started humming her three-tone song. Her mother joined her in the simple notes, and then Sami's deeper voice accompanied them, weaving in a harmony around the child's tune. For a moment, Alice felt wrapped in the comfort she had received at the end of her vision, of being totally understood and accepted. As her daughter fell asleep, the music stopped, but she held tight to the conviction of being on the right path.

"It will be OK, Sami. I'll find Corey's cave and wait for you or

Pete there. And you have a tough road too. I wouldn't want to face Dinah and Dean Darryl when they discover we've left."

"Don't worry about me." He heaved himself to his feet, grabbing the pack to set it upright. "I'll stick to the story we came up with, and Manuel is backing up my alibi. I better get going soon, though. If anyone checks and finds you're gone tonight, I want to be in bed, fast asleep."

Alice stood up with the baby and settled her in the carrier. She got the contraption on her back and the straps adjusted with some help from Sami. He dug in a pocket and brought out a headlamp, adjusting its band across her forehead.

"Remember, move only in the dark. No one else should be on the trail, and there's nothing in the forest that can harm you except humans. If the path branches, turn to the right. You should come to Corey's clearing sometime on the third night. The cave must be around there—probably north of where we sat and talked to him. I'll get word to Pete to meet you, but don't go any farther, even if nobody is there. Dinah is sure to send someone to investigate my great-grandfather first thing."

"Right." Alice reached up to give him a hug, awkward with the backpack. "Thank you, Sami. I realize what you're risking for us. Thank you."

Then she turned and faced the darkness, the lamp brightening only a few steps of the path in front of her. She leaned forward and began her journey, the baby once again asleep on her perch. If she had looked behind, she would have seen Sami standing motionless on the edge of the forest, outlined by the moonlit meadow, watching her bobbing light until it faded from sight.

Three nights later, Alice limped into the clearing where she had met Corey. The sun just kissed the top boughs of the christmas trees, with gloom still engulfing the glade as she sank to sit on a log by the creek. She eased the backpack off her raw shoulders, careful not to wake the sleeping baby.

The trek had pushed her to the edge of her endurance. She had spent the last few hours praying Pete would be here to meet her, but only the buzzing of awakening bilbugs high in the branches greeted her. Tears welled in her eyes as she tried to weigh her next move. She needed to reach cover before the sun rose higher. *Should I try to locate the cave now*, she wondered, *or catch some sleep before Aria wakes?*

She decided to enter the forest on the north side, where Sami suggested she should start her search. She had eaten all the food and knew that her milk would dry up soon if she couldn't find nourishment, but exhaustion threatened to overcome her. Removing the water bottles from their pockets, she filled them in the stream. *I'll have to wash the diapers out later*, she thought as she swung the pack onto her aching back once more and headed into the shelter of the trees.

As she had for the past few days, she looked for a clear spot to lay the child with bushes concealing them. They went one yard, then two, into the forest, but nothing suitable presented itself. As she searched the area in the dawning brightness, desperate to rest, her eyes picked out a little patch of worn dirt. Peering, she saw it extend back into the woods as an almost imperceptible track. Since no large animals lived on Goldilocks, human feet must have made this. *Corey scuffed it coming down to the creek*, she guessed. She breathed deeply and followed the faint markings on the earth, listening for any sign of pursuers.

The baby stirred on her back, whimpering as she woke, and Alice picked up her pace. They soon arrived at the bottom edge of a cliff, which loomed about twelve feet above them. *The cave must be here somewhere*, she realized, even though no hole or opening presented itself. The sun reached down in between the christmas tree needles, dappling the forest floor. Alice spoke to her daughter in as calming a voice as she could command, but the child began to cry and thrash.

Casting about, the young mother saw a dak alight in an enormous christmas tree and noticed a wide bush growing beside it, against the side of the natural wall. She headed toward it, thinking, *If there is enough space between that shrub and the rock face, this will do.*

She swung the carrier off her shoulders, bending over Aria to protect her from scratches. On hands and knees, she dragged herself and the awkward pack under the bush and collapsed beside it, extricating her daughter. A narrow strip of earth lay between the thick brambles and the sheer flat wall of the hill. The branches formed a roof, allowing her to sit upright. "This will have to do," she told the child, who was already rolling over and lifting her head to survey the unfamiliar territory. As Alice glanced in the direction the baby faced, she saw it: a vertical crack just wide enough for a person to wiggle through.

Was this the cave? The headlamp Sami gave her had exhausted its charge and would need several hours of sunlight to replenish itself. Alice decided to nurse and rest before she explored the possibility. She had settled Aria in her lap when the sound of human voices wafted in on the breeze. She strained to discern the words but could only be sure she heard the voices of multiple men. Quietly, she pushed the pack into the crevice in the rock wall and then squeezed in with the baby. Hopefully, the fallen leaves which littered the bare space would conceal any trace of their passing. *Pete or Corey will know to come here,* she reasoned, *but if it's anyone else, this is the safest place to hide.*

The narrow crack, she discovered, widened immediately into a spacious, cool emptiness smelling of old smoke and damp. Alice crawled a yard along the wall before she propped up the pack, leaned against it, and settled again to nurse. As her eyes grew accustomed to the slice of light filtering in through the opening, she noticed the ceiling hovered a good six feet above her. She couldn't see how far back the room extended. Several baskets leaning against the inner wall assured her that this was indeed Corey's cave. They also held hope that he had left some food behind.

The voices, deadened by her move into the hill, came again, louder and clearer. She realized they had probably found the same little path she followed. One man called, "I don't think this is a trail. She must still be on the main route."

"Are you sure?" the second voice sounded farther out.

"Yeah, there's nothing here."

She heard branches breaking close to their hiding place. Even Aria stopped sucking to listen, but she seemed instinctively to understand she had to keep quiet. Alice held her breath until the blundering through the undergrowth ceased. Would they head to Pete's next? *Oh please*, she prayed, *let him be safe at home and not coming to find me.*

Realizing there was nothing she could do to help Pete, the young woman took stock of her situation. As soon as the baby finished nursing, she crawled out through the crevice and found a sunny spot to charge her headlight in. Aria, cooing with excitement, was eager to get down on the ground and explore everything in her reach. Her tired mom sighed and steeled herself to stay awake until nap time. During the strenuous journey, this had proved the hardest task—caring for the child when already exhausted from a night of hiking—but she didn't dare leave her unsupervised for even a moment.

Today, hunger compounded the problem, and her thoughts turned to the baskets she had seen in the cave. Corey might have food stored here, but without light, she couldn't tell. Instead, she considered looking for plants and berries that would halt the gnawing in her stomach. Dinah taught all her students some survival skills before leading them out into the wilderness on field trips, including which species were poisonous and which they could eat in a pinch.

Alice didn't want to get too far from the cavern's entrance, but chanced crawling out from under the bush and searching the area nearby. Aria seemed happy to be carried in her arms, but she sensed she was reaching the end of her strength. *I'll forage somewhere I can keep an eye on her*, she thought.

It was the baby who discovered Corey's garden. Alice set her under a tree and turned her back for a second to examine berries on a bush. When she looked over her shoulder to check on the child, she saw her picking up something bright red from the fallen needles. She rushed to take it from her and, as she pried it out of the tiny fingers, realized the small round object resembled a tomato. As soon as she recognized what Aria had in her chubby hands, she hunted around and found rows of cultivated plants hidden in the tangle of native overgrowth.

Even though the plants had gone untended for at least a third, her hungry eyes quickly picked out more tomatoes, the fronds of carrots, the straight green shoots showing onions, and the broad leaves which signified sweet potatoes hiding in the dirt. Laughing, she popped a few of the ripening fruits into her mouth and began to dig out her dinner. Thankfully, she wouldn't need Dinah's lessons yet.

After a few quiet hours in the garden, they retrieved the headlamp, now charged, and retreated into their cave. "I don't know how long we'll have to stay here, baby girl," Alice told her daughter. "We might as well get comfortable."

The baskets held only cooking utensils and blankets, so finding the vegetable plot had become even more welcome. Near the back of the spacious room, they discovered a firepit, vented by a crack high on the wall. The discovery of some dry wood stacked in the farthest curve of the cave cheered Alice too. She decided that as soon as the sun set, she would risk a small fire. Even if searchers smelled the smoke, the vent leading out the backside of the hill would misdirect their search.

Pete and Corey didn't show up the next day, or the third or fourth. Alice, grateful for a respite from hiking, concentrated on setting up a safe space in the cave to contain her daughter, who was perfecting the ability to roll. She wove a series of low screens out of flexible bush branches stripped of their leaves, which she then configured into a large playpen area. At night, she lay sleeping Aria in this confined space and then anxiously left her to gather more wood and water in the dark.

Even with all the activity that caring for a child in the wilderness required, the young fugitive had occasion to ponder the consequences of her actions. As the days passed, she felt the weight of her decision to step outside the norms of society sap her hope. It was one thing to give up the dream of an Academy career, but her gut told her that Dinah would never forgive her. She had abandoned her lover, and the guilt she suffered at betraying all they had planned together ate at her. Only her daughter's bright face held her steady. The future spread out before her as a vast, unknown plain with no recognizable markers showing her the way forward.

On the fifth day, rummaging through the baskets one more time, Alice found packets of seeds, tied up in bundles. She took them out into the sunshine filtering through the bush which covered the entrance to the cave (their porch, as she came to consider it), and began sorting them. "Look Aria," she murmured to her daughter, who was practicing pushing up on her hands and knees, "here are carrot seeds, and these must be zucchini. I see we have melon and tomato as well. We should replant the garden. What do you think?"

Aria gave a non-committal grunt as she lost her balance and rolled over with a thump on the leaves which carpeted their porch floor. She ignored her mother, struggling to push herself up once more.

Alice laughed. "Right you are, child. I need to be as persistent and hardworking as you are. I'll get to it."

The fact that they were in the second third of the rev leading into Bleak, when little would grow and starvation ran rampant, spurred Alice's resolve. *I'll keep us fed until we move into a village again,* she resolved. *Surely, if we can make it for a third or two, they'll accept me back at Far Meadow.* But the young woman realized if supplies were low, no one would welcome them. And who knew what new dangers the Earth spaceship would bring? Still, the act of planning a garden cheered her.

For the rest of the week, she fashioned small starter pots from moss and good soil and planted the seeds. Some of them she didn't recognize. "Well, babes," she told Aria, "It'll be like a birthday party when these grow up. They'll give us a grand surprise."

She kept her plant nursery hidden behind the bush, knowing the next step—venturing out during daylight to clear the overgrown garden space—would be the most dangerous. She had heard no one else since they arrived but remained on alert. On the eighth day of their sojourn in the cave, she took the risk.

Early in the morning, Alice grabbed the only tool left in the storage baskets, a rusty hand trowel, and stuck it in her pocket. She dragged the woven panels out through the crevice and then, with Aria in her backpack, walked to the garden and set up a play area in the shade where she could monitor her. When plunked down, the baby seemed content to explore the ground within the confines of the enclosure.

Her mother knew that wouldn't last long. She hurried to the nearest edge of the plot and began pulling back the trailing ivy-like plants overgrowing the rows, using the sharp side of the implement to hack at the stems. The work, without gloves and proper tools, had blisters rising on her fingers immediately. When the child started fussing, she took a break and went to entertain her.

"This is going to take a while, baby girl," she told her daughter, distracting her by building pyramids of pinecones for her to knock over. "One step at a time, though."

She had just gone back for a second work session, Aria happily examining sticks and stones in her enclosure, when a dak flew through the trees and over her. Pausing to determine what upset the bird, she heard someone moving through the brush.

Alice ran and scooped the baby out of the playpen, knowing there was no time to hide the screens. She had planned to run back and shelter in the cave if anyone came, but the sounds seemed to come from there. *It might be just another dak,* she hoped, as she fled into the forest. She considered making a wide circle and coming to their cavern home from the other direction, but she halted first to assess the situation. Aria looked content for the moment. *Damn, I should have grabbed the pack,* Alice thought, tiptoeing even farther into the trees and peering through the branches to see who would emerge at the garden site.

She heard him before he appeared in the clearing. "Alice," the voice called, low and urgent, "are you here? It's just me, Sami. Alice?"

Stunned, the young mother stayed where she was and watched as her friend stepped through the trees and halted, taking in the homemade playpen, Aria's backpack, and the disturbed dirt around the garden area. He looked thinner, his brow wrinkled and eyes anxious, bowed under an enormous load on his back. "Alice?" he called again. "Come on out. I'm alone."

"Here," she answered, hoisting the baby onto her hip and pushing through the brush to get to him. "I'm here, Sami."

Then they were hugging, cheek pressed to cheek, laughing in relief at being found.

They sat under the trees, sharing the bounty of bread and fruit he brought. Alice asked him to fill her in on what had happened.

"It's a long story," he said, frowning. "I got word to Pete, but Corey fell ill about a week before you escaped. Pete couldn't leave him. It turned out for the best though, because the dean sent people to investigate him right away and found him consumed with nursing duties, able to say honestly that he hadn't seen you or the child. I was beside myself with worry, but unable to leave without raising suspicions."

"Did they accuse you of hiding me?"

"No. I showed up at the birth center the next morning just like we planned, with the muffins Manuel baked for you. The dean's partner was sure you ran away to keep the baby, but since Manuel, Jamie, and I were all in Seaside, they didn't know where you would go. The midwives told them about Emily and Dion visiting you, so they questioned them. They got the connection to Pete from Emily, as well as me. When none of their leads panned out, Dinah came clean about who you are and what your relationship with her really is. She told the dean your father might have kidnapped you both."

Sami paused, studying her with his mouth pursed. *He's wondering what to edit out,* Alice realized.

"Dean Darryl must have been furious," she said. "Does Dinah still teach at the Academy?"

The young man nodded slowly, looking over the tattered garden. "Yeah, but keeping her position came at a price. He insisted she tell him everything about you she knew. In the end, she revealed Elena was a dreamer, the Bridge to Before."

"No." The denial tumbled out of her mouth before she could think about it. She leaned forward to catch Sami's eye. "No, I don't believe it. Dinah wouldn't give Nainai away. I told her how dangerous it would be for anyone else to find out. Please, Sami, are you sure it wasn't Emily or Manuel who slipped up?"

He allowed her to search his face, his mouth still and his eyes soft and sad. "I was in the room, Alice. I came every day, pretending to help them. We needed to know where they would hunt next. She told him everything on the fifth day, including the fact that the baby hums. I think she hoped he might give up then. Unfortunately, the dean understood the implications right away. He told her that your father wasn't the prime suspect, but that Elena would be the magnet that drew you home."

She felt the blood drain out of her face and her hands clutched Aria tight to disguise their shaking. "The family will disown her,

Sami. She'll have nobody to help her. And the cold is coming soon. If they reject her, they won't share food with her."

"I know." He reached out a hand to steady her shoulder. "Don't panic yet. They're planning to search Far Meadow soon. I hope when they see you aren't there, they'll just leave. No one suspects Pete anymore, and if your family rejects her, we'll move your Nainai in with him."

"But he took in Corey. How can his garden sustain another person?" Alice heard the squeak of desperation in her voice. "God, what have I done?" She started to get to her feet, but Sami pulled her down by her forearm, so she crouched beside him.

"Wait a minute, OK? There's more to the story." He paused long enough for her to refocus and then continued. "Corey died, Alice. Pete tried his best, but he was sick with a cancer, it turns out. We had no medicine for it. It was probably too late, anyway."

"Corey is dead?" The news blew more fog through her already socked-in mind, and she sat back down. "But he seemed fine when we met him."

"It's a shock, but think about it, Alice. At least he didn't die alone. Pete and I were with him at the end. He knew friends surrounded him, that he was home."

Alice allowed the squirming baby to escape her grip for a moment. Sami scooped her up and deposited her in the playpen and then returned to sit next to his friend.

"That's why you took so long to come," she said. "You had to be there with Corey."

"Yeah, we hoped he would tell us where to locate the cave. In the end, he couldn't even speak. I didn't know if I would ever find you."

"So, what do we do now?"

"That's the right question. The dean figures you've found a safe hiding spot and will wait at least a month before you try to contact Elena. As soon as he sends investigators to Far Meadow, I'll ask

Manuel to discover what's happening there. In the meantime, you and Aria need to stay lost."

The young woman looked down at her dirt-streaked hands lying in her lap and noticed that they trembled. "Did I do the right thing, Sami? Are the spaceship and Earth people even real? Am I going crazy?"

"Hey, you're not crazy." He put his hand over her fingers, steadying them. "Remember, Singers have contact with Goldilocks too."

"But I haven't had any more visions. Maybe it was something else. Maybe I hallucinated or dreamed it."

"No," he said, bending to meet her eye. "Listen—what you saw is valid. The Singers came together, and I told them about it, like you shared with me. Alice, they have confirmation from Goldie. The spaceship is coming, and she's returning home with it. Remember, Elena's vision of Before only happened once, and that was genuine. Sometimes that's just how it goes."

She looked up, her eyes bright with unshed tears. "Really? Did she explain it to you guys—how she could leave us? Does this make sense to you?"

Sami gave a short, hard laugh, shaking his head. "No, those who have dreamed of Goldie lately agree about the ship and her arrival, but are at odds about how, why, and when. We got together to figure it out, but I had to come to find you. I left them all arguing over the finer points. They might have it solved by the time I return."

Alice blinked and freed her hand to brush away a stray tear. "Oh, you're leaving?" Her fingers quivered even more.

"Yeah, I have to show up in Seaside, or they'll put a tail on me." He aimed his warm grin at her. "It'll be OK. I'll stay today and tonight, and then Pete will come in a few days. We'll take turns bringing you food and supplies until the dean gives up looking for you and everyone moves on. Until then, I need to keep my guide business going and turn up where people expect to find me."

"Right. That makes sense." Alice looked over at the playpen and her daughter, pushing at the screens, trying to escape. She rose and stepped over to lift the baby out. "Well, let me show you the cave. If you can send a message to Pete, would you tell him I'd appreciate gloves and a hoe? I'll never get this garden in shape without some proper tools."

Sami called Alice to his side as he rearranged his pack the next morning, preparing to hike to Seaside. They had finished a breakfast of leftover stew with a slice of bread and jam from the supplies he brought for her, and she had just settled Aria in for her nap. As she tiptoed over to him, he indicated they should go out on the porch, where they wouldn't disturb the baby.

When he squeezed through the crevice after her with his pack, Alice saw he was holding something else behind him. They sat cross-legged on the fallen leaves, and she asked, "What's that?"

He brought out the flat rectangle of his com-pad and handed it to her. "I'm giving you this until you get yours back."

She gasped and then looked into his warm brown eyes. "But Sami, I can't accept this. They may let you return to school again soon, and you'll need it."

"Look, Alice, you might be in the wilds a long time. I understand it takes most of your energy to care for Aria and survive, but you have other goals to pursue too. You stored your notes on the daks on your jump drive. Add more observations while you're in this area. I've seen several nests around here."

She looked into his earnest face and frowned. "Well, if you get me a notebook and pens, I could do the research longhand and transpose it later. Really, Sami, I'd feel bad taking your com-pad."

She offered the tablet back to him, but he didn't raise his hands to take it. Instead, he sighed and bowed his head.

"There's something else we—the Singers—would like you to do, Alice. It's important to continue studying the daks, but we also need you to read through the rest of Elena's stories. You may find a clue about what to expect when the people of Earth land. There might be information about why Goldie left us and how we can reconnect. Emily and Lucio will research her writings too, but you know your Nainai best. We're hoping you'll share whatever insights you get from her history."

Alice's fingers reached up to touch the pouch around her neck, feeling the familiar bump of the drive inside the soft fabric. On her other hand, the weight of the com-pad increased, and she set it down.

"OK. I'd like to do that. I've been wondering if Nainai could help me figure out what my vision means. I miss her." Tears welled in her eyes. She scowled, averting her glance. "I won't have much time to work on it, though. I hope they're not expecting a lot."

Sami smiled. "Yeah, I know, Alice. Anything you can do will help. Thanks."

He leveraged himself up to his knees, preparing to crawl through the bush. "I should go now. I'll get Pete to bring those gardening tools and some more seeds."

"And any news of Nainai from Far Meadow too please."

"You've got it. Take care, friend." He dove into the branches and was gone.

"You too," she whispered as his heels disappeared and she was alone once more. On their own, her hands found the com-pad, and she hugged it to her breast.

CHAPTER EIGHTEEN

Two days later, Pete showed up with a hoe and shovel on his back and several seed packs in his pockets. He found Alice and the baby by the garden, just as Sami had, but this time, the young fugitive was expecting him and welcomed him right away. She had made some progress in the old plot, but almost wept with joy when he handed her a pair of gloves.

"Hope these fit you, girl. They were Sami's mother's. I discovered them in a box under my bed."

"Pete, you saved my life," she said, pulling on the reinforced gloves over her raw hands. "I'll be able to get twice as much work done now."

He smiled at her enthusiasm. "Well, don't start just yet. Let's sit and talk awhile. It's a long trek from my place to here."

"Oh, of course. We'll go to the cave and fix you something to eat. You can play with Aria on the porch."

She made up a lunch of bread, jam, and nut butter with clear river water to wash it down. As they lounged on the leaves under the bush, the old man tickled the baby with a grass stem. Alice could see the tenderness of his soul coaxed out by the attention of the child. *He must have played with Sami's mom this way when he was young,* she thought. *I bet he was a wonderful father.*

Alice retrieved the baby to nurse her, and Pete lay down on his back, arms folded under his head. Addressing the flicker of sun and shadow above him, the old man said, "Manuel hasn't gone to Far Meadow yet, so I don't have any news to share about your folks or

Elena."

"Sami told me not to expect anything for a while. Dean Darryl is smart enough to realize I wouldn't go there right away." She shifted the baby in her lap. "Do you think Nainai is in danger, Pete?"

He sighed as he looked at the branches. "The coming of the cold season increases pressure on our already shaky society. Yes, Elena's at risk, but so is everyone else. Folks get nasty when they're afraid and search for a scapegoat. Even if they don't banish her from Far Meadow, I hope Manuel can convince her to come to the forest. If the realization that she's a visionary doesn't turn the village against her, just being old might, when food runs low."

"Are people really so awful?" She posed the question, looking down at her daughter's downy head, which weighed heavy with sleep. She looked over at her guest as she laid the child on a blanket. "I guess I should know by now that they are, but I can't quite make myself believe it."

The old man was silent. Then he shifted to sitting and faced her. "It's not that they're awful, Alice. Or not only that—we all have crap inside of us. In my experience, the fear of losing dominion over the future brings meanness to the surface and drowns out the good in people. If folks feel certain they'll be alright, they act in positive, even generous ways."

"When have we ever been the masters of life?" Her voice came out more sarcastic than she intended. "Sorry, I'm a bit out of sorts."

"No, that's a fair question. That's what we should ask ourselves, because you're correct. We're never in control until we give up control."

"And what do you mean by that, oh Wise One?" She smiled so he wouldn't miss the tease in her words.

Pete grinned too, looking her in the eyes. "I mean, we are all going to die. Accept that, and everything else becomes easy."

Later, after the old man left and Aria napped, loneliness overwhelmed Alice again. She took out Sami's com-pad and

inserted the jump drive. The list of all Nainai's stories popped up
on the screen. *Which of you has the answers?* She inquired, scanning
for ones she had not yet read. Then a title caught her attention:
Facing Death. *You and Pete must be on the same wavelength, Nainai,* she
mused. Something here might help me, even if it doesn't shed light
on the situation with Goldie or the spaceship.

She began to read.

Facing Death

(This occurred in the first third of rev fourteen, when I was
five and two-thirds revs old or sixteen in Earth reckoning.)

When I went to the Academy, I was a full third younger
than any of my classmates. I wasn't any brighter than other
children. The fact is, something happened that scared my
fathers and terrified me—an event which convinced them
I would be safer away from my home than with them. Of
course, they were right. I escaped the plague, which took
them all. But a natural illness didn't worry Pops and Da. It
was the villagers themselves.

This occurred two revs after my vision of Earth and
Before, when I met the woman Old Ma had been. Forest Edge
came through the Bleak in Rev 13 hungry and mourning for
the children and elderly who hadn't made it. We sowed the
fields as soon as they thawed out and, while waiting for
harvest, subsisted on vegetables growing more quickly in
the bio-domes.

It should have been a time of hope and good-natured
working together, but the brush with death affected people
deeply. Some of them became hoarders, hiding extra food
in their huts and not sharing with those whose families
were in greater need, as we had always done before. Others
turned to the old religions, trying to bargain with God for

benevolence in exchange for righteous deeds. A significant chunk joined the Gladiators, who promised they could fight their way out of bad times. Everyone felt apprehensive, but Glads obsessed about the future. They couldn't let go of their anxiety or acknowledge it, so fear of scarcity and illness became the central motivator of their lives.

One day, a villager fell ill. Since an epidemic had hit Seaside and Touch Down, the elders monitored any sickness to make sure it wasn't contagious. This man's symptoms eluded diagnosis, and nervousness among the villagers grew. Cautiously, they isolated the sick man in an unused hut. Only his partner and the doctor could enter to tend to him.

On the third evening of his illness, there was a knock on our door, and when Pops answered it, all the Gladiators were there—about thirty people. They wanted me to predict the future. Since I'd had a vision of the Before, they figured I should be able to move the other way on the timeline too. As my father tried to reason with them, saying that visions are gifts which no one can force, the mayor stepped forward and opened his hand. In it lay a fungus shelf—the kind they warned us never to eat. Da and I had joined Pops but, when he saw the offering, Da pushed me behind him, blocking my sight.

Somehow, my parents stood against the crowd and convinced them to go home. I thought that would be the end of it, but Pops made me promise not to leave our hut by myself. For a week I hid inside, only going to the field or the bio-dome with one of my fathers.

The shock of the night visit wore off, though. On a day when the rest of my family went into the village without me, my best friend came by and begged me to come with her into the forest to hunt pink berries. She swore she had seen a patch ripening, although the season still ran cold, and I believed her. Was I imagining my gratification or the joy Davy would have for a little sweetness after first supper? Probably a bit of both. I accompanied my friend, and the moment we stepped into the woods, her dad and several other Gladiators grabbed me.

I can see Rowena's pale face even now, as her father praised her for catching me. She didn't smile or respond to him at all—only kept her eyes on me. I shouted to her to get my Pops and Da until someone stuffed a rag in my mouth. She stood immobile, just staring.

They dragged me to the tool shed on the far side of the village's barley field. There, they sat me in a chair somebody set up in the back between the hoes and rakes. There were no windows, and the five grown men crowding in stared down at me. I felt more anger than fear. After all, I'd known these people all my life. And Pops and Da would come. I trusted my fathers to protect me.

The leader of the Gladiators was a man with four children whose heart-bond had died even before the Bleak. He took out the fungus shelf they had presented a week before. He crouched down beside me and held it out to me in the palm of his hand. "Elena," he said, calm and reasonable, "you're a special girl, a girl who saw the Before. I'm sure you want to help everyone in our village. If you chew this, concentrating on the future, you'll be able to tell us what danger is coming to our town."

"My Pops told me never to touch those," I responded. "Let me go, or you'll be in big trouble."

He didn't like me talking to him that way. He grabbed my chin, forcing me to face him. "Look, kid, if my children had your gift, I'd make them eat the fungus. Your fathers will be happy along with everyone else if you can give us a glimpse of what we are up against this rev."

His gray eyes looked hard as stones, and I felt fear lick at my heart, which made me even angrier. I jerked my head away and screamed until someone slapped me across my face. It was Rowena's dad. I spat at him, and blood came out. A man I couldn't see said, "Bill, maybe this isn't the best idea. If she won't do this willingly, how can we be sure it's a true vision?"

"She'll agree to do it," the leader growled, "because if she doesn't, we'll burn her house down tonight with Armel, Stephan, and Davy all in it. Is that what you prefer, Missy? Do you want us to kill your family? Because—look at me—" and here he grabbed my chin again, forcing me to stare into those flinty eyes. "I'll do it. If I have to, I'll sacrifice your fathers and brother."

At last, the terror that overtook so many neighbors swallowed me too. These men outnumbered my fathers. More villagers supported them than would stand up for us. I couldn't let my family be in danger if there was any way to save them. I still hated that man in front of me, but I understood now what drove him. My heart steeled itself to die. I held out my hand for the fungus.

The dry, spongy curve of growth, which I had often seen sprouting out of christmas tree trunks like a step to nowhere, smelled musty and old. Its pale, wrinkled surface bore flecks of bark and dirt. I blew it clean before setting my teeth on it. Finding it impossible to bite through, I asked for a knife to cut it up. Rowena's father grabbed it out of my hand and, with his carving blade, shaved it into several long, thin strips. I put one into my mouth and chewed and chewed and chewed. The men watched without comment, and someone handed me a water bottle. I took a swig, swishing the liquid around the lump, but when I swallowed, I choked on the fibrous mass.

"Spit it out and have some more." The man who seemed most knowledgeable about the fungus held out his handkerchief for the masticated mess.

"How much should she take?" the leader asked.

"Don't know for sure. Most adults who use it chew the whole thing."

They put another long strip in my hand, and I stuck it in my mouth with a snarl. *These guys don't understand what they're doing,* I realized. *They probably got the wrong fungus, and nothing will happen to me at all.* I chomped it with fury, looking into each of the men's faces, determined to remember who forced this on me: Rowena's dad, a middling, round man with reddish hair like his daughter and a face flushed with zeal; the leader, Bill, with his gray pebble eyes, who lived across the outer circle from us, puffed up with authority and importance; little Bobby's father, who always played ball with the children and now would not meet my gaze; the mayor's son, barely an adult—nervous and pale with excitement; and a stranger, dark and tall—he must have been from Near Meadow, twenty miles east of Forest Edge—who observed me as if I were a mere bilbug he was experimenting on. My glare told them all they would pay. Bobby's dad and the mayor's boy backed up a bit. The boss gave me more water.

As I swallowed this second dose of fungus juice, my body heated, and my eyelids drooped down on their own. The stranger from Near Meadow bent over me.

"Stay awake, Elena," he commanded. "Concentrate on the future. Think about what's coming, coming, coming, coming."

Why did his voice echo like that? I forced my eyes open to look at him. His face, so close to mine, startled me. As I tried to focus, his bulbous nose spread over his cheeks and his sharp green eyes swam up over his forehead. Instead of spitting at him as I had planned to do, I screamed. He continued to melt in front of me, the colors and shape of his skin, hair, and clothes wavering and running into each other. I tore my gaze away to beseech for help and saw them all lengthening, thinning out, folding in on each other, and melting into a gray haze.

I drew as far away from them as I could, the back of the chair digging into my shoulders. My movement seemed to push them in the opposite direction. As I watched, they all siphoned away, like liquid going down a funnel. Nothing stood behind them—and I mean nothingness, a darkness so complete I thought, *this must be Death.*

I realized a vision had overtaken me, but not the same as the Before experience. My heart pounded. I couldn't catch my breath. The fear I felt for my family turned into terror for me.

I forced myself to look deep into the nothingness. *If I die,* I figured, *I want to see where I go.* As I stared, I found I could pick out a tiny dot of silver. Somehow, I understood the men had funneled down there—except I also perceived I had moved, while they had stayed in the present...which was that point of light. The impenetrable blackness I saw was not nothing. It contained everything—every color, every shape, every movement and experience of life. That's why it was so dense it could only look black. At that moment, I heard a voice from outside, in the darkness. It murmured, "All is well. Stay in Eternity, where you are safe. Soon, your fathers will take you back to the Now."

I clutched onto that promise for dear life. I sensed my hands gripping the old chair. The smell of urine and sweat fogged the air, but I wasn't there. I embraced the darkness and the peace of that space and told myself to wait. The Gladiators wanted me to see the future. They couldn't comprehend that no future exists there. Only the bright point of Now abides in the dark everything that held me. It swallowed even the Before.

I hid in Eternity and waited.

Then, I felt a frigid breath of fresh air as the door crashed open, and angry voices boomed around me. The ground swelled and dipped with fury, but I hung onto the darkness. I felt strong arms lift me and then knew nothing for a long time.

I learned later that Rowena had gone into the village and found my fathers. She didn't see where they were taking me, though, so it took a while to find me. When I woke from my trance, Da held me as I puked and puked and puked some more. Days passed before I could hold down even broth. I remember Pops standing in the doorway, looking small and helpless, while Da used all his skill and knowledge of medicine to pull me back from the edge of death.

The thing is, I didn't know if I wanted to return. Eternity, that blackness—packed with life but empty of conflict and violence—enticed me. The strife and worry which had defined living for so long was gone. It's hard to explain even now, but I no longer feared dying. I yearned for completeness. When I reached to join fully with this feeling, though, the voice I'd heard before said, "Not yet. You are needed in the present." I listened, but it took me a week to accept. Once I came back, I gained strength and then some weight—and then, somehow, Pops arranged to have me accepted at the Academy.

Pops and Da never inquired about my vision. Some villagers showed up, asking if the fungus worked, hoping I could make predictions, but my parents wouldn't even speak to them. I told my fathers about it anyway, one night before I left.

"Is there truth in what I saw?" I asked them. "It felt so different from the Before experience, but it still seemed right."

Pops shrugged. "I don't know, Laney. I only understand we almost lost you. No vision is worth that risk."

Da said nothing for a while, humming into his beard as he thought. Finally, he spoke. "I'm surprised you are with us today, child. I wonder if what you experienced is valid, not because of the fungus, but despite it. Perhaps God sent Goldie to reach you and keep you safe in this crisis, in a way we don't understand. If that's what happened, then what you saw is true, but it may be beyond our comprehension."

This made sense, but it scared me too. I didn't tell anyone else about the experience. Just remembering the violence those men used on me brought back panic for years. It's only been since Jay died that I've taken this memory out and looked at it again. I believe this was a true vision. It comforts me to know that soon I will go to that deep, dark everything that is Eternity and be at home there.

Aria, sleeping in a nest of pine needles under the porch bush, rolled her head and issued a mewling cry as her mother finished reading the last sentence of Elena's story. Shifting to look at the baby, noting how she yawned and returned to breathing deeply, Alice calculated she had another few minutes before the child awakened.

Nainai's acceptance of her impending death shook Alice to her core, and she reached out to the embodied affirmation of life her daughter represented, stroking the rounded curve of her tummy. If she didn't have this child to protect and nurture, would the fulfillment of Eternity tempt her? The description of the darkness in which everything existed, every conflict ended, every break in relationship resolved, watered some unknown seed deep in her soul, which took root and grew as a desire for...Alice couldn't articulate what it made her yearn for, but she sensed the tears in her eyes had gathered for herself and not for her elderly aunt.

She sighed. Something in Elena's story reminded her of her own vision. Hers wasn't such a difficult glimpse into the beyond. Unlike Nainai, she had not traveled back to Before or into Eternity. Compared to those adventures, her own waking dream was a hop across a few million miles of space to experience Earth travelers in their present time.

Then she realized: Goldilocks had spoken to them both—to Nainai in Eternity and to her in the Now but far away. That's the shared element, but what did it mean? Did Goldie exist in both realities at once? Was she unbounded by the present in a way that restricted humans rarely experienced? And, if true, what difference did it make to those struggling to survive, stuck in time?

"Oh Nainai, I wish you were here to talk to about this," Alice sighed, speaking to the surrounding emptiness. Then she considered: *Maybe I'm supposed to meet with Nainai in person.* Her eyes sought her sleeping daughter. *But how can I leave Aria? I haven't even weaned her yet.*

They had come so far. How could they discover whatever their world wanted them to find out? But leaving the child was out of the question. If the old woman came to Pete's cabin, could she sneak in with the baby and contact her there?

A plan formed in the recesses of Alice's brain. When the baby's eyes flickered open five minutes later, she found her mother bent over her notebook, furiously writing. "How would you like to see our Nainai, little girl?" Alice asked her.

She had the message ready to go when Manuel stopped by in a week. He stepped across the stream into her glade early in the morning, bringing gifts (diapers and biscuits for Aria, bread and beans for Alice). Although his plan was to continue on to Pete's before heading up to Far Meadow, he couldn't resist sitting for a while, swapping news and playing with the baby.

"Dion wants to have another child when the semester is over," he told her. "This time she'll keep it and raise it with me."

"I'm so glad her parents allowed you to be together. That's like a miracle."

"Your disappearance convinced them to let us bond. They didn't want her to get desperate and run away too. She had to promise she would finish her course of study at the Academy, though. She's studying to become a doctor, with a focus on women and children."

"I can see that in her. She helped me through my pregnancy. So, you're planning to settle in Seaside, near her parents?"

"That's what they prefer. We're letting them presume that's going to happen." The young man looked into the trees as he admitted this. "We realize we need to get away, though. I've got my work with Sami, leading scientific expeditions, and we hope to expand that to include people who want to explore the parts of Goldilocks no one's seen yet. I have friends who are considering dropping off the grid to live in the wilderness. Perhaps Dion and I will become settlers with them."

Alice thought of the willowy dark beauty whose highest aspiration, before she met the Wood Lawn brothers, had been to get through school with the least effort possible. Her friend's growth inspired her. "I wish you could tell Dion that Aria and I are alright."

"Yeah, so do I." Manuel shook his head, frowning. "She misses you. I'm afraid she, like most everyone else, thinks you're lying dead somewhere. But it's safer for her to know nothing."

Alice nodded, fighting back tears. Dion's friendship had been precious to her. "Well, maybe when you start a new village on the other side of the planet, Aria and I can come." Her smile was lopsided as she imagined all of them—Dion, Manuel, Jamie, Sami, and her—living somewhere far away from the pain and worry of the present. Then she sighed, reached into her pocket, and took out a tightly folded sheet of notebook paper.

"When you get to Far Meadow, I realize you're just supposed to assess the situation and not bring attention to yourself. But do you think you could deliver this to my Nainai?"

Manuel's dark brows drew together, and he scowled. "I don't know, Alice. If Dean Darryl's guys are there and assume I've got something to do with your disappearance, they may frisk me. They don't need much of an excuse to suspect anyone from the outback. If they find a message from you, well...."

"Yeah, I thought of that. Here—I'll show you what's on it." She unfolded the paper.

> *A Riddle for Eternity:*
> *Close to death but still alive*
> *Bridging over the great divide*
> *Black and dense and out of time*
> *yet still connected, life divine.*
> *Who can say where we have gone?*
> *What will finally bring us home?*

Manuel frowned and read the passage twice. "So, what does this mean?" he said. "I don't get it, Alice."

"Right—and neither will anyone else, except for Nainai. She'll understand. If you show her the poem and then suggest she travel to Pete's, she'll go. If all else fails, give her this." From her hip pocket, Alice brought out a tiny bronze feather. "It's from a dak. People pick them up all the time. There's nothing suspicious about you having one stuck in your clothing somewhere. After all, you're a forest guide."

The young man scanned her earnest face, still frowning. "Do you really want her to leave her home, Alice? Sami told me she's in her twenty-ninth rev. How can she make the journey? Nobody's going to lend me a hummie to drive her to Pete's."

Her head bowed for a moment, copper hair hiding her eyes.

When she looked up at him again, they brimmed with tears. "I don't know what else to do, Manuel. I'm so afraid she'll get ousted when there's no one there to help her. At least this way, you can accompany her. And I admit I need her. I can't figure out what's happening. She's the only person who might understand."

He blew out a sigh of acceptance as she turned away to wipe her tears. "I'll do my best to bring her back to the cabin. I'll tell Pete the plan when I pass through and have him make up the guest room. But Alice, listen: Don't come out of hiding until we signal the coast is clear. OK?"

"Yep. There's more than enough to keep me busy here."

The young man gave another gentle squeeze to the baby, who had pulled herself over him to steal the biscuits lying out for their snack, and then lumbered to his feet. "At least my pack's a lot lighter now," he said, his eyes twinkling.

Alice hoisted Aria onto her hip as she rose to say goodbye. "One more thing: There is someone in Far Meadow you can trust. If you need a hummie or any other help, look for Micah. Nainai always depended on him, and he stood up for me too, when I needed it."

"Micah—right. Got it. See you soon."

A quick hug and he strode off into the trees, leaving mother and child looking after him.

She dreamed that night: fog, a wind that didn't touch her, and someone singing in the distance—somebody she had to find. Alice recognized the dream described to her by the Singers. She couldn't move, so she concentrated on the music. Something about it seemed familiar, and she focused, holding her breath. There were lyrics. Did anyone speak in the dream that others had? She didn't think so. But, just on the edge of comprehension, she heard words in the melody.

And then she knew: The words were her own. Goldie sang the riddle poem she had sent to Nainai. The revelation shocked her awake. In the dark womb of the cave, she curled around Aria and whispered in her ear, "We're not alone, baby girl. We're not alone anymore."

CHAPTER NINETEEN

Sami returned to Alice just a week after Manuel passed through to Far Meadow. She heard him whistling a few dak-like notes in the pattern they agreed on and peeked from under the bush hiding the cave entrance.

"Hey, come on in. You're out late. Aria and I are making first supper, but there's plenty for you too."

He bent down to crawl into the porch area, shoving his backpack before him. As soon as his face cleared the brush, he clearly caught the fragrance of smoke and vegetable stew.

"Oh man, that smells great. I didn't realize how hungry I am, but I hope the smell doesn't travel far. It's a dead giveaway that someone's camped out here."

"I only light the fire at sunset, when I'm sure no one is hiking through." She smiled at him as he crawled over to the playpen and lifted Aria out for a hug. "You stay out here and keep her occupied while I finish dinner. It'll be dark soon, but it's nice out here under the bush. I'll bring the lantern."

Sheltered from the wind, the porch proved a lovely alfresco dining area. As they finished the meal, Alice took Aria on her lap to feed her bits of zucchini. Sami asked, "When did she start eating solid food? She was just nursing when we left Seaside."

Alice chuckled, but the corners of her mouth drew down. "It's only a month, but babies change quickly. I guess we do, too."

"Yeah." Sami studied her. "Manuel's back from Far Meadow already, and I have news to share. Let's get the baby to sleep and

271

talk about it."

They squeezed through the opening to the cave. While Alice settled her daughter down on a bed fashioned of dried grass and a soft blanket enclosed by the playpen panels, Sami eyed her other improvements: another sleeping nest close by Aria's, mats woven of reeds, the firepit encircled by rocks, and fragrant herbs hanging from lines strung high on the ceiling.

"You've made the place homey," he said as she settled on a mat next to him by the dying embers.

This time, a genuine smile lit her face. "Thanks. It's been fun. You know, Manuel told me you guys had a dream of becoming settlers in places on Goldilocks that people haven't explored yet. I imagine it would be like this, only better with partners to help."

"Yeah, it's a lot of work for just one person."

Alice noted his voice held genuine admiration, and she felt a flush of gratitude. "Well, keeping busy makes it easier to be away from all my friends and the Academy." She paused, looking into the glowing embers. "My life might be like this for a long time. Who knows?"

Sami nodded, then took a jump drive out of his pocket and handed it to her. "Elena made it to Pete's, Alice. She wrote what happened in her journal and sent a copy for you. Why don't you look at it and then we can decide what to do."

"She's at the cabin? Why didn't you say so, for goodness' sake? Is she OK?" The young woman jumped up to get her com-pad even as she peppered him with questions.

"If I had told you right away, I wouldn't have gotten dinner. Just read her account, and then I'll tell you everything else I know."

She settled back down with him, inserting the drive, the screen lighting up her face as she began scanning the latest entry. She was aware of the young man scrutinizing her as she read, but soon lost awareness of him as she immersed herself in Nainai's writing.

Last Story

(This is happening in rev thirty-eight, and I am twenty-nine revs old, eighty-nine years in Earth reckoning.)

Eventually, your stories catch up to you. I've written about the past for so long, I never thought I'd have anything to say about the present. What's an ancient woman like me know about the new and now, with one foot already standing in Eternity? And yet, here I am—ready to write the tale of what happened to me in the last few days.

It started when Nettie brought over first supper on Monday, full of the news that Dinah Seaside was back in town. We both hoped she would tell us about Alice and the baby, so I sent the girl right home to ask her parents if they had talked to her. As Nettie opened my door to leave, Dinah stood there, hand raised to knock. Of course, I invited her in and asked her to sit down and eat. She sat but refused food or drink. She wanted to talk to me alone, so I shooed my niece out, knowing she would run to get her folks.

I remembered Dinah as an intense, serious scientist. It hadn't surprised me when Alice and she hooked up. They both have a fierce quality about them. But today, the Academy professor seemed even more focused than I recalled. Her sharp green eyes darted around my room as if looking for something. When the door slammed shut behind the girl, she leaned forward, her elbows on the table, and fixed me with a steady gaze. She got right to the point.

"Elena Far Meadow, we don't have much time. I told the mayor I would speak to you first, but I have to appear to interview others in the village, too. I'm here to find out what's happened to Alice and her baby."

"Really? We hoped you had news for us about them."

"You have long associated with Singers, and I know you are a dreamer. Alice spoke to me about your vision of the Before. I also realize how much she depended on you, respected your opinions. I believe you convinced her to leave with the child, and you're hiding them." She sat back with the air of one who has delivered an indisputable truth. Her intense gaze dared me to disagree.

I poured myself a cup of tea from the pot Nettie had set to steep and took a sip. Then I said, "It's good to hear that you believe they are alive. They've been gone for four weeks now, right? The others from the Academy thought they died in the forest."

"You know where they are," Dinah hissed. "If you don't tell me, there'll be repercussions."

I drank some more tea, assessing the threat she threw at me. "I wonder why you think Alice ran away and why I would have encouraged her. If she spoke to you about me, she would have told you I supported her ambitions at school. Why would I suggest she do the one thing that threatened her career there?"

"She was besotted with that child." For the first time since she entered my house, the professor mask cracked a bit, and in her frown, I saw a tremble on her lips. "She didn't want to give it up. After everything I did for her, she threw it all away for that kid."

"Why did she have to choose between you and her child, Dinah? Why didn't she just exercise her right of motherhood?"

The wiry woman, unable to contain her energy, stood and paced around my small front room. "You hicks in the outback may still play those games, but in the cities, especially when a girl bonds with an important man like Darryl, contracts must be kept. And I set up that first-bond. My job's on the line if we don't get the baby back."

"What? Will the dean fire you?"

She shook her head. "No, I'm tenured, but he made it pretty clear that there'll be no promotions and no money for research in my area if I don't fix this. And Alice should have known her actions would undermine me. I told her over and over how politically charged the Academy is. God, she's a selfish bitch."

When she slurred Alice in that way, I knew she had disconnected from my niece. Two questions popped into my mind: First, did Alice realize her love affair was over? And second, how did Dinah plan to betray her? The answer to the last became clear quickly. I was looking into my mug, thinking, when suddenly she slammed her palms on the table and leaned forward, her face nearly touching mine.

"Look, old lady," she said, her eyes sparking, "you may remember the settlers and their fantasy of talking to the planet, but that's over. No one wants a child who sings. The sooner Alice faces that fact and gives the kid to the dean, the better. He can get it help. She can't do anything for it now."

I looked into her grim face. "The child sings?"

She straightened up. "Hums. Alice must have told you about it. She tried to cure it with breastfeeding, but it didn't grow out of it."

"I see."

"I'm sure you do," Dinah sneered. "In fact, I'm betting you encouraged her to let her baby keep humming. That's why she ran away, isn't it? So the kid could learn to sing. Where did you tell her to go?"

I sighed and took another sip of tea.

"OK, this is what we're going to do, old woman." The professor sat down facing me, her hands gripping each other on the table. They reminded me of Alice's fingers, rough and callused with dirt in her knuckle creases from working in the forest and fields. I focused my eyes on them, reminding myself that Alice loved this person deeply, even if Dinah no longer returned that feeling. She leaned closer, and I could smell her sweat, sharp with aggression and fear.

"I'm staying in this godforsaken village another day, interviewing anyone who might know anything about Alice's hiding place. If I don't find out where she is by tomorrow night after first supper, I'll come back here, and you will tell me where she and the baby are. Do you understand?"

I looked at her but said nothing. She didn't want the truth, after all. Better to arrive at the punch line—which she did quickly.

"If you don't, I'll share your history with everyone here. I'll convince them you're a Singer and that you and your mystic friends spirited the girl and her baby away with promises of peace and love, only to have them get lost in the forest and perish. They'll believe Alice's death is your fault. And you know the penalty for murder: They'll kick you out of the village to die of starvation and cold."

I nodded. She probably had the villagers pegged. The harvest hadn't been great, and the dark season approached. They wouldn't need too much convincing to get rid of an unproductive crone, especially for a righteous reason.

But she wasn't quite done.

"And if you don't care about yourself, Elena Far Meadow, consider this: I'll make sure that no child of this village ever gets into the Academy again. The faculty will never send another teacher or scientist to this place, which caused the death of the dean's baby. Your home shall become the most isolated and ignorant of the outback towns, doomed to extinction by the end of Bleak."

Then she stood, knocking over her chair, and stomped

out of my house, slamming the door behind her.

When Nettie returned half an hour later with her father and mother, I told them only that Dinah wanted help in finding Alice. The rumor already had reached them that the mayor set the professor up in one of the common rooms to interview villagers. Janelle took heart in this development, concluding, as I had, that it meant she thought Alice and her child still lived. They hurried away to tell her everything they knew about their daughter.

My niece lingered long enough to share that a student, a young woman about Alice's age, accompanied Dinah to record her findings. "Do you think she's already taken another lover, Nainai? I saw them walking toward the community room, and she had her arm around this girl's shoulders, just like she sometimes walked with Alice." Her brow wrinkled as she tried to figure out this development.

"They were not heart-bonded, Nettie. Dinah is free to find love elsewhere since your sister left. But don't jump to conclusions, OK? We don't yet understand what happened or how Alice feels about Dinah now."

Nettie looked down at the floor. "Pa thinks if they find her, Alice will come home and bond with Micah. He hopes that's what happens."

I chuckled and lifted her chin so she gazed into my eyes. "And how did that work last time he tried to make your sister do what she didn't want to do?"

The girl rewarded me with a grin, and then I sent her away. I had so much to think about....

I sleep fitfully since Jay died—and get up often to relieve my old, cranky bladder. That night, I retired early, worn out with worry, and got up before the Rose Moon set. I noticed her round face shining through my window as I shuffled back to bed. When I lay down, I noticed a warmth run over my body from head to foot, as if someone had drawn a blanket over me the wrong way down. I wondered if I was coming down with an illness, but the heat felt good and eased my joints. I fell into a deep sleep and, for the first time, dreamed the dream of the settlers. This is how it went:

I found myself standing in the middle of a cloud, solid earth under my feet. A wind blew. It sounded like a real gale, fierce and insistent, but the surrounding fog never moved, and it disturbed neither my clothing nor hair in the least. Under the storm, I heard a lonely voice singing. I knew I had to reach the singer, but I couldn't move a muscle. All I could do was listen, so I put all my energy into hearing that song. And as I focused, words seemed to emerge, carried by the notes, as a message to my ears. Over and over, the same verse wove through the haunting music:

> *Close to death, but still alive,*
> *Bridging over the great divide,*
> *Black and dense and out of time*
> *yet still connected, life divine.*
> *Who can say where we have gone?*
> *What will finally bring us home?*

When I woke from the dream, the cold light of dawn had already filtered through my window. I got up immediately to record the details. As I did, I realized something had happened differently in this version. Long ago, I read the first colonists' journals and had also listened to several Singers describe this signature vision from Goldilocks. Now, I wracked my mind to remember if I had ever encountered specific lyrics. *Never*, I thought. The music was sung, but never understood. Why did I hear words which seemed directed at me? The reference to bridging reminded me of my initial out-of-body experience when I Bridged to Before. The images of black, dense, out of time, and life and death could all refer to my incident with a fungus-induced vision of Eternity. Was Goldilocks trying to contact me specifically?

The more I studied the dream, the more I felt called to act. I had no idea what to do, though. And so I waited, all my senses tuned to what might reveal the dream's meaning.

It wasn't long before I discovered the action Goldie required.

As I sat down to my first cup of tea, a soft knock sounded on my door. Before I could rise, a young man I had never seen before stuck his head in and said in a quiet voice, "Elena Far Meadow, I'm sorry to show up so early, but I have to talk to you before anyone else is awake. May I come in?"

I nodded, and he slipped in, shutting the door behind him.

"Sit and have some tea." I reached another mug off the shelf. "No one will drop by for at least an hour."

He sat down and accepted my hospitality, even as he fidgeted to find something in his pocket. As I handed him the cup, he put a tightly folded piece of paper on the table in front of him.

"I'm Manuel Wood Lawn," he said. "We haven't met before, but I'm a friend of Pete's. I've heard a lot about you. Pete and some friends—they're worried about you."

I looked at him over the rim of my mug. He had a solid build, with big, square hands. I doubted he feared any physical confrontation, and yet his tight lips and flitting eyes telegraphed nervousness.

"Are they? I wonder why."

"You realize that Dinah Seaside is here asking questions about Alice, right? Pete suspects she knows you're a Bridge. He thinks she may, well, hurt you."

"Ah, and why would an Academy professor want to harm me?"

He set his tea down and bit his lip, studying me now. "She'll try to force you to tell her where Alice and the baby are."

"I see." I put down my cup too and nodded. "You're right. That's exactly what she wanted last night. And she threatened me. But I don't know where my niece and her child are, so...I guess whatever Dinah's going to do, she'll do."

At the mention of the professor's visit, Manuel's face drained of color.

"She's already been here?"

"Yes, and she's coming back tonight. If I won't give the answers she wants, she'll accuse me in public of luring Alice to her death. She was quite clear about her intention."

Manuel's gaze darted around the room. "I have to get you out now. There's no time to waste."

I reached out to pat his hand, trying to calm him. "Young man, where can I escape this dilemma? I'm an old woman. If I leave, the result will be the same as the villagers casting me out: I'll die of cold or starvation in the woods."

"No, you have to survive. We'll go to Pete's. He wants you to come stay with him. He has enough food." His eyes widened as he pleaded with me.

"Stop and think about this," I insisted. "I haven't long to live, anyway. If Dinah Seaside tells everyone I convinced Alice to run away, which resulted in her and the baby's death, then people will quit looking for them. That's the best thing that could happen to my dear niece. What better way for me to die than by helping her?"

I smiled into his wild eyes, willing him to be reassured. He took a deep breath and pushed the bit of folded paper toward me. I had overlooked it during our conversation, but accepted it now and eased it apart, flattening it on the table so I could read it. My confident smile faded. The words in that note—they were the same words as in Goldie's music in last night's dream. The vision held true.

I looked up to scan his face for answers and saw him digging into his pocket again. This time, he pulled out a tiny, bedraggled dak feather and laid it beside the paper.

"She needs you," he said.

And that is why, Alice, I'm sitting in Micah's bedroom with Manuel. This is the best scheme we could devise. We took only my computer and coat, hurrying over here before anyone else was up. We roused Micah out of bed and explained the situation. Later this morning, he plans to borrow the town hummie to drive to Seaside for fresh fish. Manuel and I will hide in the back. Your father is keeping Nettie busy in the fields, so she won't be by until first supper. We should be out of reach before Dinah even discovers I'm gone. If all goes well, we'll part with Micah at the rest stop and I'll make my way to Pete's with Manuel's help from there. If you're reading this, dear girl, then our plan succeeded, and I'll see you in person soon. May God grant it. Together we'll figure out: "What will finally bring us home?"

Alice sat looking at the screen, concentrating on breathing. The fire's last flames flickered out, and Sami rose to feed it some small branches, blowing it to life again. His back toward her, he said, "It's a lot to take in, isn't it?"

"Yeah." She wiped a tear off her cheek and then faced him with a smile as he settled down. "Her dream, Sami. I had the same one on the same night. Goldie used my words as her lyrics. It must be real, right? Goldie's communicating with both of us."

"You aren't the only ones. I dreamed it last Monday too. In fact, the Singers are gathering soon to talk about it and your vision of the spacecraft. They'd like you to come, if it's possible."

Alice bit her lip. "Will they gather at Pete's? How can we be sure it's safe?"

Sami shook his head, stray curls bouncing on his forehead. "That's a problem. Manuel's gone back to Seaside. He'll let us know if the dean buys Dinah's assertion that you and the child are dead. We'll have to lie low until they give up the search, which worries some Singers. The older ones felt an urgency in the message, but it may be months before it feels safe to gather."

"Months." She sighed, rocking her body back and forth. "I can't wait even another week to see Nainai, Sami. I'm the one who got her into this situation. This has to be worth something. I need her to help me figure out what my vision means, what Goldie wants us to do." Tears gathered in her eyes again, and she bit down hard, trying to contain them.

He touched her knee to quiet her, and Alice concentrated on his long brown fingers. She took a breath and laid her scratched and blistered hand on his, hanging on for balance, for life.

"You're right," he said, his voice steady. "That's why I came— so you can see her as soon as possible. But Alice," he paused and turned his palm up to hold her hand in a warm clasp, "I have to tell you that Elena's not well. Pete thinks she suffered a stroke the night she got to his hut."

"A stroke?"

"Yeah, she can't walk now, and it paralyzed half her face. Her mind's all there, though. We can communicate with her. It's just," he leaned in and, with his free fingers, brushed back a stray strand of her hair, letting his palm linger on her cheek, "we don't think she has much time left with us, dear."

"Oh no, no, no. Sami, I've got to go right now." Only his hand holding hers kept her from jumping up.

"Yes, you do. You'll leave as soon as possible."

"But what about Aria? Will it be dangerous? Do you think the dean will search for Nainai at Pete's?"

"Take a breath, Alice." His thumb brushed away a tear that refused to be contained. "I need you to listen and decide. It might be risky. Several Singers are camping out around the paths leading into Pete's meadow. They're keeping an eye out for anyone from the Academy. We can't move Elena, though. If the dean's accomplices find her, I don't think they'll do anything. She's obviously ill, and she'll pretend she can't speak. But it's a different case with you and the baby.

"Pete and I came up with two plans. I can stay here and look after Aria for a few days, if you think it's unsafe to take her with you. It can't be for long—I have to get back to Seaside, or people will become suspicious. Also, I only have three days' worth of formula."

"No, no—I can't leave her here, Sami." Her voice shook as she clutched his hand. "That's the one thing I'm sure of—we have to stay together."

Sami's mouth quirked up into a half smile. "I told Pete you wouldn't go for that. Plan B is to have me take you and Aria to the cabin. You'll talk with Elena, see if you can figure out what's going on with Goldie, and then I'll bring you back. Hopefully, if anyone comes searching for you, we'll have enough warning to get you into the forest before they know you're there."

"OK," she nodded, looking around the shadowy cave. "I guess I won't need anything but food for the road, right? Everything else should be safe here."

"Yeah, we'll leave after first supper tomorrow and walk through the night. That way, we'll avoid anyone else on the path. We'll get to Pete's at sunrise. Does Aria still fit in her backpack?"

"Well, just barely." She looked up at him, eyes wide and adrenaline coursing through her body. "Why don't we go tonight, Sami? I'll make some sandwiches, and we'll take off now."

"Alice, I've been up two nights straight and made the trip out here in record time. I'm dead on my feet. We'll be safer if I get some rest, so I can be alert tomorrow."

"Oh God, of course. I'm sorry. You're probably ready to crash." She looked him in the face, noticing the dark half-moons under his eyes. "Why don't you take my bed, Sami? I'm too wired to lie down for a while, anyway."

The young man sighed. "I am tired, but where will you sleep? I can sack out by the fire."

"No, use the bed. I'll lie down with Aria soon."

He frowned as if he might argue, but then got to his feet. "Don't stay up all night. I'll need you to help me wear out that little girl tomorrow, so she'll nap through most of the trip." He bent to kiss her on her forehead. "It's going to be OK, Alice. Elena will hang on for you."

Alice nodded and then bowed her head to read again the story of Nainai's ordeal.

CHAPTER TWENTY

They hit the trail the next day as the sun set. They'd eaten first supper early, and Aria, perched on Sami's back, showed no signs of sleeping on this exciting adventure. For fifteen minutes, she swiveled her head, taking in the unfamiliar landscape with delight. Then, as she grew bored and fussy, her mother tickled her from behind with grass stems, keeping her occupied and relatively quiet. As the light faded in the shade of the christmas trees, though, neither adult worried too much about other travelers.

After a couple of hours of walking, the baby whined, and they took a break so Alice could nurse her. The tired mother leaned her back against a trunk not far off the path and cuddled her daughter close as she fed, while Sami dug around in the pack for a snack of nuts and berries. He settled next to them and offered a handful.

"Thanks. Nursing makes me ravenous." She smiled down at the child, just visible in the gathering darkness. After a pause in which both adults satisfied their hunger, she said, "You're putting yourself at risk, helping me again. I guess it's a recurring theme in our relationship. I want you to know how much I appreciate it."

When he didn't respond right away, she turned her head to look at him beside her. He wasn't facing her. Instead, he gazed straight ahead toward the path. "Sami?"

The young man cleared his throat and murmured, "I would do anything for you, Alice."

She directed her eyes downward. Aria had detached, so she adjusted the child to nurse her other breast before hazarding a comment. Still watching her daughter, she said, "You're the best friend I have."

They sat awhile in silence, true darkness settling on them, and then Sami sighed. "There's something I want to ask you, but don't answer if you'd rather not."

His voice sounded carefully neutral. She stared at him, straining to see his expression. "OK. Shoot."

"I realize you're upset about Elena being sick and having to leave her home, but you haven't said a word about Dinah. Did you two break up? Did you know she would threaten your Nainai like that?"

High in the tree they leaned against, a dak landed, and branches rustled. Alice tilted her head back against the trunk, disregarding the sap that would mat her hair, and looked up. Although she couldn't see the creature, just knowing it nestled there above her in the darkness, with the warm, spiced smell of the forest enveloping her, broke something open in her heart. The tears she refused to shed last night now spilled down her cheeks.

When she trusted her voice not to crack, she cleared her throat. "She wanted nothing to do with the baby, Sami. I told her about the humming, and she warned me to hide it and hand her over. So, I guess, by choosing Aria instead of her, I ended our bond. Until yesterday, I hoped we might still patch it up, eventually." She wiped her face dry. "If I'm honest, as soon as I joined her in Seaside, the relationship seemed different—off somehow. I fantasized about us living together, having adventures, sharing what we learned, being close. What it came down to, though, was good sex once in a while. Maybe she never shared my vision of our future. I don't know if the Dinah I loved really existed at all."

Aria stirred, her head rolling back with a contented sigh, eyelids closed. Her mother wiped a drool of milk off the child's chin and pulled her shirt down. "I'm angry about her betrayal, but furious at myself for being so foolish."

She heard Sami shift beside her and saw the glint of his eyes as he turned toward her.

"Hey, everyone screws up their first love affair. Sometime I'll tell you about mine—or, better yet, about Manuel's. His crashed spectacularly. "

"Yeah?" She chuckled and then sighed. "Did he expose his family and friends to danger and end up raising a kid on his own in a cave?"

"Well, you have a unique storyline, but my point—that you're inexperienced at deep relationships and allowed to make mistakes a couple of times—stands. That's one reason the settlers established the bond system."

"I learned that too, but Sami—Dinah and I were supposed to be forever. I felt so sure of that. She chose my first-bond partner. She promised to wait for me. When I had Aria, I thought she would love and protect her too. And I was wrong." The tears dropped hot on her shirt, and she scrubbed her eyes. "You're a better friend to me than Dinah ever was. But since I was mistaken about her, I could be deluded about everything." She gulped back a sob. "How can I tell who I am anymore?"

His hand found her damp fingers and squeezed them. "Hey, life gives us so many more choices than just right or wrong. Your actions led you down unexpected paths, but you've been true to who you are."

She left her hand in his. "What do you mean?"

He took a deep breath and let it out.

"OK, tell me who you think you are. What defines you as Alice?"

"What defines me?"

"Yeah, when you consider yourself, what do you like and want to keep? What did you depend on in yourself that you can't trust anymore?"

Grateful for the darkness hiding her face, Alice stammered, "I-I wanted to be a scientist, but left that to be a mother. I always tried to put community before my own wishes, but I ran out, not only on my household in Far Meadow, but on my agreement to give my baby a decent home. And..."

She paused, rocking Aria and looking into the dark forest before her.

Sami prompted her. "And?"

Suddenly, the sadness engulfing Alice flamed into anger. "And I thought Dinah loved me and we would be a family, then. Now...I don't know if I'll ever love someone in that way again." She took her hand out of his and stumbled to her feet, holding the child close to her chest. "Look, we better walk. We've got a long path to hike tonight."

Sami rose too. "Right. Let's get her loaded up."

As they eased Aria into the pack, Alice said, "I'll carry her," and without waiting for a response, swung it onto her back.

The young man picked up her lighter backpack. "You go first, and I'll keep an eye on her from behind."

As they walked, the fury in her soul drained off with each step. After half an hour, her breathing deepened, and her feet slowed on the path illumined by her headlight. She looked over her shoulder and saw the tall young man, in his own halo of dim light, trudging after her about three feet away. *He's always there*, she thought, *right where I need him to be.* She said, "Hey—sorry about that outburst. I guess I'm a bit on edge."

A grunt told her he had heard, and for a minute she both feared and hoped that would be the end of it.

Then she realized he had moved closer behind her and was whispering.

"If the baby wakes, I'll shut up. But I want to share something with you that my mom taught me. You're a potter like she was, right?"

Remembering the beautiful plates and bowls which graced Pete's table, she smiled. "Sami, your mother created real art. My attempts at making dishes aren't in her league at all."

"OK, but you know about glazes and firing the pieces?"

"Yeah, I've glazed my work. I'm just saying it takes a lot of experience to get them to come out as lovely as her stuff. My bowls were never the same size, and I couldn't always create the colors I wanted."

"Exactly. You need experience. I never used the pottery wheel, but when I was little, I'd make these pinch pots while Mom worked on her pieces. When she fired up the kiln, she'd help me glaze my creations. She had all these buckets full of whitish gray liquid. I couldn't see the difference between them, but she'd tell me, dip it in this one if you want a blue or here if you'd like an orange. And then, of course, she'd get all fancy with her creations and combine different glazes into amazing patterns. But everything looked dull when they entered the fire. Her stuff wasn't much prettier than mine."

Alice's smile grew bigger. "Then, after you fired them, they came out better than you thought they would, I bet."

"Yeah, it was like a miracle. Even my little pots transformed into these bright, cheerful vases."

"That's the part I liked best too. But what's your point, Sami? Are you interested in creating pottery?"

He snorted a gentle laugh that tickled her ear. "No. This is my mom's metaphor for making choices. She didn't believe in right or wrong decisions. She said that when you choose to do something, it's like dipping a pot into a glaze. You think you know how your action is going to come out, but when the heat of life fires it, the color or consequences may look different than you expected."

Their footsteps crunched in unison as Alice tried to make sense of this.

"So, she thought nobody is responsible for their actions?"

"Not at all. She just made room to learn from experience. For example, if I screwed up by going out to play instead of studying for a test, she'd question my intention. I'd say something like: I planned to study after the ball game, but there wasn't time. Then she'd ask me, 'So, what did you discover?' I'd reply, 'Study before play,' and she'd tell me, 'Remember that—you know now what color you'll get, glazing with the play-before-study choice, and it's not pretty.'"

Alice smiled. "That's good. I'll have to recall her philosophy when Aria gets a little older."

"OK, but I want you to think about your decisions too. You said you made the wrong choices. I'm saying the question is not whether they were right or wrong, but what did you learn?"

"Ouch." The young mother kept her eyes on the road as Sami's query prodded the painful spot in her heart. "I guess I learned I'm not a scientist, or a valuable member of the community, or even a decent lover."

"No." Sami reached out to catch her elbow, bringing her to a stop and swinging her toward him, the beams of their two headlamps spotlighting each other's faces as she looked up at him. "Cut it out. Those are just roles—the colors you hoped to create. Life happened. The glaze didn't turn out the way you wanted. So what?"

His vehemence caught her off guard. She couldn't remember him ever being angry with her before, and it jarred her brain out of its self-pity. "OK, if I'm not a role, am I my ambitions? My hopes?"

"You're getting closer. Try your passions. Your inner compass too. The question to ask isn't, 'Did you fail?' It's 'What's the next pot you're going to dip yourself in to make yourself shine?'"

"I don't have a lot of choice here, Sami," she said. And, sensing the tunnel of despair closing around her, she reached for her anger. She spit out, "What do you see that's so great in me, anyway? Why do you even care?"

Immediately, the young man's face relaxed, and a smile replaced the scowl.

"Oh, Alice, how can I tell you? The first time I saw you hiding under that tree on the edge of our meadow, so brave and so alone, you showed a courage and hunger for truth greater than anyone else I knew. You throw yourself into what you love. You have such curiosity, such tenacity." He paused to take in her wide-eyed astonishment and then bent his head to touch her parted lips with his.

She leaned into the kiss. For a moment, all the heated questions and conflict in her brain evaporated. The weight of the baby on her back balanced her perfectly as she rocked forward on her toes—just the right pressure, warm and welcoming and somehow tasting of home.

She broke the kiss, leaning back on her heels, then laid her cheek on his chest and took a shaky breath. Her body's desire surprised her. She had felt no attraction to Dean Darryl and assumed she would only gravitate sexually to women. But the ache that rose in her urged her to draw closer to her friend, to become one with him. It felt solid and deeper than the excitement of those first sweet times with Dinah. Was this real or just a moment of neediness? "Sami, I don't know. I'm sorry. I'm not sure where this could go."

"Shhh. You don't have to know. Look at me, Alice." He pulled away from her, and she looked up, flooding his face with her headlight. Releasing one of her arms and placing his hand over the lamp to dim it, he aimed his over her head. Chuckling, he said, "We're blinding each other. The truth is, neither of us can see where this will lead. But we care for each other. So, let's dip that pot and let the heat of living reveal what kind of relationship it is. It could be best-friend affection, or heart-bond love, or somewhere in between, but something precious exists here. I want to discover what color it might become. Don't you?"

She looked away and nodded. "OK. But can we take this slow? I'm on the rebound and still confused. I don't want to hurt you, Sami."

As she said this, she realized how true it was—her desire to not cause him pain almost equaled her protective instinct toward Aria. It trumped anything she felt for Dinah now. *He might be right,* she thought. *Maybe what I'm feeling is more than attraction or simple vulnerability. This could be love.*

The young man gathered her into his arms. "Slow it is, dear heart. But we go into the future together—whatever that future brings."

She hugged him, letting his warmth surround her, breathing in the musky scent of his sweat, and nodded her assent against his chest. In her pack, Aria roused and emitted a small cry.

"Here, let me take her for a bit." Sami helped Alice ease out of the contraption before swinging it onto his own back. "She'll fall asleep once we get moving."

He proved right. Not a minute into their continued hike, the youngster fell quiet again. Watching her baby snooze, her face cradled between the shoulder blades of this man who loved both of them, a contentment crept up on Alice that took her by surprise. *If he's willing to risk something new, I should be open to it too,* she thought. The way forward now looked a little less daunting.

They walked the rest of the night, stopping only twice. Darkness had just eased into a lighter shade of gray when Sami called a halt and led them to a sheltered spot off the path. "We're about half a mile from the cabin," he said. "You and Aria hang out here while I make sure there aren't any visitors at Pete's. It shouldn't take long, but if I'm not back by tonight, return to the cave and wait."

He helped her extract the baby and settle into nursing before stooping to kiss her before he left. *Second kiss,* she thought. *It feels right.* She noticed her heart beat faster than she expected, listening to his movements through the brush until they faded away.

The sun was high in the sky, Alice dozing in its warmth, when the rustle of leaves jerked her awake. Aria, a string connecting her ankle to her mother's wrist, heard it too, pausing in her exploration of the undergrowth to look to her mom. The young woman silently crawled across five feet of forest floor to her child and, catching her up in a hug, stood, facing the muted noise. If an enemy was coming, there was no escape route.

Then Sami's tall form emerged from among the tree trunks, and mother and daughter both laughed with relief.

"Sami, you were gone so long. I thought we might have to go back."

"Sorry." One stride brought him to their side, and he enveloped both in a hug, kissing the tops of their heads. "A couple of Academy staff came yesterday and stayed the night. They were just leaving when I arrived. Luckily, the lookouts warned me before I blundered in."

"Oh, no. Is everyone OK? Pete and Nainai?"

"Yeah, I had to wait a bit to make sure they were gone, but evidently Elena was pretty convincing. They'll tell people at school she can't talk and is at death's door."

Alice scrutinized his face, noticing he wasn't looking at her directly. "Was it an act, Sami?"

He sighed and smoothed her tangled hair off her forehead. "She isn't getting better, Alice. She didn't speak to me. I told her you were coming, but we don't have any time to waste." He shook his head, and his brown eyes swam. "I won't lie to you, dear heart. She may not last the day."

"Oh." She tried to catch her breath. "We need to go, now. Help me with Aria."

He reached for the backpack, and they headed down the trail again.

Pete met them at the top of the steps leading down into the courtyard. He said nothing as he spread his arms wide to Alice, but as he enveloped her in a hug, the grim determination fueling her evaporated. She shook against his chest, gulping down sobs.

"Hush...," he whispered into her ear. "She waits for you. You have time yet."

Alice pulled away, wiping her eyes. "I'll go right to her then."

The old man studied her. "Be prepared. She's very ill. And be patient. If she speaks to you, it will take all the strength she has. Don't hurry her."

The young woman nodded, steeling herself, and headed past him down the stairs. Behind her, Sami eased the pack with Aria in it off his shoulders and handed the baby over to his great grandfather. She listened to the old man chortle with pleasure as he received her daughter.

As Alice entered the cabin, she paused to let her eyes adjust to the dim light. The sun shone, but only a few rays found their way through the clerestory windows. None of the artificial lights were on. She walked past the kitchen and dining table, noticing that the beautiful plates Sami's mother created sat uncleared from breakfast—or was it lunch time now? Memories of cheerful meals with Pete and Sami crowded her as she moved across the area to stand in front of the curtain which sheltered her room—the space they had made for her in their lives. She hesitated, visualizing the place as it had been when she left: empty of possessions, with new shelves waiting for Pete's stored food. Then she lifted the hanging and ducked inside.

Ledges still lined one long wall, half stocked with jars of vegetables and bags of grains, but a bed now stood beside them, with a stool pulled up close. The form under the comforter didn't move. Alice took a breath. The familiar scent of dirt, heavy and moist, didn't quite cover up the sour tang of urine. A chamber pot hid in the corner by the door. Next to it, a small table held a bowl of untouched porridge. Cool air trickled in through the high window alongside the cot, and Alice moved to stand there, looking down at her Nainai.

Elena lay on her back with only her head outside the covers. In sleep, her features looked peaceful and less wrinkled than Alice remembered. The left side of the colorless mouth drooped a bit, but it wasn't as bad as she expected. She sat on the stool, bringing her even with Nainai's face. She could hear breath stirring in the old woman's lungs, a raspy wave of life moving in and out.

"Nainai," she whispered, "Nainai, I'm here." She reached out to touch the slight bump of shoulder hiding under the quilt.

The old woman startled, her eyes opened, and her breathing sped up.

"Nainai, I'm here," Alice said again, tracing the covered arm down to the hand and patting it.

Elena turned her head on the pillow, and now Alice saw the extent of the stroke's damage. Her left eye remained half closed, and her mouth pulled down more, distorting the beloved face into a split image: One side dead, the other struggling for life.

"It's me—Alice." She recognized wistfulness in her own voice, willing her identity to give Nainai back her own. She could not read, on that twisted visage, any sign of recognition.

Elena struggled to lift her arm, weighed down by covers, so Alice peeled them off to hold the fragile hand. This was not what Elena wanted, though. She pulled her fingers from Alice's light grasp and fluttered them up to her niece's face, brushing her cheek and tracing her chin with her thumb.

"Alice?" The word barely escaped her lips.

"Yes, Nainai, I'm here." She kissed the cool palm, and the hand wafted down to the bed.

"I can't see well, dear." Elena's right eye squinted, seeking her.

These words were clearer. Alice thought, *maybe it's not so bad. She might recover.*

"It's OK, Nainai. I'm here."

She held her hand again, noting the mottled purple and gray of the translucent skin, the sharp bones and yellowed nails. This time, Elena sighed, as if satisfied it was Alice. She closed her eyes, taking a labored breath.

"Did you dream last night?" Elena spoke the words slowly, distinctly, but the question took her niece by surprise.

"No," she stammered. "No, I walked all evening, coming to

you."

"Ah." The right eye opened wide and searched for her. "She wants you to dream with me. We must see it together."

"What, Nainai? What does Goldie want us to see?"

The old woman shut her eye again and sank into the pillow.

"Too many words." She smiled, the right side of her face emphasizing the disobedience of the left. "Not enough breath."

"Nainai?" Alice's voice trembled, her eyes welling with tears. She thought, *Don't die, please don't die.*

As if she sensed Alice's fear, Elena said haltingly, "Don't worry, dear. Tonight, we'll dream together. Then you'll know."

"Know what, Nainai?" Alice felt panic clutch her stomach. Was Nainai even in her right mind? Was she mistaking her for some powerful Singer? The entire visit took on a surreal aspect, as if she already inhabited a vision with Elena.

But her great aunt had settled into sleep once more, and she didn't dare wake her with her questions. She tucked the icy hand under the quilt and reached over to kiss the smoothed forehead. Outside the small room, the low voices of Pete and Sami mingled with laughter and coos from Aria. Alice stood, picked up the bowl of congealed porridge, and ducked under the hanging, back into the main room with its firm reality.

CHAPTER TWENTY-ONE

"I don't know if I can dream what Nainai wants me to," she told Pete for the third time as they cleared the table of last-meal dishes. Aria already snoozed in Sami's arms as he rocked by the fire.

The old man placed the bowls in the washbasin, then turned to face her. Alice noted he tilted his head up to look at her. Had he shrunk? His bushy brows pulled forward, obscuring his faded blue eyes. She swallowed hard, thinking that he too had aged during her absence. *How long does he have left?*

"Don't try to dream anything." His raspy speech held a familiar edge of impatience. "You can't control Goldie."

"But what do I do?"

"Nothing and everything."

"Not helpful, Pete." Sami's voice intruded from over by the hearth. "Give her something to work with, for goodness' sake."

She would have laughed at how quickly they settled into their testy relationship, except for her anxiety. She nodded her thanks to Sami and turned again to the old man, who motioned her to sit with him at the table.

"Look, whatever you do is irrelevant. It's your openness to Goldie that creates an environment she can access. And before you ask me how to be open, think for yourself, girl. You dreamed her before—twice. How were you feeling in those experiences?"

Alice scanned the craggy face in front of her, realizing he would not give her any more help. Powerlessness swept over her.

"How do you suppose I felt?" She spat the words out, flushing red in the firelight. "I had no one to turn to, no idea of what to do, all this responsibility for a tiny child, and nothing in my life prepared me for it—nothing. Of course, I was afraid and helpless."

Pete reached out and placed a gnarled hand over her clenched fist. "That's it, isn't it?" he said, his voice unexpectedly gentle. "Stick with being vulnerable instead of trying to control the situation. Allow yourself to not know. Accept your limitations."

Alice's fury drained off with his words, a bone-deep weariness overtaking her. "OK, I'll lock my dragon away and face the dark."

The old man patted her hand. "There you go. That's the best you can do. The rest is up to Goldie, and none of us controls her. Either she will come or not."

In the corner, Sami stood and made his way over to them, handing her the sleeping child. "Whatever happens, we'll be here when you wake, Alice."

Earlier, they had moved Elena's cot over and created a raised pallet right next to it, so she could see Alice with her good eye. The old woman refused food and had dozed most of the day. When Alice and her daughter entered the small room, though, she lifted her head a bit off the pillow.

"Come to bed," she croaked.

Alice didn't know if it was a demand or a question. "Yes, Nainai, I'm here. I have to feed Aria before I sleep. Is that OK?"

Elena flashed her crooked smile. "Aria."

Her hand struggled to free itself from the blankets, so Alice liberated it, guiding it to her daughter's fuzzy head. The baby's eyes half opened, and, as her mom snuggled close and prepared to nurse her, she began to hum her two tones.

"Ah," Elena breathed, "she sings."

"Yes, Nainai. I think she'll be a Singer. That's why I kept her,"

Alice whispered, arranging pillows to keep the child from rolling away. "Sleep now, and I'll join you soon."

Her great-great aunt had already closed her eyes. Alice sighed, shutting her own, allowing herself to receive the sadness of Nainai's impending death, along with her desperate love for both her and the fragile life of her daughter nestled between them. The surrounding darkness grew deeper, and she sensed herself drifting off. Then, the two-tone hum of her child seemed to surround her, evolving into a more complex song, plaintive and haunting. *Goldie's coming*, she thought. *Aria has called her.*

Alice awakened at dawn, the dim light sneaking through the high window, tempering the dark. Still lying on her left side, with the baby cocooned against her breast and her right hand extended to hold Nainai's, she hesitated to move, although her muscles ached. She rolled her head a bit to test the stiffness and noticed that a shadow loomed over the bed. Her breath caught for a second until the indistinct form resolved into Pete's wiry frame, bent almost double over Elena.

"Pete," she murmured, "don't bother her yet. She feels better than she has in years."

A weight settled on her pallet next to her hip, and she looked over her shoulder to see Sami. He reached out to rub her shoulder and arm.

"He won't wake her, dear heart. She's not with us anymore."

"No. No, I saw her healed." Alice struggled to sit up, looking at the two men. The dim light picked up the sheen of tears on their cheeks. Directing her gaze to the form on the bed beside her, she studied the beloved face—still, both eyes shut half-way, and the mouth relaxed, slightly open. She reached out and touched a wrinkled cheek, already beginning to cool. "But just now, she looked strong and happy. I thought we would be together again."

Pete cleared his throat. "I'm glad you were with her." His voice cracked, and he wiped his eyes. "She deserves happiness."

He set his broad, gnarled hand over the old woman's eyelids, closing them completely. "Goodbye, dear friend," he whispered. He nodded at the two young people sitting in shock across from him. "Come. We need to attend to the dream."

In the main room, Sami lit a fire, laid ready on the hearth, and pulled cushions forward so they could sit close together, warmed by the blaze. Directing Alice to settle between them, Pete brought over a comforter and created a little nest for the still-sleeping baby, then lowered himself onto the floor, facing her. He handed her his handkerchief to wipe her overflowing eyes.

"The time to mourn will come, child. Right now, we need to listen to your vision. The other Singers won't be here for a while. You'll share this with them too, but while it's fresh, tell us. We'll help you remember."

Alice gulped, trying to contain her tears and the tremor which shook her from head to toe. She opened her mouth, but nothing came out.

Sami leaned in but did not touch her. "You can do this. Take a deep breath. Go back to the beginning when you started to dream. Nainai gave you this last gift. Let us help you bear it."

Alice nodded, still shaking, looking at the floor. A gift...it was a gift, but an awful responsibility too. How could she make them understand? She inhaled and began.

"Aria dreamed too. This belongs to her as well."

And then she told them.

Alice's Vision

I only had the common dream once before. This one started out similarly, but different too. Instead of being alone in the fog, I heard Aria humming. When I opened my eyes, I knew she was beside me and Nainai was too, even though I couldn't see them. Goldie took up the baby's notes and sang a beautiful song. It resembled the one in my dream before. She wasn't visible, but she came so close I smelled her, a scent like christmas trees and daks.

But this is important—I think Aria called her.

I felt so happy, so hopeful. It lasted for a long time, and I thought, *This could be the experience we're meant to have.* Then Nainai...I don't understand how this happened, but she seemed to push me to go with Goldilocks. I tried to protest that I didn't know how, and as I turned to speak to her, the entire scene shifted.

There was no more fog, no more singing, no more Aria and Nainai. Darkness surrounded me so completely that I couldn't believe this place had ever seen the sun. And I sensed no other presence—not Goldie, not anyone. I couldn't move my body either. Somewhere, far away, I felt my heart hammering in my chest. I decided I was dying, but then I heard a swooshing noise and the ping of lights coming on, flooding my prison with a brightness that blinded me at first.

I recognized it: I had seen this in my vision at the birthing center—the silver room on the spaceship. I faced down, as if someone had glued me to the ceiling. A man and woman who looked familiar came through the door—the estranged couple. I wondered if I had transported back in time, but when they started talking, it became clear they were together again.

The woman, Judy, sat down at a console. She said, "I want you to see this, dear. It worries me."

Esteban (the young man) put his hands on her shoulders, bending to peer at the screen. Even though I couldn't view the panel, I noticed his brow wrinkle as he watched.

"So, are they trying to communicate?" he asked. "Have you helped them identify us?"

"That's the problem," she said, nodding her head. "I responded at once, and they immediately shut down. I thought it might be a random signal they send out—similar to the Earth's old SETI program. Instead of continuing, though, it's like they touched fire and snatched their hands away. I picked up another ping later, and the same thing happened."

"At the same time?"

"No, the first one came in the morning. The one today would have been in the middle of their night. That makes me realize that it's nothing automated."

"How much information do you think they got?"

"Not sure. Our size and trajectory at the most. They only touched us for a few minutes." She looked up at him over her shoulder, lips pressed together and brows drawn.

Esteban patted her shoulder and settled on a stool next to her, searching her face. "What about Goldie? Is she aware they're reaching out?"

She shook her head, her long ponytail of straight black hair jiggling back and forth. "All I get from her is anxiety these days. Some excitement too, but she's worried about this homecoming. What about you?"

"About the same." He sighed, exhaling dramatically. "Do you want to try together? Sometimes that helps clarify issues."

Judy nodded and positioned herself to face him, taking both his hands and resting them on their knees, which now touched. They closed their eyes and began humming—first Judy and then Esteban, matching her tone an octave below. It sounded like Aria's contentment hum: two notes, one higher, then lower, over and over. The sound vibrated in my consciousness, up by the ceiling. The music seemed to find me and solidify my presence, making me more real. I felt heavier, more embodied somehow, and I worried I'd fall.

My anxiety made me miss the moment they succeeded. They both stopped chanting at the same time, and Judy breathed, "Hello, Goldie. Thanks for coming."

The two young people kept their eyes closed and hands linked. They were in contact with the entity now. As soon as I noticed that, I caught a whiff of christmas trees and the warmth of her presence touched me too. I realized how close she must be and became so excited, I let go of my fear. All the emotions and images she communicated to them found me too.

It overwhelmed me. I had a hard time separating Goldie from my identity. It felt like being thrown into a lake before you learn to swim and losing track of which way leads to the surface. I wasn't afraid so much as stunned by the mystery surrounding me, and I lost sight of the room and the people. For a while, I just existed.

Then Judy gasped, "There's another presence here." I snapped back up to the ceiling, separated from Goldie, and was myself again.

"The mother..." Esteban's calm voice responded. "The mother sees us."

"Yes," Judy whispered and sat up straight, extricating her hands from his and sighing.

"OK," said the young man, running his fingers through the short curls on his scalp, "that was intense. Shall we go to the mess for coffee and compare notes?"

Judy cocked her head as if listening. "No, we need to review this here and now. Whoever was with her waits and needs something." Her voice sounded unsure, but her eyes blazed.

Esteban looked around and nodded. "You may be right. OK, I'll start." And they shared back and forth the images they had received, debating what they meant.

I don't remember all the words, but they summed up the gist of their experience with Goldie in three points. Esteban got out his tablet to write them down.

First: Danger awaits us on the planet we approach.

Second: The threat comes from the people who reached out and know we're on the way.

Third: We must wait until we hear from the mother (not "a" mother, but *the* mother, Judy insisted) and receive landing instructions, which will lead to a welcoming group.

His long fingers paused in their tapping. "As usual, we have no idea when this mother is going to contact us, do we?"

"Not that I could tell." Judy bit her lip. "This won't go down well with Al or the crew. Everyone is so eager to set their feet on the ground."

"How much time before we arrive at the planet?"

"Just a few weeks, according to the gossip last night. Ellen said they almost finished retrofitting the shuttles for landing. In the biosphere, they're working on securing travel tanks for the fish."

"Maybe we'll get lucky, and the mother will contact us soon."

"Or we could try to reach her."

They turned as the door swished open and the round-faced man, the leader of this expedition, walked in.

When I looked at him, the scene shifted again....

The dream fog surrounded me once more, and I sensed both Aria and Elena nearby. I heard wind and the Singer, and the urge to find her came over me. Just as I thought I might move my stubborn feet, the gale stopped. The music...how can I describe this? The notes got crisper, sharper, cutting away the mist. I looked up, and, above me, the sky shone with darkness. This blackness appeared completely different from the absence of light on the ship. It was like peering upward through clear glass to the bottom of a well so full of water it swallowed every ray.

I turned and saw Nainai standing there looking up too. She laughed and held up her arms to the darkness—both her arms. She looked healed, strong—more vital than I've ever seen her. And then, I don't know whether she rose or the clear blackness came down, but she touched it. She welcomed it. And the singing surrounded her...and then I woke up.

"How did they even realize a ship was out there?" Emily's voice quivered, and her wrinkled face looked older than Alice recalled.

Eleven Singers now sat with Alice, crowded around the dining table, sipping tea from mismatched mugs and cups. Manuel and Jamie had arrived an hour before sunset, bringing with them Emily, Lucio, Dean Agatha, and Edie, the young fisher. Sarai and Michel, who lived in Wood Lawn, had been there since late morning.

A tapping sounded at the door just before they settled, and a middle-aged woman had entered. Pete introduced her to Alice as Dove. She was tall and thin to the point of emaciation. Her wiry hair created a gray halo framing a serene brown face with deep-set, moss-green eyes. Alice noticed that all the other guests greeted her one by one with a pronounced deference. She sat with them, listening intently.

"It might not be the Gladiators," offered Lucio, patting his wife's hand. "There could be other sentient life in this universe."

"No," Dean Agatha said, her voice brittle. "It's the Academy branch of the sect, all right. First, we're aware the threat is here because Goldie worries about coming home. Second, we do have the ability to reach out to spaceships. The Academy began building a communications array in Seaside after the one in the Armstrong's village was destroyed. Monitoring the heavens for aliens has been going on for about twenty revs."

Beside her, Edie glared. "Why don't the rest of us know about that?"

"Because knowledge is power," the dean said, "and those with power want to hold on to it."

A tense pause ensued while those congregated considered this old truth.

Emily directed her bemused gaze toward Alice. "Do you know what the Gladiators plan to do about the Earth ship, dear?"

"No, sorry." She looked down at her cooling tea, a flush rising on her cheeks.

"Not our problem," an unfamiliar voice offered.

Alice raised her head and contemplated the strange woman across the table. A smile played on that thin face, and she met Alice's eyes.

"Visions rarely tell you details. They give callings. What are we supposed to do?"

Several people spoke at once.

"Sounds to me like..."

"Clearly we should..."

Dove held her hand up, and the voices fell silent.

"What does the seer say?"

Alice sighed and shook her head. "Well, the main thing is that we need to welcome the visitors from Earth."

No one said anything in response. Dove kept her eyes focused on the young woman's face, which heated again.

"OK," she stammered, "there weren't many details. The mother is expected to contact the ship—that's how they'll identify the right group. I guess that has to be me, and I suppose Aria should be there too. But I don't want her in danger, so..."

The gray-haired woman across from her interrupted. "First, state facts. Then create strategy. What else are we supposed to do?"

"Ummm." Alice scanned the faces watching her around the table before staring back into her teacup. "We have to give them coordinates to a safe landing place where we can meet them. I think that's all I got." She glanced up at Dove, who nodded and then addressed the entire group.

"Any other facts that she's missed?"

Beside Alice, Sami cleared his throat. "The timing seems important. Didn't you say Judy thought they would enter orbit in two to three weeks?"

"Yes, that's right." She gave him a little smile. "The crew is impatient to land, so she's worried they won't want to slow down."

"But how can we contact them if we don't have any communication gear?" Edie broke in, her voice edged with tension. "And what does welcoming them mean, anyway?"

Frowning, Alice studied her intense dark eyes and firm mouth. She had spent no time talking to Edie when they met at the Singer's community in Seaside. The fisher woman couldn't be much older than she—but had such confidence. And her concerns echoed the doubts in Alice's mind.

Dove nodded. "Good questions. Let's start with the first."

***

The planning took all day. By lunchtime, they had figured out a tentative scheme for contacting the spaceship, featuring Manuel and Jamie's ability to access the Academy's communication array. The brothers didn't think luring workers away from the site would be hard. Coordinating the effort to sneak in Alice and Aria for a broadcast, though, would take the combined efforts of the whole Seaside Singer community.

As they broke the circle to prepare food and more tea, Alice noticed Dove lifting the curtain and slipping into the bedroom where Elena's still body lay. Soon, Agatha and Edie joined her. As she cut the vegetables for the first-supper stew, Emily and Sarai approached her to fill a basin with water and ask where they kept the household towels. The elderly Singer from Seaside took her arm with a frail hand as she brought out a stack of clean cloths. "This is your work too. Leave the cooking to the men and join us."

Behind the curtain, three women lined up on the far side of the bed, gazing down at the empty shell that had been her Nainai. Sarai placed the basin of water on a small table and guided Alice to stand between her and Emily on the near side. Dove began to sing a haunting melody, which they all took up. Alice sang too. Every child heard the song which accompanied preparing remains for burial many times before adulthood. She realized, for the first time, that this was a Singer hymn, part of the legacy of the early days which each person on the planet still possessed. Her thoughts raced as she went through the ritual of washing and wrapping the beloved body in a dark blue shroud: Maybe more people could recognize their roots in Goldilocks. *Those who remember the importance of this heritage might help us welcome her.*

They reconvened after first supper, and Alice started talking before everybody even sat down.

"When we bury Nainai..." Speaking the fact of her dear aunt's death struck her in the gut, and she paused to steady her voice, concentrating on her hands in front of her. "When that happens, we should invite everyone who recalls that where we end up is where we began: in Goldie's arms."

Complete silence around the dining table made her look up. Eyes searched her face, heads nodded.

Pete said, "You're right. We'll take her body back to Far Meadow and spread the word of her funeral. The people who honor her will be ones we can most likely trust."

"We only have three days," Sarai warned. "That's the law's limit for burials."

"Yes, but we need to hurry anyway, dear," her husband said. "If we settle on a date, I'll borrow a hummie and travel up the road, spreading the word to Last Stop and Mountain View. Mourners can make it to Far Meadow in time if they leave immediately. And our boys can take off tonight to deliver the message to Seaside and Touch Down. We won't get everyone, but those who come could share about the ship's landing after the ceremony."

Alice gave Michel a grateful smile. Their whole-hearted acceptance of her insight convinced her she belonged.

Pete leaned his forearms on the table, inclining his head toward Dove. "Will you lead the service? Your witness might pave the way for the rest of us to recruit support for our welcoming committee."

The tall woman frowned, closing her eyes while the others waited silently. Finally, she took a deep breath and looked around at the gathered friends. "Yes, I believe the time to act has arrived. I'll lead the service, but the seer, the mother, shall speak the eulogy."

"What?" said Alice, the warmth of being included blown away by this expectation. "I've never spoken at a funeral before. I don't—"

To her right, Sami put a hand on her arm, interrupting. "She can't go. Dean Darryl's sure to realize that's the place to catch her. She needs to stay hidden."

Murmurs of distress ran around the table, but Dove didn't move a muscle. The moss-green eyes remained steady and confident. She held up her palm for silence. Into the quiet, she said, "We will all sing. The seer will speak. The time to leave the shadows has arrived."

CHAPTER TWENTY-TWO

In the end, the twelve gathered around the table developed a tight schedule which, given the unknown variables, seemed held together more by hope than reality. They would round up as many people as possible to come to the burial at Far Meadow in two days. After the funeral, Manuel, Jamie, Sami, and Alice with Aria would go back to Seaside, where the brothers, who majored in engineering, would break into the communications lab. Alice would then contact the spaceship, giving them coordinates to land outside the wayfarer's hut by the path which led into the forest. While that happened, Pete, and anyone else the group could recruit, would clear a landing strip for the shuttle on the plain of five-foot-high grass which grew there. They had three weeks to accomplish everything.

The last of the visitors left Pete's home after first supper. The light of both moons guided them down the trail to the main road. Dove alone struck out into the thickest part of the forest, without benefit of any track that Alice could see. As she sank down by the hearth to nurse Aria, she found her tired mind preoccupied with the mysterious newcomer. When Pete and Sami finished with the dishes and joined her, the question nagging at her all day insisted on being asked.

"Who is Dove?" She spoke softly, so as not to disturb her daughter, who now dozed in satiated bliss. "And why do you all accept her as your leader?"

Sami looked at her, eyebrows raised. "You don't know...?"

But Pete stepped in with, "Our leader, huh? How do you figure she leads us?"

"Well, you all listened to her whenever she spoke. And you kind of deferred to her."

Pete nodded his head. "Uh-huh. And what about you?"

"What do you mean?" Alice frowned.

"Did we listen to you? Even Dove conceded your expertise when you shared your vision."

The young woman tilted her head, scowling. "That's because I'm the only one who saw it."

"Right." He sat back as if her reply ended the conversation.

Alice rolled her eyes at Sami, who laughed.

"Old man, you love being difficult."

Pete shrugged, and Sami continued. "The point he failed to make is that we don't have leaders per se, but we do believe everyone has a gift to bring into our midst. Just like yours, Dove's talent shows up sporadically and uniquely. We value it, not above others, but as something to pay attention to when it appears."

"Dove herself only shows up once in a while." His great grandfather pursed his lips. "I thought you'd know about her though, because she's related to Elena."

A family member she hadn't met? Alice's heart beat faster. "I never heard of her before. Where does she live?"

"Do you remember where we saw the fairy dragons?" Sami asked. "She lives out there in the broccoli tree forest somewhere, with her partner. They've always been off-grid. We just figured out her grandmother descended from the friends of Elena's fathers who took care of the Armstrong's communications array until the Gladiators destroyed it. Those women never came back to civilization. A few people wander out to their settlement every once in a while, so it keeps going."

Alice thought about this for a minute. "That's a long way off,

Sami. How could she have made that trip in one night? And where is she now? Will she arrive at the funeral on time?" More questions threatened to tumble out, but she bit her lip and waited.

Pete frowned and gazed at the ceiling. "It took her three days to get here." He shifted to study Alice. "Her gift is the ability to hear Goldilocks even while awake. We think it's because she's directly related to Xander, one of the original settlers who heard Goldie most clearly. Goldie must have alerted her the day you and Sami decided to travel here."

"That's why we trust her when she says the time to show ourselves has come," added Sami. "It's also why we believe she's right when she insists you have to attend the funeral. She'll be there with you. I'm hoping she's gone to find some more help."

"I don't understand." Alice swiveled her head to take in both men. "If Goldie communicates so well with her, why doesn't she tell Dove what we should do?"

"Doesn't work like that," Pete said.

The old man's curt replies annoyed Alice. She bit her tongue before she could snap back at him and shot Sami a glance. Again, the young man came to the rescue.

"Not even Dove can always access Goldie. She's only had two or three contacts since I started singing. In fact, I think it surprised her that the spaceship is so close and she hasn't heard more." He sighed and looked at Pete. "Perceiving the truth but not being able to prove it stresses everyone, especially the Singers who've been faithful for so long. We all wish we understood what we should do."

"It would help if Goldie relied on those of us who've known her all our lives," came a muttered response from the rocking chair.

For the first time, Alice considered how it must feel to the old timers to have her barge into their world, achieving a closeness to the entity they defended which had escaped them. She looked down at her child, tears gathering in her eyes. She hadn't sought for this gift any more than Aria had asked to hum. Now, she alienated those she wanted most to love her.

A gnarled hand patted her arm, and she turned to Pete, leaning forward in his seat to reach her.

"I'm a jealous old codger," he said. "You're a treasure for the Singers and the best thing that's happened to me since Sami came to live here. Forgive me, dear girl. I'm tired and grieving tonight. That's my only excuse."

A tear escaped, and the young mother brushed it away. She nodded her acceptance of his apology. "It's all right, Pete. I'd feel that way too in your place." But the hollow space in her chest remained.

Sami murmured, "We're exhausted and need to get going before the sun comes up tomorrow. Let's skip last supper and turn in now. I'll take the first watch over the body. Which of you can handle the second?"

"Let me do it," Alice offered. "I'll have to nurse Aria then, anyway."

"And I'll claim the third one, hopefully getting enough beauty sleep to wake up a prince instead of a curmudgeon," Pete said, while Sami shook his head in mock despair.

As Alice settled down to rest beside her already sleeping child, all her unanswered questions converged to haunt her. Where was Dove now? Would the mayor allow Nainai to be buried in Far Meadow's cemetery? Would her family rejoice to see her or shun her? She felt sure Dean Darryl would send men to arrest her, and what would happen to Aria if they caught her and.... Weariness crept in, blanketing her fevered mind, and she too slept as heavily as her daughter.

"Is that Dove coming out of the forest?"

Alice detected Lucio's shout over the howling wind and the hum of vehicles warming up. It had taken Sami and her all morning to tote the stretcher bearing Elena's body through the woods to the wayfarer's hut, sharing the baby's weight back and forth, while Pete struggled to hike beside them. Now, she crouched in the back of one of seven hummies filled with Singers from Seaside and Touch Down whom Dean Agatha and Edie had rounded up. Her bandaged hands and sore shoulders protested any more movement, yet Sami insisted that she and Aria ride in the rear bed of the little ATV so she could duck under the blankets that draped the body and avoid detection if necessary.

Now, she sat up tall and craned her neck so she could observe what Lucio saw. Sure enough, a thin figure with a staff, her wild hair blowing in the wind, strode across the field to join them. Something else stirred in the branches at the forest's edge too.

"Fairy dragons!" Alice stood, shouting and pointing. "Can you see them? Fairy dragons are coming."

The three dark shapes she had first noticed perched in the trees now soared on the gale, following Dove in loops and dives, dancing in the wind. The bright sun caught the membranes of their wings, sparking brilliant colors: red, green, yellow, and turquoise. Although their matte-black bodies measured only about four feet long, the unfurled pinions and snaking tails created the illusion of much bigger creatures. Several people bailed out of the hummies and crouched behind them.

Michel, sitting in the driver's seat of her vehicle, clutched the wheel and said, "My God, they're real. What should we do?"

Sami, sandwiched between him and Pete, yelled, "Stay still!" He jumped down over the hood and headed toward Dove, calling to the others. "Just keep calm and wait."

As the young man met the Singer several yards from where the hummies idled, one creature uttered a bell-like note, then swooped down and settled on his shoulder. Alice noticed the long tail wrapping itself around his neck and sensed her own throat constrict. She remembered that tail's embrace—dry and leathery, smelling of wood and dirt. She could almost feel the talons of six feet pricking her back too.

The other two fairy dragons circled above while Sami and Dove came to some agreement. Together, they turned and began walking toward the hummies again, the dragon still perched on Sami. The ones in the air shot ahead, swooping over the nervous little crowd. As they approached Alice's vehicle, the flying duo emitted clear cries and landed on the roll bar, their shining eyes level with her face. Pete and Michel, in front, hunkered down, trying to avoid their lashing tails, but she welcomed them, throwing her arms wide in greeting.

A movement at her feet redirected Alice's attention for a moment. Her daughter had awakened and now sat, a small fist pressed against the seat back for balance, the other reaching up toward the bizarre creatures above her. One of the fairy dragons bent its long neck down and met her wide eyes with a gold-foil stare. Aria laughed and leaned forward to hug the wide, scaly snout. Alice interpreted its chittering sound as affection. She put out a hand to steady the child.

The other creature now reached its forearms onto Alice's shoulders, tilting its broad head to gaze into her face. The same comforting acceptance she had experienced in the forest when she first met these beasts engulfed her. *This is joy*, she thought. *On the day I'm burying my Nainai, with all the danger and grief this involves, I feel joy. Whatever happens in Far Meadow, all will be well.*

The caravan arrived in her home village just before the sun set. They drove around the town boundaries to the east until they came to the burial grounds marked by two tall christmas trees and the mounded stones of gravesites. The wind, which had gusted all the morning, completely disappeared. Alice remembered how Nainai hated windless days.

The vehicles stopped by the trees marking the border of the cemetery. She could see the dark hole in the earth, some twenty yards away, and the traditional blankets strewn with Elena's possessions laid out to one side. Tears of relief gathered in her eyes. Her family and neighbors would accept Nainai back into their midst.

Someone had been on the lookout for them. Soon, the villagers flowed out of their hamlet, moving in a huddle to pool behind the vehicles. Seven hummies traveling together would have commanded their attention, even without the fairy dragons. Adding the fantastical beasts kept them at a respectful distance, murmuring their astonishment.

Alice saw her father, with Janelle holding Jaren's hand by his side. Nettie stood behind them, meeting her sister's eyes but shaking her head. Alice scanned the crowd for strangers, noticing her own birth mother and a few others from the outback villages, but nobody she recognized as an Academy plant. *That doesn't mean someone I know won't try to arrest me,* she reminded herself. Somehow, though, the fairy dragon, who now draped itself around her neck, shielded her from anxiety and fear. She took a deep breath and clambered off the ATV bed, balancing the weight of the creature on her shoulder, then reached up to lift Aria down and settle her on her hip.

Micah, pushing his broad shoulders through the gathered crowd, stopped about six feet in front of her.

"Your father asked me to help bear the pall," he said, never taking his eyes off the fairy dragon.

"Thank you. You were a good friend to Nainai. Why don't you lead, and Sami will take the other end?"

Her companion came up and directed the older man to the rear of the hummie, where they pulled out the stretcher bearing Elena's body. Dove strode to the path which led between the two christmas trees into the cemetery, letting the pall bearers and then Elena's family assemble behind her. Alice took her place right behind Sami, her parents and siblings coming next, but even Nettie kept a safe distance from her. Dove began to sing the funeral song, leading the procession toward the open grave.

They had done this so often, Alice noticed, that even the children joined in. The wind picked up, swirling the dust from the path and sending the two other fairy dragons into the air to circle the cortege as it crept to the burial site. As they came up to the blankets laden with Elena's possessions, Humphrey stepped forward, but Dove held up her hand, indicating that Alice should go first. The young woman moved to the blanket, carrying both the fairy dragon and her child, to pick a remembrance for Aria.

Every familiar object spoke to her as she gazed at the jumble of things before her: the teapot she used each time she visited and the lumpy cups Nainai treasured because she and Nettie had made them, the soft poncho that served as her coat, the picture of Rose Moon-rise that hung in the bedroom. What would Aria grow to cherish? What would teach her little daughter a bit about this wonderful and wise woman? Then, a gust of wind lifted the corner of a shawl and she saw a glint of metal: Nainai's com-pad. Had her family been trying to hide it? With this, Aria could connect to all the stories and the knowledge of their world.

She picked up the computer, noticing her father's hard stare and frown, and addressed the waiting crowd. "I'll accept this for my child. Nainai gave me gifts before I left. I won't take anything else."

She stepped back as the rest of Elena's close relatives came forward, one by one. Each claimed a remembrance. Then, other friends and neighbors moved in until nothing remained.

The final details of the funeral blurred together in Alice's mind: the lowering of the body into the grave, the beautiful music of the Singers as dirt filled the hole, the fairy dragons adding their crystal cries as the wind rose and the crowd turned back to the village. They gathered in the community room for a meager feast, ready to hear stories about the deceased. Her heart beat fast, knowing this was the time for her to tell the truth about who Nainai was.

Respect for her elders decreed she should let her father and Micah speak first. Humphrey stepped up on the small podium and shook his head, looking askance at the packed room in front of him.

His daughter noticed that his hands, so capable when planting crops or fixing a roof, trembled. He stuck them in his pockets.

"There's not much to say," he mumbled to the assembly. "Elena was my grandfather's sister by blood but not household. She lived a long life here in Far Meadow and, in the end, deserted us—for what? A fantasy that's ruined my daughter and brought strangers into our midst."

His words threw a haze of uneasiness over the crowd. He turned away and stomped over to the door, stopping to lean against the frame as if ready to leave at any minute. Micah, lined up to speak next, froze and looked between Humphrey's scowling face and Alice's wide eyes.

From the back, Dove resolved his indecision, calling out, "Humphrey has challenged his daughter. Let Alice reply."

A murmur of assent rippled through the throng, and Micah retreated, motioning the young mother to stand up front. She handed over her child to Sami, glanced at her father's angry face, and, for a moment, rage at his unfairness threatened to derail her. She took a deep breath, containing her inner dragon, and turned to look at the crowd. These were the people she came to address— not Pa. What hope could she give them? Her heart pounded. She reached up, touching the pouch which lay under her shirt at her breastbone, and the warmth of all the gifts Nainai had given her radiated through her chest.

"My father speaks out of his pain and dread." She let the words come of their own accord, trusting the moment. "I too feel sad and afraid today, but the most important thing Nainai taught me was to control anger and act out of love and hope. She instructed me through both her stories and her life.

"You all experienced Elena as mayor and teacher and neighbor. What you don't know is that she had visions: first of Earth, before the settlers came here, and then of Eternity. Her gift, rare and valued by the Singers, would have been rejected here in Far Meadow.

Her husband Jay, a dreamer and Singer himself, would have been suspect. Still, they settled here because you needed their skills. They loved you, their community, and so chose to serve you all their lives. Nainai hoped to see the day when we all would listen to Goldie, when the harmony between people and the planet would again be established. This desire did not diminish with age. Instead, in the last days of her life, Nainai also dreamed of Goldie. Her hope grew.

"You may wonder how I know this. The night Nainai died, I shared her dream. I saw her embrace Eternity without dismay, but with amazement and joy. I felt the love which enfolded her and experienced her faith fulfilled. And so, I can tell you today that while I mourn her passing, Nainai's death gave me assurance that her way of compassion will conquer fear and pain."

Alice paused, looking out at the people in front of her, all quiet, all staring. She took another breath. "Goldilocks is coming home. If you have any ability to access her, even just vaguely, you know I speak the truth. A spaceship from Earth is entering an orbit around our planet in less than a month, and our full connection with Goldie has the potential to be restored. We have a decision to make—either to reject her, deluding ourselves about human mastery over nature, or to give ourselves to interdependence once again. Nainai made her choice long ago. I have made mine. What will you choose?"

As she scanned the shocked faces in front of her, she wondered if any would join her to welcome Goldie. A buzz of talk rose to a clamor, and Micah stepped to her side. He put an arm around her shoulders and called for quiet.

"She speaks the truth. Last night, I dreamed the common dream for the first time. I didn't know what it meant. Today, Singers and fairy dragons, both believed extinct or fantasies, helped honor our kinswoman at her funeral. Alice is right—Elena and Goldie are calling us to life and hope. I'm with her all the way."

After Micah's declaration, Pete and a few other villagers spoke, but Alice watched her father, glowering by the door. As it became apparent that nobody would vilify Elena or question her motives, his frown deepened, his face growing darker. At one point, Janelle approached him, their young son still in tow, trying to pull him back into the room, but Humphrey snapped at her. A moment later, Alice saw him exit into the sunken courtyard. She looked around to see if anyone else noticed, and Dove caught her eye, nodding. It was time to disappear.

As the Singers led the others in a brief meal blessing song, Sami, Alice, and Aria moved to the door. Micah followed, and, as they stepped into the empty patio, he detained them.

"Alice, you need to be careful. Your father's in contact with the Academy Gladiators. They'll realize you are here."

"We'll leave now," Alice said, shifting the baby to a more comfortable position. "Get word to everyone who wants to welcome Goldie that the Earth spaceship lands in three weeks by the wayfarer's hut between here and Seaside."

Sami added, "We also need help to clear a landing strip. I'll send a message to you when I know the time and day."

Micah nodded to them both and then bent forward to kiss Alice and Aria on their foreheads. "You were right to follow your heart, Alice. It didn't turn out like you thought it would, but still—you were right. Elena knew that."

Tears pooled in Alice's eyes, making his solid presence waver in front of her. "Thanks," she whispered, before turning and hurrying up the steps and away from her childhood village.

CHAPTER TWENTY-THREE

It seemed to take them forever to circle around to Seaside. They drove a hummie to the familiar wayside hut but then hiked on obscure paths, sometimes bushwhacking through the undergrowth of the forest, trusting Sami's sense of direction. Alice, her emotions and physical energy exhausted, staggered behind, unable to even think about the mission before them. Each night now, when she lay down to curl her body around her child, the dream visited her. The song grew more urgent. Her feet still refused to move. She woke to the certainty that they had to hurry. The captain wouldn't wait. The coordinates must be delivered.

They arrived at the outskirts of Seaside four days after Elena's funeral. Dion, waiting in a stand of broccoli trees, spotted them through the dusk and made her way to join them. When Dion materialized by her side, Alice thought dreams had overtaken her. Hugs and whispered greetings convinced her otherwise, and her friend guided them to a house on the edge of town, where the warm light spilled into the sunken courtyard and arms reached out to pull them into the comfort of warmth, food, and rest.

The respite didn't last long. The next night, she approached a small construct on the outskirts of the Academy complex that she had never noticed before. Around the standard moat, someone had erected a seven-foot stone wall, allowing no one to see the structure inside. A locked gate kept strangers at bay. She waited in the shadows, Aria snuggly asleep in her backpack, with Sami, Dion, and Jamie beside her. Soon, she observed Manuel trot up to the forbidding door and begin banging on it. The noise brought out a tall, burly, middle-aged man, annoyed at being disturbed. They talked for a while, Manuel gesturing wildly. Then, together, they hurried away, but not before she saw her co-conspirator surreptitiously slip something onto the doorjamb before the heavy panel swung shut.

"He's done it." Jamie whispered behind her. "We have less than an hour before they have the communication system we disabled up again. Let's get going."

Luckily, the technician left all the lights on in his rush to leave. Dion stayed as lookout in the deep shade of the wall, while the others filed through the gate and down the courtyard stairs. Inside the building, no bigger than Pete's hut, Alice's eyes widened at the sight of a single room lined with silver panels and a console with screens and buttons. It was a miniature of the area she had seen on the spaceship—except there was no evidence it worked.

"Why is nothing lit up?" she asked.

"Wait for it." Sami helped her ease the backpack off and leaned it against the wall, cushioning the baby's head with his jacket. "Manuel's going to reconnect us while they're working on the main com unit. Hopefully, everyone will be too busy to notice."

Jamie hovered over the console, muttering, "C'mon, c'mon."

"When he connects, you have to be holding Aria," Sami said. "They need to recognize you as the mother."

"Right." She consulted her wrist band. Fifteen minutes gone already. What if the technician came back early? She picked up the baby, even with the risk of waking her, not wanting to waste a second.

Sami propped open the door to the courtyard in order to hear any warning from Dion. Alice padded around the crowded room, the weight of her sleeping daughter in her arms, both a comfort and a worry. They would take her away if they caught them tonight.

Hurry, hurry, she prayed silently. The watch band showed twenty minutes gone.

A sharp beep startled her, and a bright light blinked on and off. She took a step toward the monitor.

"Wait a minute. The system has to boot up again," Jamie said, staring at the panel.

The console bloomed into life, buttons popping into red, yellow, and green, and the screen in the middle lightening from black to gray.

"OK now," muttered Jamie to himself, "this one must transmit, and this receive."

He pulled out a hidden typing pad and entered a string of numbers and letters, pausing to gauge his effectiveness. Nothing happened. Alice consulted her wrist band: twenty-seven minutes. They needed to convey the message and get out. Her breathing grew shallow, and she resumed pacing.

Sami leaned over his friend and whispered, "It's now or never. We're almost at the half-hour mark."

"Yeah, yeah. Let me try this." Jamie's dark head bobbed as he typed a fresh set of numbers and letters. "Nobody may be in the com room. They could just be recording. They know it's the middle of the night here."

All three adults stared at the screen, willing it to come alive. Just as Alice gave up hope, she heard a crackle and then a voice as a wavering picture resolved into a face.

"This is Earth spaceship Shepherd to Planet KOI-3284. Do you copy Goldilocks? Are you trying to communicate? Over."

Jamie flicked a switch. "Yes. This is Goldilocks. Please stand by for an urgent transmission. Over." He got out of the chair and beckoned for Alice. "Look at the screen. Hold the baby up a bit, so the camera catches her."

As she sat down, she saw Judy's face, eyes glued to hers. The image spoke, but no sound came through.

Jamie leaned over her shoulder. "OK—to hear them, click this, and to speak, press that. Remember to say 'over' when you're done."

"Got it." She reached up to position her fingers on the small metal tabs. "Judy, this is Alice. See, I have my baby Aria right here. We need to hurry. I have to give you landing coordinates and a time. Are you ready to receive them? Over."

She flicked her switch off and the receiver on, never taking her eyes away from the astonished face in front of her. Judy snapped her mouth closed, took a breath, and then began speaking.

"Are you the mother we're supposed to listen to? Is that how you know my name? Over."

"Yes, that's right. I was there when Goldie told you I would be in touch. But we are in danger here. I have to be quick. Prepare to receive the information. Over."

The woman, so far away in space, grabbed a com-pad. Alice noticed Alan and Esteban arrive behind her, bending over her and the screen.

"I'm ready. Please proceed. Over."

Alice read off the coordinates the Singers had agreed on, marking a spot in the grassland close to the wayfarer's hut near the forest, and then repeated them. She saw Alan turn away and lost his image. Now only the two lovers were in view, nodding encouragement at her.

"We need to know if you can be there early in the morning in fourteen days. Over."

Both young people turned to consult with Alan off-screen. Then Judy said, "Yes, but we could arrive earlier too. Over."

"No, we want time to create a landing strip. How much room do you need? Over."

Esteban leaned in. "We require a minimum of one thousand twenty meters long and sixty wide to land the shuttle. Over."

Alice glanced over her shoulder at Sami, who nodded. "We'll have it ready in fourteen days. Please try to arrive in the early morning. The Singers will welcome you. Over."

"Singers?" Judy's voice rose in question, and Alan's face reappeared beside her. "Over."

"Goldie's friends." Alice said. The child on her lap, awake now, reached for the screen, laughing. "We have to go. We are in danger here."

Sami inserted himself into the picture from behind her. "Please don't respond to any other communications from this planet. There are people here who wish you harm. Over."

Aria leaned on the monitor, trying to touch the figures in the box. Alice glimpsed Judy laughing and reaching out to her. Then Jamie ushered them both out of the way and typed instructions to shut down the array and erase what they had been doing.

Sami moved back to the door to listen for Dion, as Alice struggled to get her now wide-awake and excited daughter into the backpack. They all froze in place as the lookout's voice echoed in the courtyard.

"Is that you, Manuel? Thank God, I've been looking all over for my sister. Can you help?"

"Quick," Jamie whispered, "Out the door and round to the back."

Sami moved to assist Alice, picking up the youngster and setting her in her mother's arms while shrugging on the empty pack. "Keep her quiet," he breathed as he pushed them through the opening in front of him, Jamie right behind.

They crept to the rear of the hut, huddling there against the outer wall. In the sunken trough, they could hear the conversation above clearly.

"Could you and your buddy help me look? I'm worried sick."

"Manuel can search," an unfamiliar voice said. "I have to get to my station."

"Oh, please help us. She can't be too far away, but I don't know what direction she went. I'm scared to be out here in the dark by myself."

Alice could imagine her beautiful friend looking up at the technician, her wide eyes brimming with tears, her elegant hand on his arm.

Manuel entered the conversation. "Why don't you two search back toward the Academy, Dan? She might be in that small grove of christmas trees. I'll check over by the town."

"What's your sister doing out this late anyway?" the other man grumbled.

"Well, she's a little slow—if you know what I mean...." Dion's voice faded as she drifted off with him. The crew hiding in the courtyard dared to breathe again.

Quickly, they moved to the stairs and crept up as silently as possible. At the top, Sami removed the tape from the doorjamb, took Aria from her mother's arms, and murmured, "Play along with Dion. Act like you're about five years old. Dan won't be hard to fool."

Manuel had circled around the wall and now came up, taking Alice's arm. "We'll meet you all at the safe house. Go on."

As her friends hurried off with her daughter, he whispered, "Can you manage to cry a little?"

Could she cry? Alice bit back a sarcastic comment and instead channeled all the anxiety of the evening into her chest. She recalled the way Nettie spoke with a lisp when young and called, "Thister. This, where are you? I'm scared, This." Just playacting fear ignited the actual feeling in her gut and tears streaked down her face.

"Wonderful," Manuel whispered. Then he raised his voice and shouted, "Hey, I found her! Over here."

Soon Dion, clinging to the technician's arm, came hurrying out of the dark. She abandoned her protector and threw her arms around her friend, hugging her tight. As she stood a few inches taller than Alice, who now slumped against her, the illusion of an older sister caring for a disabled, younger girl held. Dan, no longer basking in the beautiful woman's attention, moved to the gate.

"You can walk them home, right Manuel?"

"Yeah, I've got it, man. You go back to work."

As the heavy door swung shut, Alice straightened up, and they hurried away toward their hideout, but the tears wouldn't stop— not until she held Aria again in her arms.

Creating a landing strip one thousand twenty meters long and sixty meters wide to accommodate the Shepherd's shuttle proved a challenge. Doing the work under cover, hid from hostile eyes, made it almost impossible. The Singers had chosen a vast swath of flat grassland on the side of the road which ran from Far Meadow to Seaside, opposite the traveler's hut. They planned to send teams of five to six people at a time to clear the site, trusting that a quarter-mile buffer of swaying grass would screen their labor. Two lookouts each day sat close to the track and monitored the sparse traffic, ready to warn both the workers in the field and those at the cabin if travelers appeared.

Three days after contacting the Shepherd, Alice and Aria arrived at the shelter with Jamie an hour before sunset. Alice immediately offered to be on the clearing crew. Pete, who directed the project, shook his head.

"Michel's out there now with a group of four youngsters from Near Meadow. Jamie will help them. You better save your strength for dealing with the Earth people when they land."

"I can't sit around for a week and a half not doing anything," she snapped. The hike back without Sami depressed her. She was worried about his safety. She couldn't sort out whether his absence or the fact that she missed him so much upset her more. If all went well, he would join her in a few days, after establishing his "innocent" presence in town. But she needed something to do, some action to keep her busy.

Dove, stirring a pot of stew which filled the small structure with a delicious smell, looked over her shoulder at the young woman.

"She could relieve the lookouts every few hours. I'll watch the child for her."

"All right," Pete said, "but not today. Have a meal, get some rest. You'll feel better in the morning."

She nodded to acknowledge his concern and left to find a spot in the area designated for the women. Both Dove and Sarai had already claimed the beds, but a mat rolled up against the far wall waited for her. She laid it out, putting her meager belongings on the end to mark it. Then she wandered back into the room where Aria entertained the older folks and made herself useful setting the table.

It didn't take long for the work crew and lookouts to show up for first supper and rest. They filed in, sweaty and dusty, leaning their hand scythes against the wall. Jamie had gone out to inspect their progress and came through the door last, accompanying his father. Alice, already dishing out the stew, noted the son's frown and Michel's furrowed brow. As all the seats at the table filled, she nodded to a corner of the hut and joined the two men with her own bowl, sitting cross-legged on the floor.

"So, how's it going out there?" she asked, peering into Michel's face.

He didn't meet her eyes and kept chewing.

"They saw a convoy of hummies and trailers traveling north this morning, but none stopped." Jamie spoke to fill in his dad's silence. "We figure they're on their way up to Last Stop for a share of the harvest there. They pull the beets and turnips out of the ground about now."

Alice nodded, "Makes sense." She paused, looking at Michel, who kept his gaze on his bowl. "How's the landing strip progressing?"

At this, the older man set down his spoon and sighed, meeting her gaze. "We'll get it done on time, Alice. But a report reached us yesterday. The Academy contacted the spaceship. It must have been just after you talked to them. They directed the captain to land near Touch Down. They've got students out preparing a runway right now."

The buzz of conversation around them seemed to fade, and the light seemed to dim as the young woman received this information. What would happen if the Shepherd ignored their directions and sided with the Gladiators? Did Goldie understand the danger?

"When?" she demanded. " Did they say when they agreed to land?"

"Yeah, that's interesting," Michel frowned. "Same time we asked them to arrive."

Alice took a deep breath and smiled. "OK, that's good then. It means the Shepherd misdirected them. Clever people. The Glads will all be in Touch Down when they land here."

"That's what Dove told him." Sarai sat down next to her husband, balancing her own bowl of stew and giving an exasperated sigh. "My men always worry too much."

Michel snorted. "You're not out there making a useless landing strip."

"I understand, dear. But if both Dove and Alice think Goldie's on to the Gladiators, I trust all will be well."

Jamie, watching this interaction between his parents, sighed. "Go on, Dad," he said. "Tell them what else is worrying you."

Michel glanced at his wife, who had leaned in to hear better. "Haven't had a chance to share this with you yet, dear. Micah stopped by this afternoon. Came cross-country. Didn't want anyone to see him." He paused, looking into his stew bowl. "Your Pa's been to Seaside and back, Alice. They may suspect we've got a landing place somewhere up here, too, even if they don't know where. He's supposed to keep in touch with them. He's got a special com unit."

Alice frowned and nodded. "We knew he joined the Gladiators. I'm not surprised he's helping the ones from the Academy. Did Micah report what they propose to do if they locate us?"

The older man shook his head. "Best guess is they'll try to disrupt contact if the ship lands here."

"OK, let's tell Pete and Dove and get a defense plan ready."

The crew at the landing site rotated workers every few days to obscure the fact that strong young adults were away from their home villages for a period. Two Last Stop men and a Mountain View woman replaced the Near Meadow residents the next day. At first supper that night, the new volunteers announced the convoy from Seaside had indeed entered Last Stop right before they left.

"I'm afraid they wanted a lot more of our crop than we can spare," Solly, the oldest of them, said. "This happened last year too. They show up with enough trucks for the whole harvest and think we'll just hand it over."

"Yeah," his younger brother, Ben, chimed in. "Luckily, our mayor came from Seaside and knows how to talk to them."

"So, how much do you figure your town can share with them?" Michel asked.

Alice noticed his frown, but remembered Sarai said he often worried without cause.

Solly shrugged. "They'll be fortunate to get one truckload this harvest. And since they've already taken away every opportunity at the Academy for our children, as well as denying us traveling teachers, they don't have a lot to bargain with."

Michel looked at his wife and the younger woman, following his gaze, noted that she also took this seriously. Her full lips bowed down and her forehead creased. Then the conversation moved on to the work needing to get done the next day.

Alice joined Sarai at the sink to wash dishes, waiting until they were alone to ask, "Why did the Last Stop men upset you?"

Sarai paused, searching her face. "Bleak is almost here, Alice. The bigger towns, especially Touch Down, depend on the produce the villages grow. For two revs, we've only been able to give them enough to keep everyone fed. They haven't been storing any of it. The harvests aren't good anywhere, so we have little to spare, particularly in this rev, as we try to stockpile for the lean months."

"They have fish and gardens."

"How many bio-domes are in Seaside?"

Alice paused, then shook her head. "Just the Academy greenhouse, and a lot of those plants are experimental."

The crease between Sarai's brows deepened. "Have you talked to Edie about the latest catches? She told me they either trawled too liberally, or the fish have migrated somewhere else. The boats bring in fewer and fewer. Last time Michel took the hummie to town to get our supply, he came home empty-handed."

Alice thought of the rough garden she spent so many hours cultivating at the cave. Even if all the seeds brought forth fruit, she knew there wouldn't be enough to keep her and Aria alive during the full third when it was too cold to grow anything. "We're all in trouble, aren't we?"

Sarai nodded. "Humanity will be lucky to survive this time. And desperate people do desperate things."

Alice grasped at hope. "Maybe having Goldie back can help."

"Maybe."

CHAPTER TWENTY-FOUR

Sami appeared five days before the scheduled landing. Just as they spotted him coming across the lawn, one lookout ran up, breathless with news. Alice and Aria's excited welcome of their dear friend had to wait while Ben told his story: He had seen the convoy which had gone up to Last Stop only six days ago returning to Seaside, every trailer laden with produce.

"Even the blue turnips," he said. "We never give those away. They're only for Last Stop people." His face crumpled, bewilderment edging into panic.

Sarai swooped in to comfort him, while Dove and Pete exchanged worried glances. Alice, still holding her daughter on her hip, read the atmosphere of fear in the room. "I'd better call in Solly. He'll want to know."

"Get the whole crew," Dove said. "Everyone should be in on this."

"Can they stop for this?" Sami asked. "The strip needs to be done in four days."

Pete nodded. "You're right. That has to be our priority. But bring Michel with Solly, Alice. We need his insight."

The young mother handed off her child to Sami, who sank down on a bench. Their eyes met, and Alice smiled. Even the upsetting news couldn't undermine her relief that he had made it back again.

Alice delivered her message, then stayed by the road, replacing

Ben as the northern lookout. The wind howled, making her eyes tear up as she searched the horizon for any movement. She hunkered down as best she could behind a slight mound in the grassland and tried to convince herself that the gale stirred up the agitation she felt, not the report of the laden trailers heading to Seaside. *At least Sami made it home,* she thought, holding fast to that scrap of good news.

An hour passed, with only the tall grass moving, tossed about by the wind. It would be another few hours before the crew came in for the night. Alice, wondering what the others were discussing and if someone remembered to monitor her daughter, looked over her shoulder toward the hut. They had hidden all the vehicles behind the tree line. At this distance, nothing revealed that the small sunken building held any visitors. Hopefully, the illusion would hold.

She redirected her gritty eyes back to the road—and caught her breath. A dusty cloud rose far up on the track. Someone was coming in a hummie. She leaped to her feet and sprinted to the hut. The southern lookout would see the dust and record who and what passed—if the vehicle continued on. If it stopped, she needed to warn the rebels inside that they would soon have company.

Jumping down the courtyard stairs, she burst into the main room. With a glance, she took in the adults gathered around the table over mugs of tea and Aria playing with Ben in the kitchen area. The general disarray testified to the number of people housed there. "Hummies approaching from the north," she gasped.

"How many?" Pete asked as everyone sprang into coordinated action.

"Too much dust—I couldn't tell." She bent to scoop Aria into her arms and turned to Sami. He already had the backpack and helped her lift the child in, then swung it onto his own shoulders.

"C'mon. We'll hide in the forest. What's the all-clear signal?"

"Sarai will come to the top of the stairs and shake out a rug." Pete handed them a bag of rolls and a canteen of water. "If you don't see that in the next hour, head toward my house and stay there."

"Right."

The trio scurried out the door, following Solly and Ben. The brothers from Last Stop headed for their hidden ATVs. They would escape with as many of the workers as possible, if it came to that. As she left, Alice glanced behind her to see Sarai and Pete picking up the detritus of their crowd, but Dove had disappeared. Whoever arrived would encounter only a middle-aged woman caring for her aging grandpa.

As they entered the canopy of the forest, Alice's panic subsided. They had done this drill twice in the last few days, and nothing bad had happened. Surely this time, the travelers would drive past too. She led Sami to the space she had found only a few feet in, where a convenient waist-high bush spanned between two great tree trunks. She helped him remove the backpack and kneeled to lift Aria out. The little girl could play amongst the pine needles under the screening shrub while the adults took turns watching the yard. She looked up to observe her friend staring toward the hut.

"It's turning in, Alice. One hummie with four people in it. Looks like they're parking in the back."

"Oh, God." Fear rose in her throat. "Keep behind the tree. They may see you if they look this way." She stayed low but peeked over the bush, locating the ATV halting in the small clearing to the rear of the hut.

"Why would they park there?" she asked. But Sami just shrugged and kept his eyes glued to the scene.

"Alice, is that Micah and Humphrey? It looks like they have two women with them."

She stood up against the opposite tree, narrowing her eyes in the wind. She recognized Micah's solid form, but was that her father? The man looked similar, but somehow different, his back bowed and shoulders drawn in. Janelle and Nettie, clinging to each other, followed them to the courtyard stairs.

She felt sick to her stomach. "Maybe we should leave now, Sami. Pa works for the Academy Gladiators. Micah says he's spying for them. I didn't realize he knew for sure we were here, though."

His dark eyes met hers. "Let's wait a bit. Something strange is going on. Why would he bring your ma and sister with him if he's trying to catch us? And I don't believe Micah would betray you."

They crouched behind the bush, keeping Aria amused and quiet, taking turns watching the hut for close to half an hour. Alice's mind ran through every scenario imaginable, but nothing credible arose. She had begun tracing the escape route back to her cave in her imagination when Sami said, "There it is: Sarai's shaking out the rug."

"What if my father forced her to? He could be threatening Pete."

Sami turned to look into her face. "Would she give you up that easily?"

Alice sighed. "No. And Pete would die before he put Aria in danger." She stood and picked up her squirming daughter. "Let's find out what's up."

They walked through the tall grass to the lawn. As they descended to the door, Sami stepped forward, indicating he would enter first, but Alice took his arm to go with him. Whatever happened, she would face it with him.

As their eyes adjusted to the dimmer light of the cabin, Alice heard Nettie gasp her name and felt the weight of a desperate body thrown against her. She released her friend to hug her sister, who sobbed into her shoulder. Janelle stood up from her seat and joined them, wrapping her arms around both young women. Aria clung to her mother in fear at this strange behavior until Sarai stepped forward to take the child.

"Come, sit down," the older woman said, shielding the baby from their distress.

As they complied, all three sitting on a bench with her sister still hugging her fiercely, Alice surveyed the rest of the room. Sami joined

Pete, Michel, and Micah in the kitchen area, where they engaged in deep conversation. At the end of the long table sat her father, hunched over, his hands fisted on the boards in front of him. Dread bloomed in her heart and seeped through her limbs.

"What happened?" Her question, directed to no one in particular, met a heavy silence in which Nettie's wild sobbing echoed.

Janelle put out her hand and grasped Alice's, tears streaming down her face. "In Last Stop...." The older woman paused, closing her eyes as if she couldn't bear to look at her house daughter. Then she opened them and continued. "Some virus hit them. They're all dead."

"All?" Sami stood behind Alice now, his hands on her shoulders to steady her.

Janelle tilted her head and avoided looking at Alice. "They had their harvest festival. Jaren wanted to go." Sobs overcame her.

"Jaren's sick?" He had been at Nainai's funeral, undaunted by his parents' stress, a mischievous two-rev-old. *No, almost three revs now,* she remembered. She had been in Seaside for more than a third. When was the last time she had played with him? The morning she went to see Nainai and had to bandage his knee. *Why hadn't they brought him here?* Sami's fingers tightened on her shoulders, and she knew. Jaren was gone. He had died, too.

Nettie raised her head and sat up. "Pa let him go. He took him up to our cousins' house and left him there." She spat out the accusation with more fury than her sister had ever suspected her to be capable of.

"I. Did. Not. Know." At the other end of the table, her father emphasized each word with a bang of both fists on the boards. Then he collapsed, laying his face on crossed forearms.

Sami's voice, tight and stilted, sounded like hail on the roof. "Did you get the new vaccination when you were in Seaside, Humphrey?"

The gray head nodded without raising. She heard him whisper into his arms, "I did not know."

***

The unthinkable had happened. Desperate people do desperate things. The haunted past they promised they would never repeat had found its way into their present. Humans let loose a weaponized virus to gain power over others. Even as her brain accepted the facts, Alice tried to find to another explanation, a less horrific story.

"Terrible plagues have hit before. Perhaps the Gladiators didn't bring it, but just took advantage of the tragedy."

Everyone went over the events in their own minds. They all sat at the table now, eyes averted from the broken man at the end. Sami, on the other side of Nettie, shook his head.

"Too many coincidences. In Seaside, rumors are flying that an unusual disease has surfaced. We all believed them, even though none of us were sick. The authorities insisted everybody get the new vaccine the prevention team developed, except for those over child-bearing years."

"No," Jamie chimed in. "Some older professors got the shot too. It depends on what you do there."

"Right." Sami nodded. "Someone's deciding who's expendable."

Aria, sensing the tension in the room, squirmed in Sarai's arms and reached out to her mother. Alice scooped her up onto her lap, embracing her.

"Are we in danger? Did Solly and Ben bring the disease here? Or did my family?"

Micah leaned forward. "I wouldn't have brought them here if I thought they were contagious. And Solly and Ben left before anyone got sick. We think it must have been in the food that the Gladiators delivered or something they slipped into the drinking water. An airborne virus would be too dangerous, even with the vaccination."

"It will mutate and find other ways of spreading." Michel frowned, his pale face whiter than usual. "That's what viruses do—change to become more efficient killers."

Pete spoke up. "Yes, I suppose that's why the Academy

distributed vaccines immediately. They're fools, though. They may have created this virus, but they can't predict how it will develop."

"Someone must warn the other villages right away." As usual, practical Sarai saw the next step to take. "No one outside of Seaside and Touch Down has been vaccinated. They have to seal themselves off from the disease until we can get them the shots."

Her husband supported her. "Our boys have the protection, and Sami does too. We'll send them out to Near and Far Meadow and Mountain View. They could lock down within two days. But how will they resist if the Glads insist on entering their boundaries? We've never had to fight each other before."

And there it was, boldly laid out before them: civil war. The oxymoron they all feared. They had fought so much united: plague and hunger, cold and wind. Would they soon kill each other?

The ignored hulk at the end of the table raised his gaze. "You have some time. They won't come to the outback now until the shuttle lands."

All eyes turned to stare at the haggard man. After a beat of silence, Micah said, "Why? Share what you know of their plans, Humphrey. Help us figure this out."

The shaggy head nodded, and the lifeless voice said, "I'm supposed to report on how your landing strip is progressing. If I say you've stopped working on it, that you don't think the shuttle is coming here, they'll assume the captain told you he was going to Seaside."

Again, silence. People shifted in their seats. Sami finally spoke up. "Will they leave us alone, then?"

The broad shoulders shrugged. "Don't know. They don't tell me much." He paused, still focused on the boards before him. "I can say I'll keep an eye on things here. I'll pretend to continue to help them."

Alice scanned the faces around the table. From the frowns, she perceived everybody's worry, but Nettie's lip curled and her eyes burned as she surveyed her father.

"It's your fault that Jaren's gone, that everyone in Last Stop died. Helping now won't make up for that. Ever. I will never forgive you." Her sister spat the words as the broken man's shoulders slumped even further. Her mother put a restraining hand on her arm but didn't rebuke her.

"You're right," he croaked, raising his reddened eyes to meet hers. "But I'll do what I can."

They completed clearing the landing strip just as the sun set the night before the planned touchdown. Sami, Manuel, and Jamie, returning from their visits to warn the outback villages, brought trusted representatives from all three hamlets to witness the event, bringing the gathered group to eighteen. The little wayside hut couldn't contain everyone, and some diners, bowls and cups in hand, spilled out onto the lawn. Alice watched the scene, nostalgia warming her heart. This felt like a village gathering in happier days, when all the world seemed right to her little-girl eyes. Then, she noticed her father, sitting alone on a boulder near his parked hummie, his hunched back toward the crowd.

Humphrey kept his promise to deceive the Academy Glads and appeared to be successful. No other inspectors had bothered them, and they heard no rumors of any planned disruption. He had also thrown himself into the labor of creating the landing strip, wearing his body out so much that Janelle recruited Alice for support in begging Pete to forbid him to work. Her old friend, however, ignored their request. "He's making up for the three young men we had to send away to warn the villages. If it kills him, he'll die knowing he tried to correct his mistakes."

Alice strode across the lawn and lowered herself down on the grass beside her father. He paused his meal, looking down at her. The memory of sitting like this with him at some picnic many revs ago flooded her body with tenderness. She met his eyes and let a small smile flit over her lips.

The big man averted his gaze, becoming as still and unmovable as the boulder he sat on. Alice bit her tongue, letting the silence lie between them. Finally, he cleared his throat and spoke, his voice rusty as an old hinge. "I loved your Nainai. I never meant to hurt her."

"Yes, I know."

"So many people died. So many children, so many friends. I wanted to stop it. I thought the Glads were powerful, that being part of their team would help. They didn't tell me what the real plan was, I swear."

A memory surfaced in her mind: Humphrey swinging his small son up to his shoulders and galloping him off to bed, both laughing wildly. *He loved Jaren more than anyone else.* "I believe you, Pa."

He looked at her, pupils dilating and nostrils flaring. "I want to kill them, Alice. I never hurt anything on purpose before, but I want to see them perish in pain before I do."

His heavy words pressed down on the bruise of a dark anger hidden in her, igniting a shiver of disgust and fear. She took a breath, finding tenderness again. Reaching up, she put a hand on his forearm. "Maybe nobody else has to die, Pa. Not you or them."

He turned his head away from her, dislodging her fingers as he began savagely to spoon up the cooling stew. After a minute, she got to her feet.

Is this what we humans have become? She wondered as she leaned into the accelerating wind and followed the rest of the diners into the shelter. *Are we willing to shed blood as freely as the Glads did?* She looked over her shoulder at the impassive back hunched over his bowl. *How many others will want revenge instead of community?*

CHAPTER TWENTY-FIVE

"They're headed for Seaside." Manuel's shocked voice echoed what everyone standing outside the wayside hut realized.

They had stepped out into a calm, beautiful dawn, all of them searching the brightening sky for some sign of the Shepherd's shuttle. Everybody cheered when the com trail appeared, but then fell silent as they saw the trajectory was off.

"Are you sure?" Alice heard panic in her voice but was still too stunned to feel it. "Maybe they're just off course. Perhaps the coordinates were wrong."

A buzz of disbelief and despair grew around her, until Dove said, "Quiet. They will come. Watch."

The wise woman's faith bolstered them, and eyes turned again to the sky. Wherever it had landed, the shuttle was down. But as the white vapor of its passing vanished into the atmosphere, a second black dot trailing a plume appeared.

"Look, another one!"

"They sent two."

"Yes, it's headed here."

The little crowd, more confused than jubilant, prepared to welcome guests which they now suspected might as likely be enemies as friends. As the rumbling of the shuttle's approach shook the air, Pete grabbed Alice's arm and pulled her over to Dove's side. Sami joined them and all four leaned in as the old man gestured them to conference.

"Did any of you foresee this? Did you sense any change in Goldie's feelings toward us?"

The forest visionary, her gray-green eyes intense, said, "We never asked how the Earthers would deal with Gladiators. Nothing has changed in Goldie's attitude. Whatever the crew's intention, her pattern has not broken."

Sami frowned and bit his lip. "Do you think they may defy Goldie's wishes?"

Alice shook her head. "No, that makes no sense. Judy and Esteban connect to her, more deeply than any of us, except maybe Dove. They would have warned her if the crew...."

Her words faltered as the shuttle screamed overhead and every face turned to the landing strip hidden in the grass. A series of tremendous thumps shook the ground beneath their feet, and then the noise settled to a hissing as the great engine cooled.

"Nothing has changed," Dove said, her voice loud enough to carry to the others. "We cannot see as far as Goldie. Now is the time for trust. We welcome them as planned." Without waiting for a response, she turned and strode toward the path leading to the shuttle.

Alice glanced at Nettie, standing by the courtyard steps, holding Aria. She stared at her daughter's face for a second, burning it into her heart. Then, with Sami, she trotted to catch up to the long-legged Singer, Pete following more slowly behind. As she passed through the little crowd, her father grabbed her arm.

"Warn them that their other craft is in danger. Tell them about Last Stop." His hand gripped her hard, then released when she nodded.

They had planned for only the four of them to approach the shuttle, not wanting to overwhelm the crew, which they suspected would comprise five to ten people. The rest of the group waited at the hut, preparing tea and breakfast. *What are we doing?* Alice wondered as she stumbled through the head-high grass. *We know nothing about these strangers, and they know nothing of us.* Her father's anxiety, she realized, infected her. *Trust*—she reminded herself of Dove's command. *But who are we trusting?* the fear whispered back. *Even Goldie is alien to us now.*

The first unobstructed view of the shuttle startled her. Just glimpsing the shiny curve of its body above the grass hadn't prepared her for the immensity of the craft, three times as long as it was high. She stumbled over the ruts its wheels had dug in the cleared area, noticing skids veering both left and right. The landing must have been rough.

Her fingers found Sami's as her feet came to a halt and her eyes widened at the sight of the opening hatch. Dove stood on Sami's other side, absolutely still. Pete caught up and put a hand on her shoulder. "Be calm. They're as nervous as we are. Your first words need to reassure them."

A man appeared in the doorway far above their heads, dressed in the familiar blue overalls, his round face catching the sunlight so that he had to squint to see them. It was Alan, the commander, Alice realized, registering that at least they sent the head of the expedition to the Singers. He raised his hand in greeting, and the four on the ground all lifted theirs in response. Behind him, she glimpsed two taller figures peering over his shoulder. A steep slope of steps unfolded, clanging in the still air. Alan started down them, the other crew members following. She recognized them: Esteban and Judy.

As the three Earthers stepped onto the dirt, they faced the welcoming committee and paused. Each group studied the other. These people, Alice realized, were taller than most on Goldilocks, but otherwise could be part of their population. They didn't look too alien.

Pete's hand on her shoulder gave her a little shove, and she took a step forward, spreading open palms before her.

"Welcome to Goldilocks. Welcome, Alan, Judy, and Esteban.

Thank you for coming to us."

All three smiled, and Judy reached out to grasp both her hands.

"Alice, we are so glad to be here and meet you in person. You must be worried about the other shuttle. We'll tell you about that and all we have planned."

Sami, Dove, and Pete moved forward to add their greetings.

Dove said, "We have much to discuss, and other Singers and villagers want to take part, as well. Will you come with us for refreshments and council?"

"Yes, yes." Alan nodded with enthusiasm. "That's just what we hoped for. These two promised me you would set up a conference." He gestured to the forest mystic to lead the way and followed.

"Wait." Alice put her hand on the commander's arm, pausing his movement. "Before we go, I must tell you—your other shuttle may be in danger. The Gladiators—those people who contacted you after we did—they've done something terrible." Her voice faltered. What would they think of her, of their entire world, when they realized some were murderers? How could she even say the words?

The small group froze, and she could sense her companions' worried eyes on her. This wasn't part of the welcoming plan, and they hadn't discussed it. She drew a breath to steady herself so she could continue, but Judy put a hand on her shoulder.

"It's OK, Alice. We know."

"You do?" She looked up into this stranger's face and saw her own infinite sadness mirrored there.

"Goldie showed us what happened in Last Stop. We're so sorry."

Sami spoke up. "You may not be aware that it's a virus that did the damage. We believe they put it in the food or water. You should warn your other crew not to eat or drink anything."

The commander nodded but said, "We think we know what they used and have taken precautionary steps, but yes—until we understand your rivals' motives and intentions, we will be careful."

"Then come." Dove stepped onto the path. "You have nothing to fear from us, and we have much to discuss."

They had cleared the hut of most furniture to create an open space for a meeting circle of thirty people. Since only three had arrived on the shuttle, there was plenty of room. Sarai invited the foreigners to take chairs in the place of honor, but it pleased Alice to see they chose instead to sit on the floor like most everyone else. As the villagers passed tea and cakes around, she was also relieved to see their guests accepting the food without concern. Clearly, they trusted this motley group of Singers and farmers. Aria, the only child present, became a focus of attention, crawling to the strangers and gazing at their faces one by one. As if satisfied by this inspection, she made her way over to her mother, sitting between Judy and Sami, and snuggled into her lap, humming.

"I think she approves of you all," Alice laughed.

Esteban nodded. "Goldie and she are in sync. We're not really strangers to her, you know."

Dove smiled at the contented little girl. "Perhaps, in the future, we will all bond through knowing Goldie."

After a pause, Pete cleared his throat.

"You said you would tell us about the other shuttle and your plans. Could we get right to that? The Gladiators probably saw your second craft and may investigate what's going on here."

Alan set his mug on the floor in front of him and looked around the circle. "Judy and Esteban have been in deep contact with Goldie since you called the Shepherd. They shared with our crew the difficulties you face here on the planet: that you will enter a cold revolution soon, and your food stores are low, your crops are not doing well. It seems to us that the horrendous action taken by the faction you call the Gladiators was a response to fear of starvation. We hope we can ease their anxiety, reducing the threat they pose."

"That 'horrendous action' was the slaughter of forty-five men, women, and children, including my son." Humphrey sat, arms crossed, on a chair outside the circle, opposite the Earthers, and glaring down at them all. "Call it what it is: murder. I hope you sent a crew to execute them all."

Heads turned and bodies shifted as the big man's fury poisoned the atmosphere. Alice saw Pete scowling at him and, before he could issue a challenge, spoke up, desperate to pull everyone's attention away from her Pa.

"Excuse the interruption, please. This is my father, Humphrey. My brother, just three revs old, was lost at Last Stop." Tears filled her eyes. She allowed them to fall. "We will listen to your plan, though." She glared at her father now, meeting his smoldering gaze. "Enough people have died."

Beside her, Judy shifted, putting her hand out to rest on Alice's knee. "You all have suffered so much. We understand. We can't bring back your loved ones. Let us help you work to change the situation, so hate, and fear, and destruction aren't your only options."

"Yes, tell us how," Sarai said. "Suggest something we can do to save everyone."

On the perimeter of the circle, Humphrey reclined in his chair, his head sinking down, hiding his eyes beneath a furrowed brow. Alice relaxed. *Pa won't disrupt the session now,* she thought—*at least not for a while.*

The plan the Earthers proposed comprised three parts. First, the shuttle which landed in Seaside held ten crew members, some of them skilled in assessing dangerous situations and others who specialized in unique farming and food-management techniques. They hoped to come up with strategies to grow produce during Bleak. They also offered to supplement at least some of the population's needs from the spaceship's bio-dome.

"Remember, though, we designed our system to feed the crew of the Shepherd, so we don't have much to share but ideas and technology. We're hoping our expertise, and what you've grown already, will get all of you through the first third." Alan's friendly face looked as serious as it could.

"And what then?" asked Michel. "Does this just prolong our agony?"

"Ah, no," Judy spoke up, smiling. "We have a surprise for you: Goldie showed us a valley on this planet, about a thousand miles from here, where hot springs come out of the cliff wall and the air stays temperate all year. The fairy dragons shelter there in the cold months. Farming is possible, even in Bleak. We hope some of you will settle there to raise food for everyone."

An excited murmur circulated through the gathering. Sami, frowning, leaned in to look across Alice and catch Judy's eye.

"There's no way we can get that far around the planet in time to plant crops before people starve. I've traveled through these forests and up the mountains. Even with hummies, travel will be slow."

Judy nodded agreement, but it was Esteban who replied. "You're right. The Shepherd offers two things to facilitate this plan, though. We can transport thirty adults to the valley, along with supplies. With shuttles, the trip should only take a few hours. We figure five round trips will suffice. We have to conserve our fuel, because we also need to fly out the produce when the first harvests come in. You'll have to establish trade routes at some point, but with our help, we hope to feed everyone through the coldest months."

Happy gasps and hopeful smiles bloomed around the circle. Alice noticed that Micah, sitting on the floor next to Janelle, looked over his shoulder at his friend, still scowling in his chair. He sighed, met her eye, and then asked in a loud voice, "You said the Shepherd had three things to offer. What's the third one?"

Quiet fell as everyone refocused on the Earthers. This time, the commander answered.

"Communications. The Academy created a perfectly adequate array in Seaside, as you know, because you broke into it." He winked a bright blue eye at Alice. "With a little help from our communication specialists and some work with the 3-D printer, we propose to connect everyone on this planet through a system of com links. The new valley settlement will have access to the towns and villages, as well as the Shepherd, and vice versa."

"Wrist coms for everybody?" Jamie gasped.

"Yup. It'll take a while to set up, but we can do it." Alan smiled so broadly his eyes got lost in his cheeks.

Pete stared at him. "And if everyone's talking to each other, it's difficult to lie about what's going on, right?"

"Yes," said Judy. "The best defense of freedom is to ensure access to the facts of any situation. The way we understand it, your governing body kept you all in the dark about many actions. It will be harder to hide in shadows with universal communication."

Again, the conversation devolved as people processed this information with neighbors, a cheerful buzz filling the room. Alice beamed at Sami, but then her friend nodded his curly head toward her father. She switched her gaze and looked into Humphrey's furious visage. As she watched, he jumped to his feet, the crash of his chair hitting the floor silencing everyone.

"So, you're just going to forget what the Glads did? They'll get away with murder, while we grow fat and chatter with our friends? What kind of plan is this? I say, punish our enemies first. Then figure out how to survive. What good is life without justice?"

The tsunami of his anger and pain bore down on them, sweeping hope aside. Several of the men nodded their agreement. Alice felt Judy lean away from her, listening to something Alan whispered, and wondered, *Is this it? Will they leave us to wallow in our self-pity and vengeance?*

But before anyone else could respond, Janelle struggled to her feet and turned toward her heart-bond partner, her face paler than Alice had ever seen it.

"Is your pain greater than mine, Humphrey Far Meadow? Have you lost more as a father than I as the mother who bore and suckled our son? Is your suffering deeper than any of these here, who have buried not only children but partners and parents and friends?

No—our grief runs together, the sorrow of all people, of Goldie, and of God."

For a moment, her unaccustomed boldness struck him dumb, and those watching held their breath. But then his fists clenched, and he brought his face close to her and hissed, "Then we need to send those murderers to hell, Janelle."

She didn't back up, but Alice knew her housemother. She wouldn't have the words to fight his anger. Not taking time to think, Alice rose, crossed the open circle, and put her arm around Janelle's shoulders, facing into the fury.

"I'm pretty sure you can't send them to hell, Pa, without going there yourself. Ma knows what she's talking about. Grief carves a great chasm of despair. Our choice now is to either build a bridge across that poisonous pit and cross to the other side together, or to descend into it. If we go down, this pain, this division, will pass to Aria and all the children, to deal with again and again and again. Is that what you want?"

Humphrey glared at her, then shifted his gaze to stare at the people around the circle, nostrils flaring, face livid.

"So, you ask me to forget my son, to ignore the betrayal I suffered trying to do the right thing for us?"

Alice winced and tightened her hold on her household mother. Would Janelle retreat as she had so many times before when faced with Humphrey's rage?

But the older woman had reached and crossed some boundary today. Alice felt Janelle's back straighten and her head rise.

"Don't be a fool." She spat the words at the angry man. "Look at me, Humphrey. I will never forget, *never*. I will always carry the pain of Jaren's death. But Alice is right. I choose to take my grief and use all my strength to transform it into life. I refuse to go into the pit with you, even though we are bonded. You must decide now whether you will come with me into a different future."

Alice sensed the vacuum created by a communal holding of

breath as she stared, transfixed, waiting for her father's reaction. His craggy face, crimson a moment ago, drained of all color, and his shoulders sagged as if he suffered a blow to his stomach. For the space of seven heartbeats, he stood frozen. Then he turned and stumbled out the door.

Janelle, shaking with the effort of such defiance, continued standing, looking at the opening until Nettie rose to hug her. Together, they eased down to sit again. Alice met her sister's eye and nodded her gratitude as everyone else in the room relaxed and returned their attention to the Earthers.

Alan acknowledged their scrutiny with a curt nod. "We won't force our plans or our values on you. If you want to pursue a different course of action, you're free to do so.

"Understand, though—we can't take sides. Also, we don't have enough crew members to settle the valley by ourselves. If you opt not to work with us, the Shepherd will have to head back to Earth."

Dove leaned forward into the circle, her cloud of hair swirling around her face. "Janelle and Alice laid out our choice well. This is the crossroads at which we stand: Do we take the short path to vengeance or the long road to a different but unified future? Are we ready to decide? From eldest to youngest, let's make our choices known, remembering that this will affect all people and Goldilocks too."

She nodded then at Pete, who spoke to the circle.

"I have little time left, but I choose the way of healing and unity. I probably won't see us get there, but that's the future I wish to give Aria and all the children of Goldilocks."

Heads bobbed all around. Oldest to youngest, everyone present elected to work with the Earthers. Then, Janelle again spoke up.

"Humphrey hasn't yet voted. I don't want to leave him out of this decision. May I go speak with him to learn his choice?"

"Of course," Pete said. "We could all use a break. I'll put on water for more tea."

During the brief hiatus, Alice noticed Dove sought out Judy and Esteban, leading them to a corner of the room for a quiet conversation. When Janelle returned inside with a subdued Humphrey in tow and all sat down again, these three stayed together.

Her father settled on the floor next to her household mother, but Alice noted he kept his head down, eyes averted. As the circle quieted, Pete cleared his throat to begin the meeting. "All have voted but you, Humphrey. Will you tell us your choice?"

The big man did not raise his gaze, but all could hear his words, tense and curt. "I'll give up vengeance and agree to go forward. But know this..." He raised his shaggy head and glared in the Earthers' direction. "The Gladiators won't hand over control easily. You'll need as much information on them as possible. I'll stay and pretend to work for the Glads. That's the best I can do for our future."

Around the gathering, his daughter could hear a sigh of relief. Micah spoke up.

"What you offer gives me hope, dear friend. I want you to know we appreciate your sacrifice. We won't forget it."

Heads nodded and Alice murmured, "Thank you, Pa."

Even her younger sister, who had not spoken to their father since they arrived at the hut, bowed her gratitude to him.

"Then we have decided," Dove announced. "We will assist the Earthers' plan to the fullest extent possible."

Across the room, the sons of Sarai and Michel both raised their hands.

"We volunteer to settle the new valley." Jamie could barely sit still as he made this pronouncement.

Manuel added, "In fact, a group of students at the Academy has been talking about exploring more of the planet for a third now. We already gathered some equipment and were waiting to get through Bleak."

The commander of the Shepherd leaned forward. "That's great— just what we hoped to hear. We need you Singers and villagers to guide us in selecting the best farmers and technicians among the younger adults to make this happen."

"Before we discuss these details," Dove interrupted, holding up her hand, palm outward, "Goldie has sent a warning to Judy, Esteban, and me. People set out in hummies from Seaside an hour ago. Goldie thinks they intend to find out who is involved here and arrest them."

The two younger crew members from the Shepherd nodded their agreement to Alan.

"She can't be sure how much danger they present," Esteban said. "She wants us to get Alice and Aria out of the way."

"Then we begin with our plan right away?" the commander asked.

"We think that's our best move." Judy said.

"OK," Alan put his hands on his knees and addressed the group. "We'd like to take Alice and her child to the valley now, with a few people from the Shepherd. After our shuttle leaves, the rest of you scatter. Humphrey, you can tell the Glads that although we met with the Singers, you don't know what we discussed and that we left abruptly. That will introduce enough doubt to keep them working with us. We promise you we'll be in contact to choose other settlers and move them within the month."

"Wait, you're taking Alice right now?" Sami scanned the faces of the Earthers and his friend, echoing her panic.

Judy said, "Yes, the danger for her and her child grows every day. Goldie fears for her more than anyone else."

"OK, then I'm going with her. She shouldn't have to do this alone. It's not fair."

"And I'm coming too," Nettie got to her feet. "She's my sister. I want to be with her."

Alice also stood and lifted Aria, clutching her close. She looked at Sami and Nettie. "Don't you understand what this means? Sami, you would have to leave Pete behind. And Nettie, Ma needs you.

You're angry with Pa now, but he's your father. If you come, you may never see them again."

"It's their choice, Alice." Judy bit her lip as she scanned her new friend's face. Then, she shifted her gaze to take in Sami and Nettie. "We have room for two or three others. But decide quickly. We leave in fifteen minutes."

The young man stood and took Alice's hand. He looked at his great grandfather, still seated, who nodded.

"Pete understands. I promised you, Alice. I vowed we would travel the road together in whatever way we could, and I meant it."

Nettie crossed the circle to cover her sister's other hand as it gripped her child. "Don't leave me behind. Please. Nainai left without saying goodbye. I can't lose you too."

Alice looked over her at the man and woman who had raised them. Her father's head remained bowed, but Janelle gave her a weak smile and nodded.

"OK." Alice's eyes filled with tears, and she lay her cheek against the smooth head of her child. "OK, we'll go together."

Half an hour later, Alice, Sami, and Nettie prepared to board the Shepherd's shuttle. The entire contingent of Singers and villagers gathered to send them off before returning to their lives. The young mother felt only numbness as she passed through the small crowd, Aria in her arms, as Alan and Esteban led her companions up the steep stairs. Before she committed to the first step, she studied once more the dear faces of friends and family who had created her history. Pete came up to her for one last hug, his gnarled hands stroking her daughter's hair for a final time. She looked into his faded eyes and matched the sadness she found there. She could just hear his cracked voice above the noise of the shuttle's engine warming up.

"Take care of Sami for me."

She nodded, blind now with tears. *Have I made the right decision?* She wondered, as the roar increased, and Judy held her elbow to move her toward the giant silver tube. Alice's free hand went to the pouch under her shirt, the only thing she took with her from home, feeling the familiar shapes of the otter, knife, and jump drive. From the midst of her anguish, a great calm rose and broke over her. Beneath the noise of the shuttle, she detected Nainai's voice.

"This is your time to act, Alice. Leave the past behind. Be present to the moment you are in."

She took a deep breath and faced the steps. For Aria, for Nettie, for Sami, for all of Goldilocks, and for herself—she set her foot on the long road of forgiveness, leading into a vast, unknown future.

EPILOGUE

DATE: REV 44.2/2207 CE

Alice knelt among the young bean plants, weeding out stray blades of grass and straightening the poles, which encouraged them to grow upward. *They're halfway to the top*, she mused. A month before, when she left the fields to bear her second child, they had just sprouted. She rocked back on her heels to survey the plot: a riot of different shades of growing green with a few bright spots of yellow and red where peppers and tomatoes ripened. They soon would have food to send home.

Home.... No, this is home now, she corrected herself, letting her gaze move up and up the valley wall across the river from her. The warm—sometimes even scorching—springs which pierced the cliff fell in steaming waterfalls, filling the cooler air with a sulfurous fog. She wrinkled her nose and smiled. She hardly noticed the rotten-egg odor today, but every once in a while it caught her by surprise. The veil of humidity was already dissipating in the steady sunshine, and she could make out the blue sky above. Soon, Sami would call her to lunch.

She looked over her shoulder at the small, rounded hut near the river's edge which she shared with Sami and Aria, as well as Nettie and Edie. *The baby, too*, she reminded herself. Little Issac—laughter after so much loss and pain. Any doubt that lingered after she had agreed to bond with her dear friend dissolved the night she gave birth. The minute he held the infant, Sami's face broke into complete joy, eclipsing (or perhaps enfolding) the haunting grief of leaving

Pete behind.

If only the old man could have seen his great-great-grandson, she thought. The Shepherd's technology restored communication between all the settlements on the planet, and Pete had followed her pregnancy with great excitement. But his heart stopped three months ago, propelling him into Eternity. It had devastated Sami not to be there, supporting his transition.

Alice sighed and turned her gaze upriver to the fishponds about half a mile away. Edie should be returning for the meal soon, with Aria tagging along or sitting on her shoulders. She saw no sign of them, though. Instead, her eye caught sight of three fairy dragons riding the currents overhead. While the creatures gathered above the deep rift for the cold season, keeping warm in the hotter air rising from the springs, they depended on wind for flight and rarely dropped all the way into the valley.

This trio seemed to look for something. She stood, shading her eyes, trying to get a better view. Suddenly, in one smooth motion, all three wheeled through the sky and plummeted toward her. The young woman raised her wrist band and contacted Sami.

"I've got fairy dragons coming. I may be late for lunch."

His anxious face danced above her arm. "Do you want me to come? This is your first day in the field. You're not supposed to stress yourself."

"Don't worry. I'll take it easy." She cut the transmission and headed toward the bridge and the narrow path leading up the cliff to a ledge on which the gliding creatures landed.

She never got used to crossing the swinging net of rope and planks suspended over the rushing water some twenty feet below. Gritting her teeth and clutching the wobbly railings, she arrived at the footpath already sweating. Humidity rose the closer one came to the steaming cliff, and the young woman took a deep breath, wiping her forehead before stepping onto to the steep trail. She glanced downstream to the sanctuary of her house and saw a lone figure standing outside the door. She raised her wrist.

"Hey, it's OK. I'll try not to take too long. Is the baby hungry already?"

"Nope, Izzy's sleeping like, well, like a baby." Sami smiled, but even in the sun-bleached image wavering above her band, she read the lines of worry between his eyes. "Take it easy up the cliff, Alice. You don't have all your strength back yet."

"Right." She glanced up at the rock face before her, noting a rounded black snout protruding over the edge of a wide stone shelf about a quarter of a mile up. A golden eye surveyed her, conveying an aura of impatience. "They've come down to the lowest bench, Sami. I'll be fine."

He's got a point, though, she thought as she labored up the narrow track. *I'm still not one hundred percent. This better be important.*

The path led to the ledge and then veered off to the left. When the young woman reached this spot, she concentrated on making the tricky transition from the trail to the horizontal haven. She ignored the head bobbing and chittering of her three greeters until she sat with her back against the cliff, looking out over the wide valley.

The view by itself is worth the climb, she thought, as the bizarre creatures settled themselves around her, flashing their stained-glass wings until content with their positions. Alice had already noted that these were the biggest of the fairy dragons the settlers knew—with bodies four feet long and tails that doubled that measure—the ones which Goldilocks most often used to communicate with her. Since returning from Earth, Goldie no longer took connection with her people for granted. She made a point of dropping into the dreams of everyone who was open to her, but she also used the fairy dragons when more specific ideas needed to be exchanged.

Alice thought briefly about a conversation she'd had with Judy which partially explained the disconnect between Goldie and her planet. Earth, it turned out, was silent when the Glenn 2 arrived. Goldie's presence awakened her from what appeared to be a coma of some sort. (Alice thought it sounded like Nainai's experience of retreating into the safety of Eternity when suffering abuse.) As the two entities slowly got to know each other, Goldie grew more aware of the limitations of humans and the negative effects to the Earth's biosphere brought about by the absence of a planet's consciousness. Her resentment at the desertion of her people's attention turned into growing concern about whether the connection with her planet was strong enough to carry her home and repair the damage that had apparently taken place.

Judy had admitted, "We should have traveled back when Glenn 2's crew initially planned, but Earth took a while to be coaxed back, and, frankly, we only slowly learned to communicate with her. Those of us who were convinced it was important to reestablish interconnectedness urged your people to settle and stay for a generation. Goldie seemed confident at first that all was well here, but later pushed for a return, while we dragged our feet. We really are sorry it took so long to bring her back to you."

On the high ledge, the largest fairy dragon demanded Alice's attention, pushing its heavy chest across one of her thighs to lay its head in her lap, a bright eye looking up into her face. She stroked its scaled brow as another dragon pressed on the opposite side, two of its six clawed feet clutching her pants, while the third took a protective stance at the edge of the shelf, with only its tail curled about her left foot. A familiar sense of safety and contentment surrounded her. Goldie was present. Even on this precarious perch, Alice sensed her body relax, drifting into a dimension that felt first like sleep and then like being more awake than ever.

Similar to her initial vision, she found herself looking down as if perched on a roof beam. This scene, though, looked very familiar. The rounded walls and small clerestory windows of an old-style hut, with a kitchen table like her Nainai's, spread out beneath her. Warm yellow lights illuminated the space, helped by sunshine seeping through the glass. Even at her height, she recognized the two people present: Humphrey and Janelle. They had gone with the Gladiators who were exiled to rebuild Last Stop—her father's choice, which Alice suspected was atonement for the death of their beloved son. Janelle's decision to go with him attested to an ability to love beyond measure. Her house daughter honored her for it.

Humphrey paced the floor as his partner sat at the round table, pouring tea for both of them. Alice noted the broad shoulders were rounded even more than when she last saw him, and his hair had thinned to a bald spot on the crown, which he didn't cover.

"Come and sit down," Janelle said. "Tell me what happened."

The big man obeyed, slumping heavily into the chair and taking the mug in his worn farmer's hands. He avoided looking at her, and they sat in silence, each sipping at the hot beverage.

Her household mother had aged, too, Alice noted. Her hand shook as she reached out to pat her partner on the arm, and she saw the gnarled knuckles of advancing arthritis. Contact with her parents had been audio only over the last months—almost a whole third, she realized. Janelle had told her that the spotty coverage from the communication array caused this, but now she wondered if they simply didn't want her to recognize the difficulties of their life.

Humphrey sighed and gave his heart-bond a weak smile. He set down his mug. "They won't let me make the trip to Seaside, dear. I think they know I overheard the planning meeting. I'm sure our wrist coms are bugged, and they've posted a night guard on the communications hut too, so I can't contact Alice in private."

The hand on his sleeve gripped and then loosened. "How long before they attack?"

"I'm assuming they'll wait for the first harvest to arrive at Seaside and then try to secure it for themselves. They can't go to the valley until the weather gets better."

"Why are they doing this, Humphrey?" Even though she kept her voice low, Alice heard the cry of desperation. "Didn't they learn anything? Don't they understand that war on other people is war against Goldilocks?"

The man shook his head, frowning. "They fear being second-class citizens. Clay and Lyssa tell them no food will come to Last Stop, that the Singers plan to take retribution by starving us. I think everyone else believes it because that's what they would do."

Janelle tilted her face back, scanning the ceiling, and Alice felt like the older woman looked right at her. She noticed tears leaking out of the corners of her ma's eyes.

"They shouldn't have let all the Gladiators come here together," she said. "They should have split them up among all the communities to defuse their poisonous thoughts."

"Yes, we've been over this, dear." He took her hand, so she looked at him. "We can't go back and remake decisions. At the time, it seemed best to prevent their dissatisfaction from infecting anyone else. We knew how hard Bleak would be and how easy it is to blame others when you're hungry. I promised to monitor the situation and alert the cities if trouble surfaced. I'll figure out how to keep that promise."

"But you didn't hear the details," she said. "We don't know if they're developing a new virus, or poison, or what."

"I'd like to get into that science lab they put together. But Janelle...." The big man leaned forward, looking into her eyes. "There must be some way to defuse their plan without hurting people, even Gladiators. Alice was right."

"How, Humphrey? How will we stop this peacefully?" Janelle's urgency echoed Alice's thought.

"I don't know for sure. Maybe we could undermine the leadership. After all, there are only fifty-six souls in this village, and, as far as I can tell, most aren't involved in planning this. Those with power in Touch Down and Seaside would have to show mercy, acknowledging our needs and proving they care. If the first delivery of food from the valley came to Last Stop, it would expose our leaders here as liars."

Janelle nodded her head. "Yes, that might work. We need to send word to—"

Loud pounding interrupted her. Before her parents could get up, the door burst open and three young men and a middle-aged couple surged into the room. Alice recognized Clay from her Academy days. He had been one of the administrative deans. He stayed by the entryway as a younger man took her household mother and two others grabbed her father's arms. As they hauled their captives up, Clay's partner, Lyssa, read off a piece of paper: "Humphrey and Janelle Far Meadow, the leadership of Last Stop have found you guilty of spying and plotting to overthrow the authority of this village. We will confine you for as long as we deem you a threat to our community."

"You can't do this." Janelle's indignation burned so hot the woman backed up a pace.

Humphrey leaned toward Clay, making eye contact. "Leave her out of this. She knows nothing. I'll cooperate, but let Janelle stay here."

The former dean's lip curled in a sneer. "Too late, traitor. You betrayed us once. You're not getting a second chance." With that, Clay stepped aside to allow his cronies to push both their captives out the door, and then he and his partner followed, slamming it behind them.

Alice tried to move, to keep her parents in sight...but no amount of intention would propel her.

The room dissolved into mist around her, and, as she fought for orientation, the scene resolved into the common dream. Now, her feet stood on solid ground and the wind howled, but fog enshrouded her. She quit struggling and listened, picking out the wild song of Goldilocks.

"Please," she shouted, but couldn't tell if the words came out of her mouth. "Help them, Goldie. Please."

Desperation overcame her, and she sank to her knees, sitting on her heels and hiding her face in her arms. *It can't end like this*, she thought. *After all we did.... How can this happen again?*

A change in the wind caught her attention, settling from a gale to a soft breeze. Now, Goldie's song sounded clearer, its tone softer and brighter. She lifted her head to hear better and noticed the fog had rolled back, exposing a night sky.

She recognized the scene. This was what Nainai saw—what she joined—the night she died: a blackness so deep and full it shined. Alice rose to her feet, not taking her eyes off the beauty shimmering above her. Was she dying now too?

No, she realized. There was no invitation for her, but a sense that someone, something, accompanied Goldie in connecting with her. She could feel Pete's presence and almost touch Nainai, as well as sense an overarching wholeness. Comfort flooded through her. It was not yet the end—in fact, there was no end. Eternity, more real than any point of time, pulsed above her.

A nudge to her cheek and a burst of spicy warm breath brought Alice back to the ledge on the wall above the canyon's river. She opened her eyes to see the blunt snout of the fairy dragon, who had been resting in her lap, almost touching her nose. As she sat up straight, all three of the creatures regarded her with golden stares. As hard as it was to read their lizard-like faces, she felt a faint shred of her dream's reassurance emanating from them.

"OK, guys," she murmured, reaching out to rub eye ridges and pat their wide necks. "I think I understand: There's more work to do to mend our world. I'd better get to it. Thanks for helping."

She struggled up to her feet, wobbling a bit until the pins and needles in her legs shook out. Then she climbed down to the path, beginning her hike home as the fairy dragons plummeted off the ledge, falling past her, catching an updraft, and soaring circles around her head. She watched them ascend above the cliff wall and disappear into the sky. For a moment, she longed to be with them, to touch the firmament and be free from the gravity holding her captive.

Hard questions posed by her vision weighed her down: Could they defuse the situation in Last Stop and save her parents? Were they going to be able to raise and ship back enough food to keep the old settlements alive? What would their life become with Goldie fully here again?

Then, she thought of her baby. The future faded, and the present sat like a jewel in the dark depth of her vision of Eternity, gleaming warm and bright. Alice turned toward the valley below and walked back to the hut, where Izzy and Sami waited for her.

The End

ACKNOWLEDGEMENTS:

Thank you to all our friends in my new Tucson neighborhood who have been unceasing in their encouragement to finish this sequel. Your delight in *Eden.2* and eagerness to find out what happens next have been inspiring.

Many thanks also to Shirin McArthur, whose deep editing and wise advice have made this a much better novel. You have been a valued partner in this work, generating insight and energy. I am deeply grateful.

Much appreciation also to my publisher, Joseph Campbell at Queer Space, whose encouragement to write a sequel allowed me to continue exploring Goldie's world.